Fated Defender

MW00988168

Fated To Royalty: Book 3

Roxie Ray

© 2023

Disclaimer

This is a work of fiction. Names, places, characters, and events are all fictitious for the reader's pleasure. Any similarities to real people, places, events, living or dead are all coincidental.

Contents

Chapter 1 - Nico

Three days had passed since Viola threw the cloak off what she and her family had been planning. Three days of chaos for me and the rest of my pack. Three days since she and the royals openly declared war on us. Not only that, but she'd called on every bigot and wannabe shifter-hunter with a gun to join in the hunt.

I'd been on the phone with all the other pack leaders in Florida pretty much non-stop since Viola's announcement and was just getting off the phone with a bear alpha from Miami when Luis stuck his head into my office.

"You seen the news lately?"

I gave a weary shrug. "No. Something else bad, I assume?"

Luis stepped into the room, grabbed the remote for the small TV mounted on the wall, and tuned it to a twenty-four-hour news channel. On the screen, a news anchor read a report. Viola's face was superimposed on the screen alongside him.

"To reiterate, The Monroe Group's marketing team says they were wholly unaware of the anti-shifter agenda being propagated by the upper levels of the organization. Even so, senior vice president of marketing and research, Allison Wiess, has been arrested in connection to the dozens of crimes now being uncovered by the FBI, NSA, INTERPOL, and the British NCA. She maintains her innocence and promises to assist the authorities in any way to help with the capture of the fugitive CEO and owner of the Monroe Group, Viola Monroe."

I looked at Luis. "This isn't news. I've been hearing them say the same or similar stuff for days. That's like the twelfth executive they've arrested so far."

Luis pointed at the TV. "This is a replay of a report I watched earlier. Wait for what this next guy says."

The anchor turned to a man sitting to his right. "With us is legal expert Shawn Montross, here to discuss how Viola Monroe's pronouncement might affect legal proceedings against the organization and what ripples we may see in the government. Shawn, welcome."

Shawn nodded to the anchor. "Thank you, Tom. Glad to be here."

"So, what does this mean for The Monroe Group as a whole?" Tom asked.

The guest gave a nonchalant shrug. "The Monroe Group as we know it is done. Bankruptcy is the most likely outcome, followed by a government-mandated dissolution of any holdings, real estate, and stocks. That is if the government actually does anything."

The anchor's brow furrowed. He looked as confused as I felt.

"I'm sorry, Shawn. Do you think the government may *not* pursue charges? Even though Miss Monroe has, more or less, declared war on a large portion of the citizenry?"

Shawn shook his head wearily. "Tom, you and I both know there is a fairly significant anti-shifter bias in the world—and it's not only confined to the general public. I think what we are about to see is a full realignment of allegiance. There are members of Congress, the Supreme Court, and the military, not to mention local police forces and the National Guard, who may lean toward what Miss Monroe is proposing. That's not conjecture, simply facts based on numbers."

Luis turned off the TV. "That dude knows what's up."

I rubbed my temples. "Can you believe how surprised that news anchor was? I mean, sure, the government will never come out and say she's right, but we all know there are people on the inside who think she is. That guy can't be that blind. I bet several have already reached out to Viola to offer support."

He nodded. "There's a reason they've only arrested executives and some of her rich dumbass cousins so far.

well."

My father strode into the office, interrupting our conversation. He nodded to us.

"How are we doing, boys?"

"Been better, Dad. We're discussing to what level of the government is helping Viola."

Dad waved that away. "Nothing to be done about it. A few crackpots on the inside trying to help her still won't be as bad as before. At least, I hope not. They can't operate in the shadows anymore."

"Have either of you seen Sinthy?" I asked. Our new pack witch was the best weapon we had.

Luis gestured to the window behind me. "Saw her out front a few hours ago. She was mumbling some stuff out of that old book she carries around. Said she was strengthening the wards."

"Good." I nodded. "That's our first line of defense. It's kept most of the crazies from barging onto our lands."

"Yeah, they can't get in," Luis said ruefully. "Except they're still coming. There has to be at least a hundred people outside the gate. I've had reports of a few stragglers roaming around the outskirts too."

Dad chuckled. "Speaking of. Did you see the footage from last night? The security cameras set up in the northern forest?"

"I heard about it, but I haven't seen it yet," I said.

"Pull it up," Dad said and walked around my desk to watch. Luis joined us.

"What's the time stamp?" I asked.

"Three-thirteen in the morning. Camera twenty-seven."

I pulled up the feed. The cameras were equipped with night vision, and I immediately saw the three men and two women sneaking quietly through the underbrush toward the boundary of the pack's land. Sinthy's protection spells went about twenty feet past all our fences. These folks were getting very close.

"They can't be this stupid," I said. "These people should know by now that they can't infiltrate our land."

"Contrary to popular thought, knowledge does not actually increase intelligence," my dad said with a smile.

Two of the men in the lead hit Sinthy's wards. They stood rigid for an instant as if they were being electrocuted. A second later, they were blown backward ten feet, tumbling and rolling through the grass and shrubs. I would have snorted a laugh had it not been so worrying that people were still trying to get inside. I could only imagine what those idiots had planned for us.

The other three picked up their injured companions and dragged them back the way they'd come until they were out of the camera frame.

"How bad were they hurt?" I asked.

"No idea," Luis said.

As though Fate stood in the corner waiting for the perfect moment to make my day worse, my office phone rang. I looked at it with unease before answering.

"This is Nicolas Lorenzo."

"Mr. Lorenzo, this is Jessica Barton with Channel Nine News out of Tampa. Do you have a few minutes to talk?"

I glanced at Dad and Luis before answering. "Uh, sure. What's this about?"

Before she spoke again, I hit the speaker button.

"Mr. Lorenzo, I'm currently about twenty yards outside your gates. We've had multiple reports from individuals who are peacefully protesting outside your compound that they are unable to get closer than twenty feet."

"Miss Barton, I don't know if you've noticed, but being a shifter these days comes with some serious security issues. Is there an issue with them staying back a safe distance?"

"That may be, Mr. Lorenzo, but they've also told us the reason they can't get to the gates or fences is because there is some kind of barrier around your lands. In fact, a group of concerned citizens informed us that two men were severely injured last night while taking a walk in the forest near your lands. Would you like to comment on the fact that two innocent men were injured?"

I barked out a laugh, and my father's face blazed with anger.

"Lady, those men were not taking a moonlit stroll. We have video footage of them trying to sneak onto our land. They, and their friends, were armed."

"The question I really want to ask, Mr. Lorenzo, is whether shifters have access to technology that humans do not? The ability to project an invisible electric fence is beyond the capabilities of any government agency. I've done the research. We are only trying to allay the fears of our audience."

"Does your audience care about our safety?" My rising anger punctuated every word.

"I think you can agree that shifters pose a serious threat to humanity. We need to be aware of any additional dangers your species presents to humans. Along with enhanced strength, speed, and healing, if there are technological secrets that you— "

I slammed the button to end the call before she could finish. Nothing I said would get through to her. She was obviously one of the people who either secretly or blatantly supported Viola's views. If I had to guess, Channel Nine News would be airing a hit piece about our pack tonight.

"It's gonna get worse, son," Dad said as he sank into a chair across from me. He pointed at the phone. "People like her are gonna make things dangerous. More so than it already is."

"I know, Dad."

"I'm not sure you truly understand the severity. That group of protestors out there have the road blocked. I've spoken to the chief of police—they're on our side, but they can't be everywhere. A lot of people still think the original attacks were from pure feral shifters. A faction of society will never believe the truth. They'll think Viola is a scapegoat to protect the shifter race. Those people are the real danger. We can't get out to get supplies, gas, or food at this point. We can't stay on the pack lands forever. Once we're forced to go out past Sinthy's wards, there's no telling what will happen."

"We can fend for ourselves," Luis said, though his bravado sounded forced. "We're still shifters."

"Yes, boy, but that doesn't mean we're superheroes. Our skin is tougher than humans, but it's not bulletproofed."

I held up a hand before their conversation got heated. "I get it, Dad. It *is* dangerous." I glanced at Luis. "I also know we do have a chance to fight. Not like this, though. If we go out to town and beat the hell out of or accidentally kill a human, it won't do us any favors. Doesn't matter if they attacked us first or whether we were *actually* in danger—it will get twisted in some way. What we need is for one of the higher-ups in the government to make a statement on our behalf. It won't deter the crazies, but it will help our cause among the general public. Hopefully, that will happen soon. The Feds have been fairly quiet since all this broke."

Elsewhere in the house, I could sense Maddy. Her anxiety coursed through our bond. Our connection was getting stronger by the day, and it was becoming difficult for us to hide our emotions from each other. I expected she'd come to talk to me about the vial any day now. It'd been on her mind almost non-stop for days.

Standing, I addressed my father and Luis. "I need to go find Maddy. Luis, let me know if anything changes or if something weird happens. Dad, can you come with me?"

Luis left to check on the guard detail. Dad stood and followed me.

"What's on your mind, son?"

"The vial," I said.

He nodded in understanding. "It's still safe, right?"

"Yeah. Sinthy hid it somewhere in the house. Only she knows where it is. She also cast a spell on it that will only allow Maddy to access it. So, it's as safe as it can be."

We went downstairs and took a seat in the living room. Sighing, I put my feet up on the coffee table.

"I don't know what we're going to do," I said. "That vial caused all this. I keep thinking we need to simply destroy it. Boom. Over and done. But Maddy and I keep circling back to us, perhaps needing it at some point. That thing contains pure power, but it's dangerous."

Dad chewed at his lower lip, thinking. After a while, he said, "You're right. You basically have a nuclear bomb. It's both a weapon and a defense. How do you give that up? Also, if you don't, how do you use it?"

"Right. We have no clue what it will do to Maddy. There's no information on it. Edemas created that out of desperation. There's never been anything like it in history. We believe it would affect Maddy, but we can't be sure. I get the feeling Viola thinks someone in her organization could take it. Her actions don't read as a person who wants to destroy something. She covets it. Maybe there's more that we don't know."

Dad raised his hands. "Okay, what if Maddy takes it? What are the possibilities?"

I counted them off on my fingers as I spoke. "One, she dies. Two, she becomes a powerful werewolf like Edemas. Three, nothing happens, and it was all a silly story, or the magic wore off or something."

"Well, you said Viola might want to take the vial herself or have someone in her organization take it. If that's true, what would happen if you took it? Take Maddy out of the equation to protect her? I don't want you to endanger yourself, but we should think about the possibility."

"I wouldn't suggest that," Sinthy said from behind us.

Turning in surprise, I found Sinthy, Maddy, and her birth mother, Doctor Sanford, standing in the doorway.

Maddy looked pissed—her hands balled into fists on her hips. "How can you even be considering that?"

Holding up my hands in surrender, I said, "We're not considering it. Just talking about the what-ifs—things we might resort to and what would happen."

That explanation didn't ease the anger on Maddy's face.

Doctor Sanford shook her head. "Do I need to remind you of the beast Maddy's father turned into when he shifted? It tormented him. I wouldn't even consider that if I were you."

I was a little taken aback at how upset the three of them looked. It wasn't like we'd been formulating a plan for me to take the vial. We only wanted to talk about what was possible.

"I swear," I said, "we were only discussing possibilities. Nothing more."

"Having anyone, including you, take the vial is not a possibility," Maddy said.

I gritted my teeth. "Maddy, we don't know how bad this will get. I was just thinking of an advantage. That's all."

"No, Nico. If you take that vial, your body could reject it. You could die," Maddy said, her face still stern but softening.

"Or you'll turn into a mindless beast and murder everyone you love along with your enemies," Gabriella added.

I looked to Dad for help, but he'd lowered his eyes. He'd apparently decided discretion was the better part of valor.

"The thing none of you are thinking of," Sinthy said, "is that this vial was created to specifically reincarnate Edemas or his descendants. If you were to take it and not die, there is a good chance Edemas would return. His soul may come back and kick your entire consciousness into oblivion, essentially killing you. You'd be nothing but a meat puppet for an ancient king mad with a vengeance using your body."

That possibility hadn't occurred to me. I pointed at Maddy. "Would that happen to Maddy?"

Sinthy shrugged. "No telling. But she's a direct descendant, plus it seems that Edemas's daughter has already staked a claim in Maddy's mind. She was reincarnated as Maddy's wolf."

"I don't think it would happen to Maddy," Gabriella said. "She's basically already a reincarnation of sorts. But it's still a possible risk."

My shoulders slumped. "Okay. Not a good plan. We won't talk about it anymore, all right?"

Maddy tapped a finger on her lips, then said, "What if we destroyed it?"

The rest of us froze at her words. We hadn't really discussed that option. Most of our conversations had been based around using the vial and keeping it away from Viola. Destroying a weapon of such power, on the surface, was crazy. But without the vial as bait, would Viola continue going after us?

"It's a decent idea," Gabriella said. "Though I doubt Viola would care."

Maddy frowned in obvious confusion. "What do you mean? It's the whole reason she's been after me, right? If it was no longer a threat to her, then she has no reason to keep trying to attack us."

Gabriella nodded. "That argument only works if you're dealing with someone who thinks rationally. Do any of us believe Viola is rational?"

That was not up for debate. The woman was as far from rational as one could get. For centuries, her ancestors had been obsessed with finding this damn thing: a legend and a desire that old wouldn't be put aside easily.

"She wouldn't believe it," I said.

"Wouldn't believe what?" Maddy asked.

"That it was destroyed," Gabriella said, picking up where I left off. "We could tell her all day that it was gone, but she'd never believe it."

"We could record it and show her," Maddy offered.

I shook my head. "She'll say we faked it. In her mind, that vial is the most valuable thing on Earth. She thinks it can bring back the werewolf shifters, and she can't allow that. The only way she would ever believe the vial was destroyed is if she did it herself, and we can't let her have it because God only knows what she might do with it. Hell, she could try to create an army of werewolves of her own to take over the world or something."

"So we're stuck with it," Maddy said. It was not a question.

"Better to have a weapon and not need it than to need a weapon and not have it," Gabriella said, turning her gaze to me. "But that doesn't mean you get to make stupid decisions about using it."

Maddy frowned at me. She was still pissed that the thought of using the vial myself had even crossed my mind. Thankfully, my phone buzzed before any of the women could chastise me anymore. A text from Donatello lit up the screen. I'd expected to hear from him immediately after Viola's big pronouncement, but he'd been surprisingly silent. This was the first I'd heard from him in days.

Watch the announcement on the news.

Chapter 2 - Maddy

Since Viola's declaration of war on TV, I'd been in a perpetual state of anxiety. It had been bad enough when she and her cronies operated in the shadows—now things were much worse. Viola had shown her cards, and that meant it was open season on is. She didn't have to cover up our deaths. Her zealots would kill us just to please her. That terrified me.

My wolf raged inside me, ready to attack, but we had no one to focus that anger on. It amped up the anger thrumming in my veins. We'd already been through so much, and it should have been over. Donatello's reveal had been our ace in the hole—the final stake through her heart that was meant to end the royals and their bitch of a spokeswoman. Yet, here we were, hiding away in Nico's compound, terrified to go out, terrified of what was coming.

Now that I was in control of my wolf and could shift at will, I longed to see Viola face-to-face again. There would be no mercy, and that was fine. I wasn't a violent person by nature, but a person could only put up with so much before they lashed out.

Before I walked in on Nico and his dad's stupid conversation, I'd been visiting my parents. They'd taken residence in one of the vacant pack houses near the forest. The one-bedroom cabin was small—much smaller than their real home—but neither they nor I wanted them to be out in the world without protection. Not when they were still targets. Viola wouldn't hesitate to kidnap them again if she thought it would help her get the vial.

Nico had offered the house to them, and I'd been relieved when they'd accepted. They'd be as safe as they possibly could be here behind Sinthy's wards. I was glad they were a bit removed from all the action and meetings at Nico's house—the less they knew, the better.

As for Nico? He and his father were sitting in the living room, looking like two little boys who had been chastised. As well they should. That they'd even entertained the idea of Nico ingesting the contents of the vial was madness. Like I'd let him risk his life like that. There was no way we could know what might happen. Nico flipped through the channels to find a news station. Donatello's text meant something important was coming. How did the man have so many connections? Of course, it was his money. Money always paved the way.

"Did he say what announcement to look for?" I asked as I sat down beside Nico.

He stopped once he'd found a channel and shook his head. "All he said was to turn it on."

A moment later, a commercial was interrupted. For them to cut off one of their precious advertisers, it must be important. The anchor looked harried, as though she'd rushed through makeup and sprinted to her chair to give the update in time.

"Good afternoon. We interrupt your previously scheduled broadcast for a special announcement from the president on The Monroe Group and Shifter Crisis. We take you now to the West Wing."

The screen switched to the president stepping toward a podium. Dozens of flashbulbs went off, and at least a half dozen reporters in attendance started shouting questions. The president raised his hand for silence.

Once the rumble died down, he spoke. "Good day. I have a statement to make. Unfortunately, I will not be taking any questions to today."

He cleared his throat. "As you all know, The Monroe Group, and most specifically, CEO, chairman, and majority stake holder, Viola Monroe, has come under fire in recent days. Their complacency in the kidnapping, experimentation, torture, and murder of shifters is now known and being investigated. The federal government is exhausting all avenues to ensure that not only she but all guilty parties are brought to justice. The Federal Bureau of Investigation is working with Interpol and several other law enforcement agencies across the world to find her and bring her in.

"One thing must be stated. And this is a direct and total affirmation. Though Viola Monroe is a resident and citizen of the United States, she does not speak for this country. We abhor and renounce the vile bigotry she has spouted, and none of America's allies stand with her.

"Until this matter is settled, shifters of all species are under protection. Anyone attempting to harm, harass, or intimidate a shifter will be subject to the harshest laws of our land. You will be charged not only with assault but a hate crime. This evening, I will sign an emergency bill into law that will make any crime against a shifter a federal crime.

"Let there be no question, any who decide to follow Miss Monroe's call to arms will face the full and unyielding vengeance of this country—a minimum of twenty years in prison, seizure of physical assets such as real estate, vehicles, and stock holdings, as well as fines beyond measure."

The president looked directly into the camera and leveled a finger at it. "Viola Monroe, I implore you to turn yourself in at the nearest law enforcement location immediately. For those watching who think they might agree with her stances? I would think twice before tempting Fate. That's all for today."

He turned on his heel and strode away as his press secretary stepped up to the podium to dismiss the reporters. I couldn't remember the last time I'd seen a president look so pissed. The speech was great and touched all the appropriate points, but it was cold comfort. I doubted it would do an ounce of good.

"That's fine," I said. "But how many of these crazy douchebags will listen to that? These people have been waiting decades for a reason to hunt us. A nice speech won't scare them. Not when they're so full of fucking hate they can't see straight."

Gabriella gave a curt nod. "They won't stop until we're all eradicated, or they've been beaten so resoundingly they tuck tail and wait a few more decades to come out of the shadows again."

"Maybe not," Nico said. "There must be a lot of people who saw that press conference and got a little nervous. A bunch of people might have been on the fence. Those might have been beaten back from joining Viola's cause. That should bring the numbers down a little, right? At least for a while?"

He sounded so hopeful, and I wished I could feel the same. He might be right, but I doubted it.

The news anchor was back on the screen. "All registered shifters should report any signs of violence or intimidation to their local law enforcement. A special fund has been set up to add bodies to the police force. US Marshals and secret service agents will be dispatched to areas in need of special assistance with shifter-related crimes."

Nico snorted. "Well, at least we won't need that. Sinthy's wards are better than a few guys with guns, from what I've seen so far."

"It looks like pretty much every other government has given basically the same stance as ours over the last fifteen minutes," Gabriella said as she scrolled through her phone. "At least it's a united front."

"Viola must be pissed," I said. "I think she probably hoped at least a few of the outlying countries might side with her and give her a base of operations."

Carlos grunted. "Yeah, but as we've discussed, there will be people in those governments who will still provide her with assistance. Hell, some of the countries might be paying lip service. I mean, does anyone think a country like North Korea won't jump at the chance to help some crazy rich bitch like Viola?"

He was right. We all knew that.

"Regardless of what the news or any politician says, Viola wants a war on shifters, but we all know what she wants most," I said.

The others looked at me intently, but they knew what I meant. I was the prize. Me and the vial that only I could access and use. She wouldn't stop until she had both. Even if she had to wade through all the armies of the world, the woman was too crazy to understand the odds. Would anything short of death ever stop her?

"I need some air," I muttered.

"Are you okay?" Nico asked as I headed for the front door.

"I'll be fine. A little sun will make it better."

He looked at me as though he wanted to say something else, but he nodded and let me go. I stepped out onto the front lawn and took a breath. It did feel better. Ever since gaining contact with my wolf, nature soothed me.

Grunting sounds came from the house next door. Glancing over, I saw Luis and Sebastian sparring in Nico's parents' yard. I strolled over and watched them.

It looked like it was nothing but training. That was a relief. I had no clue whether the two had completely buried the hatchet or not, but the fact that they weren't bloodying each other was a good sign. If nothing else, the animosity between them had markedly decreased since Viola's announcement.

"Hey, chick," Abi said from behind me.

I turned, surprised to see her there. "Hi."

Abi was the reason for the friction between Luis and Sebastian. Everything that had passed between her and the two friends still hung over them like a dark cloud.

"So, have you worked things out with Sebastian yet?"

She visibly deflated. "No. We haven't really talked about it."

"Abi, I told you weeks ago you needed to lay it all on the table."

The little charade Abi had pulled had turned the two best friends against each other. Sebastian had nearly believed she and Luis were a thing. Luis, for his part, had played along to goad his friend but had stopped when he saw how upset it was *actually* making Sebastian.

"I know. That's what I wanted to talk to you about."

I sighed with relief. "Good. Are you going to do it today? Is that what brought you out here?"

Abi chewed at her lip uncertainly before saying, "No. At least not yet. I... uhm, I think it's time I leave the compound."

Her words rooted me to the spot. Not only that, but Luis and Sebastian stopped sparring. Their shifter hearing must have picked up her statement. Abi went red in the face when she saw them look our way.

"Hold up," I said, throwing my hands into the air. "You want to go back to your apartment? You do realize this is the safest place for you, don't you? You're still a target. Viola may try to take you again. Christ, my parents are staying until all this is over."

Abi shook her head adamantly. "No. I don't think I'm still a target. Things have gotten bigger. I'm probably not even on her radar anymore."

I couldn't believe how dense she was being. Of course, she was still on Viola's radar. The one thing that woman wanted more than anything was me. Why the hell did Abi think she wouldn't try to kidnap her again? What I had to say next wasn't pleasant, but it was the truth.

"Abi, you're not going anywhere. I'm sorry, but I won't let you put yourself in danger."

"She's right." Sebastian stalked toward us, adding his two cents. Luis hung back.

"You shouldn't go anywhere," Sebastian continued. "Maddy's right. It's safe here."

Abi scoffed. "You don't get a say in this."

"The hell I don't. My friends almost died trying to save you and Maddy's parents. We put our lives on the line to get you guys back. Of course, I get a say."

Abi whirled on him and dug a finger into his chest. "I've already thanked all of you for that, but it has nothing to do with this."

"Wait," I called out, an idea suddenly springing into my mind. "Is this about you two?"

Sebastian's eyes slid off Abi and onto me. His face told me the thought hadn't occurred to him until I said it.

"Oh my God, Maddy. Seriously?" Abi asked incredulously.

She could say what she wanted, and she could put all the feeling and emotion into the words, but I knew her. The look in her eyes told me I was right.

Sebastian must have seen the same thing I did because he leveled a grim smile at Abi. "You can't run off and put your life in danger because you can't face the repercussions of the decisions you've made."

When Abi rounded on him, I thought for a split second she was going to deck him, but she didn't. Instead, her lips trembled as she slammed her palms against his chest, knocking him back a step.

"That's really fucking rich, Sebastian. You're a goddamn hypocrite. What about your actions and what you did?"

Things were quickly going sideways. If I didn't step in, one of them would say something they couldn't take back. Luis looked nervous, but he hung back. I stepped between them and gripped Abi's shoulders, staring into her eyes.

"Abi, try and remember who you were before all this started. You've been through a lot. So damned much. I understand that. Through it all, I think you've lost yourself. You need to find that." I stopped talking, suddenly realizing what I was going to say next. "You… maybe you're right. Maybe you do need to leave."

Sebastian threw his hands up and stomped away from us toward Nico's house. Heat built in my belly and chest, hot and strong. I'd never felt it before. Probably a response to the fight. I shook off the feeling and gestured at Sebastian's retreating figure.

"Once you're back to yourself, you better fix that."

Abi huffed and rubbed a hand across her face.

"And," I added, "if you do decide to go, you won't be leaving unprotected, and you won't be going back to your apartment. I have an idea."

I headed back toward the house.

Abi called from behind me. "What idea?"

"Come on, and you'll see."

Abi hustled to catch me. We found Nico standing in the kitchen, making a sandwich. He glanced up, and the smile forming on his face died when he saw our expressions.

He slapped the sandwich on the counter. "What now?"

"Okay, hear me out," I said. "Do you think Donatello might be willing to hide Abi for a while?"

Chapter 3 - Nico

I stared at Maddy in exasperation. There was far too much going on for me to worry about the drama between Abi, Sebastian, and Luis. If it hadn't been for the imploring way Maddy looked at me, I'd have totally brushed it off. I looked from her to Abi, who promptly lowered her head in embarrassment.

"Are we being serious right now?" I asked.

Maddy glanced at Abi, then back to me. She nodded. "Yes. It's important. She needs a safe place where she can get her mind right. Between the situation with the guys and what happened when she was captured... it's too much. She wants to go back to her apartment, but that isn't safe."

I looked forlornly down at the turkey and salami sandwich. My appetite had vanished. Would Donatello be willing to give Abi a safe haven? He'd offered to house my entire pack, going so far as to say he'd send in transport helicopters to prevent us from having to drive out of the pack lands into danger. But this was a single person. Was it even worth his time?

"I'll ask him," I said. Seeing Maddy perk up at that, I raised a brow in warning. "That doesn't mean he'll say yes, though. He may tell us to go and pound sand."

Maddy nodded vigorously. "No, yeah, I get that. Thank you, Nico."

The relief in her voice had my irritation fading. I could actually sense her relief. It came off her in waves, calming my own fears and worries. I tugged my phone out of my pocket and sent Donatello a text.

Less than three minutes later, my phone chimed with his response.

I can do that, but you'll need to get her to me. I can't risk using too many of my resources for one person. Get her to Miami. I'll take care of the rest.

Maddy peered over my shoulder, trying to see what Donatello had said.

She sighed in defeat. "How are we going to get her to the airport? She's a human, so she'll be fine once she's away from here, but once she's past those gates, who knows what those crazies out there will do."

The trip to the airport would be the most dangerous part of the entire thing. Sinthy's wards protected everyone within the boundaries of the pack lands, but once we were out in the real world, it was open season on shifters and shifter allies. Maddy was right, though. If we could get Abi away from here without anyone noticing, she'd be fine.

"Can Sinthy teleport her to the airport?" Maddy asked.

I shook my head. "She could, but as soon as Sinthy leaves this area, the wards come down. Even if she came right back, it took her over a week to build and cast the spell big enough to protect this large piece of land. We'd have no defenses from anyone wanting to harm us. From what we've seen already, I doubt we'd make it a week. And God only knows how many spies Viola has situated outside our gates. The moment they see the wards are down, the royals will be on us in no time. Sinthy can't leave."

The cracking sound of knuckles popping interrupted our conversation. I looked up to see Sebastian leaning against the wall. I hadn't seen or heard him come into the room. He looked pissed.

My irritation returned. I waved a hand at him. "Sebastian, I don't want to get into this. We've got plans to make."

"I'm not here to argue about Abi," he said, and the woman in question looked like she wanted to be anywhere else but right there.

"Then how can we help you?" I asked.

Sebastian pointed a thumb at the front door. "I'll be the one. I'll get Abi out of here and to the airport safely."

Maddy's jaw dropped, and I was certain I had the same surprised look on my face.

Abi glared at him—her jaw set in determination. "I don't need you taking care of me. You're the last person I'd pick to escort me anywhere."

Sebastian ignored her. "If Abi isn't comfortable here anymore, we should help her get someplace safe. I can do that. Better than her moping around here, pouting like she's being held hostage."

"I am not pouting!"

I had to admit that there *was* a bit of that going on. I knew better than to point out something that would make the situation worse, though.

"Look," Sebastian said, finally turning to face Abi. "I want you to be happy. I can't live with you here making me feel bad about something I've already apologized for a million times." His face had a pained expression I'd never seen in all the years I'd known him.

He took a breath, then spoke again. "I want you to find yourself again because this—" He gestured toward Abi. "Is not the person I first met. This is not the woman that I... it's not the woman I fell for."

Sebastian turned and walked out of the room. His cheeks were red as he called over his shoulder. "Let me know when we need to leave."

The three of us stood in stunned silence as his footsteps receded down the hallway. Tears streamed down Abi's face—whether they were from anger or sadness, I couldn't tell. I'd had enough. It had gone on for far too long, and we had bigger things to deal with. I adored Abi, and she was Maddy's best friend, but I needed to put my stamp on things.

I walked around the kitchen island, folding my arms across my chest as I stopped in front of her. "Listen," I said. "I'm done, Abi. Do you understand? Things have happened to you. Awful, horrible things, but it's time to end this. Stop yanking my guys around by their dicks. If you can't, then you'll never be welcomed back here again. Understood?"

Abi nodded, clamping her lower lip between her teeth. Her tears were streaming faster now. Without another word, she ran from the room. I heaved a deep and weary sigh and turned to look at Maddy.

"Too much?"

She hesitated for the barest of seconds before shaking her head. "No. It wasn't. You've been telling her the same thing for weeks. She needs time away. I think that will help."

"I freaking hope so. I can't have two of my best friends being weird around each other like this. Not now. We need to be laser-focused on what's coming."

I pulled Maddy close and kissed her forehead. She pressed herself into me. "I really hope some time alone will help her. I want my friend back."

"I know," I said as I looked at my watch. "Shit. I need to go to my office. I've got a call with a few other alphas in a minute. Will you be okay?"

Maddy nodded and reluctantly stepped out of my embrace. "I'll be fine. I'm more worried about those two."

"It'll all work out. I promise," I said. After brushing another soft kiss over her forehead, I headed up to my office.

Tiago and I were running the call, with over a dozen other shifters scheduled to join in. It took almost ten minutes for everyone to get on the line.

"Okay, guys," I started. "Thanks for being here. I don't really have an agenda for this call. We're here to discuss ideas about how best to deal with the royals at this point. So, if anyone wants to start…"

Tiago broke in. "Yeah, Nico. I think Howard from the Destin bear clan has something to say. He texted me an hour ago."

I rubbed the bridge of my nose. I'd been dealing with so many people lately, I couldn't even remember what this Howard guy looked like.

"Okay, Howard. What do you have?"

"Hello," a deep voice answered. "Have we spoken about taking Viola down? I mean, isn't that the best course of action? Smoke her out and put her down. It's what you do with a rabid dog—why not this crazy bitch?"

"I think that's a little aggressive," Tiago said. He sounded a bit shocked at the suggestion. Old Howard must not have given his full idea when they spoke.

Tiago was quickly shouted down by several other alphas who were in agreement with Howard. The call devolved into chaos, with men talking over each other.

Once Tiago and I regained control, I said, "Okay, hang on. I know a bunch of you think we should take the war directly to her, but it's not that easy."

"Why not?" a man asked.

"She's shown her true colors to the world," I said. "But she still has her foot soldiers and bodyguards. That's one thing. The other is that even though a ton of her assets have been frozen, she still has funds coming in from somewhere. Money equals power. That alone will make it tough. Hell, for all we know, she could be in Japan or Australia right now. It's hard to kill someone who's hidden over five thousand miles away."

There was a moment of silence as my words sunk in. Then another voice I didn't recognize spoke up. "But if we do kill her, this all ends, doesn't it? Everything goes back to the way it was before."

That was the hope and prayer of shifters everywhere. It would be nice if it were true, but I had a hunch it wouldn't be that simple. I didn't want to be the one to break it to these guys, but someone had to.

"I don't think so," I said. "I've got a feeling we've got a war coming with or without Viola at the head. Over the last few months, the royals have stoked anti-shifter sentiment across the globe. Guys, we've got a fight on our hands no matter what happens with Viola. That's my belief, anyway. The news reports and statements from the president helped, but there are people who wish us harm, and that won't stop because one powerful guy said so."

"Nico's right," Tiago said. "I'm getting to be an old man. I don't want to fight. I don't want to see my boy fight. He's just now become the alpha of our clan. He should have years of peace to learn and do what we all did as we were coming up. But there's a cloud over the world. No other way to say it."

"Thanks," I said. "We need our packs to prepare for battle. Whether that comes in the form of a full assault from the royals or from sympathizers who want us dead, either way, we all need to be ready to fight back and kill if need be. I know that sounds savage, but it is what it is at this point."

"You're saying we should get ready to kill humans?" Howard asked, sounding shocked and a little sick.

"If it was between the people you loved and some crazy anti-shifter humans? For me, that answer comes easy. I'm not saying we bum rush the towns in our area and lay waste to them like some heathen feral shifters. That's not what we're doing. We're getting ready for what I believe is coming, to pull the metaphorical trigger when and if it does happen. No one in any government will punish us for protecting ourselves. Even if people get hurt."

"One issue, Nico," Tiago said. "I know all these boys here are law-abiding like your pack and mine, but you and I both know there's some dirty sons of bitches out there who will take this as open season on the human population. I know there's far more bigotry toward us, but there are shifters who aren't too fond of humans either."

That was the real dark horse of the whole plan. If this went sideways and some shithead shifters started taking their frustrations out on humans, public sentiment might flip back against us. Rape, murder, and lawlessness were guaranteed ways to get on people's bad side.

"I'm aware, Tiago, but we have to hope that those people are few and far between. Hopefully, things will stay calm. I guess that's the keyword for this whole meeting. Hope. That's all I can give or ask from you all. Our people need to be ready to fight hand-to-hand as well as with weapons. If we can agree on that, then I'm not sure what else there is to discuss.

"Does anyone else have anything? Or are we done?"

There were some murmurs but nothing of significance. Tiago took over and ended the call. By the time I'd ended the call, I was even more stressed than I'd been before I stepped into my office. It felt like nothing had been accomplished, and there was still so much to worry about. Rubbing a hand through my hair, I went to find Maddy.

She was on the porch with Sinthy. It would have been a lovely afternoon if I couldn't hear the faint shuffle of feet and chants from the crowd down by the gates. I dropped down beside her. The anti-shifters in town wouldn't be giving up anytime soon.

"Still there, I see," I said, nodding in the direction of the gates.

"Yup," Maddy said.

"They're as annoying as gnats. I'm thinking of adding a little something to the wards," Sinthy said.

The glimmer in her eyes had me cocking an eyebrow. "And what would that be?"

Sinthy smiled and bobbed her shoulder in a half-shrug. "Oh, A little razzle-dazzle," she said, waving jazz hands around.

I chuckled. "Do I want to know what 'razzle-dazzle' means?"

"I'm glad you asked. I'm thinking of making the wards shoot confetti or glitter whenever they zap someone. You know, to sort of spice things up a bit. It would be a good show if nothing else."

Maddy and I both laughed, unable to help ourselves. The witch tended to have a bright outlook on almost everything.

After a few minutes of silence, Maddy nudged me. "How'd the call go?"

"Like shit."

I gave them a rundown. That we'd all basically decided to prepare for war, that humans who attacked us would not be safe, and that we weren't going to go after Viola directly—at least not yet.

Maddy shook her head in disbelief. "I still can't believe this is happening. I mean… it feels like yesterday I was happily running my bar. Now I've been all over the damned world, and my entire life has been turned into one never-ending drama.

"I guess, deep down, I realized a war was coming. Whether I wanted to believe it or not." She gave a resigned sigh. "I trust you, Nico. Whatever your judgment, I trust you."

"Same for me," Sinthy added. "Since I guess I'm technically part of this pack now."

"Thanks. I'm glad you guys have faith in me."

Maddy's eyes were clouded with worry. There was a deepness to the look that hurt my heart. She looked exhausted and worn out.

"Nico, we have to end this. We have to win and put this entire thing to bed. Do you think we will?" Fervent hope blazed in her eyes.

I wrapped my arm around her and kissed her. When I pulled away, I looked at her, and with absolute confidence that I didn't truly feel, I said, "We will."

Chapter 4 - Maddy

The next day, I watched Nico, Luis, and Felipe carry three heavy cases up from the basement. The ones Nico and Felipe had looked like really long suitcases. Luis carried one that looked like a thick, bulky attaché case.

"What are those?" I asked as they came up the stairs.

"Stuff Dad bought years ago. I can't even remember the last time we took them out," Nico said. "As evidenced by the dust."

The cases were caked in dust. Nico flipped his case up and rolled the little combination locks until the snaps popped open. When he lifted the lid, my mouth dropped open. Inside were four rows of what looked like assault rifles.

"What the hell, Nico?"

He looked at me and smiled. "Don't worry. We aren't some anti-government militia or something. Dad got these about ten years ago when a shifter group that was on the bad side of both our *and* Javi's pack rolled through. They weren't afraid of packing heat, and Dad figured it was best we were prepared if they started trouble. We can die as easily from a gunshot when we're in wolf form as we do as a human. We heal faster as wolves, but still."

I gaped at the weapons. "Are we going to use these?"

Felipe opened his case. It was loaded with six pump-action shotguns. Luis's smaller case held what looked like a dozen pistols—revolvers as well as semi-autos. I'd never even touched a gun. The only reason I had any idea what I was looking at was from movies and books. The sight of the guns was both scary and exhilarating.

Nico nodded. "The guys and I go shooting every few months, but we need to train everyone to use them.

Like I told the other alphas, it won't only be a brawl if stuff goes bad. And our natural speed and power will only do so much when our enemies are shooting at us from two hundred yards away."

"Yup." Felipe grinned and cocked his shotgun.

I flinched at the sound.

Felipe's smile faded. "Oh, shit. Sorry, Maddy. The guns aren't loaded. We still have to grab the cases of ammo."

"Right," Nico said. "There's another case of handguns and rifles down there."

An uneasy chuckle escaped me. Seeing the weapons in front of me brought home how dangerous things were. Nico had said the pack would start training again, but I hadn't known exactly what that entailed until now. Before, Nico had everyone training to fight a stealth or surprise attack. Now? If the royals or anti-shifters came, it would be in the open, without fear of publicity or the police.

"I've… uh… never actually held a gun before," I said.

Nico's lips twitched. "I figured. I've been worried about how things would go if the time came for you to use one of these." He stood and scratched his head. "Do you think you can?"

I looked from his face down to the weapons and back again. Could I? If I really thought about it, I wasn't sure I could.

I shrugged. "I don't know, Nico. I mean… that's murder."

He took my hand and squeezed it. "That's the first thing you need to get out of your head." He pointed toward the front door. "If a half-dozen anti-shifters with weapons busted down that door right this minute and wanted to kill all four of us, and I picked up this rifle and shot them, would that be murder or self-defense?"

When he put it that way, it didn't sound like murder. "Self-defense. I guess."

I still didn't like the idea. My parents were pacifists. We'd never owned a gun, and Dad was adamant about not ever having one. Nico must have seen the hesitation on my face.

"Listen," he said, rubbing his hand up my arm to my shoulder. "I don't want you to be part of any battle. I know the strength you possess from being Edemas's heir would be an asset, but I plan to keep you as far from any fight as I can. However, I need to know you can protect yourself. I know you can when you're in wolf form, but I need to know that you can in human form as well. We'll practice fighting as a wolf later. Right now, this takes precedence."

I nodded and stepped back as they unpacked the weapons. They brought up the other cases and ammunition before taking some of it outside for shooting practice in the open field. Luis ran home to grab some aluminum cans for targets, and Nico and Felipe started heading out. Before I could follow them, my parents walked up the road toward us. Shock and confusion warred on their faces.

"Hang on," I said. "Nico, I'll meet you guys in a few minutes."

He glanced at my parents and nodded. "Okay. See you in a bit."

To make matters even more awkward, my birth mom, Gabriella, stepped out the door, holding a glass of tea. It was like a rule that, no matter what, parents got the chance to question their children's actions.

"What the hell is going on?" Dad asked, pointing toward the men carrying guns. "Why do they have those weapons?"

"Is there something we need to know?" Mom asked.

Gabriella said nothing as she took a seat on the porch couch, watching quietly.

"We're gonna go down to the field. Nico's going to teach me how to shoot."

My mom looked aghast. "Is that safe?"

I did my best to keep from rolling my eyes. Even with my own hesitations and fears, I didn't sound as terrified as she did. Dad, however, looked more furious than anything.

"No, it's not. Maddy, I don't think this is a good idea," he said.

"Dad, it's for my safety. Nico wants me to know how to use one if the time comes. If a big fight or battle breaks out, he wants me ready."

Sneering, he waved back at the house. "Well... wouldn't the best thing be for you to hide? I mean, isn't that safe room in there a better option than blasting away with a gun?"

"Right," Mom added. "We don't want you involved."

"That's a nice thought but unrealistic," Gabriella said.

I groaned inwardly. This was not going smoothly.

"What do you mean?" Dad asked. "Of course, it's realistic. If someone is in trouble, the safest thing to do is to hide. You've seen what these people are capable of."

"Oh, I know," Gabriella said, setting her tea aside. "That's why I'm sure it is the best thing for Maddy to learn how to fight. Both as a wolf and as a woman. If learning how to use a weapon will help keep her safe, I'm all for it."

"Well, that's your opinion, Gabriella. But aren't bullets flying around more dangerous?" Dad asked.

"Enough! Enough, okay? I'm going. For God's sake, I'm an adult. If I want to go and shoot a damned gun, it's my prerogative. Gabriella is right. It's like what Nico told me. If someone broke in and I had to choose between dying and knowing how to use a gun, I'd rather know how to use the gun."

"So you're taking her side?" Mom asked, pointing at Gabriella.

I wanted to scream—to tear my hair out. Of all the stupid shit for them to get in a fight over, this was at the top of the list.

"I'm not taking anyone's side, Mom." I thought about it for a second before changing my mind. "Actually, no, I am taking a side. *My own.* I'm doing it. There's a war coming, and I need to be prepared. Honestly, I think it would be good if you were too, but that's your decision. I'm leaving." I stormed off before any of them could say anything else to piss me off.

By the time I got to the field, I'd managed to calm down.

Felipe and Luis looked at me, then quickly continued loading the guns. Nico grinned. "So, that went well."

"How would you know?"

He tapped his ear. "Shifter hearing."

I sighed. "Let's not talk about it, okay? Show me what I need to know."

"Okay, we've got some time before Sinthy comes down."

"Uh, Sinthy?" I said. "Is she also gonna learn to shoot? Is that necessary with what she can do?"

"Not really," Nico said. "But she told me she had worked out something to make training more realistic. Not gonna lie, that sounds a little scary, but I guess we'll see what she has up her sleeve."

Nico showed me how to load, unload, and turn the safety off all the different gun types. A dozen more of his pack mates arrived, and eventually, we were all taking shots at cans sitting lined up on an old wooden fence. Nico and his two friends kept grumbling about how out of practice they all were. That irritated me because, from what I'd seen, they could hit the targets without issue. Me? I was struggling my ass off. I'd fired off at least thirty rounds before I finally put a shot through an old beer can.

"I am terrible at this," I said as Nico took the pistol from my hands.

"You hit that one," he said, pointing at the can lying in the grass.

All around us, the *pop pop pop* of gunfire was going off, muffled by the earplugs I wore. I was about to tell him to be honest and tell me how bad I actually looked, but from the corner of my eye, I saw Sinthy strolling through the grass toward us.

Nico held his arm up and shouted for the shooting to stop. Sinthy was grinning and looking very proud of herself.

"Okay, what's this surprise you've got for us?" Nico asked.

Sinthy clasped her hands together and bounced on her toes. "Oh, you're gonna love it. First, I need you all to put the guns back in the cases—can't be too careful."

Nico sighed and frowned. "Sinthy, this is the whole point of the exercise. How are we gonna teach people to use the weapons if we aren't holding them?"

She pulled a piece of paper out and waved it around. "I'm telling you that I've got it. This took me, like, a week to create. You'll see in a second."

For the next fifteen minutes, Sinthy went about whatever strange ritual she'd written. She spent time with everyone in attendance, placing a hand on them and muttering strange words she read off the paper. After touching each of us, she went around the entire field, stopping every few feet to either draw a weird symbol in the air or mutter some more. The language was like nothing I'd ever heard before. Even though it looked like she hadn't done much, when Sinthy walked back to us, she looked utterly depleted. Her face was pale, and sweat ran down her cheeks.

"Okay," she said with a heavy breath. "All done."

"Are you okay? You look like hell," Felipe muttered to her.

She waved him off. "This was some intense stuff. Weaving a spell as complex as this takes a lot out of me. It's hard to explain. Are you guys ready?"

The twenty or so people, including me, shrugged. We weren't sure what was about to happen. Nico looked more impatient with each passing second.

Sinthy sat down cross-legged and said, "In a second, you guys are gonna have a battle to fight. You'll be safe, nothing can hurt you, and the weapons you hold will feel real, but they are also totally safe. You'll probably have about forty minutes, maybe thirty if I get really tired."

"What weapons?" Nico asked. "You made us put the weapons away."

Sinthy rolled her eyes. "Men. No imagination at all. You'll see soon. I won't be able to talk. I'll be concentrating on keeping the mirage together. Otherwise, it'll flutter away like dandelion seeds. Ready?"

"Uh…" Nico looked at me for some kind of help, but all I could do was shrug.

"I guess so, sure," Nico finally said.

Sinthy closed her eyes and began muttering in her strange language again. A few seconds later, she went quiet and opened her eyes again. I gasped. Instead of the pretty blue, I was used to, her eyes were totally white. No iris, no cornea, not even any thin red blood vessels. Pure white.

A weird crackle, similar to static electricity, filled the entire field. The feeling tickled down my arms. Some of the others cried out in surprise as they felt it. There was a half second where I worried that Sinthy had done something wrong. That feeling vanished when a heavy weight appeared in my hand. Blinking in surprise, I looked down and saw my fingers curled around the butt of a pistol.

"What the hell?" Nico said. He was holding an assault rifle.

I looked behind me at the gun cases and was shocked to see that all the weapons were still safely tucked away. Everyone had a weapon. Luis even pointed his shotgun to the sky and pulled his trigger experimentally. The earth-shattering *boom* made me jump. It sounded exactly like a real gun. When he turned the gun toward the grass and fired, the sound exploded again, but the ground and grass were untouched.

"This is insane," Luis said, his eyes so wide they might have fallen out of his skull.

"She wasn't lying about realism," Nico muttered as he inspected the rifle in his hands.

From the forest at the edge of the clearing, a shout echoed across the field.

"Filthy fucking shifters."

As one, twenty heads turned toward the sound. Fear jolted through me. Had the anti-shifters somehow gotten through the defenses? Had Sinthy used too much of her power to create the guns, and that had decreased the efficacy of the wards? Could that be it?

As if in answer, three gun-toting men stepped out of the trees and sprinted toward us. There were some shouts of surprise and shock from the pack. One man stopped running and raised his gun, aiming directly at us. Without hesitation, Nico lifted his rifle and fired. Two bullets slammed into the guy's chest. His arms and head went flying backward as his body tumbled away. An instant before the intruder hit the ground, he vanished in a small puff of what looked like smoke or steam.

"Holy shit," Nico muttered, then turned and shouted. "They aren't real. It's part of the spell. This is what Sinthy created. Everyone defend yourselves."

As though spurred on by his words, another ten people came running from the forest toward us. I watched them begin to get taken down, each one getting shot and then vanishing. Even though I understood that they weren't real people, the effect was so uncanny that I was unable to push away my fear. The intruders were all screaming out how much they hated us and wanted us to die. I couldn't tell myself I wasn't *really* in danger.

Forcing myself to act, I joined the others in firing on the magical creations. The gun bucked in my hand, so real that in seconds I totally forgot it was all make-believe. When any of our people were shot, their guns vanished from their hands, effectively *killing* them.

Anytime all of us were killed, or all the intruders were killed, the spell reset, and we started all over. It was awe-inspiring and gave me a whole new appreciation for Sinthy's powers. After three straight cycles of us defeating the intruders, the human forms and weapons all vanished.

It was so surprising and fast, like a light switch being flipped. I turned and saw Sinthy making her way to her feet, a tired smile on her lips.

"How was that?" she asked.

All I could do was laugh. "It was amazing." I stepped closer so no one could hear our words. "Just how powerful are you?"

Her smile faded, and a shadow passed across her eyes. "Powerful enough for my family to be killed for it. My parents and I were probably the strongest witches on Earth. The royals coveted our power."

It reminded me of all the young woman had lost. She had as much to gain from the fall of the royals as we did. Sinthy had spent her whole life working toward this final fight.

"Sinthy, that was outstanding," Nico exclaimed. "It was so real. How often can you do that?"

"The first time is always the hardest. It should get easier to harness the spell each time I do it. Though, I doubt I could ever hold it for more than an hour."

"This could be a game changer for training. I wish the other packs could experience this."

"I can work on a spell that would work at a distance. It may not feel as real for them, but it might be better than nothing."

"I don't want you to drain yourself," Nico said.

"It won't drain me. Not as long as I get a chance to refuel and rest between trainings."

"Amazing." Nico took her hands in his. "Thank you. You've already done so much for us. You'll have to tell me how I can repay you one day."

Sinthy smiled sadly. "You've given me a family. Besides, we're gonna take down Viola. That alone is enough for me."

He patted her shoulder and nodded. "Thanks." He turned and addressed everyone. "That's enough for today. Get some rest."

The crowd dispersed, leaving Nico and me alone. As Luis and Felipe hauled the gun cases back to the house, Nico pulled me aside.

"You did great, but next time I'd like you to stay farther from the action. I want you to learn, but if this were to happen for real, I'd prefer you have to defend yourself be a last resort."

I'd been shot—and *killed*—multiple times during Sinthy's little mirage. If that had been a real fight, I'd be dead. I nodded. "Got it."

He then grinned and looked over his shoulder toward the woods. I could almost taste his pent-up energy. Even knowing the fantasy hadn't been real, my adrenaline had still spiked, and I wanted to work it off. From the look he gave me, Nico felt the same.

Grinning, he nodded to the trees. "You wanna go for a run?"

As an answer, I sprinted away from him, shifting as I did. Nico laughed behind me before he shifted and joined me. The wind in my fur and the scents and sounds of the forest exhilarated me. As we ran through the trees, an overwhelming sense of longing and desire hit me, along with a surge of heat across my whole body. I ran faster, my feelings toward Nico building with each minute. It was a strange and wonderful sensation.

Chapter 5 - Nico

That evening I called Tiago and shared the training mirage Sinthy had come up with. "Do you think the other alphas would want similar training?"

"If what you're saying is true, I'd damn sure say so," Tiago said.

"Okay. She said she needs to tweak the spell a bit, but she can do it. Apparently, it'll get easier for her each time she does it. I really think this will help."

"That sounds like a plan. I'll discuss it with my son, and then I'll get reach out to the other alphas. I think they'll be on board."

When I hung up, I was in a great mood. But my mood quickly soured when Maddy walked in, a look of frustration on her face.

"What's wrong?" I asked.

Maddy flopped into a chair and groaned. "It's Abi. She's refusing to go anywhere with Sebastian."

"Are you kidding me?" I could feel the familiar irritation building again. "I thought this was all settled. Donatello could call any minute saying he's ready."

"I know. She told me she really wanted to grin and bear it, but she can't. It's too much for her."

"Damn it. What other choice does she have? I guess I could try and sneak her out and get her to the airport."

"Nico, it was probably too dangerous for Sebastian, but I know it's too dangerous for you. The airport is thirty miles away. That's a lot of ground to cover. I'll be honest. I don't know that it would have been safe in the first place. I want to talk to Sinthy about it."

I waved my hands in dismissal. "No. We can't ask more of her. She's already burning herself out with everything. Plus, if she teleports away, the wards will fall."

"Maybe she can think of something else. Look what she did today. Surely she can do something to get Abi to the airport safely. After everything we've seen her do, that should be an easy ask," Maddy said. She sounded more hopeful than assured.

"We'll talk to her," I said pointedly. "But if Sinthy has any hesitation at all, we call it off. I'm not letting that poor girl kill herself because Abi can't get her shit together. Deal?"

"Deal. I don't want Sinthy hurting herself, either."

When we peeked into Sinthy's room, she was eating a massive king-sized candy bar. She shrugged when we saw it. "Need carbs. Big spells are super draining. What's up?"

I sighed and took a seat. "Speaking of big spells— "

She brightened. "The other alphas want me to do the whole virtual reality thing?"

I was glad she looked excited about helping. "Umm, I think so. Tiago is going to get in touch with them all. That's... shit... that's not exactly what I came to you for today."

Sinthy looked from me to Maddy and raised an eyebrow. "Something I should know?"

"It's Abi. We need to find a way to get her to the airport. Donatello is going to hide her because she doesn't want to be here anymore, and that was the safest thing I could think of."

Sinthy rolled her eyes. "That guy. So slick and smooth. Nice dude, but not my type. How can I help?"

"We're trying to figure out how to get her there without having to go through miles of anti-shifters. Do you have any thoughts? Like... I don't know—can you make her face look different or something?"

Sinthy took another bite of her candy bar and shrugged. "I can just teleport her."

I frowned. "No, that won't work. You said if you left the pack lands, your wards would fall."

She gave Nico an incredulous smile. "Well, duh, but I don't have to go with her to teleport her."

I looked at Maddy, and she stared back in wide-eyed surprise. When I looked back at Sinthy's face, it was obvious she was confused as to why we were confused.

"Wait, did you guys think I had to be present at the arrival and departure points? I don't. I can send her. It's even more exhausting that way, but it's easy enough."

"Well... damn. I guess we should have asked earlier. Can..." My words trailed off as a thought occurred to me.

Sinthy, reading my mind, shook her head. "Nope. I know what you're thinking. Won't work."

"What was I— "

"You want me to teleport Viola here."

It was like I'd been smacked. The woman was eerie. That was exactly what I'd been thinking. If she could send Abi to the airport, why couldn't she bring Viola here?

"Umm, why wouldn't it work?"

Sinthy sighed and set her candy aside. "Teleportation is something that can be used as a weapon. It's sort of like hypnosis. You have to *want* to do it. It would be super easy to bring her here and deal with things once and for all. But nothing in life is that easy. Like I can't teleport us to her until I know where she is."

"Well, I guess it was a good thought, at least," I said. "Sinthy, I really don't want you doing this if it'll be too much for you. You've done so much already."

"It's fine, Nico. Seriously. Let me know when, and I'll take care of the rest."

Maddy and I both sighed with relief. Maddy gave Sinthy a hug. "Thank you for helping my friend."

I left to give Donatello a call. He answered quickly.

"Nico? I was actually getting ready to call you. The island is prepared. When can you get Abi to me?"

"Apparently, faster than I thought. When's a good time?"

"I can have a jet ready in two hours. It'll be at the private airstrip beside Tampa International. I trust the pilot with my life."

"Okay, let me get everyone ready. We can probably be there by then. I'll text you a confirmation time."

"All right." Without another word, Donatello disconnected.

An hour of chaos followed as I got everyone on the same page, helped Abi pack, and tried to find a basic floorplan for the airport so Sinthy didn't accidentally teleport us into the middle of a wall.

"I think I know where to put you guys," Sinthy said after inspecting a visitors' map we found online.

"You're sure?"

She nodded. "It'll be great, wait and see."

Sebastian sat in the corner of the kitchen, nursing a soda and a bag of chips and shooting sullen looks at us every now and then. Abi was completely ignoring him. His anxiety was palpable. Regardless of what they'd been through or done to each other, Sebastian was worried about her.

He wouldn't meet my eyes, even though he had to know I was staring right at him. Abi and Maddy were double-checking the small suitcase Abi had packed, but all I could do was worry about my friend. It would be nice if they figured all this shit out soon. If things did end up turning out okay for all of us, that was the first thing I would put my foot down about. Dealing with the two of them was almost as stressful as dealing with Viola.

Maddy wiped a hand across her forehead. "Dear lord, isn't anyone else hot?"

Living in Florida, I always made sure the air-conditioning was working and turned on. Shifters ran a little hotter than humans to begin with, so my house was almost always set below sixty-eight degrees. It was comfortable.

"No," I said. "I think it's fine."

"Are you serious?" she asked.

Gabriella stepped into the kitchen and eyeballed Maddy as she kept asking Abi and Sinthy if they were hot. Maddy's cheeks did look a little flushed. Was she getting sick? There was a tug on my sleeve, and I turned to Gabriella.

Without taking her eyes off Maddy, she whispered, "Can I talk to you really quick?"

"Yeah, sure," I said.

Finally locking her eyes on mine, she added, "In private?"

I led her upstairs to my office before closing the door. "Well? What's up?"

She chewed at her lip for a few minutes before answering. "Have you noticed anything… *off* about Maddy lately?"

"Not really." My brows knit together as I tried to think where she was going with this.

"I'm pretty sure she's about to go into heat."

I froze, remembering the run Maddy and I had gone on. Her scent had been different. Stronger. She'd been uncomfortably hot downstairs as well.

"Fuck," I muttered as it all came together in my head.

"Exactly," Gabriella said. "Not a great time for it. I know they make heat suppressants for shifters. I still have my medical license, so I can get them. We'd only have to get off the grounds."

"Sinthy can help with that. We can teleport out and grab whatever we need." I raised my eyebrow. "How much time do we have? Best guess?"

Gabriella shrugged. "Based on what I witnessed downstairs, her body is flushing. Hot flashes mean it's coming soon. Maybe a day or two."

"Shit," I hissed.

When female shifters went into heat, it wasn't terrible. Usually. The problem was that most women's first heat was intense. She'd have a hard time concentrating and doing anything. We did need those suppressants. However, I wasn't sure how happy Maddy would be about taking them. After all, she'd taken shifting suppressants since she was a child, and that was part of how this whole problem started. It was a different medicine, so I hoped she'd understand. I needed her fully focused.

"Make whatever calls you must. Get the meds prescribed, and I'll figure out how to get someone to a pharmacy."

Back downstairs, I found the others basically ready. Maddy looked like her usual self. Did she even notice a change happening? Could she even understand she was going into heat? I needed to discuss it with her, but that would need to wait until Abi was safely off.

"I'm going to see her off," Maddy stated as I came back into the room.

"Is that the best idea?" I asked.

"I don't care if it's a good idea or not. I'm going. It won't be dangerous. Sinthy will bring us back quickly. I'm going."

Her tone brooked no argument. Her mind was made up. I couldn't wait for life to become boring again— whenever that might be. I turned to look at Sinthy.

"If Maddy's going, then so am I. Can you send all three of us?"

Sinthy blew out a breath, puffing her cheeks as she did. "I'll need to eat a whole pizza and go to bed early, but yeah. Shouldn't be an issue."

"Well, let's do this. Before anything else comes up," I said.

Sebastian tossed his drink and snack into the trash can and stomped upstairs. He didn't spare us a second glance.

"Everyone ready?" I asked.

Abi was watching Sebastian go. She pulled her eyes away and looked at me. "Can I have a second? Real quick. I'll be right back."

I waved at her to go. The day couldn't end soon enough. She jogged up the stairs, and in a few seconds, I heard her having a murmured conversation with Sebastian. I blocked it out, giving them the privacy they needed. When she returned, Abi's back seemed a little straighter. Her eyes were more focused. It was like she'd finally figured something out. What that was, I had no clue. All I knew was that I was happy we were ready to go.

"Hold hands. Abi, keep your free hand on your suitcase," Sinthy said.

We did as she asked, then the witch mumbled a few words, and that same sensation hit me as it had when she'd teleported with Maddy and me.

Sinthy caught my eye and winked. "Have fun, Nico."

Before I could ask what the hell she was talking about, I blinked, and we were gone. Tugged along into whatever magic plane facilitated this fast travel. When I blinked again, the three of us stood in a bathroom stall. It was a large handicapped stall, but even so, we were crammed in tight with Abi's suitcase. Outside the stall, two women were having a conversation at the sink. I gritted my teeth, finally understanding Sinthy's joke. She'd sent us all into a women's bathroom. Very funny.

We waited for almost five minutes before things sounded quiet. Hustling out of the bathroom, I managed to get into the main hallway without anyone spotting me. The rest was fairly easy. It took some before we figured out how to get the private airstrip. We had to leave the main terminal and walk down a short sidewalk to a separate building with a few small planes out front on their personal taxiway attached to the airport's main runway.

A man stood on the tarmac holding a big cardboard sign that read: *Abi*. As we neared, the pilot waved to us and met our group halfway.

"Abi? Are you Nico?" the pilot asked.

I nodded. "Yeah, this is Abi. She'll be your passenger."

"Well, all right then. Only one bag, Miss?" he asked as he took her suitcase from her. "Mr. Moretti is very excited to have a guest."

"Umm, is the island nice?" Abi asked.

The pilot's smile grew. "Paradise, my lady. That's the only description."

"Is it a straight shot from here?" I asked, eyeing the small plane. Could he get all the way to the island with that tiny thing?

The pilot stowed the bag in the luggage compartment near the tail of the plane before answering. "We go from here to a small airstrip in the Keys, where we'll transfer to a chopper. From there, I'll get her the rest of the way."

"You can fly airplanes *and* helicopters?" I was surprised and a little impressed.

The pilot grinned. "Mr. Moretti only hires the best." He turned back to Abi. "Are we ready, my lady?"

Maddy and Abi shared a quick but strong hug.

"I love you, Abi. I'll see you soon," Maddy said.

"Maddy, I love you so much. I'll send you a picture of me sunbathing on the beach tomorrow."

"You'd better."

Maddy and I went back inside and watched as the small plane taxied out to the runway, and then, ten minutes later, it vanished into the clear blue sky. I sensed Maddy's sadness and worry and wrapped my arms around her, pulling her close.

"It's all going to be okay," I said.

"I hope so. I really want her to be okay again. Maybe some time alone will do that."

We found a spot out in one of the parking lots behind a palm tree that mostly hid us from prying eyes before I texted Sinthy that we were ready to go home. Within seconds, we were back in my living room. I didn't think I'd ever get used to that.

I glared at Sinthy. "The ladies' room? Really?"

She chuckled. "It's the small things in life." She yawned and stretched. "It's been a day. I'm going to have a little power nap."

That meant we wouldn't see her until the next morning. She wasn't lying when she said her body needed to recuperate after exerting herself with such powerful spells. Maddy and I were both mentally and physically exhausted and decided to turn in early as well, a couple of hours later.

We lay curled up with each other as the sun set. Maddy's head rested on my shoulder, and I could tell she wanted to say something. It was in the tension of her shoulders and in the scent coming off her.

"Go ahead and say whatever's on your mind," I said.

Maddy huffed a little laugh. "That's creepy."

"Maybe, but go ahead and give it to me."

She pushed herself up so she could look at my face. "I still feel kind of useless."

My face crumpled into a deep frown. "Useless? How?"

"I want to help more, do more. I get that when things get bad, I should stay as safe as possible, but it's frustrating. How would you react if everyone you cared about was out fighting while you were shoved away somewhere safe and sound?"

"I'd be pretty mad," I admitted. "But Viola isn't after me."

"Does that make it any better? I don't think it does for me."

She had a point. I couldn't imagine how bad I would feel in that situation.

"Then there's the vial," Maddy added.

I stiffened, and she must have noticed it because she quickly said, "I'm not drinking it. I only wanted us to think about what could happen. We can't dismiss it completely. Not if push comes to shove. If my becoming a full werewolf could save us, then it has to be on the table."

"But what about what you said to me the other day? What if it turns you into something terrible? Some creature you'd have no hope of controlling?"

"We've been wrong about a lot of things. We thought I'd shift into a werewolf when I first shifted. Instead, I'm just a regular shifter. We could be wrong about the vial. What if it really is a weapon we can use against the royals? I think we're being a little short-sighted if we think all Edemas did was create something that would turn his descendant into a monster. Right?"

I had no argument for that. We couldn't know what would happen to Maddy if she ingested it. I remembered

Isme's story about the past. All the lies that had been passed down as history. Speaking of the ancient witch reminded me of something.

"I get that," I said. "We also need to think about what Isme said about using it. She said it wasn't meant to be used in malice. Only for protection."

Maddy nodded. "I remember. That's why I think we should plan on me only taking it if there is no other way to win. If our backs are against the wall, and we're all gonna die anyway"—she shrugged—"what's the harm?"

That was a good enough plan for me. She was right. Who really cared what happened if the alternative was death? I lifted my hand, sticking my little finger out.

"Only as a last resort. When all hope is lost. Pinky promise?"

Maddy burst out laughing but twisted her pinky around mine. "Sure."

Ten minutes later, with the lights out, I could hear Maddy's breathing slip into deep, steady breaths of sleep. No amount of planning could erase my worry. It would hover over me until all this played out one way or another. Maddy shouldn't have to be a part of this war at all. It was horseshit that her whole world had been turned upside down. And the fact that she might be our last hope to win was terrifying. There was no way to know what the end held. We were going into this blind.

As I slipped off into my own world of dreams, I realized I'd never talked to Maddy about her going into heat. My eyes drifted shut, and I told myself it would be fine to wait until the next day.

Chapter 6 - Maddy

Darkness and heat. I couldn't tell where I was, but the heat was scorching. Hands were all over me, caressing my skin — four, five, maybe six pairs of hands. A cascade of groping, caressing fingers trailing across my breasts, through my hair, and slipping between my legs. I groaned in pleasure. When I finally opened my eyes, it was Nico, but a half-dozen of him. Multiple versions, all naked and exploring my body. One of them lowered their face to my pussy—

A blink and I was in a bathtub. The water was scalding; sweat trickled down my cheeks. I rested my head on the edge of the tub. A cock slid into me. Gasping, I looked down and saw no one. The feeling was there. It was like I was being fucked by a ghost. I spread my legs wider, letting it have its way with me. All I could think of was my desire. The water sloshed over the rim of the tub as I was taken roughly. I wanted to come, but—

A blink and I was in bed with Nico, his eyes closed, breathing deeply. A hunger unlike anything I'd ever known enveloped me. I didn't just want him. I needed him. Like I was going to starve if I didn't have him. I ripped his underwear down and slid his cock into my mouth, shoving my fingers into my pussy at the same time. He sat up, gasping, and looked into my eyes. "Maddy?"

"Maddy? Maddy? Wake up."

With a startled grunt, my eyes sprang open. I was covered in a cold sweat, and my hand was in my panties, two fingers inside my pussy. It had been a dream? No, not entirely, because I was still horny. I'd never been so turned on in my life. My clit was swollen and throbbing under my fingers.

Nico knelt over me, checking to see if I was okay. "Maddy? Was it a nightm—" He sniffed the air twice, and his eyes widened. "Oh, shit."

Before he could say anything else, I was on him. Tearing—literally tearing—his underwear off. The fabric ripped away, and exactly like in my dream, I had him in my mouth in a millisecond. I swallowed him until his tip reached the back of my throat. Nico grunted with surprise but then moaned as I slid my lips up and down his shaft; my pussy was so wet, my arousal dripped down my thighs. Another surge of heat burst within me, and I felt like I was in a sauna.

Pulling his cock from my mouth, I looked into his eyes. "Fuck me," I growled.

There was hesitation in his eyes, but I had him. His delay lasted only an instant before he flipped me on my back. Smiling with satisfaction, I wiped away the sweat that sheened my body. Nico yanked my panties off, and a second later, he buried his cock inside me.

"God, yes," I murmured as his glorious length slid in and filled me.

He ground his hips against my body, rocking inside me. I ran my hands through his hair and across his chest. Sex had never been so good. Ever. A myriad of thoughts spun through my head. I wanted him in every way I could think of. I wanted him to fuck my pussy, my mouth, my ass. I wanted him to pull my hair and ride me until his balls were empty, and then I wanted more. What the fuck had gotten into me?

Desire urged me on. I raised my hips again and again, fucking him from below. Nico lowered his face to my chest, taking a nipple into his mouth. The sensation made my eyes roll back in my head. I wrapped my legs around his waist and flexed my thighs, pulling him as deep as he could go. It was like I couldn't be satisfied—like nothing was enough.

"Fuck me. Fuck me hard, Nico," I murmured into his ear.

"Oh God," he moaned as he slammed into me.

A smile formed on my lips as his body crashed into me. Our sweaty flesh clapped together with each thrust. My orgasm came fast and hard. A quick buildup that exploded like a bomb, surprising me with its speed and power. Slamming my head back into the bed, I clutched the sheets and gritted my teeth. I felt the veins in my neck pop out as pleasure cascaded over my body.

Sucking in a breath, I realized that, instead of satiating me, the orgasm had only strengthened my desire. Digging my nails into his back, I urged him on. My mind had short-circuited. I'd never experienced anything like it, but I couldn't think about anything but having him.

Nico clutched at me, grabbing my breasts as he fucked me harder. Sweat dripped from his nose onto my chest.

"Maddy, I'm gonna come," he hissed.

"Not yet. Please, God, not yet. Harder. Fuck me harder."

He fucked me hard. Taking me like a madman, crushing me into the bed as his cock thrust in and out of me. A second climax swirled deep inside my body, ready to burst. Nico picked up the pace, then started to shudder and gasp. He grunted, and the muscles of his back flexed under my palms as his cock spasmed inside me. It sent me over the edge. I screamed, guttural and animalistic, as I came. It was even stronger than the first. Rippling across my body and pulsing between my legs.

By the time Nico rolled off me, I was a twitching, shivering mess. I was satisfied, but I still felt a little twinge deep inside. A spark that I already knew was going to rage into a fire. How could I still be so horny? We'd just fucked each other's brains out.

"Maddy?" Nico asked, panting for breath. "You're going into heat. I should have told you. I shouldn't have done that without telling you."

"Oh, holy shit," I whispered.

I was an idiot. Now that I was a full wolf, of course, I'd go into heat. I was like any other shifter now. With everything else going on, the new bodily processes had been the least of my concerns. It never even occurred to me to think about it.

I rolled over and placed a hand on Nico's cheek. "It's okay. I wanted it. Don't feel bad."

He exhaled heavily. "I know. I kinda thought we'd have a few days to get some heat suppressants, but I guess I was wrong."

I'd heard about heat suppressants my whole life. It was a special drug female shifters took when their heat was coming on. The combination of herbal and synthetic ingredients helped tamp down the urges. After feeling what I'd experienced, it was a good thing they were readily available. Otherwise, female shifters would have been humping out in the streets. The need was so strong, I didn't think anything could have stopped me. *Nothing.*

"Let me go get Gabriella. She's a doctor. I want her to make sure you're okay."

"Uh... okay. I guess," I said.

Nico and I both put on robes, and then he vanished to go down to the room Gabriella had been staying in. They reappeared about five minutes later. Gabriella looked like she was still half asleep.

"Maddy? How are you feeling?" she asked as she sat next to me.

I thought about that for a second. "Umm... well... uh."

"Horny as hell?" she asked bluntly.

Heat rushed into my cheeks, but I nodded, unable to meet her eyes. Gabriella sighed, then pulled a thermometer out of the pocket of her robe and pressed it against my forehead. After checking that, she took my wrist in her hand, pressing her forefinger against my pulse. A few more checks and she was done.

"She's in heat," Gabriella said. "It's already fully manifested. Suppressants won't do anything now. She'll have to ride it out."

"What does that entail?" I asked.

Gabriella gave me an embarrassed smile. "Well, I have good news and bad news. The good news is you and your mate get to... um... *enjoy* each other. A lot. The bad news is it could last anywhere from two to five days."

"Five days?" I asked, mouth agape.

The desire I'd had when waking had been more than I could handle. It had been like my conscious mind had vanished, replaced by nothing but the Id—my instinctual desires—of my mind. Only wanting to fulfill whatever urges might flash across my mind. I couldn't imagine enduring a week of that.

"Up to five days. The average is three. It..." She glanced at Nico, then at me. "Well, it might get more intense before it subsides." She looked uncomfortable. "I think I'll stay at one of the empty guest houses for the next few days. The two of you will need some privacy."

"Oh, Jesus," I grumbled, covering my face with my hands.

Gabriella patted me on the shoulder. "Don't be embarrassed. It happens to everyone at least once. Some women even choose to totally forgo the suppressants and just... enjoy their time with their mate."

She got up to leave, then turned back before walking out the door. "I'll spread the word that everyone needs to stay away from the house for a few days."

Nico locked the door behind her and turned to look at me. "I'm sorry. Like I said, I should have told you as soon as I suspected."

I looked at him as I chewed at my lower lip. The now-familiar warmth started to radiate out of my stomach and pelvis. "Well, since you want to apologize for something, I think I know how you could make it up to me."

Nico's eyes widened in surprise. "Already?"

We had sex twice more that night, finally passing out from exhaustion near dawn. The next few days were interesting—to say the least. Was this how hormonal teenage boys felt? Like clockwork, every hour, I was ready to go again. When the urge came on, there was no holding off or waiting until later.

In the kitchen, Nico knelt on the floor and lapped at my pussy while I was bent over the sink. My cries of pleasure echoed through the empty house as his tongue assaulted me.

In the middle of lunch, I dropped my cutlery, pulled his cock out, and rode him right at the dining room table. I was the aggressor, taking him and satisfying my needs. There was very little guilt—my heat pushed those thoughts away.

In the shower, we experimented with anal. Feeling him fill me in a new and kinky way sent my head spinning. By the time we really got used to it, I was nearly losing my mind as his cock slid in and out of my ass. I came so hard that I collapsed to my knees while I recovered.

Over and over it went. After a day, it seemed like I was living in a porn movie. I didn't feel ashamed or embarrassed, though. I had a need, one that was so instinctual that all I could do was follow it. I did start to pity Nico a bit. There was only so much the guy could do, and after a while, he had to revert to only oral or using his fingers because his cock was too fatigued to give me what I needed. Then every morning, once he was rested, I used his body again. It was sort of liberating. Taking control. It was something, as a woman, I don't think I'd ever truly done. Not with sex, anyway.

Even though it was being forced on us by my heat, I still had the feeling that Nico and I were growing closer as it went on. Sex was an act of intimacy, and each time it bound us closer. As I demanded more of him every hour, he didn't act like he was being forced or put out. If anything, he tried even harder to bring me to orgasm— working diligently to give me what my body needed, even as he exhausted himself. I fucking loved the man.

Chapter 7 - Nico

When I woke, it felt like I hadn't slept at all. The night before, Maddy had roused me from sleep by tugging on my hand and pushing it between her legs. My sixteen-year-old self would have rejoiced if he'd known he'd live to experience the last three days.

At no point in my life had I ever been so tired. I'd stopped counting at the nineteenth time Maddy pounced on me. So, it had probably been at least twenty-five times. Everything hurt. My legs hurt from holding her against the wall on the second night, and my feet were raw from bracing against the tile to keep us steady while we fucked three different times in the shower. My balls actually ached. I hadn't known that could even happen just from sex, but here I was. I wasn't sure I could get it up again for at least a couple of hours. Even my tongue was sore from the slightest movement.

Rolling over, I found Maddy sound asleep. Giving the air a cursory sniff, I sighed with relief. Her pheromones had dropped like mad since the previous night. She smelled like her old self. The heat had subsided. As exciting and fun as it had been, I was more than ready to recuperate for a few days.

I'd surprised myself with how well I'd kept pace with her. It was shocking that I had any little swimmers left after the first day. The trash can beside the bed was overflowing with used condoms and two bottles of empty lube. I wrinkled my nose in disgust as I crawled out of bed. Pulling on a shirt and pajama bottoms and slipping my feet into a pair of flip-flops, I quietly took care of the trash.

Three condoms littered the shower floor, and six dirty towels were flung about the bathroom from when we'd cleaned up after our little romps. It took about ten minutes, but I managed to clean the house of all sexual paraphernalia. At least, I really hoped so. The last thing I wanted was for my mother to open the pantry the next day and find a gross, flaccid condom on the floor.

As though Fate heard my thoughts, I glanced out the front window and saw my dad walking up the sidewalk toward my house. Maddy's dad was beside him. A blush rose to my cheeks. I couldn't help it. All the dirty things I'd done to his daughter over the last couple of days flashed through my mind. I was an adult, and so was Maddy, but that didn't change the whole father-boyfriend dynamic.

Not wanting them to come in until I'd had a chance to *really* clean up, I tied the trash bag and tossed it into the laundry room before jogging over to the front door to meet them outside.

Dad smiled when he saw me and reached out to pat me on the shoulder. "Glad to see you survived Maddy's first heat."

"Is she okay?" Maddy's father asked, his voice tinged with rage.

"Uh, yeah, she's fine. Sleeping it off," I said.

"Why did none of you know this was coming?" he growled. "Shouldn't you all have done something to stop this? I know they make drugs for it, for Christ's sake."

I held my hands up, surprised by the fury in his eyes. "Mr. Sutton, I'm sorry, but we had a lot going on. I'll be totally honest, but it was the last thing any of us were thinking about."

From the corner of my eye, I saw Gabriella walking up an opposite path, my mother beside her. Dear God, was I going to have to talk about my sex life in front of every goddamned parent in the pack lands?

Maddy's father shoved a finger at my chest. "That's not good enough. You're her mate. You're supposed to take care of her and make sure she's okay."

"That's enough," Gabriella said. "Maddy is a wolf now. This is totally natural. You're acting like it was something dangerous or something to be ashamed of."

"You told us to suppress her wolf!" Maddy's father barked at her.

"Yes, I did, but that was a long time ago, and it was for her own protection. Those days are over. It's time for her to live her life the way she was meant to. You have to embrace her for who she is now."

Maddy's father scoffed. "I'm supposed to embrace my little girl being used like some sex doll every eight or nine months?"

"Stop it!"

We all spun to see Maddy standing on the front porch, tying her robe around her waist. I looked back and saw the color drain from her father's face.

"Maddy, I didn't— "

"No." She cut him off. "I don't care what you *meant*. All I know is what I heard."

He lowered his head in shame. I was having a hard time not lowering my own head. Maddy was furious. It wasn't that she was mad at me, but she was still terrifying when she got mad like this.

She stomped forward on bare feet. "I understand that you're viewing things from a human perspective, but that isn't what this is about. Apart from that, Nico is my mate. That's the same as a human spouse. Whatever we do in our bedroom is our business, not yours." Her face softened, and she lowered her tone. "Nico loves me. He locked himself in the house for three days to attend to my needs. If he hadn't, I would have been under an extreme amount of discomfort. If you think he was *using* me, you have it backward. I was the one using him."

My parents chuckled, and I could have lit a match on my face. I'd never had a more uncomfortable conversation in my life. I stared intently at the ground, but a sideways glance showed me Maddy's father was still scowling but looking chastised. Gabriella ignored him and stepped closer to Maddy, putting a hand on her shoulder.

"How do you feel, sweetie?"

Maddy gave her a small smile. "I feel fine. Thank you for *your* concern."

Maddy's father sucked in a breath. Realizing, too late, that he hadn't even asked about her well-being, he looked up and opened his mouth to say something, but Maddy cut him off with a disappointed shake of her head.

"Dad, you and Mom need to realize things have changed. I'm a wolf now. I am, and always will be, your daughter. That will never change, but you have to come to terms with the fact that I've changed. I'm not your helpless little girl anymore. You can't look at me from a human's perspective anymore. Those days are gone."

She turned on her heel and went back inside without sparing a glance back at her father. Her dad stood there, looking crestfallen, heartbroken, and embarrassed. I nodded at my parents and Gabriella to give us a minute. The three of them strolled around to my backyard, leaving me standing with Maddy's father.

"Mr. Sutton, I'm sorry about all this. This wasn't how I would have wanted it to happen. In a perfect world, none of this would have been so sudden or surprising. But we aren't living in a perfect world. I can only imagine what you and your wife are going through."

"You can't," he murmured. He didn't sound mad anymore, only sad.

Nodding, I said, "She isn't the same girl you raised. Not physically, anyway. She's still your kid. A child you raised, and you turned her into an amazing person. I can never thank you enough for that. But as much as you love her and want to protect her, you have to realize that she isn't weak. She may very well be the strongest of all of us. Her life has changed. She's a wolf. A descendant of the strongest shifter to ever live." I shook my head, not sure if he was understanding. He just kept staring at the ground.

"She's a wolf—a wolf with a target on her back. Everything you see on the news, all the crimes and deaths and horrific things the royals have done over the last year, have all been to get to her. The very last thing she needs is her parents judging her over something that is both beyond her control and very natural for our kind. For *her* kind." I took a breath and eased my tone. "Now that we know, we can plan for the next time and buy plenty of suppressants."

Maddy's father finally looked up and locked eyes with me. They were bloodshot and wet like he was on the verge of crying. I couldn't discern anything but sorrow in his eyes.

"I'm sorry, Nico. All you and your family have done is try to protect us. Without you... I probably wouldn't be here."

I waved him off. "That's nothing. I would do it for anyone—"

"That's the thing," he said. "Not many people would. Human or shifter. You've put everything you know at stake for Maddy and for us." He kicked a pebble in anger. "And all I'm doing is standing here bitching like a child. Again, I'm sorry. I'll... uh... head back to our cabin. Okay?"

He turned and started trudging back to the cabin he and his wife were sharing.

Before he got too far, I called after him. "Mr. Sutton?"

He turned back mid-stride. From the look and his face, I could tell he was ready and willing to get another reprimand or warning. I groaned inwardly.

"You're a good father. Never forget that."

His face almost crumpled into tears. He wiped at his eyes and nodded before heading on his way.

I put a hand to my head, watching him go. I was getting a headache. Deciding to get inside before anyone else stopped by to make my morning uncomfortable, I walked up the steps and through the door, shutting and locking it behind me.

Upstairs, I heard the water going into the shower. Undressing, I stepped into the bathroom and joined Maddy. She grinned at me as I closed the shower door.

"Looking to get lucky *again*?" she asked, one eyebrow quirked.

I laughed and shook my head. "Lord, no. My downstairs needs a good long rest. He's spent the last few days running a marathon. Even Olympic-level athletes need to rest."

"Oh, so it's Olympic level, is it?"

Shrugging, I said, "Didn't hear many complaints the last three days."

Maddy chuckled. "Fair enough."

My smile faded when I saw the sad expression that slid over her face. "Are you okay?"

"I don't know," she stated simply. "It seems like my parents are sort of at odds with everything. Gabriella has been more supportive and understanding of everything. I don't understand it."

Wrapping her in my arms, I pulled her flush against my chest. "They're nervous and scared. It's confusing to have your whole life flipped upside down. They, *literally*, don't know how to help. This is outside their area of expertise. They're human. Gabriella is a wolf. It's natural that she'd be more understanding."

"I guess you're right. It doesn't make it any easier, though."

I rubbed my hand up and down her back as the water streamed down our bodies. "We'll talk to them. Sort it all out and set things in stone. They both love you. I know they'll get it together for you. Anyone would."

Maddy lifted her face to mine, stealing a quick kiss. "Thank you, Nico."

"I will do anything to keep you safe. Not just your body, but your mind too. Whatever it takes."

She pressed herself against me and slid a hand between my legs. "So, are you sure you need to rest?"

The stirrings of desire pricked up inside me, but not even that could convince me I'd give her the pleasure she needed.

Sighing, I rolled my eyes. "How about tonight? Maybe I can take a nap today. Prepare to make your toes curl again."

"I'll take that as a promise," Maddy said and kissed me one more time before I got out.

Drying off, I left her to finish her shower. I dressed and went to my office—I hadn't checked my phone or emails in days. I'd been too busy fucking Maddy. Not a bad way to spend three days, but things still needed attention. I had dozens of texts to answer from Luis, Sebastian, Felipe, and Donatello. There were at least ten emails from some of the pack leaders and multiple voicemails. As I worked my way through them all, the back of my mind slipped into the introspection of the previous three days. It was one flash of sex after the other. Writhing bodies, warm wet holes, moans of pleasure, and exhaustion.

A memory flitted through my mind, and my fingers froze on the keyboard. That very first moment. The morning Maddy woke up. It had been so fast and furious. A blur. My own hormones had gone haywire at the scent of her heat. I frowned. Had I put on a condom? I couldn't remember. Maybe I had, but…

Chapter 8 - Maddy

When my eyes opened the next morning, I could sense something was wrong. A dark foreboding settled on my mind as soon as I was fully conscious. I sat up, quickly glancing around the room. Part of me was worried there was an intruder, but I was alone. The other side of the bed was empty. Nico was nowhere in sight.

I grabbed my phone, and my eyes widened when I read that it was almost nine in the morning. That was later than I'd been sleeping. Ever since shutting the bar down, I no longer slept until noon. Nico must have let me sleep. I definitely needed it after three straight days of nothing but sex. Still, I wondered where he was. Part of my sense of impending doom was that I could sense Nico's worry. I could tell he was upset and scared. I needed to find him.

Jumping from the bed, I yanked on my clothes and hurried out of the room. At the top of the landing, I heard the faint murmuring of the TV. The sound was loud but still unintelligible. As I came down the stairs, I heard a voice— Sebastian.

"Holy shit. I can't believe this is happening." He sounded heartbroken and terrified.

A thin spike of fear sliced through my heart. I didn't want to know what was happening, but I had to find out. Once I was at the base of the stairs, I noticed Nico sitting on the couch, leaning forward, intent on the news broadcast. Felipe, Sebastian, and Luis were all there. My parents were sitting on the other couch—twin looks of horror and shock on their faces. Gabriella stood in the kitchen, her eyes trained on the TV screen. Her face was a stony mask of anger. She was the first to see me.

"Maddy? You need to see this," she muttered.

Nico spun in his seat, and my heart almost shattered at his expression. I'd never seen him look so broken. Devastation and sadness marred my mate's handsome face.

He raised a hand, beckoning me forward. "Come on."

I moved toward him in a haze, almost like I was in a dream. I took his hand and sank into his lap. The news seemed to be of a war zone.

"They've been playing the same report on repeat for the last fifteen minutes," Luis said. "It'll start over again in a second." He sounded weary beyond words.

True to his words, the report started over with an anchor in a studio. The words *Emergency Special Update* scrolled across the bottom of the screen in large red letters.

"Good morning," the reporter said. "We come to you today with a report out of Virginia. Early reports have come in that local anti-shifter activists, under the assumed direction of Viola Monroe, have attacked a wolf-shifter compound near Roanoke. A local affiliate is on site. Before we go to them, we have to caution our viewers. If children are present, it would be best if they left the room. What you are about to see is… disturbing, to say the least. We go now to Johnathan Moyer."

The camera switched to a man standing in the rain, a blue raincoat with the network's logo on the chest covering him. He looked shell-shocked. Someone shouted his name off-camera. He blinked twice and seemed to come back to himself.

"Yes… uh… thank you, Clarice. This is Johnathan Moyer with Channel Twenty-Two News out of Roanoke. I'm standing here at a Roanoke County wolf-shifter enclave. The compound houses nearly three dozen families, with the Harris family being the alpha seat of power in the pack.

"At approximately three-thirty this morning, a group of seventy-five to a hundred anti-shifter activists approached the fences and gates, demanding that the shifter population inside bring themselves out for some form of lynch-style justice. The local police force had nearly a dozen officers on site to guard and protect the compound. Surviving members of that police force tell me that when the officers refused to allow them access and asked them to turn around and return home, a second group of anti-shifters, hidden in the forest, opened fire on them. This resulted in the deaths of nearly all the officers before they had time to draw their weapons."

"Oh my God," I whispered, slapping my hand to my mouth.

"Once the officers were down, the activists flooded into the pack lands." The reporter glanced behind him, then turned back to the camera, his face ashen. "The activists proceeded to attack... all members of the wolf pack. Semi-auto weapons, shotguns, homemade Molotov bombs, and simple hand tools like... like axes and hammers were used in the attack."

Behind him, I could see EMTs, police officers, and firefighters walking through the remains of the compound. Fire had gutted several homes. I glimpsed human and shifter bodies littering the ground. Most were covered by sheets or already placed in body bags. The body of a young girl, no older than seven, lay face-up in the rain, eyes closed. Closed forever.

Pain pricked in each of my fingertips as my claws threatened to extend. The anger roiling inside me was almost enough to force me to shift right then and there.

The reporter went on. "Thankfully, one mortally wounded officer was able to radio for backup before succumbing to her wounds. The Harris family pack defended themselves, but both sides sustained heavy losses. By the time officers arrived, the battle was over. Officials are still tallying casualties, but as of right now, we know that thirty-seven of the activists were killed, along with at least that many wounded to various degrees. Nine officers were killed in the line of duty, with six more hospitalized with severe injuries. The shifter pack sustained a loss of twenty members, and of that number, five were adolescents." Tears glittered in the reporter's eyes. "That includes two twin children, one year of age, who perished in a fire started by the activists." He broke down and chopped his hand across his throat, telling the cameraman to cut.

The original anchor returned to the screen. "Thank you, Johnathan. I can't imagine what it's like there. We now have Glen Harris, alpha of the pack that was attacked last night. He comes to us live from the local Roanoke hospital where his pack mates are being cared for."

The screen split in two, and a man appeared on the other side. A bandage covered his left eye. Fresh, red scratches ran all the way down to the thick salt-and-pepper beard that covered most of his face.

"Mr. Harris, I would like to extend my condolences to you and your pack."

"Thank you, Clarice," he said, his voice thick with emotion.

"How is your pack dealing with this tragedy?

He shook his head slowly. "Not well. I lost friends last night. I… I watched a pup, no more than four years old, get murdered right in front of my eyes. These people are vicious and have no morals." Tears streamed from his one good eye. "All they do is hate."

The pain and grief in his voice cracked me in two. My knee bounced nervously as he spoke. My wolf and I yearned to go to this man, this pack, and help them. To tear and rend and brutalize those responsible.

"Mr. Harris, did these people give any indication who sent them? Most reports say they were working on the belief that Miss Viola Monroe of the disgraced Monroe Group was speaking directly to them through her various online videos and posts. Was this the case?"

The alpha nodded grimly. "They were screaming about how we shouldn't even be alive. That we were abominations. It was the same damn hate that woman spews. I wouldn't wish this on anyone." Resolve suddenly formed on his face, his one bright blue eye staring into the camera full of fire and rage. He held up a finger. "I will tell you this, and I hope every anti-shifter in the world is watching. We killed a bunch of you. We killed more of you than you did of us. If you keep following this woman's orders, this is your fate. My brothers and sisters around the world won't stand for this. Bear, wolf, panther—any species—won't lie down and die. We aren't made that way. If you don't want to die, you better turn tail and run."

After a few more words of condolence and thanks, the news anchor ended the interview, and the broadcast went to commercial. I looked around at all the others. The room was so quiet I could hear my own heartbeat. Several of them were sniffling and wiping tears from their eyes. Nico nudged me, and I moved so he could stand.

"I'm afraid this won't be the end. It feels like the start of something," Nico said.

"What do you mean?" Mom asked.

He pointed at the screen. "Others will see this and try to take things into their own hands. Yes, a bunch of those anti-shifters died, but more people will see this as a call to arms. Instead of being scared to act, they'll see those dead humans as an act of war by the shifters."

"That's bullshit," Sebastian barked. "Those fuckers attacked them."

Nico nodded. "I know that, but that won't be how they justify it. All those people will see is dead humans, and they'll gnash their teeth and rage about how good clean humans are dead because filthy evil shifters killed them. Fuck the truth."

It was insane, but he was right. Once people aligned themselves with one side or the other, they were typically blind to the truth. You saw what you wanted to see, and there was no changing their perspective, not without something major and indisputable.

Nico slapped a hand on the wall in anger. "You know, the worst part is that we can't protect everyone. We've got it better than almost any other pack. Between Donatello and Sinthy, we're better off than others. All I want to do is help everyone, but I can't. It's like I'm fucking impotent." He turned and glared at his three friends. "You all make sure everyone is training every day. Every. Damned. Day. Increase the guards on the fences. And we need to figure out where that bitch, Viola, is. The only way this all stops is if their damned figurehead is taken down."

He walked over and pressed his lips to my forehead, kissing me, then headed upstairs.

"I've gotta make some calls. I'm sure the other alphas have all seen this." Without another word, he jogged up to his office and slammed the door.

Felipe nodded to Luis and Sebastian. "Come on. Let's grab some people. Anyone who hasn't gone through a training session. We need to make sure everyone is ready to fight if it comes to it."

The three men nodded their goodbyes and left me with my three parents. Mom was wiping at her eyes. Dad had an arm around her, and Gabriella was still standing in the kitchen, a cup of coffee clutched in her hand as she stared at the floor.

Mom looked at me with terror in her eyes. "We were right to hide you all those years," she said. "These people really are crazy"—she pointed at the TV— "and I don't want that to happen to you."

"I know, Mom, this is bad. Nothing can be done now, though. Not until we find Viola."

She shook her head. "We need to hide you. Like you did with Abi." She heaved a sigh and slapped the couch. "None of this would have happened if you hadn't taken that stupid ancestry test. I wish you'd just left it all alone."

It was like I'd been slapped. Was she blaming me for this? All because I took some silly at-home DNA test? There was no way I could have ever known any of this would happen. Never in a million years. Yet here she was, telling me that I'd screwed up. My face twisted into a scowl. Dad leaned toward Mom and whispered angrily into her ear, but before I could open my mouth to defend myself, Gabriella spoke up.

"This isn't Maddy's fault. It's mine. I did this. It goes farther back than that test. I knew exactly what Maddy was and what she could be. I told you to put her on suppressants. I lied and never told you she was my daughter. If Maddy knew what she was from the beginning, things might have turned out better." She looked into Mom's eyes. "You can't blame Maddy for what's happened."

Mom looked stricken, both by what Gabriella said and by whatever Dad was hissing into her ear. She shook her head and cried more. "No... I'm sorry. I didn't mean it like that." She looked at me. "Maddy, I'm sorry. It's just that I'm so scared I'm going to lose you. I shouldn't have said it like that. The last thing I want is to lose you—I'd rather die than let that happen.'

I nodded, my breath huffing through my nostrils. I understood. Things were tense. Everyone was afraid. She couldn't help being terrified.

"Look," I said. "Nico and the other packs are going to do everything they can to prevent what we saw on the news. We're going to train, and we're going to fight. I know, deep down, that everything will be all right."

"You can't know that," Dad said with a sad shake of his head.

"Right," Mom added. "We can't assume it will all work out. I'm sure those shifters in Virginia thought things would work out fine too."

Gabriella sat beside me and put a hand on my knee as she looked at the couple who'd raised me.

"Maddy is strong," she said, her expression incredibly sad. "You never knew her biological father, but he was the strongest person I ever met. That strength is in Maddy. I can sense it. All she needs to do is believe in herself."

Inside my mind, my wolf rumbled happily at her words as if she agreed. Was she even stronger than I thought? Was that what my wolf was agreeing with? The idea surprised and frightened me. Even after all this, was I still suppressing my wolf's true power?

I looked at Gabriella, and she gave me a knowing smile. Mom and Dad still weren't totally sold on the prospect of Nico and me being safe. The thought still tickled my mind that there might be something more lurking inside me. My wolf had nearly pounded her chest with pride when Gabriella talked about how strong I was.

An hour later, the guys had organized another training session with Sinthy, ready to create another magical simulation. Nico was there, and most of the pack had come out to watch, which wasn't typical. Everyone must have seen the news. They wanted to see what kind of chance we would have.

Nico nudged me. "Let's work on a fighting retreat. We have to plan for all possibilities. Then we can see how it goes with us trying to get you and the others out if things go bad."

I shook my head. "No. Not this time. I want to do a full-scale assault. A lot of people attacked that shifter compound."

Nico seemed like he was going to argue, but I cut him off by looking over at Sinthy. "I want at least a hundred enemies this time. All of them were armed with guns. Can you do that?"

Sinthy shrugged and smiled. "It's your world. I'm just living in it."

A few moments later, the magically simulated anti-shifters came pouring out of the forest. I reached deep inside and touched my wolf. There was a moment of understanding between us. With a flex of my mind, I told her to take full control, to give me all she had, and I would guide us. She howled in excitement, and a moment later, I shifted.

I'd thought I understood my wolf. But there had been so much more I'd suppressed. Unconsciously, I was afraid of what might happen. The power was immense. I moved faster than ever, my paws barely touching the ground as I sprinted. My instincts were honed sharp as a razor, my body able to see, hear, and smell the bullets as they whizzed toward me. I dodged and ducked the projectiles before they had a chance to strike.

My teeth snapped through throats and arms, dropping the faux enemies to the ground in a puff of smoke. I moved faster and faster, almost like I would never get tired. Soon the sounds of my pack mates vanished, almost like they'd disappeared. I was locked in the dance of battle, more graceful and savage than I'd ever been in my life. The wolf inside me was like a goddess of war, dragging me into battle.

When the final enemy tumbled to the ground, I shifted back and turned to see where everyone had gone. The entire pack—everyone—was staring at me in wide-eyed shock. They had all backed away to watch the show. Even my mother and father were staring at me with slack-jawed surprise.

I pushed my sweat-soaked hair out of my face as I walked toward them. Nico looked me up and down with an approving and somewhat turned-on expression.

"What's everyone looking at?" I asked.

"Holy shit," Sebastian shouted. "You were… like… holy shit."

Nico grinned. "You took out ninety percent of the enemies by yourself. It was madness. I've never seen a wolf move like that."

The entire pack broke out into spontaneous applause. I blushed and glanced over at Gabriella. She was clapping, too, a secret smile playing on her lips. She'd been right. I was strong. I was more powerful than I'd ever realized.

Chapter 9 - Nico

Later that afternoon, when the adrenaline had faded, I was sitting in my office when Donatello called.

"I assume you've seen the news," he said before I could even say a word.

"First thing I saw this morning. I can't believe they attacked the police. It's madness."

"Zealots tend to be quite corruptible. They have no sense of place, no understanding of repercussions. There's a reason it was so easy for the Nazis to convince people to do terrible things. Once one powerful person verbalizes their deepest darkest beliefs, they take that as acceptance to bring about the endgame they want. It's not a surprise to me. And the worst part is that rather than acting as a release valve for tension, this situation will escalate things."

I sighed and rubbed the bridge of my nose to stave off the massive headache forming behind my eyes.

"That's basically what I told my people. People are gonna be emboldened by what happened in Virginia. It won't be long before we see more of these attacks," I said.

"That is my fear as well, my friend."

"We have to find Viola. That's the only way this ends."

"You are correct. The best way to kill a snake is by cutting off the head. Things won't completely die down, but without their figurehead to look toward, the extremists won't be as foolhardy."

"How's that going, anyway? Finding Viola, I mean."

Donatello hummed. "The shifter alliance I've formed is scouring the globe. So far, nothing."

Donatello had banded together with over a dozen other shifters of influence from around the world. Together, they had a fortune in the tens of billions. More money than the royals ever had. Plus, they weren't being hunted by every law-enforcement agency known to man. They could move in the shadows and weren't bound by diplomatic ties or international laws. With the money they had, they could go into the dark places people, like the FBI and Interpol, couldn't.

"We have increased our reach, though," he went on. "Sometime today, an anonymous website will go live and, with some prodding, will be mentioned on most media sources around the world. It will proclaim a fifty-million-dollar award for anyone pointing us in the direction of Viola Monroe. That alone should cut down on the number of dark holes she can hide in. Even if she has safehouses and allies, fifty million dollars is a lot of money. More than enough to get someone to flip on her."

"Jesus Christ," I muttered under my breath. "Fifty million? Can you guys afford that?"

Donatello chuckled. "My friend... For one, yes, of course, we can. For another? I would double or even triple it if it meant getting that smart-mouthed bitch off the streets."

I blinked. Donatello had never used such foul language with me before. He was always so composed and well-bred. It showed exactly how upset he was with what was going on, that his control slipped for even a second.

"She's the face of this war," Donatello said. "The sooner she is taken in.... Or dealt with in another way... the sooner it's all over. No one else in her organization carries as much weight or power as she does. End the Monroe line, and the royals fall apart.

"I'll contact you again if anything important happens. I hope you'll do the same for me?"

"Of course, of course, yes. Don? Can you give me an update on Abi? How is she doing?" If I told Maddy about this call, she'd want to know.

"Maddy's little friend? Quite well so far. She doesn't come to the main house much. She's residing in one of the small cabins near the ocean. My staff takes her three meals a day, and we stocked the pantry there, but it's not as luxurious as the other rooms throughout the island. I think she's taking a hard look at herself. I see her in the distance sometimes, either strolling the beach or simply staring off toward the ocean. Tell Maddy her friend is doing fine."

"Thank you," I said, relieved. "I'll talk to you later."

I shoved my phone into my pocket. I was happy that Donatello and his friends were working on the problem, but it made me feel even more worthless. I was sitting here, under the impenetrable protection of a witch, completely safe while other packs were being attacked and killed. The heavy weight of guilt filled me like a thick stone right in my chest, weighing me down. I thought of Tiago and all the others. Some of them didn't even have fences around their pack lands. My God, if the same thing happened to them like in Virginia… It would be a massacre. No amount of training could overcome sheer numbers. Time was ticking. A bomb was about to explode and soon.

Before I could go further down that rabbit hole, Maddy walked in. Her eyes were bloodshot from crying.

"Hey? What's wrong? What happened?" Panic seized my heart.

She waved me off and flopped into a leather chair. "Nothing happened. I was downstairs watching another news report about that pack. They updated the death toll. Apparently, five more shifters who were in critical condition at the hospital died. Two of them were children."

"Son of a bitch," I hissed, pounding my fist into my desk. I beckoned her over.

Maddy shook her head. "Not now. I swear to God, if you hug me, I'll probably break into tiny pieces. I hate this, Nico. It's worse than it's ever been. I really thought that once we exposed her, Viola would fall apart. I truly believed it would all be over."

"I know. It's not what we thought would happen."

Crying wouldn't solve anything. I knew that, but what else could we do? Again, I felt like my hands were tied.

"What's the next move?" Maddy asked. "Are we gonna sit here safe and sound until the world falls down around us? I mean, it's like your dad said. Eventually, we'll need to resupply. We've got tons of food, but it won't last forever. And Sinthy is acting pretty nonchalantly, but I'm not sure her power is never-ending. She's been getting tired a lot more lately. Eventually, the wards she put on the pack lands might go down. Or worse, she'd be forced to keep them up for years and end up draining herself. We promised Isme we'd take care of her. Using her as a tool isn't right."

There was a truth to Maddy's rant. Sinthy was strong-willed as all hell. She also hated the royals even more than Maddy, and I did. Sinthy would never tell us if she was being pulled too thin. I didn't want to push it because Maddy was right. The problem was that I was starting to formulate a plan. One that would, most definitely, require Sinthy to push herself to the breaking point.

"You're right, Maddy, but we need her to help us with one more big plan. Perhaps the biggest ever."

Her brow furrowed. "You mean bigger than making a fantasy army five times a day for multiple packs and putting up an impenetrable force field around three-hundred-square acres? Do tell."

A grim expression crossed my face. "I want Sinthy to help us get some of the other packs here?"

Her eyes widened. "You mean teleport them all onto our lands? I thought you said that wasn't possible."

"I know what I said. Things are different now. What we saw on the news this morning. The way those terrorists murdered shifters like they were nothing. I can't sit by and do nothing. Not when we have Sinthy. What if Tiago's pack was attacked next? If he and his entire clan are exterminated, could you live with yourself? Hell, could Sinthy if we all knew we could have helped and didn't?"

"But the wards, Nico. It's our only protection."

I grimaced. "I know. Let's talk to her and see what we can figure out. Maybe things aren't as dire as we think."

Maddy looked well past tired, but I could see she understood what was at stake. She nodded. "Okay, sure. Last I saw her, she was in the backyard. She enjoys being outside. She's almost like a shifter that way."

Maddy and I went downstairs and out to the back porch. Sure enough, Sinthy was right at the edge of the woods, scraping something off one of the pine trees. As we got closer, she scraped whatever she'd gotten into a small glass jar.

"Hey, guys," she said.

"What are you doing?" I asked, curious.

"Oh, this?" She held up the glass jar. "You've got some great fungi on a few of these pine trees. Its scientific name is *Cromartie Quercuum*. Humans generally call it Fusiform Rust. In Wiccan circles, it's known as Heart Skin. Deadly to the trees but really good for attack potions. You know, like poison. If you slip it to people and you do the right spells over the potion, their hearts will literally explode in their chests. Like *pop*, you know?"

She swelled her cheeks out and then made a bursting sound like a balloon being stuck with a pin. Maddy and I stared at her in shock and horror.

Sinthy rolled her eyes at us. "Ugh, no imagination. It's also used with other stuff to cure things like heartburn, arrhythmia, and heart attacks—anything to do with the heart, but man, the bursting chest thing? That's where the real excitement is."

I waved my hands for her to stop. "Okay, good, got it. Evil tree fungus. Ten-four, good buddy. Can we talk to you about something else?"

She shrugged. "Sure, what's up?"

Dark circles ringed her eyes, and I realized we were right when we thought she might have been stretched thin. It made this next part more difficult.

"Sinthy, hypothetically speaking, what would happen if you had to leave the pack lands. Say for... I don't know, a day or two?"

She frowned. "Well... it wouldn't be great. If I left right now, at this moment, the wards would crash within an hour. You guys would be defenseless."

I nodded thoughtfully. "Is there a way to, maybe, keep them up longer?"

She raised an eyebrow. "I smell a plan. What are you guys getting at?"

Maddy chuckled. "She's too smart for you, Nico. Tell her."

My shoulders sagged. I really hoped she wouldn't take this the wrong way. The last thing I wanted was for her to think we were taking advantage of her.

"So, you saw the reports of what happened in Virginia, right?"

A darkness clouded her eyes. "Assholes. Baby killers. I saw it, all right."

"I've been sitting in my office, thinking about how blessed we are." I pointed at her. "Blessed to have you. You're keeping my pack safe. You've stepped in and done things we never dreamed of. The training sessions for us? The ones for the other packs? It's amazing."

She smirked. "Thanks. I appreciate that. I will tell you, the magical-enemy thing for the other packs is exhausting. I'm sleeping like twelve hours a day now, doing that. I'm not sure how long I can keep it up."

"That's part of what I wanted to ask you. I don't want you to have to do that anymore. What if we brought our other ally packs here instead? With your help?"

Her eyes widened. She stared into my face, and I knew her well enough to know she was going over a dozen different ideas in her head. I didn't know what kind of algebra or alchemy witches used, but she was scrolling through a thousand pages of knowledge in a few seconds.

"You want me to teleport that many people here? How many is that?"

"Well, my pack is one of the biggest in the country, so not nearly as big as this. I'm thinking maybe five hundred? Seven hundred at the most."

"Fuck me," Sinthy gasped.

I was quick to shake my head. "If it's too much, say it. We only wanted to ask. Maddy and I are afraid for our friends. We don't want what happened in Virginia to happen to them."

Sinthy shoved the glass jar into some hidden pocket of her robes and turned away from me. Crossing her arms behind her back, she started strolling down the edge of my yard and the forest. She didn't say a word, almost like Maddy and I had vanished.

Maddy tugged on my shirt sleeve. "Is this, like, a negative answer? Is she saying no?"

Shaking my head, I said, "I have no clue. Let's see what happens."

Maddy and I sat down right where we were and watched Sinthy. At one point, she snapped a small branch off a tree and started drawing something on the ground. After nearly ten minutes, she shrugged, then scratched it out with her foot. This went on for almost two hours. Eventually, I had to step into the trees to relieve myself.

Finally, she walked back to us, a confused frown etched on her brow. "You guys have been sitting there the whole time?"

I looked at Maddy, feeling embarrassed for some reason. Were we not supposed to? It had seemed like the obvious thing to do while she thought about it.

"I... uh... yeah?" I said dumbly.

Sinthy let out a laugh. "Anyway, I think I have a plan that will work."

I jumped to my feet. "You do? Can you help?"

She nodded, giving me a pious look. "I think so. It won't be easy, and I'll be out of commission for at least three or four days afterward. You guys are gonna owe me big time."

"Anything," I said, the words bursting out of me. "Whatever you need."

"A lobster dinner, twenty-ounce wagyu ribeye, baked potato with a lot of bacon and sour cream... oh, and cheesecake. That will be a start."

"Are you serious?" I wasn't sure whether she was joking. Sometimes she was hard to read.

"I most certainly am. As I said, that's only a start."

A massive grin spread across my face. "Sounds great. Hell, once this is all over, I'll fly to Maine to get the damned lobster."

Maddy patted my chest. "Sinthy, are you sure this is possible? What about the wards?"

Sinthy bobbed her eyebrows up once. "That is a conundrum. But there is a way to keep them in place. The longer I'm gone, however, the less powerful they'll be. There's a sort of kinetic spell I can cast. It's very powerful, and it can be used to continually feed energy into another spell, even when the witch is gone. The problem is that it is *very* difficult to get right. I'm not worried about that. The issue will be getting the wards back to their full strength once the other packs are here.

"It will have to be done quickly. I'll be weak when it's all over, and the wards will be susceptible to tampering. Don't forget. We saw Viola had some kind of magic at her facility. They have a magical being on their side, most likely being forced to help them, but either way, if the royals get any inkling that the wards around your pack have weakened even a bit, they could come. I have confidence in my ability to fight another witch, but that will take my attention away from protecting everyone here. Do you see what I'm saying?"

I did. We could bring our friends here, but it had to be done fast—and preferably under the cover of darkness. If any royal spies outside the gates saw a huge mass of shifters appear out of thin air, Viola would be informed. She'd pounce. I could save my friends, but it would be dangerous.

Nodding solemnly, I said, "I understand. I'm okay with the risks if you are."

Sinthy put one hand on my shoulder and her other on Maddy's. "I'm your witch. This is *my* pack, *my* family. I'll do whatever I can to help. I don't think I could stomach another massacre." She lifted one hand and punched me playfully in the chest. "You better not forget my lobster, though."

Maddy and I laughed in unison. Rubbing at the spot she'd punched, I said, "When can we start?"

"Now, actually," Sinthy said. "I need to grab a few things. I'll be right back."

The witch ran inside, leaving me with Maddy. The day looked even brighter than it had before.

"I'll go with her," I said. "Will you go find the guys and tell them the plan? My dad and my brothers, too?"

Maddy nodded. "I will. You know, we really don't deserve her," she said, nodding toward the door through which Sinthy had vanished.

"You're telling me. But at least she's on our side."

Maddy went inside, and Sinthy reappeared not long after. She held what looked like a pewter or silver tub with a small lid. She pocketed the cap and walked toward me.

I peeked into the tub. It held some kind of wax or grease. It was a pale yellow and looked thick. Sinthy held it with reverence.

"What's that?" I gestured to the container.

"This is one of the most precious things in all of Wiccan culture. It was legendary even a thousand years ago. Isme was considered the greatest witch ever to live, and part of that reputation stems from her having this."

I stared at her for a few seconds, then said, "You, uh, still haven't told me what that is."

Sinthy blinked and shook her head. "Shit, sorry. I was being too mysterious. It's a reliquary embrocation. Created and strengthened over hundreds of centuries. This"—she held the jar up toward my face— "is basically the emulsification of dozens of legendary magical figures throughout history. The blood of Odin, a snippet of the hair of Samson, a piece of the mummified remains of the sun god Ra— "

"Hang on," I interrupted. "Odin? Ra? Those... they were real?"

She arched an eyebrow. "There are more things in Heaven and Earth, Horatio, than are dreamt of in your philosophy."

The implications were astounding and made me dizzy. I stared down at the strange yellowish gel. "What about… you know?"

"Oh, Mr. Christmas-time himself? There's a bit of the cross that bore him in this as well. Like I said, very powerful."

"Holy shit," I murmured in awe.

"Literally," Sinthy said with a grin. "Shall we begin?"

I spent the next two hours with her walking around the boundaries of the wards she'd created. Every ten or twenty feet, she stopped, dabbed an almost minuscule amount of the substance on a finger, and touched it to a tree. As she muttered an incantation under her breath, I could actually sense the change to the wards—like a weird pulse that rattled my eardrums.

"I can feel it," I said after an hour.

Sinthy looked at me and grinned. "These are your lands. Your soul and the soul of your pack are imprinted upon them. I'm surprised this is the first time you've had a physical sensation to my magic. You need to connect with nature more often."

I laughed at that and nodded. "I don't get out as much as I did when I was younger. Too much to worry about and work on most days. Do you think that would really help?"

With a knowing look in her eyes, she said, "It would. The more connected you are to the earth itself, the more you'll notice not only my magic but the magic that binds the world together. If you can connect to that, then you can pull power from it. Where do you think I get the power I use to implement my spells and potions?" She touched a tree, pressing her hand against the bark, and frowned.

"What is it?" I asked.

"Witches have walked here before. There are still remnants of their power. It's very old magic. But this place was blessed once before. A strong witch, and if I'm not mistaken, it was blessed for an ancient alpha and his pack. Long gone, but the magic is still here. Wisps and shadows, but still there." She cast her eyes over to me. "Connect with your home, and you'll see. Get down deep with nature, and you'll be surprised by what you find."

"Huh," I said, at a loss for words.

Later that night, after finishing with Sinthy and eating dinner, I called Tiago. It took a while, but I explained what we had planned and that his pack would be the first we were bringing in.

Tiago let out a shudder of relief, and it was the first time I understood how scared my friend was.

"Thank you, Nico. You have no idea how much this means to me and my son. There are dozens of people outside our hideout. It's safer than our pack lands, but word got out. The protestors tracked us down. We have to fight off an incursion almost every day. The police are trying, but... well, you understand."

"I do. There's a large building on our land which we'll use to house as many as we can. It's an old Moon Mate ceremony house. It should fit a couple hundred. The plan is to house the men there. The women and children will bunk in homes with members of my pack."

It had been decades since the building had been used for its intended use. When my grandfather built it, our pack was the most centrally located in the state, but once a wolf pack was founded south of Kissimmee, it was rarely used for the ceremony. The pack had kept it clean and usable, though. It would be more than big enough for our purposes.

"Thank you again, Nico. I'll let my people know. When can we expect you?"

"We want it to be done as quietly as possible. We also want as few prying eyes as possible. I'm thinking we'll come to you at around two a.m. Does that work? I hate to say it, but if your people can pack up any food you have, it would be a big help. We're well-stocked on supplies, but not for this many people."

"Totally understand. I'll get the word out. I'll have everyone pack a small bag of clothes and personal items and whatever food they can carry. I'll see you tonight."

Later that afternoon, I found Maddy sitting in the field we used for training, lost in thought.

"How's it going?" I asked as I settled on the grass beside her.

"Fine. How'd the call with Tiago go?"

"Stoked. He sounded like he was on a razor's edge. I think the anti-shifter activists near his compound are getting antsy. Looks like we may have done this in the nick of time."

"Good. And Sinthy has the wards strengthened? I didn't get to ask you about it when you returned."

I told her about our walk in the woods, the strange substance she used, and the sensation of ancient power she'd felt.

"So, a pack ruled these lands before?" Maddy asked. "And a witch? Sort of déjà vu, right?"

I nodded. "It is. I keep thinking about what she said. That I should have felt it a long time ago, but I wasn't fully connected to the land. That's difficult for a shifter to hear. All we do is commune with nature—at least, I thought we did."

The sun had tucked itself behind the horizon, and the lands were cast in dark orange light and shadow. I had a sudden urge to go into the woods.

Nudging Maddy, I said, "You wanna go try something?"

"I think I'm still sore from the past three days, but thanks anyway."

"Not that. I want to see if I can do what Sinthy said. I want to give it a shot."

A few minutes later, Maddy and I stepped into the small clearing I enjoyed coming to. The woods were almost fully dark now as the moon began to rise. Maddy seemed at peace as she smiled at me. It was a weird, knowing smile.

"I think I can feel what Sinthy's talking about," Maddy said. "I wouldn't have noticed if you hadn't pointed it out."

I sighed in irritation. I'd lived on these lands my entire life, and I was only now figuring out their history. I sank to the forest floor and crossed my legs.

"Do what you had me do when I was trying to contact my wolf. But... maybe, instead of looking inward, look outward. At the land? I don't know. I sound like some new-age hippy," Maddy said.

Closing my eyes, I did as she said. I cleared my mind and pressed my palms to the ground. The residual heat from the sun baked into my hands from the pine needles. The smell of the ocean drifted on the light breeze. The ocean was dozens of miles away, but I could still smell it. I slipped into an almost complete trance. I shoved everything out of my head—all thoughts of the war, of Edemas, Viola, even my pack, and Maddy. It was just me and the forest. No one else. Two entities, nothing more.

A peace unlike any I'd ever known descended on me. Now that I was fully open to my land, the earth responded. Like a wave or clap of thunder, something surged up through the ground and into my fingers. Images. There were glimpses in my mind. An ancient group of dark-skinned shifters huddling by a fire. An old crone, tracing symbols of protection on a tree. An alpha cutting his hand and binding a spell with his blood. There was power—unfathomable power coursing through me all at once. It didn't scare me, though, only filled me with even more calm as the ancient spell's remnants swirled within me. My body and mind seemed stronger, but in a way, I couldn't describe.

When I opened my eyes, the woods looked more colorful and vibrant, as if I could see things that had been hidden before. I didn't know the world could look so beautiful. I slowly got to my feet and looked at Maddy, who was biting her nails, but her eyes gleamed.

"Did... did you notice anything?" I asked.

Nodding, Maddy said, "That was weird. Maybe your pack lands needed you as much as you needed it. It was like a pressure wave or something. I don't know how to explain it."

My legs were shaky as I took her hand and started to walk out of the forest. As we went, I touched the leaves, branches, and needles. Everything was warmer than it should have been. Like I could *really* sense the life inside. If I had to guess, I would say I now had a much closer relationship with my home than I had before. It thrilled me.

We walked up to my house, the night sky now fully dark. Sinthy sat on the front porch. Her eyes lit up when they fell on, and a wide grin crept across her lips.

"Was I right?"

"Uh, you could say that," I said.

Sinthy looked out at the woods, then looked back at me. "I think we're gonna be okay. I've got a good feeling."

Chapter 10 - Maddy

Since the strange meditation session in the woods, there'd been something different about Nico. It wasn't any one specific thing I could put my finger on, but he seemed surer of himself. He'd always been a confident man—something that came from being a pack alpha, I was certain. Now though, that confidence emanated from him. It affected everyone else as well. Each person who interacted with him said the same thing. It was like his confidence touched them, and so increased their own.

My wolf sensed it as well. Being near Nico calmed and relaxed her more now, like she was completely at ease near him and trusted him even more than she had before. Something had changed, and I was glad for whatever it was. Nico needed it. He'd struggled so much with the weight of the situation. He took so much on and wanted to be the one in charge, the one who took all the stress. It was nice to see that whatever power he'd tapped into in the forest was helping him. It might not last long, but the peace I saw on his face lightened my heart. I'd take it.

It was late when we gathered in Nico's office. Sinthy came in, chugging an energy drink out of a brightly colored can.

"Are those things healthy?" I asked.

She drained the can and tossed it in the wastebasket by Nico's desk. "Don't care. Need the energy. This is gonna be rough."

Luis and Sebastian stood at the far wall of the office. Nico's dad sat beside Felipe, and two of Nico's brothers were squeezed in there as well. The room had always been larger than the average office, but now it was absolutely cramped. The clock on the wall read one-thirty a.m.

"Luis, do we have anyone at the Moon Mate building?" Nico asked.

"The rest of your brothers are there," Luis said.

"I'd like you to head down there too. I trust Tiago, but his people will be a little disoriented. I want as many hands there as possible."

I remembered the first time we'd teleported. It had been disorienting for those first few moments. Vanishing from a place you know and ending up in and strange place would be scary as hell, especially for the children.

"Got it," Luis said. He left without another word.

"Are you ready for this?" Nico asked with a wary look at Sinthy.

The woman shrugged. "Why wouldn't I be? I'm only teleporting like fifty people. No big deal."

I couldn't tell whether she was being sarcastic or serious, but Nico nodded as though he took it for assent.

"When do you want to do this?" Nico said.

"Whenever they're ready. Call Tiago and let him know I'm ready when he is. I'm sure it'll take some time to get everyone ready, but I shouldn't be gone for more than ten minutes. If it's been longer than fifteen, something has gone terribly wrong. That's a heads up for you."

Nico nodded. "Duly noted."

He pulled out his phone, and a moment later, he was talking to Tiago. "Sinthy is ready to go. Are your people ready?" He listened for a moment, then nodded. "Sounds good. And you're sure the coordinates are totally accurate, right?" Another pause. "Okay. Be ready."

Ending the call, he slid a map across his desk. A large red dot had been drawn in the general location of Tiago's pack. The latitude and longitude were written beside it, with a photo Tiago had sent pinned next to it. It was a large open area that looked like it was underground or in a cave.

Nico gestured at it. "This is enough, right? I don't want you teleporting into the middle of a hunk of stone or something."

Sinthy grimaced. "Oh, good. New fear unlocked. Thanks for that." Nico looked stricken until Sinthy smiled.

"It's fine. This works. I have enough to astral project to that spot. My body will follow behind a millisecond later."

"Okay, let us know when— "

Nico's words were cut off by the small clapping sound of her vanishing. A little whoosh of air filled the room, and that was it.

"Damn," Sebastian said. "Not even a countdown or anything?"

The minutes passed with agonizing slowness. None of us wanted to talk. At least, that's how it looked. Each of us waited in silence as our friend worked on bringing the others back here. When Nico's phone rang ten minutes later, we all jumped.

Nico lifted it and read the screen. "It's Luis," he said as he swiped the screen to answer. "Are they here?" The smile faded into a confused frown. "Okay, we're on our way."

"What's wrong?" I asked.

"Let's go. Everyone. Luis said they're all here, but Sinthy looks like shit. We need to get to her."

Our entire group hurried downstairs and out the door. In hindsight, we'd been dumb to have her leave from Nico's house. Sure, it was a more comfortable location, but why the hell hadn't we simply had Sinthy depart and arrive from the same damned place? My stomach was in knots as we sprinted toward the Moon Mate building. Before we even reached the door, I could hear the rumble of many voices.

Chaos greeted us as we entered. Nico's brothers were trying to direct everyone to different areas, and Tiago and a younger man—who I assumed was his son from their similarities—were working with their betas to get cots spread out for the men. Several members of Nico's pack had come here to have food ready for the new arrivals should they be hungry. A line had formed for the soup and sandwiches set up against one of the walls. The sound of children crying echoed through the room.

Nico and I shoved our way through the throng until we found Luis sitting with Sinthy. Her face was ashen, and she was slumped in a chair, her head lolling back against the wall behind her.

"Sinthy?" I called out as I ran forward.

She opened her eyes and gave me a tired smile. "Hey, Mom. Sorry I didn't call. Am I grounded?"

I ignored the joke. "Are you okay?"

"My body is worn out. It's like I did a million burpees or something. I feel like a blob of jelly," Sinthy said.

Nico's brother Gabriel ran forward, holding out a couple of orange slices and a bottle of water. "Here you go. Found what you asked for."

Sinthy grabbed the oranges and devoured them. I frowned as I watched her eat everything—including the peel. That couldn't have tasted good, but you couldn't tell it from the look of relief on her face as she chewed. Swallowing, she uncapped the bottle of water and downed the entire bottle of water in three large chugs.

"Oh, God. That hits the spot," she said as she wiped her mouth with the back of her hand.

Relief flooded through me as her face regained some of its color. Nico bore the same look of relief. I could almost sense how happy he was that Sinthy was all right.

"Did everything go well?" Nico asked.

"Yeah," Sinthy said. "Couldn't have really gone any better."

Tiago walked forward and shook Nico's hand. "That was weird as hell."

Nico chuckled. "It does take some getting used to. Are your people getting settled?"

He nodded. "We found the cots, and I've got my guys setting them up. You didn't have to feed us. That was too generous."

"Nope," Nico said. "You're our guests. The Lorenzo pack takes care of guests. Also, for now, we'll house all of you here. Once we start bringing other packs in, we'll keep the guys here, as I said on the phone. We'll fill up the meeting house next. After that, I've got a list of volunteers who are gonna house more."

Tiago seemed on the verge of tears. "Thank you. You… you don't know how bad it was. I think we were literally hours away from something happening. Like Virginia, or maybe worse. These people are alive because of you, Nico. Maddy, Sinthy, all of you. Thank you so much. My pack and I are forever in your debt."

Nico gripped the older man's shoulder. "You are in no one's debt. This is what friends do. I have no doubt you'd do the same for me if the situation were reversed."

"You have a high opinion of me," Tiago said as he wiped at his eyes. "I appreciate it. Hopefully, one day I can return the favor."

Nico swatted Tiago's arm playfully. "Go get some grub. It's late."

Tiago leaned down to take Sinthy's hands in his. "Thank you. You'll never know how grateful I am to you."

He turned and headed to the food line. I glanced at Sinthy and saw the blush creeping into her cheeks. The young woman was barely past being a teenager, and sometimes she still acted like it. She was silly and sarcastic but also worldly beyond her years. She could be sweet as well as kind. Once again, I was happy that she'd come into our lives. Not only for her magical prowess but for who she was as a person.

"Why are you looking at me like that?" Sinthy asked.

I shook my head. "No reason. Just happy it all worked out."

She narrowed her eyes. "You aren't gonna get all sappy on me, are you?"

I chuckled. "Maybe? Would that be so bad?'

Sinthy rolled her eyes and stood. She looked a lot less shaky than when we'd arrived.

"I'm going to go to sleep for about eleven years. Don't wake me until it's time for lunch. Deal?"

"Deal," I said.

She shuffled off, and other than looking weary to the bone, she seemed perfectly fine. She would be tired, but I thought she'd be okay to bring the other packs in.

That would relieve a lot of Nico's stress. Once our close friends and allies were here and safe behind our wards, it would allow him to focus on the main situation.

My phone buzzed with a text from my father.

What's going on at that big building by our cabin? Lots of activity.

I huffed out a breath and tugged Nico aside. "I'm going to head over to my parents' place real quick. I guess the noise from here woke them. I'm going to update them."

With a nod, Nico pulled me close and said, "Do you need me to go with you?"

He was remembering the situation with my parents and didn't want me to deal with something like that again. Admittedly, that hadn't been great, but I could handle Mom and Dad fine. No reason to make things awkward this late at night by taking Nico along.

"I'll be good," I said. "Don't worry. If you're asleep when I get home, I won't wake you."

He kissed me, and I left, leaving the madness behind me. The cabin Nico had offered my parents was closer to the building than I'd realized. No wonder the noise had woken them. From here, I could hear the scraping of cots on the floor, voices, and the cries and screams of children. There'd probably been some sort of loud noise when Tiago's pack arrived. There was no way that many people appearing out of thin air had been silent. It had probably sounded like thunder or something.

I knocked, and a few seconds later, my dad opened the door.

"Come in," he said as he tightened his robe.

Mom was sitting at the kitchen table, her hands wrapped around a steaming cup of tea. She smiled at me as Dad closed the door.

"Sorry if the noise woke you up," I said, gesturing toward the other building.

Dad waved my words away. "We were in bed, but we weren't asleep."

I wrinkled my nose. "Eww."

My mother blushed. "Not like that."

"No, we were talking," Dad added. "We've watched more news about that attack in Virginia and were discussing how worried we were. I know we're as safe here as we could be anywhere, but it's still a bit worrisome."

I sat down and poured myself a cup of tea. Mom was fidgeting with her cup, and I wondered if there was any way to alleviate their fears. Probably not.

"We'll be fine. We have Sinthy, Nico, me, and the whole of Nico's pack. This is the safest place we can be. That's what all that noise was. Sinthy teleported another pack here. We're gonna bring in as many as we can. That's how safe it is."

"Part of our worry is mired in guilt," Dad said, unable to meet my eyes.

"Guilt about what?"

"About not telling you that you were a shifter," Mom said. "Maybe, if we'd told you sooner, you could have been better prepared to defend yourself. That attack in the bar may have gone differently. I'm so sorry. You can't imagine how awful your father and I have been feeling since this all started."

I'd long since gotten over their deception. Gabriella had put the fear of God into them when I was little. Had basically made them believe I would be dead within weeks if my real self ever came out. They weren't to blame. And who knew, maybe the royals *would* have come for me as a child. Then all three of us would probably be dead.

"I know who I am now. I'm in full contact with my wolf. I'm as prepared as I could ever be."

Dad let his hand flop to the table. He looked like he'd aged ten years in the last few weeks. "Who you are is another reason I'm worried. Yes, you can defend yourself, but you aren't any ordinary shifter. Viola and her group will literally burn the world down to get to you. No one on Earth is more at risk than you are. I'm terrified of what happens if you end up in a fight. If they can't take you, they'll kill you."

I reached out and put my hand on his, then reached over for Mom with my other. "I'm not fighting. Nico's made that clear. The only reason I'm training is for the worst-case scenario. He's said a million times that he wants me safe and sound if any fight breaks out. You trust Nico, don't you?"

They shared a look, then nodded. Their nerves seemed to have calmed a bit by the time I left. When I got home, Sinthy and Gabriella were asleep in their rooms. Nico hadn't returned yet. Too tired to wait up for him, I fell into bed and was asleep almost instantly.

I woke a little after ten the next morning. The bed beside me was ruffled and slept in but empty. Nico had gotten home after me *and* got up before me. Knowing that Sinthy would need to start refueling, I dragged myself out of bed and went downstairs to make brunch.

I was making omelets, biscuits, and gravy when she came down the hall, looking like a zombie. The dark circles under her eyes made her look older than her years.

"Hello, sleepyhead," I said. "Food will be ready in five minutes."

"I was gonna have Pop-Tarts. You didn't have to do all this," Sinthy said, waving at the spread.

I nodded at a bowl of fruit. "Eat some fruit. No magic until you're fully reenergized." I pointed my spatula at her. "Got it?"

Sinthy held her hands up in surrender and sat. She grabbed an apple and bit into it.

"You're bossier than my mom was," Sinthy said. Her face fell as what she said sunk in.

I had to keep reminding myself that she had not only lost her birth parents but also her adoptive mother, Isme, who only passed a couple of weeks ago. The wound had to still be fresh, regardless of how well Sinthy masked her grief.

Guided by my instinct, I circled the kitchen island and embraced her. Sinthy didn't pull away. Instead, she sank into me. She didn't cry or sob, just wrapped herself around me and let me offer her some comfort. It didn't last long, but I could feel some of the sadness lift away from her.

Sinthy cleared her throat and looked around, obviously embarrassed. "Thanks for caring about me, Maddy."

"That's what I'm here for," I said as I nudged a plate of food her way.

Despite her complaints, Sinthy ate like a teenage boy, scarfing down three servings before proclaiming she was stuffed. I wondered if this was what it was like to have a little sister. That's kind of how I saw Sinthy. I'd been an only child and had no experience, but so far, it was nice. Almost like having an older child, maybe?

That thought sent my head down another path. It seemed like I was doing a decent job in the role of big sister. What would it be like to have a different job? The job of a mother? As I ate, those thoughts swirled through my head. No matter what I did, the daydreams wouldn't dissipate.

Chapter 11 - Nico

None of us had gotten much sleep the night before, but we couldn't afford to sit around and recover. I was out of bed when the first rays of sunlight came through the window. Careful not to disturb Maddy, I dressed and went straight to the Moon Mate building. Tiago and his men were already awake. He'd said his son was taking over as alpha, but from all I'd seen and heard, it looked like that had been reversed or delayed until the crisis was over. Tiago was completely in charge.

He and some of his men were doing an inventory of the food his pack had brought along. When Tiago saw me, he raised a hand in greeting.

"Did you even sleep?"

I chuckled. "I could ask you the same thing. I got about three hours."

Tiago nodded. "Same here. Too much to do."

Glancing at the huge pile of items, I asked, "What do we have?"

Tiago took a clipboard from one of his men. "Two hundred pounds of flour, a hundred pounds each of salt and rice. A dozen cans of condensed milk, two dozen cans of fruit, and about three dozen cans of vegetables." Tiago slapped the clipboard on his thigh. "It's not a lot. Not for how many people we have, but it was all we could carry. Even this made Sinthy's eyes bulge when she saw it. I'm thinking the more mass or whatever she has to move, the harder it is on her. That's the way it seemed anyway."

"That's amazing, Tiago. Thank you. There should be plenty. We appreciate it," I said. I tried to put as much emphasis into my voice as I could. I didn't want him to think he could have done more.

"What's the plan for today?" Tiago asked.

"Good question. First, I wanted to walk the perimeter with you and your men and let everyone get a good idea about the layout of the land. After that, if she's up to it, I'd like Sinthy to set up one of her simulated battles."

"We've done two of those," Tiago said. "It's strange as hell."

"You haven't seen the real deal since you were too far away from her power to have the full effect. You just had shadows. This will be… pretty real."

From the look on Tiago's face, I could tell he was skeptical that the simulation could be more realistic than what he'd already experienced. I looked forward to seeing his face when he saw what Sinthy could really do.

Tiago, his son Alfonso, and six of his top betas followed me as we walked the perimeter. The gate was the first stop. The anti-shifters were still there and had pushed a little closer. The power of Sinthy's wards had definitely decreased. You could feel it. The energy wasn't what it had been. As soon as she'd vanished the night before, I'd felt it. Whatever spell she'd done had kept the wards in place, but it would need to be re-strengthened before we sent her off to gather any more shifters.

We trudged through the forests and fields surrounding the land, I pointed out security cameras along the outer edge, and we had guards patrolling the area either in wolf form or in their human form and armed. It took three hours, and we were all starving when we got back.

I ate with the men outside their makeshift barracks, and it was nearing noon when Maddy and Sinthy came down the hill toward us. I waved to them, and both women waved back. Maddy looked refreshed but still tired. Sinthy looked better than I'd thought she would. The dark circles under her eyes had faded, and her skin wasn't as pale as it had been the night before.

"Hey," I said as they walked up to the picnic table.

"Hi," Maddy said, kissing my cheek. "Did you get enough sleep?"

Waving away her concern, I looked at Sinthy. "I'll be fine. How is our miracle worker doing?"

Sinthy smiled brightly. "It's amazing what sleep and about ten thousand calories will do."

I glanced at Tiago and his men. My next words were hesitant. "Do you feel up to a simulated training battle?" I raised my hand quickly. "If not, I totally understand. It can wait for another day."

"After last night," Sinthy said, "that'll be child's play. I'm fine. I'll only do one, though. I need to strengthen the wards again later."

Relief surged through me. She seemed well-recovered. I didn't hear any hesitation or forced acceptance in her voice. If her tone had even suggested either of that, I'd have called it off.

"Great. We'll meet you at the field in a minute."

After we finished eating, Tiago rounded up all the men of his pack who were old enough to fight and followed me to the field. Shooting off a quick text, I had my dad, brothers, and my best friends meet us there as well. It pleased me to see Luis and Sebastian cracking jokes with each other as they walked down with Felipe. At least that drama had resolved itself.

Sinthy walked the perimeter of the field, casting her spell.

"What kind of things did you see during your training time?" I asked Tiago.

"Kind of like shadows running around. No faces or anything like that. It did help us figure out how to organize and work under pressure, but it wasn't as realistic as what you mentioned," Tiago said.

With a grin, I nudged his arm with my fist. "Get ready. You're about to see something that's gonna knock your socks off."

Ten minutes later, Sinthy sat cross-legged on the hill overlooking the field and activated her spell. Tiago and his men murmured curses of surprise when the weapons, solid and heavy, appeared in their hands.

Tiago looked up with wide, shocked eyes. "Holy shit."

"Wait for it,' I said, nodding toward the trees.

A moment later, dozens of armed men and women stormed toward us from the tree line. Each one looked as real as could be. Murmurs of confusion erupted through Tiago's pack. Confusion and panic.

I held my arms up. "It's an illusion! No one freak out."

After a few minutes of explanation, I told Sinthy to let the battle commence. Tiago's men went to work firing on the fake enemies, and I pushed my way into the battle, letting my mind slip into the dark place it went in a fight. It only took a few seconds for me to totally forget it was all fake.

Gunshots and screams assaulted my senses as I sprinted around the field, dodging volleys of bullets. I took down four enemies before I witnessed Tiago's gun vanish from his hands, a kill shot removing him from the game. He cursed and walked to the edge of the battle.

The new power surged within me, and even in my human form, I moved more surely than I ever had before, my shots more accurate, my reflexes faster. Sweat drenched my back as the battle wore on.

"Nico!" Maddy screeched.

I spun and saw her on the hill, an enemy's arm around her neck, a pistol to her head. The image of her like that, helpless and in danger, froze me to the spot. How had she gotten there? When did she enter the battle? I couldn't move. All rational thought vanished from my mind.

I never saw the enemy coming up behind me. I didn't see him raise his rifle and fire at my head. In a flash, my weapon was gone. I'd failed the simulation. The enemy holding Maddy fired his gun into her temple, and she fell over with a puff of smoke.

Spinning, I caught sight of the real Maddy standing beside Sinthy on the hill. Alive and safely out of harm's way. Stomping away from the fake battle raging around me, I kicked at the dirt and cursed.

Sinthy shrugged. "Sorry. Was that too much?"

I jammed my hands into my pockets. "No, it was fine. I'm not mad at you. I'm mad at myself. I froze. I lost all control when I saw Maddy in trouble. Even though deep down, I knew it was part of the simulation, I still froze. It was a good lesson for me. Thanks."

Sinthy gave me an embarrassed half-smile. I needed to make sure I didn't hesitate like that if the actual fight went the same way. I sat with them and watched until my pack and Tiago's destroyed the last of Sinthy's fake enemies. Sinthy ended the simulation, and all the guns vanished.

Tiago's son Alfonso had a shit-eating grin as he joined us. "That was crazy!"

"I agree," Tiago said. "Nico, you weren't lying. That was... I don't even know. For a bit there, I forgot it was fake." Tiago stood beside me and waved around, gesturing to my people and the land itself. "Did she do something else too? Things feel different here. Like your pack is more confident. Like *you're* more confident. I got a sense of it when we walked the pack lands, and I don't think it's the wards. I can't quite put my finger on it, though."

My mind flashed back to my experience in the forest and tapping into the ancient power shrouded in my lands. I was surprised that the change was noticeable. Connecting to nature and to my own land had done something incredible.

I put a hand on Tiago's arm. "Probably us realizing we do have a chance to win this war."

"If you guys are done bro-ing out..." Sinthy said. "I'm going to add some strength to the wards, then eat and nap. Because I'm now, apparently, a cat."

"Hang on," Maddy said. "You need to drink something before you do that. I don't want you getting dehydrated."

Sinthy started walking toward the house with Maddy behind her. "Oh my gosh, I'll be fine, Maddy."

"I'm sure you will, but you're still gonna do what I say."

I grinned as they left. They bickered like a mother and daughter. It was strange to see. Strange and wonderful. With as much as Sinthy had done for us, I was glad we could at least give her a semblance of a family.

Tiago and I walked back with his men to join the rest of their pack. Grabbing two bottles of water, Tiago tossed one to me, and we sat outside.

"I talked to a friend of mine near Virginia," Tiago said after a few minutes.

"Virginia?" I asked, feeling fear bubble in my gut. "Was he— "

"No, he's a panther shifter. He wasn't at the massacre, but a friend of *his* was there. It was horrible, Nico. Worse than what they're saying on the news. That pack never stood a chance. The news reports don't do it justice. It was a total surprise. The cops and the shifters never knew what hit them. The only reason they were able to fight them off and kill so many attackers was that the shifters knew the layout of the land. If the anti-shifters had another ten or fifteen people on their side, it would have been a different story."

"It won't be the last one," I said.

Tiago nodded sadly. "Yup. Like I told you, the protestors outside our compound were getting angrier and more violent. Had you not sent that little lady to us, I truly believe we'd be on the news right now. That's how bad it was."

"Well, maybe the loss of human life from that attack in Virginia will scare enough of them off until we can figure something out. Many people died. We can hope that will be a deterrent."

As though the world, God, or Fate decided I needed a swift kick in the ass, my phone buzzed. It was Donatello: **Turn on the news**.

"Oh, for fuck's sake," I hissed.

Tiago looked confused. "What's up?"

"Grab your phone. My contact, Donatello, says there's something on the news we need to see."

We both pulled up a news app, and a growl burst out of both our mouths as we saw what was on the screen. Viola Monroe, wearing what looked like military fatigues, her face, calm and composed, was on the opposite side of a split screen with a news anchor.

"Everyone, we have a special interview tonight. Miss Viola Monroe, coming to us from an undisclosed location, has agreed to an interview with this network.

"Miss Monroe? Can you tell us what your motives are for this proxy war you seem to be waging against the shifter population?"

Viola smiled a thin smile. "I would prefer you not refer to the abominations as part of the *population*. Do you refer to fungi, bacteria, or viruses as part of the population? I think not. They are something to be weeded out and destroyed."

The reporter looked uncomfortable with that statement but continued. "The attack in Virginia must have given you pause. So many human lives were lost as a result of extremist actions. If you truly are for so-called human rights, then doesn't this atrocity fly in the face of what you preach?"

Viola shrugged. "War is war. Casualties are to be expected in battle. In Virginia, brave human warriors finally took the fight to the shifter scourge. The bravery they showed is immense. I can only hope that other brothers and sisters of humanity will take up the fight that these courageous souls started. That loss of life is the cost of winning a war."

"Miss Monroe, you must see the futility of this fight. Every nation in the world has decried your actions and all violence against shifters. You must realize you cannot fight the entire world."

Viola laughed. "My sweet, simple friend. The world only follows what the majority says. Right now, most people know I am right, but due to centuries of propaganda and brainwashing, they've suppressed their true beliefs. No true human can look at the shifter menace and say they *belong* here. They are an evolutionary accident. No human truly wants to share the world with that. As my followers wake up and start pushing for action, the truth will come out, and the leaders of the world will see what their constituents really want. This is a long game, and my organization and I are prepared to play and win. In fact, this war could end quickly and decisively with minimal loss of human life."

"And how would that be possible?" The anchor looked less and less happy about the path the interview was taking.

"Well, there is one person who has exactly what I need to end this shifter curse once and for all. I admit we experimented on shifters of all ages and species trying to find this person. I now know her name. The last in the ancient line of the semi-mythical Edemas. The so-called Werewolf King. If I have this woman and the ancient blood that flows in her veins, I could end this war in a day. I could eradicate shifters from the earth and give humanity a safe and clean home. A home without the filthy stink of these animals polluting the air." Viola leaned toward the camera, a hungry gleam in her eyes. "This descendant is a woman by the name of Maddison Sutton in Florida. Any true human who wants a world expunged of these animals should go there. The person who brings me this woman will be greatly rewarded, not only with money but with respect. Their name will go down in history as a hero. Statues will be built in their name. Children a thousand years from now will study them in history books. Bring me Maddy Sutton and become a god among men."

The screen cut to black. The anchor blinked in surprise. Inside the Moon Mate house, voices filled with anger cursed and called out. They'd seen the report. I stared at my phone, the metal, glass, and plastic cracking under the rage that trembled in my fingers. Viola had escalated. Instead of putting a price on all shifters, she'd slid all her chips onto Maddy. She'd told the world there was a bounty like no other on my mate's head. I was fuming, and my wolf growled in fury. Things were about to get worse.

Chapter 12 - Maddy

I stared in stunned silence at the TV screen in the living room. Donatello had texted me to put on the news. Nico must have received the same message. Sinthy glared at the screen, and Gabriella had her face buried in her hands, a deep growl resonating from her throat.

This was bad, but not the worst that could have happened.

Nico burst through the front door with Luis, Sebastian, and Felipe hot on his heels. "Maddy? Maddy? Have you seen the news?" His voice had a barely contained tremor to it.

"Yes, calm down, Nico. It's gonna be all right."

"How is it gonna be all right?" he said, gesturing to the TV. "She told everyone where to find you."

I was surprisingly calm, given the circumstances. I shook my head. "No. She said my name and that I lived in Florida. She didn't say Clearidge. She didn't give an address or anything like that. It'll take time for them to figure it out."

"Maddy," Gabriella said sadly. "We're living in the age of the internet. People will figure it out in a day. A few web searches, and it's done."

I shook my head. "They'll find my old address, the bar's address, but there's nothing that links me here to Nico's house. DMV? IRS? As far as they know, I still live at my old address."

Gabriella nodded hesitantly.

"Plus, there has to be a bunch of other women with my name. That may muddy the waters a bit."

"Not many women, but there should be some," Sinthy admitted. "It may take a little while for them to narrow it down."

My lips peeled back into a snarl. The thought that other Maddison Suttons all over Florida were now in danger didn't sit well with me. God only knew how many were now in danger because of what Viola had said. I almost wished she *had* been more precise in her revelation. If I had to guess, that was exactly why she'd done it. Viola knew what would happen, and she just didn't give a fuck. The bitch probably thought she could smoke me out by threatening so many innocent people. We'd never be able to live with ourselves if someone got hurt because of me. It was a sick game played by a sick woman.

Nico's rage was all-encompassing. It flowed off him in waves. His newfound power forced his will on all of his pack. When he cursed, the three other men winced almost in pain as the anger washed over them. Sebastian even let out a tiny whimper and lowered his head in submission.

"Nico?" I went to him and put my hands on his face. "Calm down. You're angry and can't think straight. You're making everyone uncomfortable."

His glower faded as he looked around in surprise. He saw his friends cowering in the corner and realized what was happening. With a sigh, his shoulders relaxed, and almost immediately, the red blanket of anger that had been on him lifted. Everyone else looked relieved.

"I'm sorry," Nico said, looking embarrassed.

"It's fine, bro," Felipe said. "You're mate's in danger, and you're the alpha. We get it."

"What do we do now?" Luis asked.

Nico shook his head and said exactly what I was thinking. "We wait. There's nothing else we can do."

"We have time, but not a lot," I said. "I'm worried about the people in town. Someone will eventually put two and two together. Someone will remember me and that I shut the bar down before moving up to the pack lands. It won't be immediate, but it'll be soon."

"No one is getting close to you," Nico snapped. "They can come, and they can try, and they'll run into a fucking buzzsaw. That's a goddamned promise. I don't want to hurt humans, but if a single one of them tries to come for you, I'll burn their world down to stop them."

A tingle of fear shot up my arms. He was serious, and I was terrified for anyone who even *thought* they could come onto his land and hurt someone he loved. There was no doubt in my mind that things would end poorly for whatever misguided soul crossed that line.

Sebastian and Felipe took to monitoring the news online, giving us updates as we attempted to come up with a plan. By that evening, things had gotten worse.

"It's bad, guys," Sebastian said, looking up from his laptop. "I'm on some anti-shifter forums, and there are lists being exchanged of any woman named Maddison Sutton. Addresses, emails, phone numbers, and places of work. They aren't even worrying about whether they live in Florida or not. Hell, most of these women are human. It's open season on anyone with your name. I've got a Maddison Sutton in Montana, for Christ's sake. There are hundreds, maybe thousands, of women in danger. This is bullshit."

"Show me," I said.

Sebastian turned his laptop to face me, and I saw three different windows open on different websites. Streams and streams of comments, posts, and pictures scrolled by. It was a disaster. Innocent people all over the country would have to run for their lives. It was playing out exactly how Viola wanted it.

My apprehension flared, and I was unable to pull my eyes away from the screen. I refreshed and scrolled and bounced between windows. My knee bounced with anxious energy. How could I fix this? I hadn't understood how fast this was going to happen.

Nico slammed the laptop shut. "Enough. You're gonna freak yourself out if you haven't already."

I straightened and rolled my shoulder. "I only want to see what's happening."

"No, you're doomscrolling. It's only making you more worried and upset."

"But these women— "

"Are in danger," Nico finished. "As of right now, there's nothing we can do. All we can do is hope the authorities will do what they can for them. How can we help a woman in Maine or Colorado with your name? We can't."

I chewed my lip. I hated it, but he was right. "This is my fault."

He narrowed his eyes. "No. Don't even let that thought slip into your head. It's Viola's fault. Never forget that."

"I keep thinking that if I go to Viola, it'll all be over. I'm stronger than I was. Maybe if I give her what she wants, I can take her down," I said, trying to convince not only Nico but myself.

"Enough," Nico murmured. "We aren't going there, and you know it."

Before the argument could go any further, my phone rang. I was surprised to see Abi's name on the ID.

"Abi?" I said when I answered.

"Oh my God, Maddy, I saw the news. Are you okay?"

"I'm… fine, I guess."

"You'd better not be doing that thing you do. You aren't gonna go be some martyr, are you?"

Was I that easy to read? "Are you reading my mind right now?"

"No, but I know you're selfless. The first thing I thought when the report came on was: Maddy is going to want to sacrifice herself. Let me guess. You're obsessing about all the women those people might attack because they think she's you?"

"I know, I know. Nico's already talked to me about it."

"Good. Are you listening to him?"

"Abi, I promise, okay? I'm not going to give myself up for the greater good or whatever."

The words made me sound selfish. They were right, but I couldn't help but think I was doing something wrong by not following my instincts. When I mentioned this to Abi, she laughed.

"Yeah, that sounds like you. Except I'd rather you be selfish than dead."

Wanting to get my mind off everything, I changed the subject. "How's life in paradise?"

Abi gave a dramatic sigh. "Oh, it's so rough. Sun, sand, endless cocktails, and food. It really is a burden to live life like a billionaire. But seriously, I think it's doing me good. I've been doing a lot of thinking. Plus, this Donatello guy isn't so bad to look at, either. I saw him swimming the other day in a speedo and… damn."

I laughed. Long and hard. Even as I tried to catch my breath, I realized it was the first time I'd done it in quite some time. Abi and I talked for another twenty minutes before we ended the call. I felt immensely better. For one, it allowed me to talk through some things and get my head right. For another, it was the first time in weeks that it felt like I was actually talking to my friend. I thought Abi really was getting back to herself. That alone lifted my spirits more than anything.

Nico was still sitting with his friends, discussing plans, when I got his attention.

"I need to go for a run." My wolf was desperate to get out.

He stood and smiled. "I'll join you. I need it."

We sprinted through the woods behind the house. The wind and the smells of the forest were calming balm to my mind. Though, as we ran, I couldn't get the feeling that something was *off* out of my mind. Like a thought or feeling was brewing just beneath the surface. My body was warmer than usual. Not a fever or sickness, but a deeper warmth. It seemed to radiate from within my belly. It was strange, but I was able to put it out of my mind. It had to be my nerves. With everything going on, it wasn't surprising. It would probably go away in a day or two.

Chapter 13 - Nico

Training took top priority over the next few days. It was all we could do to keep our minds off what was happening in the outside world. The only thing we could do was stay ready and hope. If we were ready for whatever came our way, perhaps everyone would feel a little calmer about the situation. Sinthy kept increasing the difficulty each time, adding more enemies, better weapons, and even barriers and buildings to the battlefield. Maddy worked alongside everyone else, even though I was always quick to remind her that she'd be at the rear of any fight.

When we weren't training with the packs, I took Maddy to the woods behind the house for target practice. Between the one-on-one sessions with me and the pretend battles, she was getting better at handling weapons. Her aim had already improved tenfold since starting, and she continued to improve.

Even with the planning, training, and organizing, tension and anxiety ran high across the pack lands. Everyone was on edge—my pack, my friends, and Tiago's pack. There was so much going on that I failed to notice the change in Maddy's scent. Again.

We were sitting at the table, having a big family dinner, when my brother Mateo walked in, looking shell-shocked and confused.

"Hey, jackass, you're late. Mom spent like two hours on the roast," Gabriel said.

Mateo slumped into the seat next to Maddy and me. Something had happened. Gabriel kept on joking, but I silenced him with a look.

"Spill it, Mateo. What happened?"

The chatter around the table ceased, and every eye turned to him. He looked at me and shook his head sadly.

"Just got word from one of your guys at the auto shop."

My auto shop was still in operation but running solely on human workers. It wasn't safe for us to go to town for work, but business had slumped as everyone knew the place was shifter-owned, run, and staffed.

"What is it? Did something go down at the shop? Vandalism or something?"

"Worse than that. A girl from town got attacked right across the street from the shop. She's lived here her whole life. Dates a bear shifter who moved here from Georgia. He's part of a pack about three towns over. They jumped them right in broad fucking daylight. Beat the hell out of her pretty bad, but her boyfriend came running out of the restaurant and beat the shit out of them for it. She's alive but in the hospital. Her boyfriend's clan is fucking furious."

I furrowed my brow. "Wait, what? Why did they jump her? What set these assholes off?"

Mateo glanced past me to Maddy before his eyes locked on mine. "The girl's name is Madeline. She goes by Maddie. These due's heard someone say her name, saw her with a shifter, and that was it." He snapped his fingers for emphasis.

My God. They weren't even trying to match last names now. Before long, they'd be going after any woman with an 'M' in their name. Megan, Mary, Michelle? These sons of bitches were off their rockers.

I understood why the bear clan was enraged. I would be, too. Not every pack or clan had battened down the hatches. Some refused to hide and revolted against the thought of living in fear. It was valiant but obviously dangerous. Things like this were going to happen, but that didn't make it right. Viola wanted things like this to happen. She knew the paranoia would spiral out of control, and it was following the plan she'd laid out.

We ate mostly in silence. What could be said? My alpha aura, fed by my anger at what had happened to that girl, pulsed out of me. Ever since I'd connected with the ancient power in my land, my alpha power had been growing stronger. Each time I went for a run, it seemed to get more powerful, almost like the old magic in the land was feeding my inner wolf. I had to be careful with it, though. Sometimes my own friends hit their knees in subservience, pushed to submit by the power of my will. I didn't enjoy it, nor did I want it. Viola might have liked that kind of power, but I didn't desire it.

Maddy whimpered beside me. I clenched my fist, worried I'd done the exact thing I'd been worried about. Had I forced my will on her? If so, it was the first time she'd ever reacted to me that way.

"Are you okay?" I asked, putting an arm around her. "Was it me?"

She shook her head. Her jaw was clenched tight, the muscles rippling beneath her skin. "I'm okay," she said through clenched teeth. "I'm an alpha too. You shouldn't affect me like that."

That was only partially correct. Lower-level alphas could still be brought to submission by a stronger alpha. But with her bloodline and the wolf living inside her, she was right. Even with my newfound connection to the land, I shouldn't have been able to exert my will on her. Ever since we'd bound ourselves together by mating, we fed on each other's energy. We were symbiotic now. I should have sensed whatever caused her pain or worried her.

"Does anyone else… smell that?" Sebastian said, glancing around the room.

I looked at him like he'd lost his mind, but then a foreign scent I didn't recognize hit me. Before I tried to place the scent, I looked down the table at Sinthy.

"Did someone get through your spells? Do we have an intruder?"

She almost spat her water out as she choked. After coughing and wiping her mouth, she shook her head. "No way. I would have known the moment it happened. Nobody's on your land."

"But…" I looked back at Maddy.

She obviously felt something. That had to be why she was whimpering and gritting her teeth.

"Oh," Sebastian said, drawing out the sound. "I know what that is."

"What is it?" I asked, annoyed that I had no clue what he was talking about. I glanced around the table, my gaze resting on Gabriella at the far end of the table, seated beside two of my brothers.

Maddy's birth mother was gazing at Maddy with teary eyes and a soft smile. I swung my head back to my own parents. My mother was also staring at Maddy, a knowing grin slowly spreading on her lips.

"Okay, what the hell is going on?" I asked. "Can someone tell me—"

The scent finally triggered a memory. I *knew* that smell. The scent of pregnancy.

"Why is everyone looking at me?" Maddy asked, shooting worried glances at everyone.

I focused my senses on her body. I wanted to know for sure. My shifter hearing picked up on the thud of her pulse, the hiss of breath going in and out of her lungs, and a tiny fluttering sound that wasn't usually there—the sound of a very small heart beating deep in her womb. A sound so light it was like butterfly wings. My jaw slowly fell open.

"Nico? Please tell me, what the hell is wrong?" Maddy asked. She no longer looked irritated—she seemed freaked out.

Unable to form words, I slid from my chair, my knees hitting the floor in front of her. Placing my palm on her belly, I could sense the tiny being inside her. I couldn't believe I'd missed it. It must have happened when she went into heat. I'd been too consumed with everything the royals were doing to realize what was happening with my mate.

Excitement, pride, fear, and protectiveness flooded my mind and heart. Maddy stared down at me, eyes narrowed. She didn't get it. She didn't understand.

"Nico?" she whispered.

Finally finding my voice, I choked out the words. "Maddy, you're pregnant."

Her eyelids fluttered as the words slammed into her. "I'm sorry, what?"

"You're pregnant," I repeated.

"That's not possible. I'm on birth control."

The corner of my mouth lifted in a wry smile. "When's the last time you took it?"

We'd only worried about necessary medicines when we loaded up on supplies—antibiotics, painkillers; anything that could be used to help save lives. No one had thought about basic items like birth control pills. She'd been out of those for weeks. Realizing this, she still shook her head.

"Still, though, we were careful."

I shook my head. "Not that first night when your heat came in. That very first time."

Her lips formed a word that I was sure was going to be another denial, but then I could practically see her replaying it in her mind.

"Fuck," she breathed.

She had to be mortified that this conversation was happening in front of my brothers, my friends, parents—everyone. I didn't sense any excitement from her, not even worry or pride. Just pure, unfiltered terror. Her fear was so strong it was almost beyond reason.

Maddy shook her head vehemently. "No, Nico. I can't be pregnant. I can't."

The fear in her eyes made no sense. Why was she so scared? Did she have a phobia I didn't know about?

"Maddy, it's definite. I can smell the baby, hear its heartbeat, and sense its aura." I reached up and cupped her cheek. "It's okay, Maddy."

It was anything but okay, though. She was vibrating with fear, shaking her head back and forth like a metronome. Maddy was terrified. I glanced furtively at everyone else. Their elated smiles had frozen in place.

"This is bad. Such bad timing," she muttered, tears sliding down her cheeks. "Nico, what will happen if Viola finds out I'm pregnant?"

That was the reason her fear was so pronounced and visceral. It wasn't that she didn't want a child—she was afraid of what Viola would do to her or our baby. I cupped her face, preventing her from shaking her head.

"Maddy, I swear, I won't let any harm come to you. Not to you, and not to our baby. I promise it. Do you hear me?"

She didn't answer. Her tears came freely, and she fell into my arms. I wrapped her in a hug, rubbing her back. Glancing over her shoulder, I noted the fear and sadness on everyone's faces. It should have been the most joyous moment, one to celebrate. Instead, Viola had infected everything with her venom. Even this had been spoiled. I gritted my teeth, visualizing the terrible things I'd do to that bitch once I got my hands on her. I was done with her stealing things from me. If it were the last thing I did, I'd make sure she paid and paid dearly.

Chapter 14 - Maddy

I was pregnant. No amount of denial could change it. Nico's cousin, Eliza, gave me a pregnancy test she had stuffed in the back of her medicine cabinet. Despite my deepest hope, two lines appeared on the stick. I couldn't turn my back on the facts—I had to live with it.

My heart was a little broken. I *wanted* kids—always had. The idea of having a new person growing and sheltering inside me had been one of my deepest dreams. The problem was, I hadn't expected it to happen while I was hiding out behind a magic forcefield with the whole world searching for me and a psychotic mastermind pulling strings to bring me to her. So much danger and so little time to relax and enjoy anything. My fear of the unknown increased a hundred percent now that there was more at stake than my own life.

Regardless of what everyone told me, if it came down to the people I loved versus myself, I wouldn't hesitate to sacrifice my life for them. Now? Now someone else was relying on me to stay alive. They were growing inside me, sleeping peacefully within my womb. All the excitement I should have experienced was marred with fear. It saddened me and overwhelmed me with anguish.

Nico found me in the bathroom, sitting on the edge of the bathtub and crying. Not pretty girl crying with delicate drops shimmering on eyelashes. No, it was that nasty, snotty, ugly crying. My makeup was running down my face, my eyes bloodshot, my nose red, and tissues piled on the floor. Definitely the sexiest I'd ever looked. Had to be. No question.

"Hey," I said, the end of the word tilting up into a high-pitched whine. I sounded ridiculous.

"Maddy, baby, are you okay?" He sat with me and put an arm around my shoulders.

I unloaded all my fears and anxieties on him and told him the thousand different terrible scenarios I'd played through my head since finding out. He listened without interrupting, not even when I shared the nightmarish visions I had about how Viola could use this against us. By the time I was done, I was pretty much cried out.

Nico ran a hand through my hair. "You've got valid concerns."

"Really?" I squeaked, my throat raw from sobbing. "Some of it sounds crazy to me."

He nodded in agreement. "Maybe a few. But you still have good reasons to be worried. This is huge. A massive change. I know you're scared. So am I. The thing is, there's still joy to be had. The little surprise is one of the best things to happen in my life. In either of our lives."

I blew my nose, then laughed. "I didn't think one time without a condom would be enough."

"Well, all it takes is one time. But you were also in heat, which increases your chances of conceiving. That's my fault. I should have thought about it and grabbed one."

I'd been insatiable that night. Waking up with my clit swollen and throbbing, my fingers thrust inside me, desperate for it to be him. The entire three days were hazy at best, but some things were still clear in my mind. I'd never experienced anything like it in my life. From the moment I woke up, I'd basically accosted him.

Rolling my eyes, I said, "Well, it's nice that you think that, but I didn't really give you a chance. Don't blame yourself. I don't."

The memories of what we'd done to each other clicked through my mind like a slideshow, sending a warm tingle through my stomach: my mouth on his cock, his tongue buried inside me, Nico's cock thrusting into my ass and pussy. My cheeks went red as I recalled the visions.

Nico put a finger on my chin and turned my face to his. A rumbling growl rose from his chest. "What are you thinking about?"

My face grew unbelievably hot. "Probably something I shouldn't. Not at a time like this."

Nico leaned forward, kissing me before I could say another word. He pulled me close, and I sank into his body, letting my thoughts and worries vanish. He urged me upward, and I stood. He walked me over to the bed—our lips melded together, tongues dancing. Our breathing became one as he led me to the bed.

Lowering me gently to the mattress, Nico broke the kiss and gazed into my eyes. "Nothing will ever hurt you. You are mine, and I protect what's mine."

The warmth that had been building inside me surged into an inferno. I grabbed his shirt and tugged him onto me, kissing him with urgency. My tears had dried, and all I wanted was him and a few moments of peace and happiness.

Nico undressed me, piling my clothing next to the bed. His hands slipped across my skin, slow and gentle. Across my belly, down my thighs, the slope of my collarbone, and the curve of my breasts. The entire time, he gazed into my eyes, connecting to me wordlessly. I ached for him but wanted this to go on forever. The feel of his body against mine filled me with hope and confidence, and his fingers gliding over my skin made me wet.

When his thumb flicked across my nipple, I gasped and arched my back as electric energy seemed to shoot from the tip of my breast down to my clit. My free hand fumbled with his zipper and quickly tugged him free. Already hard, I stroked him and watched as the blanket of pleasure fell over him. His eyes glazed over, and a grunt of satisfaction burst from his chest.

Nico slid a hand between my legs, his fingers finding me hot, wet, and ready. One finger slid inside me, then another. I sucked in my lip, clamping my teeth down as he curled his fingers to stroke me. A breathy moan escaped me. Our eyes remained locked. The rigid flesh in my hand pulsed with heat, and I wanted it inside me. I'd never wanted anything more.

"I want you," I murmured.

With a nod, Nico shimmied out of his pants and nestled himself between my legs, his cock resting on my belly, his balls pressed against my pussy as he leaned down to kiss me. I ran my hands along his back, pressing my tongue into his mouth. He cupped my breasts, gently pinching my nipples in a way that was sure to drive me mad.

With a slight flick of his hips, his cock slid down my slit. With aching slowness, he entered me. My mouth dropped open in a silent scream as he filled me. I looked down and watched as inch after inch of him vanished within me. When he was fully sheathed inside me, he pulled me to him, hugging my body to his, holding me like that without moving like we were one being. One living thing. Nothing had ever felt so good. So *right*.

Nico raised his face and looked into my eyes again, then pulled his hips back and thrust into me. All conscious thought vanished from my mind. Instead, I was swept away in an avalanche of pleasure. Nico stroked a hair from my face as he moved within me. He placed his palm on my cheek, his eyes never leaving mine. My nails dug into his back, pulling at him, urging him on.

"I love you," he whispered.

Whimpering with my own feeling of adoration for the man I loved, I leaned forward and kissed him. "I love you too."

I slipped a hand down between us and began to stroke my clit as he made love to me. The combination was a dizzying, heady sensation. Nico's body flexed, his breathing quickening into near-panting. He was getting close. My own orgasm was building. A delicious pressure started erupting inside me, swelling with each thrust of his hips and each twitch of my fingers.

Nico buried his face in my chest, sucking a nipple into his mouth. The suction of his lips was like a hammer, shattering glass. In an instant, I catapulted over the edge, my body jerking, his name falling from my lips as wave upon wave of ecstasy crashed over me. A moment later, his hips picked up speed, short-circuiting my brain as another fresh wave of climax washed over me. His shoulders went rigid, and a satisfied groan of release oozed from his chest. Collapsing on me, we lay still, caressing each other as we caught our breath.

After we'd cleaned up, Nico slid under the covers with me and pulled me against his chest. I breathed a deep, contented sigh.

Without thinking, I said, "I hope I'll be a good mom."

Nico raised up on his elbow and looked at me. "Of course, you will. You'll be the *best* mom." He stroked my cheek again. "Things are gonna work out. I know it. We'll end this shit with Viola, and then we can enjoy the rest of your pregnancy."

"I hope so," I said. "There's still a fight coming. That's obvious. It terrifies me."

"Well, as far as that goes, I hope you realize there is zero chance of you being on the frontline. I know that's always been part of the plan, but it's non-negotiable now."

Something that had been bouncing around in my head since I found out I was pregnant floated to the surface again. In my despair and worry, I hadn't really given it much thought. I was more calm and content at the moment than I had been for the last two days since I'd found out. I let it out, saying it out loud for the first time.

"I wonder if there will be any side effects for the baby when I drink the vial."

Nico stiffened. "When?"

"No, sorry, not when but if. What might happen, you know?"

"Absolutely not. No way. It's not worth it."

I sighed. "I know that, Nico, but there are a million doomsday scenarios that *theoretically* could make it a necessity."

"Name one."

"Okay, Sinthy's wards fail, and the royals descend on us. We have no recourse without all of us dying. Or someone betrays us. The government decides they actually *do* want to side with her, or— "

"All right, all right. I get it, but that doesn't change anything." He looked me in the eye as intensely as I'd ever seen. "Even if I'm on the brink of death, I don't want you taking that vial."

Unbidden, my mind formed an image of Nico bleeding out on the floor, blood bubbling from his lips, his chest torn apart from multiple bullets. The very thought sent me into a panicked rage, and a growl vibrated in my chest.

"Promise me, Maddy," Nico said. "Promise you won't take it."

I wasn't sure it was right to make such a promise. Deep in my mind, the decision had already been made. If it came down to all of them dying and me taking that vial to give us one last chance, I wouldn't hesitate. My baby was already precious to me, and I didn't want to do anything to harm it, but if the only other option was both our deaths, was there really any choice? Still, I wanted Nico's mind at ease.

I nodded. "I promise. I swear. I won't do it. Okay?"

Nico's body visibly relaxed, and his face softened. "Good. That's good." He leaned forward and kissed me again. "This is all gonna be fine. We probably won't even have to think about that damned vial."

Snuggling in close to him, I rested my head on the pillow. As I closed my eyes, more images flashed into my mind. The pack lands on fire, dozens of wolves dead at my feet, my parents lying lifeless in the grass, and again, Nico gasping out his last breaths as blood seeped from his body. In the background, I could hear Viola's high, cackling laughter.

I'd lied to Nico. Not purposely, but I had anyway. When it came down to it, I would do whatever it took to save the ones I loved. To save Nico, I wouldn't hesitate to drink the contents of that vial.

Chapter 15 - Nico

Two more attacks, equal in their brutality to the disaster in Virginia, occurred the next week. I'd known it was coming, but part of me had hoped I was wrong. It was such a senseless thing that the human part of my mind revolted against the idea. Yet there I was, watching yet another tragedy play out on the television.

The first attack had been on a panther clan in New Mexico. The mob that went for them hadn't been well-armed and had come in the daylight. That gave the panthers the advantage they needed to fight them off with only seven dead. *Only*. Every lost life was one that didn't need to happen. But they'd been lucky compared to the lizard-shifter clan in South Carolina.

Their enclave was near the ocean. The anti-shifters went at night, and it was a slaughter. Lizard shifters didn't have the same advantage that wolves, bears, or panthers did. They shifted into creatures that were small and inherently less dangerous. The destruction of their pack hit me harder than it should have, but I'd had dealings with lizard shifters before. Two of them had gone to Europe with me and the others. They'd put their lives on the line to rescue Maddy. They were good people and didn't deserve what happened.

Footage of the latest attack rolled over the screen, showing how bad it was. Maddy was beside me, silently crying, unable to look at the screen. The worst was the small black body bags. Children. Kids killed by psychopaths who thought they knew which beings were allowed to live and which weren't. My eyes locked on the bags as the footage showed EMTs loading them into coroner vans. I didn't hear a word the reporter was saying. All I could think of were the innocent lives that had been lost.

Maddy being pregnant with my child made it all the worse. I refused to allow that to be our child. I'd do whatever was necessary to prevent that from happening here in our pack. I'd die before that happened. I made the promise to myself then and there that I wouldn't allow it to happen.

I tugged on Maddy's arm until she was nestled in the crook of my shoulder. "Are you okay?"

Sniffling, she nodded. "Yeah. I fucking hate this."

Before I could say more, the news report switched to a live report from the White House.

"Let's see what this guy has to say."

The president stepped forward and laced his fingers together before resting them atop the lectern.

'Good afternoon, my fellow Americans. As many of you have seen, the anti-shifter movement has again brought terror to our cities and towns. My heart and prayers go out to the Sanchez panther pack in New Mexico and the Brennan lizard clan in South Carolina. I cannot imagine the heartache and devastation these two familial groups are going through right now.

"FEMA has been dispatched to both locations to assist with temporary housing. What I want to tell you all today is that this scourge must come to an end. As the leader of freedom in the world, The United States was founded on the ideal that all men and women are created equal. Those of you who believe otherwise are traitors to the ideals of this nation and, as such, will be branded as traitors.

"As of today, Congress has enacted the Every Shifter is American act. From this moment onward, any citizen, immigrant, non-immigrant visa holder, or visitor who participates, facilitates, or assists with any anti-shifter activity will be tried as a traitor to the state. For any who are not clear on what it means to be convicted of treason in the United States, I want to remind you that the penalties are severe and can include death. Congress has taken this extreme step, with my blessing, as a means to ensure that all shifters everywhere know that we *are* on their side.

"We are still working with worldwide law enforcement agencies to find Viola Monroe and her collaborators, but as of this moment, we have not made any inroads we can discuss here. Again, I call on her to turn herself in and stop the tragedies that are unfolding.

"In the meantime, the Department of Housing and Urban Development and FEMA are in contact with the United States Military to supply and retrofit closed military bases into housing and safe havens for any shifter populations who want the fullest protection of the US military. As of ten minutes ago, a link has been put up on USA.gov for any shifter alpha who wants to apply for their pack's acceptance to their nearest housing facility. Other updates will be forthcoming. No questions."

The president turned and walked off the stage to a chorus of questions. I sighed and slumped against the back of the couch, rubbing Maddy's back.

"Do you think people will take him up on that?" Maddy asked.

I shook my head. "I doubt many will. Those who do will probably be really small packs or those who live a more nomadic existence. If you have no home base to hunker down in, it would be a hell of a deal. Most of us are gonna be too amped up and paranoid. Hell, three months ago they were telling us FEMA would have collection facilities, and we were gonna be rounded up against our will. Now? Oh, now they want us to go there so they can protect us. Nah, I don't like it. It's probably not a trap, but it feels like a trap. I think most of us will stay put."

Most of us. That didn't count the ones who we'd brought here. Sinthy had been true to her word and, over the last week, had brought most of our allies here. The final pack was a smaller wolf clan from near Daytona. Sinthy was completely exhausted. I doubted I'd ever be able to thank her enough. Neither could the other alphas. They'd be even more in her debt after today's news.

We'd almost run out of room, and the newest pack alpha, Norman, was being housed with my parents. His people and betas were all spread out among my brothers' homes. They were all resting, which was good since we'd need them to start training soon. I wanted everyone on the same page if something went wrong.

My phone rang, and I was surprised to see Javi's number on the screen. He'd been running for cover for a few weeks, moving his pack around the county, trying to stay hidden.

"Javi?" Maddy looked at me questioningly.

"Hey, friend. How goes it?" Javi asked. His voice sounded haggard.

"Sounds like it's going better than you," I said.

"Yeah, listen. My pack is tired. We're scared. I hate asking this, but is there anything you can do for us? I'm getting the creepy crawlies up my back. I can't get over the feeling that Viola's actively searching for us. I don't even want to know what she'll do to me if we're found."

Javi's pack had been one of the few shifter packs that pledged fealty to the royals hundreds of years ago. His pack had done their bidding until the whole thing went down with Maddy. Eight months ago, I'd have assumed Javi was trying to get close to slit my throat. Now? He'd proven himself a friend and ally after turning his back on Viola and her group. Still, Javi was a stubborn son of a bitch. I'd offered him sanctuary at the beginning when Sinthy first put up the wards, but he wanted to protect his pack himself. I couldn't blame him for that. If the roles had been reversed, I would have hated relying on someone else.

"I think I can help. You remember Sinthy, our pack witch?"

"Hell, yeah, I do. That's part of why I called. I remember you talking about the forcefield or whatever she had around your land. We need protection, Nico."

"All right. We've been bringing in packs from around Florida, our closest friends. Mostly the alphas who came for the big gathering a few months back. I'll be honest, we're bursting at the seams, and this is gonna sound shitty, but all I have left is an old barn on the far end of my property. You and yours will have to sort of camp out, but you'll be within the wards and safe."

"I'll take it. It doesn't matter. Whatever you got," Javi said without hesitation.

His quick acceptance told me all I needed to know about the state of things out in the world. Javi's original pack lands were right on the city limits with Clearidge. It was fine as a location when relationships between humans and shifters were civil, but now? Who knew where they were hiding out? And God only knew where they were getting supplies. His pack was smaller than mine, but the stress had to be taking its toll.

"Here's what we'll do," I said. "Get someplace safe, and I'll contact you when Sinthy is ready so we can bring you in."

Maddy excused herself as I talked over the details with Javi. When we were done, I dropped my phone and simply sat for a while. I couldn't stop thinking about how Maddy was taking this. Her fears about having a baby had to have skyrocketed with the news of the fresh attacks, and hers and her wolf's emotions were fluctuating from the pregnancy hormones. I could smell the changes taking place within her. I needed to find Viola and end this, but how? Even with every government scouring the planet for her, there'd been no success. Not even a whisper of her whereabouts.

But I knew the one person who might know something.

I dialed Donatello's number, and he answered on the first ring.

"Nico, how are things? I trust you, and yours are safe?"

"I am, yes… I mean, we are."

"Fantastic. I know things have gotten rather intense today. Abi, as sweet a girl as she is, has almost tread on my last nerve with questions. Every hour she's back at my door, demanding to know more. It really is tiresome."

I winced in embarrassment. "I'm sorry, Don. If it's too much with her there, we can work out something else."

Donatello huffed a dismissive laugh. "Nico, you shame me. I'm not so fragile as to break at the incessant questions of a young lady. No, she's fine. Now, let's get to the point of this little call. You want info on Viola's location, do you not?"

That caught me off guard. Whenever I dealt with Donatello, I always had the faint but nagging feeling that he had everything figured out before any of us had even managed to start thinking.

"Well... yes, actually. How did you— "

"No time, dear Nico. I'll go ahead and get into what my and my associates' teams have worked on.

"First, we've had the world's pre-eminent cybersecurity experts trying to trace Viola's location. You've seen the little 'interviews' she's been doing on different media outlets? Always from some unknown location that no one can recognize?"

Gritting my teeth, I nodded to myself. "Yeah. I've seen them."

"Dressed for the cameras in guerilla uniform, no less. If the bitch is one thing, she's committed to the show. Well, these videos are coming from somewhere, but her team is doing a fantastic job preventing a trace. She's using dozens of shadow servers and mimicked IP addresses. The last interview traced back to the International Space Station of all places. I'm one hundred percent certain that's not where she is." Donatello chuckled to himself.

"Damn. So, there's still nothing? No trace at all?"

"Not actionable, no. There are rumors of someone with lots of money buying weapons on the outskirts of Saudi Arabia, but that could be any rich, wannabe terrorist or drug kingpin. My people are also running down leads on a rumor of a mysterious woman running some sort of cult-like compound near Guanshan in Taiwan, but I don't hold out hope for that one.

"Our teams are on it. I'll make sure you're the first to know if we find anything. I promise you, Nico. Also, I think congratulations are in order, are they not?"

His question tugged me out of the depressive spiral I had been about to go in. Coming back to reality, I managed to speak. "What? Oh, shit, yeah. Yes, I guess so. How'd you find out?"

"Abi. She was at my door five minutes after getting off the phone with Maddy. She says lovely Miss Sutton is a bit of an emotional mess over it, though. Fear of the unknown, perhaps?"

I grunted noncommittally. "She's terrified Viola will find out and use it against her. It pisses me off because this should be a really happy time, but this situation has ruined it."

"My friend, never let the evils of the world drain away your joy. I promise you this, in the times of the greatest darkness, a sliver of light can change everything. Babies were born in the ghettos of the Holocaust. They were born during the Great Shifter Purge of the twelve-hundreds. Children have entered the world during every great tragedy. That is what God does—he grants us moments of blessed happiness to get us through the bleakest of days. Never forget that, and when your child is born, hold them tight, raise them high, and remember what you fight for."

Tears sprang to my eyes. I wiped them away and laughed. "You know, Donatello, if you hadn't become a billionaire, you could have been a poet."

"Ugh, perish the thought. I like poetry, but… Lamborghinis are really fun."

After talking some more, we hung up. I'd hoped the call would ease my worries, but it didn't. Viola still being a ghost in the wind, irritated me more than I'd thought possible. I was becoming antsy. I loved my pack lands, but it was becoming claustrophobic. Being unable to go out and do what needed to be done made me feel helpless.

I was trying not to feel sorry for myself when it hit me. A small change, but noticeable. Almost like a surge or push on the pack lands. I was more in tune with the land since my experience, and this did not seem natural.

Thundering footsteps rushed down the stairs, and Sinthy burst into the living room, her eyes wide with panic.

"The wards! Someone is trying to tamper with them."

I was on my feet in an instant. "What? Are you sure?"

She nodded and scrunched her face in concentration. After a few moments, she shivered. "It's wrong. All wrong."

"What's wrong, Sinthy? Is it Viola? Is she here?" Dread flooded through me. If she was here in broad daylight, she must have been very confident she'd win.

Sinthy shook her head vehemently. I couldn't tell if it was an answer or not. It almost looked like she was trying to throw something out of her head.

"The magic feels wrong. That's what I mean."

I had my phone, my fingers flying over the screen as I texted my guys. "Sinthy, can you pinpoint the location? Do you know where they're trying to get in?"

"I do. Yeah."

"Let's go."

I grabbed her by the hand and sprinted for the door. Before we'd even made it twenty feet from the house, Luis and Felipe came loping toward us in wolf form, running at full speed to catch up. Sebastian was running from the opposite end of the pack lands, also sprinting to reach us. Not wanting to stop and explain, I continued running with Sinthy, letting her lead. She was so fast, and it shocked me. She started leaving me behind, and I had to shift in order to keep up. She was full of surprises.

The closer we got, the more I sensed it, almost like someone was pounding on my chest. Whoever was trying to get in was beating on the wards, almost like a door. That shouldn't have been possible. Anyone touching it should have been damn-near electrocuted.

Sinthy led us deep into the woods, toward the very edges of my lands and the wards, until we came to an opening in the trees. I froze and shifted back. The wards were shimmering, almost rippling from where someone was touching them. A dark hooded figure stood at the wards, running their hands over the barrier. The wards didn't touch them.

Then a crack, like a thunderbolt, exploded around us. I slammed my palms to my ears. It sounded like a grenade going off. Luis crumpled to his knees—his hands clutched at his ears. In the distance, the hooded figure took a step back and froze when they caught sight of us. We growled, deep and threatening, at the intruder.

"God," Sinthy whispered, fear and awe laced in her voice. "This can't be."

"What can't be?" I snarled.

"The wards. They're broken. Gone."

My eyes nearly bugged out of my head. "What?"

Ignoring me, Sinthy was still shaking her head and talking to herself. "They shouldn't be able even to crack them, much less break them down."

She turned menacing eyes toward the intruder. Moving almost too fast to see, Sinthy raised a hand and uttered words I didn't understand under her breath. The intruder jerked as if hit and raised both of their own hands back at her. I watched in confusion as a strange pulsing energy flowed between them. At times it looked like water, at others a colorful wind. The intruder and Sinthy both grunted with exertion, each flicking with that strange energy.

Was this what it looked like when witches fought? Because that's what this intruder must have been. Nothing else could have taken Sinthy's wards down. But the fact that they'd done it at all showed how dangerous this person was.

"Please… don't hurt me." The figure grunted, gasping in exhaustion and struggle. The voice of a man, but slight and wavering—young.

"Who are you?" Sinthy growled, her voice as deep and angry as any shifter's. Her hair floated about her face, raised by the energy emanating from her. I'd never seen her so enraged. She was fucking terrifying.

The intruder was now on their knees. Whatever power they had wasn't enough to survive a full onslaught from Sinthy. One of his hands lowered, the other barely staying up to hold off her full power. Bark peeled off trees, moss ripped away, and stones flew backward. If he dropped his guard, Sinthy's power would strip him to the bone.

"Please," the man pleaded in a broken, terrified tone.

Following my instincts, I put a hand on Sinthy's shoulder. "Enough."

"What?" She turned her fiery rage-filled eyes on me.

I looked back at her, calm and steady. "You've beaten him. That's enough."

Hesitantly, Sinthy lowered her hand and dropped the multitude of spells she'd been sending toward the man. The new arrival sagged to the forest floor. Sinthy shrugged my hand away from her shoulder and stomped toward the man. With a flick of her wrist, his hood flew backward, revealing the face of a young man. Barely more than a teenager. Twenty-one at the oldest. He looked at Sinthy with fear and shock. I hurried to catch up with Sinthy.

"Explain!" she screamed. Her face inches from the boy's. "Explain it."

With wide, fearful eyes, the boy wordlessly shook his head like he didn't understand.

Still consumed with rage, Sinthy kicked a clod of dirt at the boy, and mud spattered across his face.

"Why does your magic feel like my mother's? How did you do it? Fucking tell me." On the last word, the air began to pulse with energy. Her anger was palpable.

In the distance, I noticed another disturbance. My ears pricked up, and I scented the air. More people.

"Luis! Radio the perimeter guards. We have more intruders incoming. I need bodies here. Now."

The boy was holding a hand up almost in supplication toward Sinthy. Tears brimmed his eyes as he continued to shake his head. "I didn't ask for it. This isn't my fault."

Sinthy screamed an inarticulate sound of rage, sorrow, and pain. She lunged, yanking the boy toward her by his robe.

"I will turn you to dust. I'll make your mind live a million years in a simulated hell. I will boil you with the blood of your own body. I will. Unless you tell me how you have my mother's magic inside you."

Chapter 16 - Maddy

I sat up so fast, my vision blurred. Something was seriously wrong. Even dead asleep, in the depths of unconsciousness, I'd sensed it. Nico was worried, almost panicked. Some kind of danger, but I couldn't pinpoint it. Then, there'd been a weird pressure shift, almost like when your ears pop going up a really tall elevator. It ripped me from sleep, and I was out the bedroom door as soon as the grogginess of sleep had washed away in a current of fear.

I sprinted downstairs, only to be greeted by an empty house. I could still get a sense of Nico's worry and terror. Our connection was so deep that I could feel his tension even from afar. He was west of the house, deep in the forest. That was all I knew.

Before my feet even touched the ground outside the front door, I was shifted into my wolf and rocketed across the pack lands. The scenery rushed past me in a green-and-brown blur. Something was horribly wrong, and it had something to do with Sinthy's protection spells. The air around the pack lands felt… more open somehow. Everything seemed less closed in, less protected.

Barreling into the forest, I let my wolf take over, dodging and weaving through the trees and shrubbery without ever decreasing in speed. It was probably dangerous and reckless, but I had to get to Nico—I had to find out what was happening.

Their scents hit me not long after I entered the forest. Nico, Sinthy, Felipe, Sebastian, Luis, and… something else. I pushed myself to go faster, the fresh, unfamiliar scent making my heart hammer in my chest.

Sinthy's screams of rage battered against my ears, and I almost skidded to a stop. I'd never heard her sound like that. Knowing I was getting close, I hurried on. Finally, I burst into a clearing to find the group standing around a youngish man in a hooded robe. Sinthy had him by the collar and was screaming something about how he had her mother's magic inside him.

I shifted back and ran forward. "Sinthy?"

Nico spun in place. The second his eyes landed on me, the look of fear grew larger. Terror blazed inside him. He turned and grabbed Sinthy's shoulder.

"Maddy's here, and the wards are down!"

Sinthy glanced over her shoulder and saw me, her face softening. Apparently, I was in some kind of imminent danger, though I was still unsure what was happening. Without letting go of the man, she swept her hand back toward me, and a shimmer of magic enveloped my body where I stood.

"Stay still, Maddy," she called out. "If you don't move, you'll be fine."

She'd cast some kind of miniature ward around only me, but that meant Nico and all my friends were out in the open. Nico had said the wards were down. How had that happened?

In the distance, through a copse of trees, two more shadowy figures emerged.

Nico pointed at them and called back to the others. "Luis, there they are. Where are the guys?" He then looked at the new arrivals. "Stay right fucking there. Don't you fucking move. You hear me?"

Felipe leaped forward, shifting mid-stride, and stalked slowly toward the two men. Sinthy's magic radiated off her, fueled by some kind of manic hatred or sadness. It was like nothing I'd ever experienced before. She lifted a hand toward the approaching intruders and clasped them in some kind of spell similar to my protection ward. They stood, rooted to the spot, apparently unable to move. They were still so far away that I couldn't even make out if they were men or women. Felipe, seeing they were now frozen, ran forward and circled them, and I could hear his growls and snarls all the way where I was.

Sinthy jerked the man's collar, making his head loll around like a doll. "Tell me what I want to know. Otherwise,

I'll start by fileting you like a fish. I'll start with the skin, then I'll do the fingernails, then the eyes, then the— "

"I'm sorry." His voice sounded so tortured and broken. The horror at Sinthy's threats sending him into a frenzy. "I'm a witch, okay, I'm a witch." Then he shook his head and closed his eyes. "Wait, that's not exactly right— "

"Enough. The truth or you're done. Five… four… three…"

"My father," he shouted in panic. "It's him. His line descended from witches. I carry the blood in my veins."

His words struck home with me, almost like an icy knife hitting me in the chest. Almost exactly like me, but instead of shifters, it was witches.

Sinthy shook him again. "That doesn't explain what you're doing here or why you have my mother's magic inside you."

The man—boy, really—was shaking like a leaf, absolutely frantic with dread. Nico must have seen it. He reached forward and touched Sinthy's arm.

"Calm down. He's too scared to tell us anything. Let him go. He's not getting away," he said.

Sinthy jerked her head around and glared at Nico. For the barest moment, I was afraid she might lash out at him. Thankfully, she didn't. She shoved the boy away, and he sprawled in the dirt at Nico's feet.

Nico knelt and, playing the good cop to Sinthy's bad, said, "Okay, son. What the hell is going on?"

The young man looked up into Nico's face. Then he swallowed hard and seemed to steel himself.

He took a deep breath and, in a low voice, said, "I'm descended from witches. Except I didn't have any magical powers. The bloodline was diluted. All I am is a vessel. A… uh, a body that was capable of holding magic. We were taken, my siblings and me, when we were very young. They experimented on us, and almost all of us had terrible reactions." Tears dripped from his eyes. "They injected us with all these drugs and serums. I was the only one whose body didn't reject it. I was told it was a synthesized serum developed from the genetic code of a dead witch. Sort of… um… sort of like a magical CRISPR treatment, maybe? I'm not good at science. I woke up the next day with magic, but I didn't understand it. It fought with me, and I fought with it. I'm not in control of it. You have to understand." He was pleading, but his voice was still low, almost a whisper.

Nico looked into the woods at the two others, then back at the boy. "Are they royals? Viola's men?"

At the mention of Viola's name, the boy flinched in fear, then nodded.

Sinthy stepped forward, hissing at the boy through clenched teeth. "That's my dead mother's magic coursing through your fucking veins."

The air pulsed again, surging with her anger. I could actually feel the wards starting to rebuild, spurred on by the rage inside her. I wondered if she was doing it on purpose to defuse some of her anger or if it was unconscious. It had taken her days and days to build them the first time, and now the wards were going up so fast, it made me wonder what kind of power Sinthy would be capable of if she truly let herself go. It was an almost God-like power.

If I were in her shoes, I was certain my rage would have overwhelmed me just as much. It was obvious what Viola had done. After killing Sinthy's mother, that evil bitch had used Sinthy's mother's blood to create drugs in an attempt to make her own witch—one wholly and completely controlled by her. The violation was even worse than pure death. At least if she'd only killed Sinthy's mother, it would have been over. This… abomination of an experiment was like Sinthy having to relive her mother's death over and over again. All this only a few weeks after losing her adoptive mother, Isme.

Grabbing the boy again, Sinthy pulled his face up to hers. "I'm going to rip the magic from your body. I will expunge it from every cell of your body. I will leave you drained and wilted like a dead leaf. And when I find Viola, I'll use that power to make sure not even a single atom of her body is left."

Heedless of her threat, the boy leaned forward and whispered, "I can help you. I can tell you things." With a plea in his eyes, he said, "I don't want to die. I need to protect my siblings. Even though the treatments didn't work on them, she's holding them hostage to get me to do what she wants. Please. I... I can tell you where she is."

Those words got a reaction. Nico stiffened, and I gasped. The one thing we'd wanted. Could it really have just walked into our laps? A way to find Viola?

Sinthy's breathing calmed a bit. "Then tell us."

"I can't right now," he said, the desperation in his voice amping up.

Sinthy shrugged. "No need. I have other ways."

She pushed a hand toward the boy's chest, never touching him, but power burst through her palm and slammed into his chest. Sinthy gripped his collar to keep him from tumbling back. He gasped in pain and grabbed at his chest. I thought she'd killed him, but soon he recovered and clutched his chest, wincing in pain.

Pulling him close again, she hissed. "I have magic you can't even comprehend. I'm the most powerful witch of the modern age, and Viola has fucked with the wrong person this time. You are now marked by me. I can find you anywhere, at any time. No magic can hide you from me. Even in death, I can find your bones, and so shall it be until the day the sun goes dark. If you tell her about it, she'll kill you. So don't," she said through gritted teeth.

Sinthy shoved him back and straightened, looking toward the two figures in the distance. With a flick of her wrist, they floated toward us, feet an inch above the forest floor. Once they were close, I saw that they were both men. They were dressed in standard military gear, AR-15 rifles hanging from their shoulders, but their arms were frozen in place, and they couldn't touch them.

Walking up to the men, Sinthy glared at them, her eyes darkened to a near-black. Again, I realized how much anger and rage the young woman had kept walled up within herself. It was scary and sad all at the same time. She was a sweet girl who deserved a normal, happy life, but the royals had ruined that, and Sinthy would have to live with that forever.

Without looking at the young man, she spoke. "Are these men evil?"

"What?" the boy asked with trepidation.

She sneered at him. "I said, are these men evil? Are they bad guys?"

The boy barely hesitated before nodding. "Very bad, yes."

Nodding to herself, Sinthy said, "I'm going to send Viola a little message."

With a wave of her hand, the spell around the men dropped, and they fell to the ground. Instead of grabbing their guns to fire on us or leaping up to run, they grabbed their stomachs and yowled, their voices going higher in pitch in the most agonized screams I could ever remember. A moment later, a red-hot flame erupted from their midsections and consumed them in a flame so hot I had to look away. When I glanced back, the two men were nothing but a pile of ashes.

"Holy mother of God," Luis whispered.

"Shit," Nico muttered with a wary glance at Sinthy.

She'd killed them with barely a flick of her wrist. Sinthy didn't even look like it had fazed her. Instead, she walked to the other witch and squatted low to look into his eyes.

"You tell Viola what happened here today. You tell her she messed with the wrong witch and her pack. Nico and Maddy are under my protection. If she really wants her life to end so soon, she can try again. Now, get out of here before I do to you what I did to them," she said with a nod toward the pile of ash.

With a shaky nod, the boy stumbled to his feet and backed away. He tried to teleport but only went slightly opaque. The second attempt was successful, and he vanished. That showed me that he was being honest and that he really wasn't in full control of his magic.

Sinthy trudged off into the woods, back toward the main area of the pack lands. A look into the sky showed me that the wards were creeping back into place, almost like a plant. It wasn't noticeable unless you knew what to look for—a faint waver in the light as it rose. Perhaps anger was a good fertilizer for magic.

Sebastian knelt over the ashes and ran a stick through them. "Holy fuck, one guy had a gold tooth. It's still here."

Wincing in disgust, I turned to follow Sinthy. The others did the same, Nico barking at Luis to get the perimeter guards' asses in a sling. He was furious that everything had gone down before *anyone* had shown up for backup. That was bad, but I couldn't think about anything but Sinthy. I wanted to see her and help her calm down.

Once we got back to the house, we found Sinthy pacing like an animal in the living room.

Stepping close, I held out my hand. "Sinthy? Are you okay? That couldn't have been easy."

Some of the old Sinthy resurfaced. Her face was no longer a seething mask of rage and anger. Shoulders slumping, she turned a pained gaze on me.

"I'm sorry. I got a little out of control. You guys shouldn't have had to see that." She shook her head in disbelief. "Once I felt my mother's magic, realized what happened… I lost it. That's all I can say."

I pulled her into a tight hug. At first, she was rigid, unyielding. After a moment, however, she relaxed and sank into me, tentatively putting her arms around me. The others stood around awkwardly, watching us warily. When I finally broke the embrace, Sinthy had even more control back. She almost seemed like her normal self.

"You said you can track that guy?" I said, asking the question that I desperately needed an answer to.

She shrugged. "More or less. It's a crest. A mark that lets me scry him out anywhere."

I frowned. "Scry?"

"Um, sort of like viewing from a distance. It has a few different meanings in magic, but that's more or less what I did."

"Does that mean we can find out where Viola is?"

"It's a little wonky. It won't be an exact location—more like a ballpark. Plus, I can't tell when he's around her or not. But it's something."

I grinned at her, unable to contain my enthusiasm. "You did fantastic, Sinthy. Thank you."

The others had gathered around the kitchen island, and we joined them there. Nico's father joined us, having heard of the disturbance in the woods. Nico gave him a brief rundown, and while he talked, I mulled over what I'd witnessed in the woods. A nagging fear had been eating at me since I'd seen how afraid that boy had been. I'd ignored it while dealing with the shock of the events, but now it surged to the forefront of my mind.

"That boy didn't look happy to be here. I got the distinct feeling he was more a slave than a conspirator. I'm worried about what Viola may do to him for failing whatever mission she sent him on," I said.

"What mission was he on, anyway?" Nico's father asked.

Sinthy waved a hand dismissively. "He was trying to alter the wards. It shouldn't have worked at all. It wasn't his magic, and he had no clue how to wield it. The only reason the spells wavered and fell was that it was my mother's magic doing the work. It has a similar wavelength to mine, which gave his power a boost. They didn't fall completely. The additional spells I did to strengthen them while I brought the other packs here helped keep the framework there. Once I had that kid under my power, the wards rebuilt themselves. Still, that was closer than I want to think about." Sinthy looked out the window toward the woods. "I need to strengthen them. The ward won't come back one hundred percent without my help."

There was a dark look in her eyes as she looked out the window. We could all feel her distress. It came off her like a tsunami. She was still thinking about what Viola had done to her parents and what she'd done with her mother's blood.

I touched her lightly as I stepped close to her. "Sinthy?"

The young woman shook her head as if she'd roused herself from some kind of self-induced hypnosis. "I'm fine. It's okay."

"What are you thinking?" I asked.

She chewed at the inside of her cheek and finally said, "I feel like... when my mother's magic was coming from that guy, that it was almost like my mother was trying to warn me about something." Her voice cracked as she spoke. "I need a minute."

Sinthy rushed out the door before I could respond. I wanted nothing more than to follow her, to comfort her. I understood what it was like to realize the royals had taken something from you that you could never get back. For me, it was my birth family and the life I could have lived. I was beyond happy with who my adoptive parents were and loved them more than life itself, but knowing something special had been taken away from me was still devastating. It had to be even worse for her because Sinthy remembered life with her parents. She'd had to grieve that loss all the years she'd lived with Isme. The best thing to do was to give her time alone.

Nico looked wired when I returned to the group like he'd downed a pot of coffee. I hadn't seen him so keyed up in a long time.

"This is what we've been waiting for," he said, jabbing his finger on the table. "That magical tracker Sinthy put on that kid can lead us to Viola."

"Right..." Felipe said. "But how do we know when to use it? He could be in a damned cage somewhere. Or worse, he's nowhere near Viola, and our advantage is lost. If she finds out he has a trace on him, she won't hesitate to kill him. I don't care how much time and money was spent creating him. She's not the type who leaves loose ends."

"True," Nico said. "That's why we have to be smart. This is our one chance to do what we need to do. We can't fuck this up."

We all understood exactly what was at stake. We had to be very careful. There was a sense of finality to this. Like God had given us the biggest, baddest weapon on Earth, but it only had one bullet. Best not to miss.

Chapter 17 - Nico

Sinthy was gone for a long time, holed up in her room, if I had to guess. My head was still spinning as I tried to make sense of the last hour. I'd never seen the witch look so upset and confused. Since I'd met her, Sinthy had been the face of calm and usually acted like a goofy kid. But that rage she'd shown when she realized her mother's magic had been stolen had... well, it had terrified me. Not only had her mother's magic been stolen, twisted, and tortured into some kind of weapon, but it had twisted that poor kid into some kind of monster for Viola's needs. Somehow, every passing showed me another layer of the vile human she was.

"I'm gonna go check on her," Maddy said when Sinthy had been gone for over an hour.

"Okay. Let me know if I can do anything for her."

Maddy returned a half hour later, looking forlorn.

"What happened?" I asked as she came in the front door.

"That girl is not okay. She's depressed and sad and a little out of it."

"Is she still out in the woods?"

Maddy nodded. "Yeah. Said she was re-strengthening the wards. She told me she was mentally tired from using so much power earlier against the intruders. She needs time alone to get her mind back on track. That, on top of learning what happened to her mother? It's a lot to process. I think she'll be all right. I guess we'll see. I do think she liked that I went to check on her, though."

"If she needs anything, just tell me. I'll even risk sending someone to town for it. Whatever she needs, I'll get it. She's done too much for us for me to let her fall apart."

"That's sweet of you. Where did everyone go?" Maddy glanced around. For once, the house was empty.

"The guys went out to check the perimeter and do some ass-chewing. Dad should be back in a minute. He went to get the alpha bunking with them. Norman. He, Dad, Tiago, and I are gonna talk. Of all the shifter packs here, we lead the largest three."

Like clockwork, Dad walked in with Tiago and Norman in tow. Norman was younger than Tiago but older than me. A broad-shouldered shifter who looked like he could handle himself.

Maddy waved to the stairs. "Go, have the boy talk. You can fill me in later."

I led the guys upstairs to my office. Once they were seated, I spent ten minutes relaying the events of the day. My father looked disturbed. The thought of our pack lands being infiltrated probably filled him with existential dread, which I guess I couldn't blame him for.

Tiago and Norman looked worried as well, especially after I told them about Sinthy frying the royals' soldiers and sending the boy back.

"Viola probably thought she was being slick as shit," Tiago said. "She probably spent weeks planning this little operation, and our resident witch gave them the beatdown before they even got near Maddy. Bitch is gonna be pissed."

Norman nodded. "Right? From all I've heard, you guys say this chick is even worse than she seems on TV and online. Are we thinking retribution—will she try to hit back?"

That was inevitable. No matter how it happened, Viola would be furious that her mission had failed. The woman didn't have enough humanity to get upset if some of her pawns got taken out. I highly doubted she had any emotional attachments. But a failed mission to get Maddy? Yeah, she'd be hitting back.

"That's why we've been training," I said. "The royals will come at some point. As for those two piles of ash in the woods? If those guys *had* managed to sneak closer and get anywhere near Maddy, they'd be dead anyway. I'd have made sure of that. So, it doesn't matter how they died."

"Can't argue with that," Dad said with a nod of acknowledgment. "I'll be totally honest, though. Was it the best idea for her to let that boy go?" He gave me a pained look. "I don't wanna be bloodthirsty, but wouldn't it have been safer to have three little piles of ash out in the woods? Aren't we worried that kid might tell Viola what really happened? What if he tells her about the crest or whatever Sinthy put on him?"

I shook my head. "No, I don't think so. You weren't there. It was no act. That kid was fucking terrified. Of Sinthy, sure, but mostly of Viola. His siblings are her hostages, and they're probably still being experimented on or tortured. He wants her dead. I could see it in his eyes when he offered to help us."

Digging in my pocket, I pulled out my cell.

"Who are you calling?" Tiago asked.

"I need to let Donatello know. Best to keep him in the loop on everything that happens."

"Good afternoon, dear Nico. Calling again so soon?" Donatello said. I could almost picture his little island paradise as he spoke.

Once again, I went over the day's events. When I described the magical trace Sinthy had put on the boy, he let out a long low whistle.

"You know, boy-o, that is possibly the luckiest thing to happen to us so far."

"That's kinda what we think," I agreed.

"What's the next play? Step two?" Donatello asked.

"Good question." I hesitated. "After what's happened, I think the pack lands might not be the safe haven we thought."

Dad lifted his head, raising a questioning eyebrow. I hadn't discussed it with him. Hell, it hadn't even occurred to me until those fuckers got through the wards. We were safer than most, but Sinthy could only do so much.

"Don, I keep thinking of that offer you made," I said.

"It still stands." There wasn't even a hint of hesitation in his voice. "There's more than enough room for you and all those you are sheltering. Say the word, and I'll arrange the transport."

"Well, if anyone comes, it won't be all of us. Probably only Maddy and a small contingent of people to ensure her safety."

I was met with surprise from the other men. This was all off the cuff, and I'd caught them all off guard. Maddy and the other pack alphas would need to agree, obviously. It was my land, but it was their lives, and that meant they got a say in anything that might affect them.

"Let me know what you decide. As always, I'm here," Donatello said, and the call disconnected.

My father and the other two men looked at me expectantly.

"Gather the alphas. We need to discuss this. It might be safer for everyone if Maddy gets out of here. It'll take the heat off a bunch of innocent shifters and get her someplace even more secure."

Dad tilted his head and gave me a wry smile. "And has the ever-so-intelligent Mr. Lorenzo spoken to his mate about this idea yet?"

I hadn't. I'd only started thinking about it since the wards had been threatened. But Maddy would see reason. She'd understand it was for the best.

"I'll speak with her and see what she thinks is best," I said.

"Okay, we'll spread the word," Tiago said as he stood. "When and where is this big meeting happening?"

"Tonight," I said. "We'll do it outside. Down in the training field. Tell everyone to be there at sundown."

Unsure how to go about the discussion with Maddy, I decided to come right out and say it. Tear the Band-Aid off, so to speak. She was surprisingly receptive to it once I laid it all out.

"You're right," she said. "Viola is targeting this place because of me. It's making it too dangerous. All these innocent people here, and I'm bringing this on them. Especially with the new packs we've brought in."

"So, you're okay with leaving?" I asked incredulously. I'd assumed there would be much more cajoling and begging.

She nodded. "I think so. We'll see what the others say, but as of now, I think it's the safest option for everyone here, especially after what happened. Who knows if Viola has more witches, she's forced to work for her. She might send more or one with more power next time. Sinthy is amazing, but she's not strong enough to fight everything that will come our way."

Tension crackled in the air at the meeting. Rumors of the enemy incursion had made the rounds. They were all well aware of how close we'd come to losing all protection from the wards. Every alpha in attendance looked desperate to hear more about it and what we had planned.

I stood silhouetted against the roaring bonfire Sebastian and Felipe had set, looking out at the sea of faces. Nearly a dozen alphas, my own friends and family, along with Sinthy and Maddy's three parents—all looking to me for leadership and answers.

I left nothing out as I spoke. The people under my protection needed to know exactly what we were up against. Their fear grew, and wary looks passed between them when I explained that the male witch had almost broken our magical protection completely.

"To that note, I think Maddy needs to be taken somewhere safer. Not only will it ensure her safety, but it will likely remove the threat from the pack lands. Do any of you have an objection to that?"

Byron, the alpha of the smallest pack here—ten members—stood. "Nico, we're happy to be here, and we appreciate your protection. This is your decision. Yours and Maddy's. I don't think I have a leg to stand on telling you what you should or shouldn't do. These aren't my lands, and this isn't my pack."

There were some nods of agreement all around. Others spoke up, saying that if Maddy felt safer somewhere else, she should go. I was surprised and proud that none of them spoke of their own danger. It was all about what Maddy needed, what I wanted, and what was best for everyone. The consensus made me slightly ashamed that I'd assumed people would be desperate to get rid of Maddy to save themselves, but that wasn't what was happening.

"That settles it," Maddy said. "I'm going. I'll join Abi on Donatello's island."

"Donatello's offer stands for anyone." I looked at Maddy's parents. "Mr. and Mrs. Sutton, Gabriella, do any of you want to go with Maddy?"

Maddy's parents held each other close, and her father shook his head. "We have no supernatural powers and won't be of much good in a fight, but we're safe here. I don't think we want to go somewhere else. I wish Maddy would stay, but… we understand. We're staying."

"Fair enough," I said, then turned to Maddy's birth mother. "And you?"

Gabriella looked torn. "I worry for Maddy. Part of me wants to stay close to her. I'm scared of what Viola will do if she ever gets close to her."

I held up a hand in reassurance. "I promise you she'll be safer on the island."

Gabriella nodded. "Viola would also love to have me locked up again. I'm not ecstatic about it, but I think I'll stay here. Separating Maddy and me might make things more difficult for Viola."

After the other alphas and Maddy's parents had gone back to their lodgings, I decided Luis, Felipe, and my brother Diego would go along with Maddy and me to the island as additional backup and protection. I'd asked Sebastian, but he declined, worried his presence would interfere with Abi's healing.

"So, this is it," I said, looking at each of them in the flickering light of the bonfire.

We were about to do something very dangerous, but in the long run, it would, hopefully, keep us all safe. I called Donatello to let him know we were coming.

"Fantastic," Donatello said. "I'll have a chopper sent out to you unless you want to use the talents of that lovely young witch?"

Sinthy's face went red, and she rolled her eyes. With a shake of her head, she said, "No helicopters. That will be a big red flag. I can get them to the airstrip."

"Fair enough," Donatello said. "My private plane will be ready. I assure you. You will be safe in my charge."

I sent the guys off to pack up and prepare. Sinthy hung back and pulled Maddy and me aside. Her steely eyes held nothing but determination as she spoke.

"I'm going with you," she said.

Maddy and I shared a look before I answered. "You have to stay here. Without you, the wards will fall. It's all that's protecting the people here from those anti-shifters out there."

Sinthy glanced over her shoulder like she was afraid someone would hear. "That's what I wanted to tell you. When that guy crossed the threshold of the wards with those two assassins, the spell didn't fully collapse. He shouldn't have been able to do anything against them, but with my mother's magic inside him, it was on the same wavelength or frequency as my own."

"I don't see how that's a good thing," Maddy said.

Sinthy shrugged. "It usually wouldn't be, but when I walked the perimeter to strengthen the wards, I found something weird. Not only had they rebuilt themselves to almost full strength, but the wards were even stronger than before. It's like his breaking through had been like a bone breaking in an arm. When it heals, the bone ends up thicker and stronger to prevent another break. That's what's happened here. The combination of my magic, Isme's spells, and my dead mother's magic created some weird confluence. This place is a fortress now."

"But you still have to be here to maintain it," I said, trying to get the fact into her head.

Smiling, Sinthy shook her head. "I don't need to. I figured a way around that."

"What way?" I asked incredulously.

She pointed at the ground and raised an eyebrow. "These lands are special. You've seen it, that power of the land. I tapped into it this afternoon. Imagine the land is like an outlet. I managed to create a cable, or plug, if you will, that uses the magic of your pack lands to maintain the spells holding the wards up. So, to repeat, I'm going with you. And everyone here will be safe. You can trust me. I've quadruple-checked it."

My mind went back to that moment I'd connected with the land and the vision of the ancient cronelike witch from centuries before blessing the land. My own strength and confidence had increased two-fold from that little encounter. I'd barely even brushed the surface of the power that lay in these pack lands. If Sinthy really had been able to harness all that old power, then she might actually be right.

I rubbed a hand across my forehead. "Are you sure? Sinthy, you have to be one hundred percent sure about this."

"Too many people are relying on you," Maddy added.

Sinthy put one hand on my left shoulder and one on Maddy's right, looking back and forth between us. The dark circles under her eyes were going away. It was a sign that the wards weren't draining her as they had been. It gave me a bit of hope that she was right about her findings.

"I swear to you," Sinthy said, "this place will be safe. With the way it's set up, even if Viola sent ten witches here, the wards wouldn't fall. And besides, even if they try, I'll know it wherever I am. I can get back here in a flash. I want to go with you. I've... I don't know, I've got a feeling."

My heart lurched. "A feeling? Like what? Are we going to be attacked or something on the way?"

"No, no, nothing like that," Sinthy said, shaking her head. "But I feel like the only way I'll ever get to meet Viola face to face is to get out of here."

"Fine," I said. "You can go, but I want you with one magical ear to the ground. If anything goes wrong here, I want you back. Okay?"

"Deal," Sinthy said. "I'll go, get packed. Also, is this a really nice island? Do I need to pack my thong bikini?"

"Would you go, pack," I growled at her.

Her laughter rang through the air as she went. I looked up at the sky. I couldn't see the magic that protected us, but it was there. If Sinthy really had worked out a way to do what she'd said, then that opened a lot of possibilities. She was no longer bound to this location. It was a secret weapon I'd have to figure out how to use.

Back in the house, I had a suitcase open on the living room couch. Luis, Felipe, and Diego had already packed—their bags lined up in the foyer. Maddy and Gabriella were making dinner. My phone rang, and I assumed it was Donatello again or one of the alphas housed here, but the unknown number made me frown. The hair on the back of my neck stood up.

I answered it on speaker. Something bad was coming, and I wanted the others to hear.

"This is Nico Lorenzo."

"I should have known filth like you would align yourselves with a witch." Viola's voice dripped with acid as she spoke.

Maddy dropped the spatula she'd been holding. The others froze in whatever action they'd been involved in and slowly walked toward me, gathering around the phone.

"Hello, Viola," I said, forcing my voice to remain calm. "What did I do to be graced with your disgusting voice tonight?"

She ignored that. "I understood when you stole Gabriella from me—she's blood. I simply never thought you'd go so far as to sully your flea-ridden home with a spellcaster of your own. Witches are an abomination like you. A dark stain on God's planet. Only the Lord himself shall wield those powers. They have stolen the powers of God, and after I'm done with shifters, I'll work on their ilk."

"I never knew you were so religious," I said, trying to get under her skin. "Isn't there something about loving thy neighbor in that book?"

"Thou shalt not suffer a witch to live is also a phrase from that book," she retorted. "You've confirmed it now. Your witch has killed my men and sent me back a broken and terrified boy."

"Speaking of that," I said. "If you hate witches so much, why'd you make one? Seems counterintuitive if you want them wiped out."

"They have their uses," she hissed. "A tool to be used in the fight against the scourge all around us. At least they have their uses when they know what the hell they're doing." Over the phone, there was a cracking sound like a slap, followed by the whimpering cries of a young man, begging Viola to stop.

My eyes locked on Sinthy, who was staring down at my phone with rage and disgust. Maddy paced back and forth across the room, her hands locked in fists so tight her knuckles were white.

"All of this can end," Viola went on. "All you need to do is give me what I want. The vial is all I need. I don't even need Maddy. Though, I could still use her. What I do is up to you. Things will only get worse. More attacks, more shifters butchered, and more innocent women attacked because they share Maddy's name.

"Here is my last bargain. Give me the vial. Spare innocent lives and accept your fate. Or watch as the citizens of the world rise up and tear your species apart. How long do you think the governments will keep toeing the filthy line of shifter support? True humans all find you disgusting obscenities. Once I get enough people on my side, the constituencies will demand action. Remember, if God is with me, who can be against me?"

"You realize many humans are going to die in this war you have planned, right?" I said.

"I will kill millions of humans, tens of millions," she hissed through clenched teeth, "if it means the end of shifters. There is no cross too heavy to bear when the fate of the world is on the line."

I was tired of hearing her grating voice. "Well, in that case, I've gotta say fuck you. No deal."

Viola chuckled ruefully. "Oh, you'll regret that. I tried to bargain with you, but I should have known that's impossible with animals. You'll pay a heavy price. Count on it."

I stared at my phone. Viola hadn't sounded desperate or backed into a corner. Crazy, yes, but that was to be expected. No, if anything, she sounded calmer and more focused. Even with the whole world bearing down on her, she managed to stay composed. Somehow. It made me worried about what might be coming next.

Chapter 18 - Maddy

A slight sliver of hope settled in my chest when the call ended. Viola had been in a rage. Psychotic and malicious as always, but her anger hadn't been as out of control as it could have been. She hadn't let on that she'd realized the Wiccan boy had a tracker placed on him. There was no doubt in my mind that she would have given us shit for that. She would have called us and chastised us for thinking we could get one over on her. It was the kind of person she was.

That was all fine, but we had other things to worry about. Viola might decide to retaliate for this latest issue. What would she do, and when would she do it? We had been talking about it for nearly an hour when I spoke.

"Is this a good time to leave? I mean, are we sure now is the time to travel away from the pack lands?"

"Absolutely," Nico said. "If anything, I'm even more certain now is the time to go. We take that vial with us and get out of here." He ran his tongue along his teeth before adding, "I'm starting to think we should take everyone."

"You're worried about the wards?" Sinthy asked, but she didn't look upset.

Nico nodded hesitantly. "I know you say the wards are strong enough, but my people are here, and it's the only protection they'll have once we leave."

Sinthy reached across the table and put a hand on Nico's. "I would never put you or your people at risk. I've checked the wards over and over again. The power of your land truly is astounding. If there were even a chance they wouldn't hold, I'd never leave. Not only is your land strong, but I'm probably the strongest witch on Earth. At least, that's what Isme always told me. You can have faith in me and in your pack lands."

Nico looked like he really wanted to believe her. Her confidence had already eased my fears. I believed her.

Sinthy hadn't done anything since we met for me to think she was anything but trustworthy. She also seemed to take the fact that she'd been brought into the pack very seriously. No way she'd ever put these people at risk. The pack was her new family, and if there was one thing I'd learned about the girl was that she desperately wanted a family. Hers had been ripped away, and this was now what she had.

Finally, Nico sighed and nodded to Sinthy. "Okay, as long as you're sure. Moving everyone would probably be traumatic, especially for the ones who just got here. There's no reason to terrify everyone if we don't need to."

"Exactly," Sinthy said. "In fact. I tested it to make sure."

She stood and walked over to the linen closet near the laundry room.

"What are you doing?" I asked.

Sinthy opened the closet and pulled out a big shopping bag. "I teleported to town as an experiment, and while I was there, I monitored the wards' strength if I wasn't around. It stayed solid, so I decided to grab a few things while I was there."

"Son of a bitch," Nico said. "So, it does work." He let out a heavy sigh.

He'd obviously trusted Sinthy, but the uncertainty looked like it had added five years to his life. Knowing the protection would remain in place if she left had a relieved grin spreading across his face as Sinthy walked over with the bag.

"Here." She handed Nico a stack of small boxes.

Nico looked at the six boxes with pictures of phones on them. "Phones?" Nico asked, looking thoroughly confused.

Sinthy nodded. "Burners, as the kids call them." She grinned mischievously. "I figured you guys would ditch your phones here and take these instead. There's a chance Viola could trace you guys with your personal phones."

Nico held one of the boxes up and chuckled. "Didn't even think of that. Thank you, Sinthy."

"No problem. And these are for you, Maddy." She handed me a few bottles of pills and a thick book.

She'd gotten me prenatal vitamins and a pregnancy book. Tears pricked my eyes. Sinthy had thought about my baby while she was out there in the real world. This sweet woman was thinking about what was best for my baby, and all I could do was complain that the timing was bad.

I gritted my teeth and made a decision. From today, I was going to try to celebrate and enjoy this pregnancy. It was a happy time, one that deserved to be observed with joy. I couldn't let Viola steal that happiness from me.

Sniffling back tears, I put an arm around Sinthy. "Thanks. I really appreciate it."

"When do we want to go?" Sinthy asked.

Nico looked across the room at the guys, raising his eyebrows questioningly.

Luis shrugged. "We're good whenever," he said.

Swinging his gaze back toward me, Nico said, "I guess we need to say our goodbyes."

Mom and Dad got to the house less than ten minutes after I called them. Nico's parents and brothers were all there too. All of them looked relieved that we were getting someplace even safer but worried about being so far from us.

"You'll check in a lot, won't you?" Mom asked as she hugged me tight.

"Yes, Mom. I promise. When it's possible, I definitely will."

Her hand moved from my back down to my belly, and she smiled sadly. "Be careful. For your sake, but also for the baby's. I can't wait to meet the little one."

I took Mom's hands in mine and looked into her eyes. "It's going to be all right. We'll be safe. Please try not to worry about us."

I said my farewells to my dad and Gabriella, then to Nico's family. Nico's mom and I hadn't gotten off to the best start, but over the last few weeks, all that had really smoothed out. Her eyes were even a little misty as she hugged me.

Sinthy came into the room with the little wooden box that held the vial. I still had no clue where she'd hidden it all this time. I could almost feel my pupils dilate as my eyes fell on the box. Something about that damned thing always called to me. Like a phantom or ghost was nudging and pushing me toward it. My heart rate jumped a little, and my palms got sweaty too.

Sinthy saw the look on my face and sighed. "That's what I thought."

Blinking rapidly to clear my head, I looked up at her. "Huh?"

She pointed to the box and then to me. "This thing is like freaking catnip for you. That's why I hid it and put a bunch of spells around it. Otherwise, your mind would have been on this thing all day, every day." She waved her hand over the box. "Hang on a second."

Indecipherable words tumbled from her mouth as she moved her hand across the wood. Then, in an instant, the strange pull of the box vanished, and I was suddenly back to myself.

"Are we ready?" Nico asked as he slung a backpack on his shoulders.

I hesitated for a moment before nodding. "Yeah, I think so."

Nico's father stepped forward and hugged his son again. "I'll keep this place safe, son. I promise. Everything will be as it was when you get back."

Nico smirked at him. "Well, you do have enough practice. What was it? Thirty years as pack alpha?"

His father shrugged. "Like riding a bike, I'm sure."

Our little group formed a circle. Each of us had a backpack and a small suitcase with clothes and personal items. Nico handed Sinthy a printout with the location and a satellite picture of the private airstrip.

She studied it for several seconds before nodding and tucking the paper away.

"Everyone, please touch the person beside you. The circle needs to be unbroken."

We all grabbed a suitcase with one hand and placed our free hands on the person on our left. Sinthy closed her eyes, and it happened.

I had time to hear Felipe let out a surprised curse, and then we were standing outside beside a small airstrip. My head was a little woozy, but otherwise, I was fine. Felipe, not so much. He'd turned and puked his guts out the second our feet touched the ground.

Sinthy watched him with an apologetic frown. "Sorry. Some people… uh… well teleportation can be weird for some people."

Felipe groaned and wiped his mouth. "That… was awful."

"Come on," Nico said.

He was glancing around in every direction, probably scared the royals had somehow discovered our location before we'd even arrived. We grabbed our things and walked onto the tarmac, where a pilot waved to us.

Sinthy bypassed the pilot and walked over to place a hand on the plane. Closing her eyes, she gave herself an affirmative nod before looking back at us.

"Checking to make sure there was nothing on the plane that could track us. We're clear."

The pilot showed us the seats and where to put our bags, then left to join his co-pilot in the cockpit. We hadn't even gotten buckled up when every one of our new burner cell phones started chiming and ringing. I caught Nico's eye, dread filling my stomach. This couldn't be good.

Diego read the text. "It says we need to turn on the news. Like, now."

Nico found a small, flat-screen TV on the wall and turned it on. As soon as the screen flashed on, I became nauseated. My face was staring back at me from the screen. My current driver's license photo. The news anchor was speaking in the background.

"…again stating that Miss Maddison Sutton of Clearidge, Florida is the woman Viola Monroe is so desperate to apprehend. We want anyone with knowledge of Miss Sutton's location to inform the police immediately so proper security measures can be taken."

"Well, the best fucking security measure would have been to keep Maddy's damned face off the news," Nico hissed through clenched teeth.

The anchor went on. "We will now replay the video we received ten minutes ago."

The anchor and my face vanished, only to be replaced with Viola's face. Growls erupted all around the plane. If I didn't know better, I thought even Sinthy may have growled.

"I'm done playing games," Viola said. "Let's get right to it. This is my quarry." Viola held up a picture of my driver's license. "Maddison Sutton of Clearidge, Florida. Bar owner and *sexual consort*," she spat the words like they disgusted her, "of Nicolas Lorenzo, alpha of the Lorenzo pack. This woman is dangerous. I want all my followers, or any who are on the fence about our cause, to listen. She is a descendant of the legendary vicious and evil werewolf king Edemas. She has the power and strength to decimate whole towns on her own.

"With her blood, my scientists and I could create something that could end the shifter race once and for all. I implore anyone who knows where this woman is to send a message to me via the secure link that will be posted at the bottom of this screen. Anyone who gives me information that leads to the capture or death of Miss Sutton, or anyone that brings me this woman—alive or dead—will be rewarded with twenty-five million dollars. The money is good, but the main reward will be that you are preventing a disaster. If she is allowed to live, I don't want to know what may happen to humanity. I look forward to hearing from you all very soon." Viola smiled cruelly at the camera, then the video cut off, returning to the news desk.

"This video was uploaded fifteen minutes ago. Our team tells us it has already been shared more than forty million times and counting. Once again, anyone with knowledge of Maddison Sutton's location needs to contact authorities or take her to the nearest law enforcement location for her own protection."

Nico clicked the TV off right as the jet sped down the runway.

He locked his eyes on Sinthy. "You are totally sure the wards will hold, right? The entire country is about to descend on the pack lands to capture or kill Maddy. Are my people safe?" The imploring look in his eyes hurt my heart.

Sinthy met his eyes with a steely gaze of her own. "They'll hold. I guarantee it. And once those assholes start dropping like flies as they try to go through, they'll get the point really fast." She shrugged. "I'm not a killer by nature, but when it comes to my family, I make sure they are taken care of."

Nico stared at her for several seconds before sighing and relaxing in his leather seat. "Good enough for me."

Chapter 19 - Nico

The flight was short and uneventful, which was good. It was a struggle to keep my mind off the fact that Viola had once again upped the ante. Sinthy was certain my family, pack, and friends were safe, but that didn't make things any less stressful. I was the alpha. It was my duty to protect my home, my lands, and all those who counted on me. Except, my other duty was to protect my mate. That took precedence above anything else. It was like I was getting pulled in two different directions. If I hadn't left Dad in charge back home, I'd be on the verge of a nervous breakdown. He'd been the pack alpha for decades before I took over. He would keep everyone in line and keep them prepared. That was all that I could hope for.

The plane descended toward a small private airstrip in the Keys. In the east, the barest glint of orange had started to color the horizon. Yet a while until night vanished, but I took it as a good sign that the world was still turning. Things continued to move along, even though it felt like everything was falling apart. It gave me some confidence.

As the small jet taxied toward a tiny building at the end of the runway, I looked out the window and saw a familiar figure standing near the small facility. Donatello, dressed in a solid white suit. On anyone else, it would have made for a ridiculous and gaudy picture, but Donatello made it look stylish and natural. At least he wasn't wearing a hat—even for him, that would have been too much.

The pilot lowered the door that doubled as stairs, and I was the first out, climbing down to the tarmac.

"Welcome, friends," Donatello said with a smile. "I trust the excursion has gone well so far?"

Still in a foul mood from the news report, I shrugged. "Suppose you've heard the news?"

His smile faded, and he nodded. "I did. It is unfortunate, but it seems we timed this perfectly. You couldn't have chosen a better time to go into hiding." As he looked behind me, his eyes widened.

I turned to see Sinthy stepping down the stairs, the wooden box with the vial clutched in her hands.

"Is that what I think it is?" Donatello asked.

"The vial? Yes."

He blinked, then turned his gaze back to me. "Oh, very good. I was actually talking about the magnificent creature carrying it."

Sinthy shook her head in derision. "For the millionth time, Donatello. The answer is no."

Donatello put a hand to his chest and sighed sadly. "If only Fate were not so cruel. Perhaps in another life, you would allow me to bask in your presence forever, my lovely friend."

Sinthy rolled her eyes. "He's been like this since the first time I teleported to him. The guy spent three hours trying to get me to run away with him. Kind of exhausting, to be honest."

Maddy came out, followed by the guys. She glanced around, her face falling.

"Didn't Abi come with you?"

Donatello lowered his head in an apologetic bow. "Unfortunately, the boat will only hold so many. She will be there when we arrive at the island, though. I decided a boat would be safer. The less air traffic between the mainland and my private island, the better. I don't want to give Viola any hint as to where you or I might be."

Even hearing her name made my blood boil. My face turned red with anger as I, again, thought about her showing Maddy's face to the world.

"Have we made any headway finding that bitch?" I asked. "This isn't just Maddy's life at stake anymore. Our unborn child's life is in danger, too."

Donatello clapped a hand on my back. "I assure you—we will make it happen. Of that, I guarantee. It's only a matter of time."

He then turned away from me and waved to the building. Two men in white polo shirts and khaki shorts came hurrying out.

"Please transfer my guests' bags to the boat on the dock. The faster you move, the bigger the tip," he said.

The men gathered up all our bags and backpacks and hustled down a pathway leading to the eastern portion of the island. We followed them. Maddy was at my side— her arm around my waist. I took comfort in her being near me. There was no way I would have survived if I'd sent her on her own, not even if I sent every male member of my pack as protection. I needed to be by her side. I had to be.

The speed boat was tied up at a small dock. By the time we'd got to it, the two men already had our bags stowed in a storage compartment at the front of the boat. Donatello thanked them, and unless my eyes deceived me, he tipped them *both* five hundred dollars.

The boat ride was nice, in that, between the roar of the high-powered engine, the hiss of the wind, and the sound of the fiberglass hull crashing through the water, it drowned out my thoughts and worries. For a short time, I enjoyed the ride. It took nearly an hour to get there, and by the time we arrived, the sun had crested the horizon, shining off the ocean and turning it into a blue-green mirror.

The island itself was exactly as I'd pictured it. If I didn't know better, I would have assumed that it *was* a resort. A few small buildings were scattered throughout, and one massive building spread across the central portion of the island. The main building was only about three stories tall, probably due to the threat of hurricanes. From a distance, I estimated the main building took up nearly twenty acres of land. Whoever had built this place had to have sunk hundreds of millions into it. Poor bastard. But one man's folly was another man's refuge.

Donatello pulled up and docked the boat expertly, then assisted us with getting the bags out and onto the wooden dock. As I slung my backpack over my arms, I looked up and saw a figure sprinting down the beach toward us. Her hair flowed behind her as she ran. I nudged Maddy and pointed toward the figure.

It took less than a second for Maddy to see Abi and run down the dock to meet her friend. They embraced, their laughter floating up toward us as they walked back toward the dock. Abi had only been gone a couple of weeks, but it was obvious Maddy needed her friend. Ever since Abi had been gone, Maddy had been down. Already, I could see how happy she was to have her best friend back. As they stepped up onto the dock, I could see Abi was crying and pressing a hand to Maddy's belly.

"I can't believe I'm gonna be an aunt," Abi exclaimed through the tears.

"Come on, everyone," Donatello said. "You'll be staying in my personal home while you're here. I'll give you a quick tour."

We followed him to a mansion fifty yards from the high tide line. It had very different architecture from the rest of the buildings on the island, and I had a feeling Don had built this after purchasing the defunct resort. Instead of a front yard, the mansion sported a huge infinity pool with a hot tub and seating for sunbathing. I still had a hard time believing anyone could be this rich.

Inside, the house was full of bright, vibrant colors, very different from Donatello's New York house. While that had been full of dark-stained wood trim, red and crimson wallpaper, and dark, lush green carpeting, this was an explosion of pastel colors, bright white paint, and light gray marble floors. Exactly how I'd imagined a billionaire's beach house.

Donatello pointed to the big staircase in the foyer. "Upstairs, I have five guest suites. Abi has one of the rooms. Maddy and Nico will take one room. The lovely Sinthy will have her own as well. Gentlemen, you'll need to work out how to split the last two rooms, or I could get you a spot at the main lodge."

Luis waved him off. "Felipe and I will bunk up. Diego can have his own room."

Diego looked at him. "Do I smell that bad?"

Luis wrinkled his nose. "Well, I didn't want to say anything, but..."

"Dick." Diego laughed.

"Go, get settled, and then we shall meet on the veranda to discuss what's been happening," Donatello said. "I texted my kitchen staff as we were approaching the island. We should have a full spread ready when you come back down."

"Hell, yeah," Felipe muttered, rubbing his stomach. "I'm freaking starving."

I led Maddy upstairs, and into the first bedroom we found. It was fantastic. Bigger than my bedroom at home, and the bathroom was beyond my expectations—a huge walk-in shower, a bathtub that was almost as big as a small swimming pool, two massive closets, and two separate water closets with a toilet and bidet inside.

"I could get lost in this room," Maddy said.

"Yeah, I think this bedroom and bathroom are bigger than your old place. Before you moved in with me."

"Uh, yeah. It definitely is. I think my old kitchen, dining room, and bedroom could all fit in this bathroom alone."

We spent ten minutes unpacking and getting situated in the room before heading back downstairs. Everyone had already made themselves comfortable at a large umbrella-covered table on the veranda that overlooked the pool and the beach beyond. Donatello hadn't lied. There was more than enough food for everyone. Multiple different kinds of brewed coffee, three different fresh juices, a massive platter of sliced tropical fruits, yogurt, granola, freshly baked croissants, and pastries, a platter of bacon and sausage, scrambled and boiled eggs, roasted potatoes, smoked salmon, and a fresh salad with citrus vinaigrette.

I looked at the spread, then with disbelief at Donatello. "You know there are only six of us, right? Not sixty."

Felipe pointed a fork at me, his mouth full of food. "Hey, shut up. I plan on finishing all this."

After everyone had made a plate and gotten drinks, Donatello began the discussion.

"So, our friend Maddy is now known to every bigot in the world. Not ideal," Donatello said.

"At least she's here and not back home," Luis said.

I nodded. "Right. But that means we can't go home until Viola has been taken care of. She'll never be safe until the threat is gone. I mean…" I gestured to the island. "This is amazing, but we can't impose on you forever."

Donatello sipped at an espresso. "True. You deserve to live in your own home free of fear. So, what do we have that we can use against Viola?"

I inclined my head at Sinthy. "We caught one of Viola's special ops groups trying to break through Sinthy's magic wards. They had their own witch, a young man, who absolutely didn't want to be doing her bidding. Sinthy… uh… took care of the two military guys, put a magical tracker on the witch, and sent him packing back to Viola."

Donatello set his cup aside and sat forward eagerly. "So, we have a way of finding one of Viola's people? At any time? Do we think Viola suspects?"

I shook my head. "We don't think so. She called me not long after the incident. Nothing in her voice or demeanor indicated that she knew. We could even hear her abusing the boy over the phone. I think it's safe to say she doesn't know."

"The tracker is still on him. I can sense it," Sinthy added. "Which means the boy is still alive. Even if they did somehow discover it, the only way to remove it would be to kill him." She shuddered. "She's an evil bitch, so I wouldn't put it past her to try and dissect him to figure it out and somehow use it against us, but that's not possible either."

They all continued to talk as I turned my burner phone back on. It was almost six in the morning. I needed to check in back home. I texted both my parents and waited for their response. It didn't take long, and as I read the incoming messages, a lump formed in my stomach. My worry and fear must have shown on my face.

"Nico? What's wrong?" Maddy asked.

My chest constricted as I looked up. "Um, Mom texted. She says there are nearly three thousand anti-shifters surrounding the gates and wards."

Luis's fork clattered to his plate, and Felipe's face went gray.

"Three thousand?" Luis asked in barely above a whisper.

I nodded. "She says as soon as the report came out with Maddy's name and last-known location, they started swarming in."

"Are the wards holding? Is everyone safe?" Diego asked.

"Uh, yeah. Dad says they aren't getting close to them. One guy rushed the barrier early this morning. He ran so hard and fast to get in and got electrocuted so badly they're pretty sure he's *dead*."

Sinthy nodded grimly. "I told you. I will protect my family."

I texted my parents, letting them know to contact me immediately if things escalated so I could have Sinthy teleport us back.

Tossing the phone on the table, I said, "Enough of this shit. What's our plan? I want this woman dead." I was surprised to find that I was totally serious.

"Well, a message would be good. Let her know that we're ready for war," Donatello said.

"Yes," Maddy added. "But do we really want to stoop to her level? I mean, if we start an all-out war, innocent humans and shifters will get hurt."

"She's right," Donatello said. "We lose our moral compass if we become as bloodthirsty as she is."

"So, we need to let her know we're ready to fight her, but we want it on our terms in our own way?" Luis said. "How the hell do we do that? What kind of leverage do we have? Other than the vial, I mean.'

"Viola is good at getting people to do what she wants because she knows how to pull their strings," I said. "She does it because she always makes sure she has something they want or need. We have to find that thing."

Donatello sighed and picked up his cup. "Well, as Luis said, we have the *thing* she wants: the vial. And the person she wants: Maddy. What we need to find is someone else that's close to her. I don't think *things* will be enough. We should find out if she cares for anyone. A lover, perhaps? I've already checked, and her parents are dead—that's how she gained control of The Monroe Group in the first place. Maybe a favorite cousin or sibling? Though we've found no trace that she's anything but an only child."

"She's a horrible person, but there must be someone. Even Ted Bundy had a girlfriend, for Christ's sake," Maddy said.

"We just said we didn't want to stoop to her level," I said. "Are we actually talking about kidnapping someone? Holding a captive is *way* further than I thought we'd go."

Maddy looked me dead in the eye and said, "Things are dire now. Worse than ever. We would never hurt an innocent person, but we need leverage. Somehow, some way."

I couldn't argue with that. Maddy was right. After breakfast, we decided that the next several days would be an all-out push to dig in and find any secrets Viola might have. Donatello and his alliance of friends had spent millions trying to find Viola with no luck, but they'd only been searching for her current location, aliases, or allies. They never delved into the past.

Luis took the lead—as a private detective, he had more experience and contacts than we did. Donatello pivoted his own researchers and detectives to the same path. For days, we combed through everything we could find. It seemed hopeless after a while. We confirmed she was an only child, never married, had no children, and didn't have any close connections to anyone. Both her parents had died, leaving her the company. She didn't even have a close relationship with her other distant relatives that helped run her company.

Near midnight on the fifth day, Abi and Maddy sat at a powerful desktop computer Donatello let us use for research. Luis sat with them as they combed painstakingly through old newspaper articles. It had been going on for hours, and all three of them looked exhausted. I sat at a table, eating a pizza, which Donatello's chefs had made for us.

"Okay, hang on," Luis said tiredly, rubbing his face. "Let's try something else. Maybe we can narrow this down."

He walked them through taking a screen capture of Viola's face and loading it on the computer. He then logged them into a program he used regularly.

"This is facial recognition software. Not quite as powerful as what the government uses, but still pretty damned good. This computer should be powerful enough to run it fairly quickly."

"But haven't other countries tried this?" Abi asked.

Luis nodded. "Yes. But, again, as Don said, they're looking for her now. They haven't been looking in the past."

I put my food down and leaned forward, feeling hopeful for the new line of attack. Luis had Maddy punch in a range of dates from Viola's birth date, which we'd found in public records, to a random date three years prior. Maddy hit the search icon and waited. Every few seconds, a picture or article with her name popped up, but they discarded it as being useless. The articles and photos were all from benefits, galas, and interviews. It took nearly an hour, and when it was done, we had nothing.

"Damn it," Maddy hissed, smacking her hand on the table.

"What's that?" I asked, pointing to a red alert icon beside the search bar on the program.

Luis glanced at the screen. "It's saying it has a partial match. Could be a traffic camera with a picture of someone who looks like her, a blurred photo, or a partial." He shrugged. "You can open it to see if you want, but I doubt it's anything."

Maddy clicked the alert icon. A picture filled the screen, and in unison, Abi and Maddy said, "Oh shit."

Chapter 20 - Maddy

We stared in shock and awe at the picture on the screen. It was obviously Viola. At such a young age, it was no wonder the program only thought it was a partial match, but I'd recognize those bitter and angry eyes anywhere. She couldn't have been more than sixteen. She was standing with a much older man, who had his arm around her. A swaddled baby lay gently in the crook of her arm.

Luis sat forward and gaped at the picture. "Holy hell. What is that from? Click the link."

I did as he asked. The link routed us to a picture from the archives of a small courthouse on the outskirts of Chicago. The tiny article had a dozen other pictures of other couples that had been married by the justice of the peace that month. Viola and the man with her were labeled as the new Mr. and Mrs. Jane and John Smith. Obviously, fake names had been used.

"Hang on," Nico said from behind us. "Use that name and check hospitals in the area. That baby looks like it's less than a month old."

We did and found a birth certificate for a baby boy named Maxwell Donnelly. Based on the dates, he'd be around twenty-one years old now—if he was still alive.

"She's got a fucking son," Luis breathed. "I did not peg her as the maternal type."

"Can you use that name and those fake names to try and find anything in The Monroe Groups servers? Can you even get into them?" Nico asked Luis.

"Uh, well. I can give it a shot. I can hack into anything, in theory. Their stuff has pretty much been abandoned as the executives, and anyone associated has fled prosecution. So, network security is probably at its lowest it ever has been."

Luis worked for an hour, meticulously combing through file after file. Finally, he found a file of legal documents. Viola had gotten pregnant by a man named Claude Donnelly. They'd had what appeared to be a shotgun wedding forced by Viola's parents. The baby was born, but three years later, the two divorced. Looked like the Donnelly guy remarried and had a few other kids.

"This document here shows that when Maxwell Donnelly was eighteen, his father and stepmother died in a car crash. Maxwell took custody of his half-siblings. Hang on... there's a driver's license photo of this kid."

Luis clicked on the tiny thumbnail picture, and it swelled to fill the screen. Nico stiffened beside me.

"Oh my God," Sinthy hissed from behind us. "It's him."

The 'him' was Maxwell Donnelly. The young man who'd tried to break through her wards. The one who had been experimented on and tortured to create a witch the royals could control. The realization dawned on each of us, filling us with equal parts disbelief and disgust.

"Her own child?" Donatello whispered in disbelief. "Her own baby boy and she treated him like a lab rat?"

Nico pointed at the soulless eyes of sixteen-year-old Viola Monroe. "This bitch probably found out about the kid's paternal family background. Once she knew her ex-husband's family were witches in the distant past, she kidnapped them and forced Maxwell and his half-siblings into the experiments. That's got to be what happened."

Viola was a different kind of monster. To do that to the child she carried in her womb showed exactly how hell-bent she was on success. All she cared about was her family's power and the destruction of any and all supernatural creatures. I could imagine her finding out her son's great-great-great-great grandmother was a witch and any love for him vanishing in an instant. That's how insane the woman was.

"Well, shit," I breathed. "There went that plan. The only person she might have had an emotional attachment to is being experimented on like a guinea pig. She can't love him. No one could and still do what she's doing to him. If she doesn't give a damn about her own son, then she doesn't give a damn about anyone. She's a sociopath, clear and simple."

The air in the room seemed to go cold as we all resigned ourselves to defeat. We had nothing to hold over Viola. No loved ones, not nothing. I said as much, but Sinthy paced the room, a contemplative look on her face.

"Hang on," she finally said. "We may still have something we can use."

"What?" Nico asked. "She doesn't care about anyone."

"That's where you're wrong," Sinthy said. She pointed at the computer. "That boy is the culmination of who knows how many failed experiments. If she sent him into the field to break the wards, that means he has to be the best thing she and her scientists have come up with. They may have been working on this for decades. That kid, that..." She shook her head, trying to find the right word. "That *forced* witch is like a billion-dollar weapon. She will value that if nothing more."

I sighed in resignation. "I don't think that's enough to get her to fold. Let's say we kidnap him. Then what? Do you really think she'd give up this crusade and turn herself in to get him back?" I pointed at the computer screen. "She's tortured him for years, ruined his life. Her own child. She's not human."

My hand curled instinctively around my belly. I couldn't feel the new life growing in me yet. Didn't know whether it was a boy or a girl, but I already knew that I loved my child. I would die to protect the child inside me. The thought that Viola could be so cruel and heartless as to take the one thing she should have loved unconditionally and twist it, break it until it was almost unrecognizable, was one of the worst atrocities I could think of.

"I agree with Maddy," Donatello said. "Viola is not sane enough to be reasoned with. Taking the boy would enrage her but not bring her to heel. It may even make matters worse. She could even put out more unhinged videos telling her followers to attack shifters."

"Wait," Nico said. "This is the first breakthrough we've had. I think we need to give this a shot. Viola can't do much more to us. Thousands of zealots have surrounded my pack lands. Most shifters are in hiding, and there's a bounty on Maddy's head. How much worse can it really get?"

Donatello sucked at his teeth for a second before inclining his head toward Nico. "You also have a good point. But I still fear that, as unpredictable as Viola is, there could still be trump cards up her sleeve."

"That's true, but honestly, we're running out of time," Felipe said. "I'm with Nico. We gotta take what we can get, right?"

Diego and Luis share a look before nodding to each other. Luis looked at the group. "Yup. We say go with Nico's plan."

Sinthy grinned. "I think this is a good plan. As Felipe said, time sort of feels like it's getting short somehow. This is our chance."

That was it. Donatello and I had been outvoted. They had a good argument. It all made sense, but something about it made me uneasy. Part of me truly thought that when Viola found out her own son had been taken, she'd simply shrug and go about her day. How did you reason with, or even threaten, a person who was a monster?

"Sinthy, I think you and I should go and get this guy," Nico said. "We use the tracker you put on him, teleport to his location, and take him. We'll leave some kind of message for Viola. If she wants him back, she'll have to call off the manhunt on Maddy and turn herself in."

The group continued with their discussions and plans, even going so far as to decide that if Viola contacts us and decides she doesn't want to end things our way, we'll give her a location to have some final all-out war if she is so dead set on it. Everything they talked about made sense, but part of me thought it all seemed too easy. I shot a glance across the room at Donatello, and he gave me a pained look. He had the same misgivings I did about the miracle plan the others had formulated. What I was really worried about was that Nico and the others were grasping at straws to end this as quickly as possible without truly thinking things through.

It was well past midnight when we all shuffled off to our rooms to crash. My sleep was dreamless, and when I awoke the next morning, I was rested but not at ease. Nico and Sinthy were set to leave that morning. At breakfast, I barely had any appetite. Nico must have noticed how stressed I was because he put an arm around me and pressed his forehead to mine.

"It's gonna be all right. I promise." He kissed me, then added, "We won't be gone long. Plus, I'll have the burner phone with me. If anything goes wrong, I can call with an update."

I shoved a pile of scrambled eggs across my plate. "And what if what goes wrong is that you and Sinthy are dead or captured? What about that?"

"Don't think like that. We've been shit on for too long. This is our chance. I have faith. I've got a feeling everything's going to go the way we planned."

My own feelings were the exact opposite, but it would be pointless to try persuading him or Sinthy. They were locked in, and I could see the intensity in their eyes. Nothing I said would stop them from going on the mission. All I could do was pray it went the way Nico thought it would.

Donatello showed Sinthy and Nico a piece of paper. "The exact coordinates for the island so you can be sure you get back right here. No good to get in and then get back out only to teleport ten miles off the coast and drown."

Nico reached out to take the paper, but Donatello yanked it back.

Nico frowned at him. "Can't I just take it?" Nico asked.

Shaking his head, Donatello said, "Unfortunately not, my friend. I know your confidence in the success of this mission is strong. Unfortunately, I must take more precautions. If one or both of you are taken, I cannot let the location of this island fall into Viola's hands. Now, both of you look at the coordinates. Memorize them."

Sinthy and Nico leaned over the table, reading and rereading the coordinates until they could recite the numbers back to each other seamlessly.

Donatello clapped and slid the paper back into his pocket. "Well done. I trust we will see you both very soon."

Nico pulled me close and gave me one last kiss. "I'll be back soon."

"Yeah, but will you be in one piece?"

Nico grinned at me and brushed a strand of hair away from my cheek. "Every limb will be intact. I promise."

Sinthy and Nico stepped out on the veranda. I watched as Sinthy took Nico's hand. A shiver of fear and worry shot through me. What if they didn't come back? What if it was a trap, or if things didn't go the way they thought they would? Those thoughts vanished as Sinthy gave a little salute, and in a flash, they both disappeared.

Chapter 21 - Nico

Like every time Sinthy teleported me, I arrived at the new location and felt a sudden and powerful feeling of dissociation. It stemmed from being in one place one moment and then in another in less than a blink of an eye. No matter how many times I did it, it never got any easier. It was worse this time since I literally had no clue where we were. Sinthy had simply tapped into the magic tracker she'd put on Maxwell and taken us to the signal.

"Where are we?" I asked, keeping my voice low.

We were in a narrow alleyway. From the sounds echoing in toward us, I could guess we were in a fairly large city.

Sinthy glanced around. "I have no idea."

"Oh, that's good. Glad we have that figured out," I hissed.

"Hold your horses, big guy. Let's head out and have a look around."

Sinthy walked toward the mouth of the alley; I followed close behind.

"This tracker thing isn't like a GPS," Sinthy said. "It only gets me *near* the target. I could be up to a half mile off."

"Information that might have been essential an hour ago," I growled.

"Yeah, yeah, it'll be fine. Once I'm in the general location, I can sort of follow the feel of it."

As we stepped out of the alley onto a busy street, I immediately knew we were in Europe. The people were less hurried, and the architecture seemed old and full of history.

"Wow. Here we go," Sinthy said, pointing down the street.

I turned in the direction she was pointing. The Eiffel Tower stood large and imposing, its spire pointing toward the heavens.

"Paris? I always wanted to go to Paris," I said with a shrug.

"Well, next time, it can be a leisure trip. Right now, we need to find Maxwell."

I followed Sinthy down the sidewalk as she tried to find the trail of her tracker. The longer I walked, the tenser I became. The citizens were glancing around and fidgety. There were absolutely no other shifters on the street. In fact, I was already getting funny looks. Shifters always had an effect on humans. A slight crackle of energy, not quite as strong as a static charge, but always there and noticeable. When they were all around, most humans either got used to it or ignored it. Eyes slid toward me as we strolled by. Many were not happy, and others were openly hostile as they saw me and realized what I was.

"Any time now would be great, Sinthy. I think the locals are restless."

"Hell, I forgot. I didn't even think of it. Come here." She pulled me into another alley and murmured a few words.

"What are you doing?"

"Covering your shifter and alpha aura. If you were a mere shifter, the humans would probably not even look twice at you. It would be too faint to pick up, but alpha energy is stronger and easier to register. You're good now."

"Are we getting anywhere? Can you tell where Maxwell is?"

"He's close," she said, holding her hand up like she was feeling a breeze. "He's nearby. I can almost taste it."

We walked down the alley to get away from the people who'd already clocked me as a shifter and walked the street until we came to a small office building. Sinthy walked past it once, never even glancing at it. Then at the end of the street, she took my hand and walked back, pretending that we were a happy couple on vacation. As we passed the building again, she cast a sidelong glance at it.

"That's it," she whispered as we stopped to browse at a flower cart.

"The building back there?"

She nodded. "I'm not sure if it's that exact building, but it's on that block for sure. We need to scope it out for a while. Make sure no one's keeping an eye out for intruders like us, and circle the block to narrow it down."

I glanced away from the flowers and into a café. Through the windows, I could see a TV on the wall behind a small wine bar. Maddy's face stared out at me from the screen.

"Shit," I muttered.

Sinthy followed my gaze. She grabbed my hand and pulled me into the café to watch the report. It was in French. I was totally lost, but Sinthy was frowning as she watched the report like she was listening.

"Can you speak French?" I asked.

"Isme taught me French, German, Russian, Third Century Wiccan, Sanskrit, Latin, and Atlantean Hieroglyphics. She always said we'd get around to ancient Egyptian, Mandarin, and Greek, but that didn't happen. I wasn't a great student when it came to languages."

"Well, what does it say? Anything new?"

Sinthy patted my hand. "My French has always been rough, but I think I've got the gist. The American president is asking that Maddy turn herself in for her own protection. That it's the best way to ensure Viola doesn't kill her."

It was complete madness that the leader of the free world was on the news, asking my mate to turn herself in. Pretty much everything that had happened since the night I found Maddy covered in blood in her bar had been bonkers, so I wasn't sure why this was so surprising.

My phone rang, and I tugged it out. Maddy was calling.

"I already saw," I said as I answered.

"The news?" Maddy asked. "You saw what the president said?"

"I did."

Maddy let out a humorless laugh. "Never in a million years did I think the president would be saying my name over and over on the news. I can't turn myself in."

"Absolutely not. If you're in the government's hands, our options are limited. Who knows what kind of spies or followers Viola might have deep in the government? All it'll take is for one US Marshal or secret service agent to turn, and then Viola will have you in her clutches. Nope. I trust Donatello's island more than I trust Gitmo or some NSA safe house. Stay there. We'll figure this out without the government."

"Where are you guys?" Maddy asked, sounding a little calmer.

"The City of Love. Wish you were here."

"Ugh, asshole. I've never been to Paris."

"Well, like Sinthy said, once this is all over, I'll bring you here. Maybe for our anniversary."

"I'll let you get back to it. Have you found Maxwell yet?"

"We're close. Sinthy is pretty positive she's found the building where he's being held. We're gonna watch it for a while and make sure it's safe before going in."

"All right. Be careful. I love you."

"Love you too," I said and tucked the phone back in my pocket.

Sinthy and I locked our arms together again, still acting the happy couple, as we circled the block. A small townhouse sat behind the office building. When Sinthy saw it, she almost skidded to a halt.

"Never mind. I was wrong. It's not an office building. That's it. That is most definitely it."

"Positive?"

She nodded. "I can almost taste the spell I put on him. He's in there."

"That's what you said about the office, though. We have to be totally sure."

"Yes, that was because the magic was so strong it was radiating through that building. There's more than my spell here. This place is crawling with magic."

The townhouse was the most inconspicuous place I could imagine. Nothing about it screamed importance. I'd honestly been anticipating a maximum-security prison with razor wire and barking dogs. This was almost too easy.

Sinthy raised her hand toward the building for a few seconds before lowering it and clicking her tongue. "Four people inside. One is definitely Maxwell. I can see what they've done now. They surrounded it in a half-assed attempt at an illusion spell. See?" She pointed to an upper corner of a roof.

It took a moment, but eventually, I saw it. The corner shimmered in and out, flickering like a bad lightbulb. Had she not pointed it out, I never would have seen it.

"What illusion are they trying to put up?" I asked.

"Sound barrier, and a very crappy avoidance charm to get people to walk past the place without giving it a second look. It's a good plan in theory, but whoever did it had no clue what they were doing. It'll work on humans, but any magical creature like us would spot it in a second. Like we just did."

We walked over and leaned against the wall of the bakery. We tried to attract as little attention as possible as we talked.

"I don't sense any other magical beings inside there. Do you want to hear?" she asked.

"Hear? Inside there? How?"

The witch held a hand up to the house, muttered a few words, then touched my ear with her other hand. Suddenly, I *could* hear some mumbled conversations going on within. I was never going to get used to this kind of magic. None of the voices were female, so Viola wasn't there. I didn't know if things would get much better. It might be our best shot.

"Are we ready to go in?" I asked.

"Yeah. As we walk up, I'll remove the charms hiding the house and whatever they have protecting the entrances and exits. I'm sure they've tried something, but if the sound barrier and avoidance charms are any example, any other spells won't be worth a damn."

I looked into her eyes, then gave a terse nod. "Let's do this."

Without another word, Sinthy and I pushed away from the bakery wall and walked straight to the house. As we stepped off the street and up to the curb directly in front of the stoop, Sinthy waved her hand across the house, and I could feel the spells collapse and vanish. The men inside must have felt it, too, because I heard shouts and screams.

Knowing our element of surprise would only last a few seconds, I sprinted up the steps and slammed my shoulder into the door, tearing it off its hinges with my shifter strength. I fell and rolled on the floor, jumping up in a fighting stance. That's when I saw that I'd overestimated the fear and surprise the men would feel. Two guys trained their machine guns on me.

Time seemed to slow down. I stared down the black barrels of the weapons. I'd made a terrible mistake. Their fingers twitched on the triggers, and explosions like the end of the world barked out of the guns. I could actually see the flash of the guns as they fired. My eyes focused on the bullets as they burst out of the barrels. It happened in less than a quarter of a second. Death surged toward me, and I could do nothing but watch. The automatic guns hurled over a dozen bullets toward my chest, belly, and head.

I had time to scream in my mind that I was sorry. Sorry to Maddy for being in this place and not returning to her as I'd promised. Sorry to my unborn child that they would never know me. Sorry to my family and friends who counted on me so much.

The first bullet slammed into my forehead, ripping my life away… or it should have, had it not frozen in mid-air. Every bullet shuddered to a stop less than an inch from my body. Sinthy stepped forward, hands raised, magic pulsing off her. With a flick of her wrist, the bullets vanished into a spray of metallic dust.

"Glad you brought me along?" Sinthy muttered.

The gunman gaped in abject shock, unable to fathom what had happened. There was no time for me to contemplate my mortality or how close I'd come to becoming a red splatter on the walls. I jumped forward, shifting into wolf form. My rage at what the men had tried to take away from me exploded into a fury I'd never experienced.

The first man tried to fire his gun at me again, but Sinthy's magic must have extended further than the bullets. His gun did nothing. I crashed into him, tackling him to the floor in a pile of limbs and screaming that cut off as I ripped out his throat. The coppery mineral taste of blood filled my mouth.

Leaving that royal soldier to bleed out, I turned on the second man. The red gore that dripped from my muzzle sent him into a frenzy of horror. He stumbled backward, dropping his gun and yanking a long hunting knife from the sheath on his belt. I attacked him with abandon, snapping my jaws at him as he swiped his knife back and forth, cutting the air with a hiss. His eyes were wide with panic. I waited until he slashed at my back with the knife to dodge aside and grab his ankle with my bloody teeth. My fangs sank into the soft flesh of his Achilles tendon, and it snapped beneath my jaws. The knife fell from his hand with a clatter as he tumbled backward in agony. He tried to clutch at his ruined leg, but as he fell, his temple caught the edge of a table. He survived but was knocked unconscious.

"He's running," Sinthy muttered as she raised her hands toward the roof.

My ears popped as some sort of spell fell around the house. I spun and looked at Sinthy with questioning wolf eyes.

"Maxwell. He's trying to run. I put a forcefield around the house to hold him," she said.

The thud of feet came from the basement. Either Maxwell, the third guard, or both. Not wanting to give them a chance to get the jump on me, I ran straight toward the basement door, my paws digging into the carpet as I ran.

The door flung open, and the first person out was Maxwell. His eyes were as big as platters. I'd never seen someone look so scared. Rushing up the stairs behind him was the last royal. I leaped over Maxwell, slamming my paws into the other man's chest. A look of comedic surprise flashed over his face as his shotgun fell from his hands, and he went flying back down the stairs. He tumbled down the entire flight and collapsed in a heap on the floor. I had no clue if he was still alive or not—I didn't care.

"Why are you here?" Maxwell shouted. He'd caught sight of Sinthy.

I shifted back and walked toward him. "We're taking you. That's why."

Maxwell shook his head vehemently. "Why, though? I'm not important."

"Pretty sure even if she tortures you, Viola still feels something for her son," I said.

Maxwell paled, leaving his skin gray and sickly. "You know?"

I grabbed his arm. "We do. We're going to use you as a hostage. Force your mother to give up and turn herself in."

"This won't change anything. I'm not sure what you thought was going to happen here, but she won't care if you take me."

Sinthy lowered her arms. "So, your own mother doesn't care about you at all?"

Maxwell's shoulders slumped, then he shrugged. "She cares. But… it's in her own way." He looked very sad when he added, "Not enough to abandon her plans."

"Well, we'll see about that," I said.

The man who'd been knocked out slowly started to groan and whimper in pain. I walked over and knelt, smacking him to bring him to full wakefulness. He hissed in pain and clutched at his mangled ankle.

"Wakey-wakey, eggs-and-bakey," I grumbled. "You're going to give Viola a message. Any form of retaliation, and the kid dies. Tell her the only way she gets her kid back alive is if she turns herself in. Got it?"

The man looked at me, sweat beaded up on his face from the pain. Even through his agony, he gave me a wicked and vicious smile. "Tell her yourself, you fucking animal." Beside him, a phone had tumbled to the floor. The screen was face up, open on a recent text to an unknown number:

Wolves are here. Send backup.

"Fuck," I hissed.

"Nico?" Sinthy shouted, her eyes going wide.

Screeching tires screamed from outside. I lifted my hand to Sinthy, and she ran over, grabbing Maxwell and me. Her fingers dug into our wrists with vice-like power. Racing footsteps sounded on the porch, and an instant later, Viola, looking more harried than I'd ever seen before, rushed into the house. Her eyes were wild with fear, anger, and malice.

When she saw Maxwell in Sinthy's grasp, her face went ashen. I sneered at her.

"You'll pay, Nico Lorenzo," Viola hissed through gritted teeth. "You'll fucking pay. I swear to God you will. No one steals my property."

That last sentence bothered me more than almost anything she'd ever said. She'd called her son her *property*. Maybe she couldn't be reasoned with if that was how she viewed him.

Six men with guns burst through the doorway, gun barrels raised and trained on us. Viola's mouth twisted in a snarl, and she shouted at the men.

"Shoot them. Don't let them take him!" She looked like a monster as she screamed.

For the second time in less than ten minutes, I watched a gun barrel aim at my head and fire, but the bullets could only crash into the drywall behind where we'd stood because Sinthy had teleported us away before they could make contact.

Chapter 22 - Maddy

A scream burst from my throat and died in an instant when Nico, Sinthy, and the young man from the forest appeared before us. He looked almost as terrified as I felt. There was a faint *pop* as they flashed into existence in front of my eyes. Everyone else seemed equally surprised. I'd assumed it would be at least another hour before they returned—if they returned at all.

The young man, Maxwell, slowly lowered himself to his knees. He had a wretched look of sadness on his face. Sinthy stood over him and waved her hands across his hands. I blinked in surprise as I watched her. Out of thin air, a coil of smoke manifested, curling and spinning before descending down to Maxwell's hands. The smoke encircled his wrists, and then a flash of light made me wince and look away. When I glanced back, the circles of smoke had turned into thick and heavy bracelets. They had the shine and color of gold, and polished silver twisted together.

"What are those for?" I asked.

Sinthy pushed her hair back out of her face. "They'll prevent him from using any of his stolen magic. It works as a block. He won't be able to get them off." She looked at Maxwell with a sideways glance. "I'll be surprised if he even tries."

Maxwell held his manacled hands up to Sinthy pleadingly. "I never wanted this damned magic. Can't you take it? Rip it out of me. All I ever wanted was to keep my siblings safe. It was all to get them away from my mother. I went along with her experiments, hoping I could steal them away and hide all of us where she could never get to us. Please," he begged. "Please get it out of me. Take it."

Sinthy's face softened, and she knelt down close to him. "Maxwell, I can't take it from you."

The look on his face was one of complete despair. He let his hands flop to his thighs. "Why? I want you to. Take all of it." His voice was so full of weary sadness, I felt a twinge of empathy for him.

Sinthy put a hand on his knee. "The ones who did this to you must have never explained how magic works. Natural or stolen, magic is a life force. Your ancestry is a magical bloodline. That's the only way you'd be compatible enough to harness magic, to begin with. It's inside you now, bound to your very soul. There is no removing it. Without magic, you'll die."

I didn't think it was possible, but after hearing that, Maxwell's face looked even more miserable. I looked across the room at Nico and Donatello. They were as mesmerized by the discussion taking place as I was. The fact that all this had been going on for years, that her own son was suffering so terribly, made me loathe Viola even more. She was a goddamned monster. All she did was rail on and on about how shifters were disgusting abominations that shouldn't exist... Well, the woman needed to take a look in the fucking mirror. Maybe she was projecting her own black soul onto shifters.

Maxwell paled as he drew his knees up and wrapped his arms around them, hugging himself. Sinthy let out a sigh and stood, joining me by the door. She wrapped her arms around me and laid her head on my shoulder. I put my arms around her shoulders, again feeling like I was a surrogate mother to her. It had to be hard for her, knowing that the man sitting on the floor had her own birth mother's magic coursing through his body. She couldn't even be angry at him for it since it had been forced on him without his consent or desire.

As he sat there, clutching his legs, his gaze darted around the room, bouncing from Nico and Donatello to Abi and Diego, then over to Luis and Felipe. So many people, and all of them, complicit in his kidnapping. He had to be assuming the worst. What else could he think after the life he'd lived? Had anyone ever cared for him? Probably his siblings, perhaps his father before he died.

"We aren't going to hurt you," I said.

Maxwell turned his head toward me, his eyes fixed on mine. I gently pulled away from Sinthy and stepped closer to the man. He *was* a man. Though I knew he was twenty-one, he had the qualities of a child who'd been abused and made to think he was worthless his entire life. Of all the travesties Viola had perpetrated, what she had inflicted on this young man might be the most depraved. He looked at me like a scared puppy waiting to be kicked.

"I promise, no one will hurt you here. You're here because we need some leverage over your mother. We need to show her that she isn't the only one who can go to extremes. We're trying to get her to end this—all of it."

Maxwell looked at me like I'd just told him two and two made five. He chuckled humorlessly and shook his head. "She'll never quit. Never. You don't know her as I do. If it meant she could get you or the vial, she'd skin me alive and make a coat out of my hide. She'd even laugh while she did it." He shook his head again. "No. You won't stop her. If anything, taking me will only piss her off more, and she was really pissed, to begin with. She hates you and despises you. Viola is used to getting what she wants at the snap of a finger. The fact that you guys have drawn this out for a year has her frothing at the mouth. She's doing anything and everything. She's burned bridges left and right."

Nico stepped forward. "Can you tell us why you didn't tell your mother about the tracker Sinthy placed on you?"

Maxwell's eyes darted to Nico, and he swallowed hard. "I guess... I hoped you guys would use it to find her. To... end this mess. I never thought you'd kidnap me. I'm worthless. I don't matter. You'd have been better off leaving me for dead."

"You aren't worthless," I said soothingly.

My heart shattered. This young man had been so broken and twisted by Viola that he truly didn't think he was worth a damn. She'd made him believe he was nothing but a tool. A reviled and disgusting tool, no less.

He was stronger than I was. If Viola had been my mother, I'd have killed myself long ago.

Maxwell ignored my words; he was still looking at Nico imploringly. "What about my siblings? They aren't Viola's children. They were born to my dad's second wife. She has no attachment to them. She'll hurt them. She might think I planned this with you all and kill them for retribution."

"Where are they, Maxwell?" I asked. "If you know where they're being held, we can try to get them out. You saw what Sinthy is capable of."

He looked at me, and before he even spoke, a cold, heavy lump formed in my stomach. Tears shone in his eyes as he shook his head. "I don't know. She's never told me."

"Damn it," Nico hissed. "That bitch might actually do it. We've got to hope she doesn't hurt them until she can prove Maxwell did or didn't have something to do with us taking him."

"What do we do with our young friend for now?" Donatello asked.

Nico's eyes darted up and locked on mine. He was thinking the same thing I was. We didn't want to imprison him, but what other choice did we have?

"Sinthy?" I asked. "There's not, like, a reverse tracker on him, is there? Viola didn't manage to do to him what you did?"

She shook her head. "No, I already checked him. He's clean. She won't find us through him."

I looked at Donatello. "I think we should put him in one of your free rooms. House arrest, you know? At least for now, just for a little while," I added, turning back to Maxwell.

He nodded as he wiped tears from his eyes. "I understand. It's probably smart. I'd do the same thing in your position."

I gave him a weak smile. "Diego? Luis? Can you find him a spot?"

The two men stepped forward. Donatello got out of his chair and joined them.

"I have a suite outside by the pool that should work for him," Donatello said as he placed a hand on Maxwell's shoulder. "We call it the pool house for obvious reasons. How do you feel about hot tubs, young man?"

Maxwell frowned. "Uh... I don't think I've ever used one."

Donatello chuckled as the group walked out the door. "You're gonna love it. You can wash away your worries."

Nico shrugged. "Now we wait."

"Wait for what, Nico?" I asked.

"We wait for Viola to make contact. Now that we have her son, she'll have to make contact. I'm sure of it."

"Oh my God, Nico," I hissed. "Do you really think that? There's no way this is going to get us the outcome we're looking for. All that's happened is that we've turned into kidnappers. We're locking up a poor kid, for God's sake."

"What do you want, Maddy? We had no other option. This was the best plan we had, and the best chance we were going to get, so we had to take it." Nico looked angrier than he should have. It was probably the stress, but it still irked me.

"Because, Nico, I told you this wouldn't work. Donatello and I both said it. Now we've done this, and it might get that kid's brothers and sisters killed."

Nico looked down at the floor, gritting his teeth. "I made the call. We all voted. It was what we needed to do. What the hell were we supposed to do, Maddy?"

My anger was growing with each passing second, and his refusal to see what a bad idea this was only spurred it on.

"You know what, Nico? I can tell you one thing that would be better. Maybe not having a goddamned prisoner of war locked up by the pool. How about that?"

Nico held a hand up and shook his head. "I get that. It's not moral, but our backs were pushed to the wall. I didn't hear you offering any other suggestions before we left."

"So, this is my fault?" I was nearly shouting now, but I couldn't rein in my voice.

"Yo!" Felipe called out. "Enough, you two. Jesus Christ, don't we have enough to worry about without you two biting each other's heads off? Damn."

I didn't like being told what I could and couldn't say. I whirled on Felipe and jabbed a finger toward him.

"We are having a conversation, Felipe. I don't think we need extra input," I growled.

He simply cocked an eyebrow at me. "Tensions are high. I get that. But you guys shouting back and forth can't be good for the baby, right?"

My jaws locked shut. I hadn't thought of that, but my anger wasn't going to go away that easily. No one seemed to be listening to me, and I needed some alone time.

"I'm going for a run. Call me if anything changes," I said and stomped toward the door.

"Maddy— " Nico called out, but I slammed the door behind me, cutting off whatever he had been about to say next.

The island was a tropical paradise—the entire perimeter was beachfront except for the back of the island, which had a cliff face that dropped down to the sea from forty feet up. Thankfully, there was a large grove of pine and palm trees near the center of the island. I shifted and sprinted toward that. My wolf took over, and I was able to take a step back and really look at things. I was scared, frustrated, and hormonal as all hell. That discussion should have never infuriated me so much. It pissed me off, and I was angry that it had made me look like the stereotypical, overexcited female.

All these months, and we were still dealing with this. As I raced through the trees, my paws digging into the sandy soil, I wondered when it would end. We had to be nearing the end. I didn't think I could survive much more of this. My baby deserved all my attention, and I couldn't even do that. Everything seemed to revolve around Viola and what she was going to do next.

My paws ascended the rocky hill at the back of the island. I padded to the edge of the cliff and sat on my haunches, breath panting in and out past my lolling tongue as I stared out at the turquoise water. What kind of world was I bringing my baby into? How could I make sure they would always be safe?

There was a moment, the barest flicker of thought, where I wondered if I could end all this. What if I let my wolf run free and wild—a raging werewolf beast running on bloodlust and rage, tearing Viola apart—all with a simple sip from the vial?

Shaking that thought from my head, I shifted back to my human form and sat, legs hanging off the edge of the cliff, enjoying the view. That wasn't a road I needed to worry about going down—not yet, anyway.

I wasn't sure how long I'd sat there, but it must have been a while. I caught Nico's scent as he hiked up the hill to meet me. My mouth stayed shut as he walked up and took a seat right next to me. We sat in silence, staring out at the vastness of the sea.

Finally, Nico said, "I came to apologize. I was a dick. I'm sorry."

"Mmhmm," I grunted.

"Is… uh, is that female for 'you're forgiven'?"

"What do you think?"

Nico's breath heaved out of him. "I really am sorry, Maddy. I know things are really messed up right now. I'm so worried about everything and everyone, but that doesn't give me the right to snap at you. All I want in life is for you and the baby to be safe. I want to end this so we can move on with our lives and build a family. I love you so much, and I already love the baby more than life itself, and I haven't even met them yet. Does any of that make sense?"

The cold ball of anger that had been coiled in my stomach suddenly unfurled itself and began to dissipate. As much as I wanted to keep giving him the cold shoulder,

I couldn't. I loved him too much to be petty for the sake of being petty.

Reaching over, I pulled him into a hug.

"I'm sorry. I was being an asshole," I whispered.

"Nope. Not an asshole. A pain in the ass? Yeah, but not an actual asshole."

I laughed despite myself and swatted his chest. "Don't be a jerk. You were so sweet a minute ago."

Nico chuckled and rested his hand on my knee as we stared out toward the horizon. Sitting like that, with the man I loved, I only had a few simple wishes—that my baby would be safe, that we would both live to raise them, and for the world to go back to normal. I began to genuinely hope that Nico's plan would work. This had to end soon. We couldn't keep going on like this.

Chapter 23 - Nico

What I would remember later was how fast everything happened. Even looking back on it, I still couldn't comprehend how it all went down so quickly. Part of it was like a dream, the rest like a nightmare.

We'd all gathered back in the building where we were staying. Donatello's staff had brought out some salads and grilled chicken for dinner. We ate as we planned our next move. I couldn't even remember where the conversation had been going. Those memories were lost in the chaos that followed.

My burner phone rang, and after swallowing my food, I answered it.

My father's voice rushed over the speaker before I could say a word. "Nico? Turn on the news right now. Hurry."

"Dad? What's going— "

"No time," he said. "Turn it on now."

The line went dead. Dread filled me. I was going to throw out every TV we had when I got home. All they ever seemed to do was bring bad news.

I looked at Donatello. "Where's the nearest television? My father says we need to watch the news immediately."

Donatello looked perturbed by that news but pulled out his cell phone and pushed a few buttons. A portion of the wall above the fireplace slid aside with an electric hum and revealed a large TV. By tapping the screen of his phone, he turned the television on.

We didn't have to wait long to see what my father wanted us to see. Donatello scanned through channels, and it looked like it was on every network. He finally stopped on a channel that hadn't finished the full report.

"Today, another message from Viola Monroe, who has been branded an international terrorist, war criminal, cult leader, and a murderer by the UN. She's put out a press release. We'll read the letter here."

The anchor raised a paper and began to read. "To the humans and rightful inheritors of this world, I tell you now that our goals remain in sight, but starting today, all attempts to capture Maddison Sutton should cease and desist."

I turned and looked at Maddy in confusion. Her face mirrored my expression.

The anchor stopped reading abruptly and put the paper down as he glanced off camera. His expression was one of bewilderment and panic. A voice off-screen mumbled something to him that I couldn't hear. Finally, he addressed the camera again.

"We now have a live video message. It's just come through. I want to caution viewers that the team at Channel Eight News has not vetted this video. We cannot guarantee what will be shown, and as such, must say that viewer discretion is advised."

An instant later, Viola's face filled the screen. Even seeing her on the screen sent me into a rage. I had to calm my wolf down because all he wanted to do was sling something at the television to destroy the screen and wipe her face away.

"Good day, everyone," Viola said into the camera. "As you may have read in my press release, I am here to tell all of you that the capture of Maddison Sutton has been called off. This monster, this vile and disturbed creature, is not to be captured. I want that explicitly stated in this message. She is abhorrent and disgusting. She has even, in the last four hours, kidnapped my own dearly beloved son. She and her cohorts have stolen him from me in an attempt to get me to end this war against shifters. A war that I know will create a safer, cleaner world for humans. Kidnapping an innocent young man shows me, and hopefully all of you, exactly how ruthless and heartless shifters can be.

"This is what my family and I have been trying to show humanity for centuries. Shifters are not to be trusted.

They are mistakes, evolutionary dead ends, beasts that have no place in a civilized society. All of my so-called crimes have been in the pursuit of the end of their stain on this planet." Viola leaned forward with a pleading look on her face. "Anyone would do what I've done. What are the lives of a few shifters and humans in comparison to the billions of humans that suffer from the very presence of these *things*? The needs of the many outweigh the needs of the few. A wise man once said that, and I believe it is true.

"So, back to my original statement. I am calling off the hunt for Maddy Sutton. She is not to be taken, kidnapped, or otherwise brought in." Viola leaned closer to the camera, the screen filling with her face. Disgust, rage, and madness were evident on every line of her face. "Maddy Sutton is to be brought to me dead." Viola became unhinged as she finished. "I want her blood to soak into the dirt. I want to see her eviscerated body dropped at my feet. I will double the current reward for anyone who brings me her fucking head."

She held up a hand, lifting a single finger. "To show her, her filthy mate, and all others who think they can defy me that I am serious. I present you with the following video."

Her face vanished, replaced by a shot of a familiar location. My pack lands. My own house, in the distance.

"Nico?" Maddy asked, her voice trembling with fear and worry.

"What the fuck, man. What is she gonna do?" Luis asked as he stepped closer to the TV.

I had no words. I couldn't answer their questions. All I could do was stare at the screen. The video seemed to be taken from some kind of drone. Viola's voice spoke over the video.

"Everything these creatures know and love will be destroyed."

"No way," Sinthy said. "The wards are too strong even with me gone. She's bluffing."

Almost as though Viola could hear what Sinthy said, a strange flash and crackle of static appeared on the screen. The flash was so bright that it washed out the video in a blaze of light.

Sinthy gasped and hit her knees. That finally pulled my eyes away from the screen. The witch was on the ground, clutching at her chest. She looked both shocked, confused, and terrified. It sent an icy finger tracing along my spine. I spun back around to check the TV. Part of me was prepared to see a massive smoking crater in the ground with a mushroom cloud ascending into the sky above the charred and dead bodies of my family and friends and what used to be my home. Thankfully, everything still seemed whole.

"Get Maxwell," Sinthy barked. "Now."

Not waiting for a second command, Luis and Felipe sprinted out the door toward the stairs.

"Sinthy, what the fuck is happening?" I asked. I'd intended my voice to sound commanding. Instead, it came out in a whine. Panic and fear mixed into my throat as I spoke.

Sinthy was still holding a hand to her chest. "I'm not sure. Whatever she did attacked my wards directly. I'm no longer powering them, but they're still connected to me. It was like I'd been kicked in the chest. I have no clue what could possibly do that. No weapon of man could hurt those wards. Especially with it pulling energy from your pack lands." She shook her head helplessly. "I don't know, Nico."

On the screen, another strange blast hit the pack lands. Sinthy gasped again and put her hands on the floor, steadying herself even more than she already was. I didn't think it was possible, but she looked even more scared.

A moment later, Felipe and Luis came in, dragging Maxwell between them. The boy looked terrified, and he should have. All sympathy I had for him had vanished. All I could think about was the attack going on back home. Right then, I was more than ready to stoop to Viola's level to protect my home and loved ones. I'd skin the kid alive if it meant saving everyone.

I stepped forward and grabbed him by the shirt collar, yanking him close, his body flopping around like a doll.

"What the fuck is your mother doing?" I screamed into his face as I pointed at the TV.

A perplexed expression replaced the confusion on his face. "What? What are you talking about?"

Sinthy stood and pulled him from my grasp. She pressed her face against his, her nose almost touching his.

"Viola. She's attacking my wards, and it's fucking working. What in God's name is she doing? Was this your plan? Have you cast a spell on me that I didn't notice? What is it? Tell me right goddamned now, or I swear to God, I'll turn your body inside out. Literally."

Maxwell turned from Sinthy and looked at the television, wincing. He *did* know something. It spurred on my fury.

"Talk. Right now, or I'll let her do exactly what she wants to do to you."

"Wait, wait," Maxwell said. "I didn't know she was going to do anything. All I know is that she was using me to try and create magical weapons. Things that could be used against other witches and warlocks. I think she knew you guys had a witch protecting your pack lands. I swear, I didn't know she was anywhere near close to having a working prototype. You have to believe me."

"What the hell is it?" Sinthy asked, shaking him violently again.

He shook his head like he was trying to clear it. "Uh, it's a cruise missile. She got several on the black market, removed the standard explosive payload, and she and her scientists used me to try and create magical warheads. Things that could break through wards, spells, force fields—basically any kind of magical protection."

Sinthy groaned again and clutched her hand to her stomach. She looked at me, and I saw the terror in her eyes.

"She hit it again. Nico... it's bad. These weapons are strong. If it wasn't for how strong your lands are and the initial spells I wove, the wards would have already come down. They could fall at any moment."

On the screen, the drone footage swept across the pack lands. My pack ran around the lands, moving in panic and terror. I could only imagine what those flashing explosions must feel like there. The footage panned over to the gates, showing a new horror. Nearly a thousand human anti-shifter activists were pressing forward, getting closer to the gates than they had in weeks—almost like they knew the spells were about to fall. Even from the height of the drone, I could see rifles and pistols being waved in the air.

"Soon," Viola's voice hissed, "all you love will be ground under my heel. Prepare yourself."

The video ended, leaving a distraught and confused anchor gaping at the camera. My family was in danger. I was the alpha. If they were going to fall, they would fall with me at their side.

"Sinthy, take me back. Teleport me home." I turned to look at Diego and my two friends. "Are you ready to fight?"

Luis gritted his teeth and nodded to me. "I was born ready."

"You aren't going without me," Maddy said.

I shook my head. "No, it'll be too dangerous. You stay here."

"Bull-fucking-shit!" she screamed and shoved her hands into my chest.

I stumbled backward, recoiling at the strength of her alpha aura. It pulsed out of her like heat from a fire. Luis, Diego, Felipe, and even Donatello went to their knees, unable to stop themselves. Even my own wolf, a strong alpha in its own right, wavered and almost succumbed to her strength.

"I'm going. You don't get to ride off into battle without me. Understand?" Maddy looked like a demon from hell as she spoke.

"Me too," Abi said from the corner of the room. She stepped forward and took Maddy's hand.

There was no time to argue. The wards could fall any second. I hissed my anger but grabbed them both, pulling them close.

I looked into Maddy's eyes. "When we get there, you go straight to the house. You got it? You and the baby stay safe. That is the only thing that matters. Promise me."

She nodded. "I promise."

"I'll make sure she stays," Abi added.

I grabbed Sinthy's hand, and the others stepped forward, even, to my surprise, Donatello.

"Don?" I didn't know what else to say.

He shrugged. "I've fought from the shadows long enough. It's time to get my hands... er... paws a little dirty."

"Screw it," I said. I looked at Maxwell. "He comes too."

Sinthy clutched the man's arm in her free hand. A moment later, we were hurtling through time and space, ripping into whatever strange passageway Sinthy opened for us. My anger and fear overrode whatever discomfort usually came from teleporting. We stumbled in the grass as we arrived in the pack lands.

Before we could even register that we were back, I heard a hissing whistle overhead. My eyes snapped toward the sky and locked on the smoke trail behind a massive missile that coursed through the air above us. I actually saw it hit the dome of the wards. The flash made me temporarily blind, and the shockwave knocked us all off our feet. It sounded like the end of the world. Like time itself had been cracked in half.

Sensing my presence, my pack started rushing toward us. My mother, father, and brothers were among the first to get to me. They all looked terrified, but they hugged me briefly. There wasn't time for a drawn-out reunion.

I grabbed my mom's arm. "Take Maddy, Abi, and this guy. Get them to the house. No time for questions. Get them somewhere safe," I said, gesturing to the three of them.

Mom didn't hesitate or ask any questions; she hustled all of them forward and rushed toward the house. Gabriella burst out of the crowd that was rapidly surrounding us and ran up beside me, digging her nails into my shoulder.

"I'm going with them. I'll protect them as long as I can if it comes to that." She stared into my eyes with a fierce intensity. "I will give up my life for Maddy. Believe that and know that she's protected. You fight. Don't worry about her."

Without another word, she was gone, shifting into her wolf form and galloping toward the house. My rage was beyond anything I could describe. It was like lava had replaced my blood.

"Nico?" Sinthy called.

I turned. Her palm was flattened on the ground. "What?"

"I don't think I can rebuild the wards fast enough. Not with the attacks coming so strongly and quickly. I'm not sure I have the energy or power." She gave a sad shake of her head. "The next strike will cause a catastrophic failure of the spells. The… the wards will fall."

My hands bunched into fists, shaking at my sides. I pulled my shoulders back and shouted out above the noise of the crowd. "Lorenzo pack? Are you ready to fight? Will you defend your home?"

The yells that answered me were nearly as loud as the exploding missile. Tiago, Norman, and the other alphas we'd brought shouted back as well. The look in their eyes told me they would fight for us, for the ones who'd offered shelter from the storm that had still managed to find them.

Sinthy stood and gave me a grim nod, pointing at the sky. In the air, another missile rushed toward the forcefield. The bizarre whistling sound filled my ears.

I turned back to the packs. "Meet them at the gate. That's where they'll enter. Go."

Following my orders, hundreds of shifters bolted toward the gates. The nearly inhuman screams of rage and war swiftly turned into howls and yelps of wolves as they rushed the gates. I shifted and ran with them. A small pack of massive black bears was right in the middle of the group—we'd brought them in a few days before we left for Donatello's island.

Donatello himself raced alongside me. His wolf was a gorgeous sleek black, like nothing I'd ever seen before. As he passed, rushing to the gate, the missile made impact. The explosion was louder than the one before. I could actually feel the magic give way, feel the power collapsing. It was an implosion of force that swept over us with a gust of wind. With each step, we drew closer to the gates. That was when the gunshots started.

The zealots were pushing forward, rushing the gates. I watched as one of my own—a man named Davis who had been manning the guard shack—was pulled down under the surge. He never even had time to fire his weapon or shift. Gunshots blasted through the air, and I knew they'd killed him. Killed a member of my pack.

I bared my teeth and ran faster, my paws tearing at the dirt, a constant growl in my throat as I darted past everyone, taking the lead. The crowd ahead of me loomed ever larger as they rushed into the pack lands. They fired on us, but I didn't flinch, I didn't slow, I didn't think. I wanted blood, and I would die for my pack, my mate, and my family.

Ten feet from the front of the group, I leaped toward the man in the lead. He was wearing a faded and torn American flag shirt, with a greasy trucker hat stuffed low on his head. He held a machete in his left hand. We locked eyes as I flew through the air. The fear in his eyes as he realized his life was over sent a burst of sadistic satisfaction through my wolf. I sank my teeth into his throat, and we tumbled into the crowd. The war had begun.

Chaos. It was the only way to describe it. Bodies were everywhere, screams, shouts, howls, and the sound of gunfire all morphed into one long and continuous hum.

I couldn't spare a moment to look around and see how the others were doing. The fight in front of me took precedence. My shifter strength and speed pushed me deeper into the battle. I ripped hunks of flesh from thighs and calves and dragged my claws over faces and across necks. In minutes, I was covered in blood and panting. The fight pushed us back up the hill toward the center of the pack lands. The anti-shifters outnumbered us by several hundred, but we fought harder than they did and held our own. The sheer force of will and strength that came from being shifters more than made up for their numbers.

Above me, a *wop-wop-wop* sound filled the air. Worried some new weapon was descending on us, I risked glancing up. A news chopper hovered overhead, probably hoping to up their ratings by recording the battle. Any anger I felt toward the reporters vanished with a searing bolt of pain down my side. I yelped and spun away as a woman tried to hack me in two with an ax. Before I could attack her in response, the silvery fur of my cousin Francisca flashed by me as she tackled the woman. Francisca's jaws clamped onto the woman's arm. As blood sprayed from Francisca's maw, I turned to rejoin the battle.

The anti-shifters were pushing closer to my house, and I started to fear that they'd get there. I didn't even know what I'd do if any of these people broke in and tried to hurt Maddy.

The group of attackers faltered as a heavy gust of wind blew across their advancing force. Sinthy stood at the top of the road. Her hands held high overhead. The wind was nearly hurricane-strength but only affected the attackers, not the shifters. Her spell gave us the opening we needed. We surged forward, pressing the attackers back.

Between the strength of the shifters and the power of Sinthy's spells, we might have a chance. The fight started to turn as Sinthy sent more magic toward the crowd—fireballs, then electric bolts, and then a shimmering flash of ice shards that miraculously missed all of us but crashed into the attackers. Sinthy was pressing her attack, doing more magic in a few minutes than I'd seen her use the whole time I'd known her. Not only was she attacking the anti-shifters, but she was also casting protection wards around as many shifters as she could see.

An instant later, a bullet pinged away from my face. Sinthy had obviously put a ward around me, and I hadn't even noticed. She'd just saved me from having my brains blown out for the third time in one day. If I survived the rest of this, I'd have to find a way to thank her properly.

The fighting became more chaotic. The humans spread out, and the battle wasn't as easy as a straight face-to-face fight. Instead of waning as I grew tired, my rage only flared brighter as the fight wore on. It also made it more difficult for Sinthy's spells to work as the fighting spread like cancer across the pack lands.

Sebastian and my brother Rafael galloped up beside me, snapping and biting at the attackers around us. Rafael jumped up and tore a shotgun out of one man's hands, taking one of the guy's fingers along for the ride. The pop of a gunshot behind me was almost insignificant— so simple and pointless compared to all the other noise that I barely spared a moment to give it a look. What I saw when I turned nearly stopped my heart.

Sebastian, in wolf form, lay on the grass, blood oozing from a bullet wound near his ribs. His yellow canine eyes rolled in their sockets, then locked on mine, and I knew he was hurt badly. I could smell the fear and pain pheromones pulsing off him, and terror tore through me. My gaze swept up to see the person who'd shot my friend. An older man in a button-down shirt and jeans stood there, his hands shaking as he desperately attempted to reload his revolver.

I didn't hesitate. This man had possibly killed my best friend. It was time for him to meet his maker. I lunged, and the man's terrified screams were a balm on my soul.

I fell upon him and allowed my hate and rage to take over. I pulled back all my humanity and let my wolf have free rein. If anyone had told me I was capable of such savagery a day before, I'd have called them crazy, but when I was done with the man, what remained could barely be called human. It sickened me, but he'd made his choice by coming here, and these were the consequences.

Spinning back, I found Sebastian had shifted back to his human form, the pain keeping him from keeping the connection with his wolf. The bullet wound was right below his left nipple. Dark arterial blood spilled from it, soaking into his clothes.

I shifted and cradled Sebastian's head in my lap. The battle vanished from my mind as I held my dying friend. Glancing up, I saw Tiago had rallied his pack and helped my own press the humans back nearly to the gates. Sinthy was directly in front of me, fingers dug deep into the ground, and I could practically see the energy radiating off her. It was unlike any power she'd shown before. It was actually scary. I had a strange feeling of immeasurable power being summoned, built, and formed out of nothing.

Her body quaked and shook, and I watched the skin on her arms and face go pale as she murmured words under her breath. Her skin took on a corpse-like quality as she seemed to pump every ounce of magical energy she had into whatever spell she was attempting. From the look of her, she was putting more than just magical power into it. I had a flutter of fear that she was going too far. Was she pushing herself over the edge to try and save us?

Moments later, the last humans were shoved back out the gate. Sinthy raised her face to the sky and screamed. Her voice was unimaginably loud, amplified by magic. I flinched as it thundered out of her throat.

"By the names of Morrigan and Dagda, Lugh and Brigid, Ceridwen and Herne, I command the powers of the four corners. Protect this land. We are the wolves of Hecate, and by her power, I close this gate."

Sinthy lifted her hands and slammed the palms together in a clap. The sound that came from her hands was like the voice of God. The pulse of energy swept over me, causing Sebastian and me to slide backward across the grass several feet. All over the pack lands, windows erupted and shattered. The ground reverberated, and through it all, I could still hear Sinthy's words echoing around me.

An instant later, Sinthy collapsed in a heap as an earth-shaking *crack* reverberated across the pack lands. The humans were blasted away from the gate, and the shifters were knocked back into the pack lands as a new forcefield burst into existence all along the fences. This time I could see it—it shimmered like water and rose twenty feet in the air. The humans sprang to their feet and ran from the pack lands, terrified by Sinthy's magic.

I didn't revel in the victory. Sebastian was deathly pale. His eyes were half open, and his labored breathing had an audible wet hiss with each inhalation.

He raised a hand and tried to grab my shoulder but only managed to slap ineffectually at my chest.

"Nico? Nico?" he whispered, his voice a gurgle as if he were underwater.

I squeezed his hand. "I'm here, Sebastian. I'm here. You're okay."

"I don't... I don't want to go." He was trembling violently. "I'm scared... so scared."

"No. No, you aren't going anywhere. You're too stubborn, you son of a bitch. You hear me?" I spoke through a haze of tears.

Members of the pack had drifted over to us, dozens of them slowly circling us.

Sebastian's eyes rolled back in his head until all I could see were the whites. I shook him. "Sebastian?" I shook him again, calling his name over and over. I could hear his breathing slowing. My shifter hearing picked up his thready and uneven heartbeat. He was dying.

Without taking my eyes off him, I screamed, "Sinthy."

Chapter 24 - Maddy

Nico's mother shoved me, Abi, and Maxwell into the living room. My parents latched onto me, hugging me tight, and my dad reached out and grabbed Abi, pulling her into the embrace. Panic flooded through me as Gabriella burst through the door, slamming and locking it behind her.

"The wards are going to fall," she said as she turned and leaned on the door. "Be ready to get into the safe room. All of you. When I tell you to go, you go. Do you understand that?"

Though her words were meant for us all, she stared right into my eyes as she spoke. A few weeks ago, I'd have argued and demanded to help fight. Now? I could sense the life growing inside me and how much I wanted to take care of it. For the first time, I truly understood what Gabriella had lost by giving me up. I also knew that if it meant saving the child inside me, I'd do the same thing. I would do it and live with the heartbreak forever. Gabriella's gaze emitted such strong, motherly love.

I nodded. "We will. You say the word, and we'll lock ourselves in."

Gabriella breathed a sigh of relief and gave me a thin smile before looking out the windows. The TV was on, showing the live report of the situation outside. On screen, we saw another of those missiles barreling toward the protection wards.

The image shown to the world couldn't come close to relaying the earth-shattering explosion echoing from outside. The house shook as the spells Sinthy had so carefully woven cracked and broke. Seconds later, the first gunshots rang out, and my blood went cold.

My father, probably knowing that I needed it, held me even closer as we watched the disaster unfold on the screen. Maxwell sat on the couch, his head buried in his hands.

A horror movie played out on the screen. I was rooted to the spot, unable and unwilling to look away. The camera couldn't get close enough to show distinct details, so they were all like ants moving back and forth across the screen. I watched as shifters fell under gunfire. Each one could have been Nico. I dug my fingers into my father's shirt, tugging and pulling as each second passed.

"They're getting close," Gabriella called out from her position at the window.

Icy tendrils of fear sank deep into my gut. The screams, shouts, and gunfire made it seem like we were in the middle of a warzone, which I guess we were. I'd never experienced anything so terrifying in my life.

"If they get to the cul-de-sac, you run for the safe room and get inside."

My birth mother's voice was strained and tight. I wanted to go to the window and see what she saw, but fear held me in place. Instead, I turned back to the television. The battle was turning a bit. Three figures were hunched near each other. One was on their knees, their hands on the ground. The other two were huddled together, one holding the other. Even at that distance, there was something familiar about all of them. Then I heard it.

Sinthy's voice thundered over us—even from inside the house, it sounded like she was inside our heads. Mom and Abi sank to the floor, covering their ears. Flinching, I buried my face in Dad's chest. I didn't think anything had ever been so loud. But I was wrong. As soon as she uttered her final word, there was a *crack* that could have broken the world. One of the windows in the kitchen exploded inward, and Gabriella had only managed to get out of the way in time. The rumbling and shaking slowly subsided, and silence finally reigned.

I'd barely managed to get my bearings when the scream came from outside again.

"Sinthy!"

It was Nico's voice, terrified and broken. Nothing could stop me from going to him after hearing that. I yanked out of my father's grip and rushed toward the door.

"Maddy, no," Gabriella said. "We don't know if the fight's over."

"Nico might be hurt!" I pushed past her and ripped the door open.

I was halfway down the porch steps when I heard the others rushing out of the house behind me. Nico sat on a grassy mound less than fifty yards from the house. He was holding someone and rocking back and forth. It was bad. Even before I reached him, I knew it was bad. Something about Nico's body language told me that whatever it was, I didn't want to see it.

Pushing through the slowly gathering throng of Nico's pack, I found exactly what had him so distraught. I gasped in horror, my hands flying up to cover my mouth. Nico had Sebastian cradled in his lap. Sebastian's head lolled back, and blood pulsed from a gunshot wound in his chest.

"Oh God," Abi whispered beside me.

I hadn't even realized she was beside me. I glanced over and saw she was crying. My own eyes were hot with tears. Abi and I sank down to the ground on either side of Nico.

"Sebastian, please. Come on, buddy. Please, God. Please." The desperation in Nico's voice tore my heart in two.

I reached forward, pressing my hands to the wound. Abi reached over and added her hands. In seconds, our fingers were slick with blood. Luis and Felipe came limping out of the crowd. I glanced up to see the grin of victory on Luis's face shatter and his steps falter.

Felipe took it even worse. He hit his knees and began openly crying, then, his voice ragged and begging, shouted, "Help! We need help."

"Shift, Sebastian," Nico hissed in his ear. "Shift, and you can heal faster. Can you hear me? You need to shift."

If Sebastian heard, he wasn't able to do what Nico asked. His chest rose and fell beneath my hands, but it was getting slower and shallower every second. He was slipping away. I could see it in the deathly pallor of his face. Sebastian was dying. The realization made me want to throw up.

I turned and shouted into the crowd. "Where's Sinthy? Where is she?"

The pack who had surrounded us were all whimpering, human and wolf sounds of sadness and despair. Nico's voice was beginning to crack as he screamed at his friend to fight an unwinnable battle. Then, like a ghost, Sinthy pushed her way through the pack. My breath whooshed out of me when I saw her.

She looked closer to death than Sebastian did. Her face was so pale that I could see all the veins beneath her skin. The whites of her eyes had turned red from the burst blood vessels inside them, making her look like some kind of fallen angel or demon. Sinthy stumbled forward and fell to the ground at Sebastian's feet, looking for all the world like she was about to lie on Sebastian's lap and die with him.

She turned her inhuman-looking red-ringed eyes on me, and through her exhaustion, she raised a shaking hand to someone behind me. I spun and saw Maxwell right behind me, standing beside Gabriella. He looked terrified.

"I… need… him," Sinthy croaked, sounding for all the world like she was a hundred years old.

Her eyes were focused and determined, but her body wavered and shook. Whatever final spell she'd done had almost killed her. I could see that, and again, I wondered what kind of strength this girl had within her. The drive and determination were beyond what I could imagine.

Sinthy waved a hand and groaned with pain as the magical bangles she'd placed on Maxwell's arms clicked apart and fell to the ground at his feet.

"I need your… magic… I have… barely anything left," Sinthy said, speaking directly to Maxwell.

Sebastian's breathing became markedly more labored, and his heart was doing odd things below my hands. He was fading fast. We had to hurry. If there was anything the two witches could do, they needed to do it soon.

Maxwell took several hesitant steps forward before kneeling beside Sinthy. He looked at his hands and shook his head. "I can't control it. I don't know how to heal anyone."

Sinthy reached a weak and shaking hand out and put it into his. "You have my family's magic running in your veins. It will flow through me, and I will guide it. I need you. This only works if you allow me to access the magic deep inside you." She nodded toward Sebastian. "His life is vanishing. He'll be gone in thirty seconds if we don't do something now."

Nico had lost all control. He was openly weeping over his friend, his tears pattering down on Sebastian's chest and face. Luis and Felipe had crawled forward, and each of them had a hand on Sebastian as though they could somehow summon magic to save him themselves.

Maxwell nodded eagerly. "I want to help. There's been enough death. Do what you need to."

Sinthy gave him a thin, tired smile and wrapped her fingers tightly around his hand. Maxwell gasped, and his eyes rolled back in his head. Sinthy leaned forward and placed her free hand on Sebastian's forehead. There was a surge of power as Maxwell's magical energy flowed through Sinthy. Static crackled in the air, and the shifters all took several steps back, expanding the circle around us.

Sebastian's eyes fluttered open, and he groaned, but blood was still seeping from his wound. Sinthy slid her hand down, pushing mine and Abi's hands away from the wound. Her fingers became slick with blood, and she pressed her hand hard on his chest. Her teeth clenched, and the hand that held Maxwell's shook with the effort. For his part, Maxwell looked nearly comatose. All I could see were the whites of his eyes as his energy fed Sinthy—his body tense as she used his power.

He must have still been aware, though, as Sinthy spoke to him in a low, whispered voice. "Concentrate. Think of healing. Focus all your thoughts on life."

"I... don't... know how. I'm scared," Maxwell murmured through his strange trance.

"If you fear your magic, you'll never command it," Sinthy hissed with renewed strength. "You can't be scared. This man is scared. He is dying, Maxwell. Your fears don't matters. Help me save him."

Sebastian's eyes fluttered closed. Sinthy looked pained as she watched him sag back onto Nico's legs.

"It's not enough," Sinthy said as tears started to trickle down her cheeks. "He's too far gone. I'm too weak, and Maxwell's power isn't flowing fast enough. I don't know what else to do."

Like a lightning bolt, Nico's hand shot out and clamped onto Sinthy's arm.

"These are my lands. I'm connected to them. Use me. Pull from me. From all of us."

Sebastian shuddered one final time, then his final breath hissed out of his lips, and he went still.

Ignoring that his friend had died, Nico shouted to everyone. "Lean in. Open your minds to Sinthy. Give her everything."

Sinthy shook her head sadly. "Nico, it's over— "

"Not yet," he screamed. "Everyone, come on. Hurry." He looked into Sinthy's eyes pleadingly. "Try. Please. One last time. Try."

Nodding. Sinthy pressed Maxwell's hand to Sebastian's chest and placed hers on top. All around us, the pack leaned in, placing their hands on each other. Those closest lay their hands on Sinthy and Maxwell. Nico never let go of Sinthy. I sat beside Nico and wrapped my arms around him, willing every ounce of energy I had into helping Sinthy to save Sebastian.

With everyone connected and concentrating, images flashed through my mind: ancient shifters hunting and running through these lands, an old crone witch drawing symbols in the dirt. In my mind's eye, she looked up and locked her gaze on mine, then nodded with a smile.

Sebastian's body jolted, almost like he'd been shocked by a defibrillator, and a surge of power coursed through all of us. There were murmurs of surprise and shock through the pack as everyone else felt it. Sebastian jerked again, his back arching so hard that he almost bent in half. Sinthy's eyes opened with surprise, and a faint smile crossed her lips. An odd glow emanated from Sinthy and Maxwell's hands. It was so bright that I had to avert my eyes.

The energy kept building and building until finally, Sinthy and Maxwell fell backward away from Sebastian's body, both looking depleted. Sinthy, still looking like death warmed over, lifted a bloody fist and smiled at me. She opened her hand, and a twisted and warped bullet fell from her palm onto the ground.

Beside me, Sebastian, in a burst of movement, opened his eyes wide and sucked in the deepest, most intense breath of air I'd ever seen anyone take. He took in two more massive lungsful of air before coughing and falling back onto Nico's lap.

"Holy fuck, that hurt," Sebastian groaned.

There was a single second of shocked silence, then the entire pack screamed and roared with a combination of relief, delight, excitement, and happiness. Nico yanked Sebastian into a heavy bear hug, and Sebastian seemed very confused by the tears on his alpha's cheeks.

"You cried for me?" Sebastian asked when Nico let go of him. "You really do care. What a softy."

Nico feverishly wiped the tears and snot from his face. "Shut up, asshole. If you do that again, I'll bring you back a second time and then kill you myself."

Before Sebastian could give Nico a retort, Abi nearly tackled him. My friend wrapped him in her arms and hugged him tight, sobbing uncontrollably. Nico detangled himself from Sebastian and pulled me to my feet. Abi curled almost completely into Sebastian's lap and pulled him even tighter. To me, it looked like his near-death had wiped away all the stupid shit they'd been going through. What was left was how they really felt about each other.

At first, shocked and surprised, Sebastian finally smiled and wrapped his arms around Abi. The entire pack was celebrating, and in the distance, I could hear sirens approaching as the police and ambulances began to arrive.

Even through the shouts of excitement and relief, I could hear Sebastian talking to Abi as he stroked her hair gently.

"You know, if I'd realized dying was all it took to get the girl, I'd have done this months ago."

Abi let out a sobbing laugh and slapped him on the back, then wrapped him in her arms again. Sebastian looked down at her, and for a man who'd been dead only a few minutes before, I'd never seen anyone so happy in my life.

Chapter 25 - Nico

Helping us push back the anti-shifters, protecting as many of us as she could, and whatever she did to lift the protection spell around the pack lands had drained Sinthy completely. She'd been on the verge of death when she still managed to find a way to save Sebastian's life, and she collapsed into Maxwell's arms not long after Sebastian had come back to us.

My friend was beaten and unable to stand and walk on his own. Diego and Mateo had picked him up to carry him to my house—Luis and Felipe were too emotionally exhausted to help. They were still crying tears of joy as they followed my brothers and Sebastian up the hill to my house.

I knelt and scooped Sinthy up. She was almost totally insubstantial, like a dried-out husk that still had the shape but no longer the mass of what it had been. Her head lolled on my shoulder, and I couldn't believe how pale she was. Her skin was almost translucent, and her eyes looked like she'd accidentally used red food coloring instead of eye drops. The blood-red sclera made her look much more intimidating than usual.

"Did he make it?" she murmured as I carried her.

I nodded, a lump forming in my throat. "He did. He's alive. I think he's gonna be fine." I pulled her close, hugging her like she was my daughter. "Thank you, Sinthy. Thank you so much. I can't even begin to tell you how much it means to me. To all of us. Everything you did."

She gave a tired sigh and closed her eyes again. "That's what you do for family."

The lump in my throat grew harder. More tears leaked from my eyes. This girl, who was barely old enough to drink, was braver than almost anyone I'd ever met. Never in my life had I been so proud to know someone. Proud to have them be a part of my pack.

Abi helped my brothers get Sebastian settled in the guest room where she'd stayed until a few weeks ago. Maddy and my mom helped me get Sinthy into bed to sleep off everything she'd done. I left so they could undress her and get her into something comfortable.

Out in the living room, my happiness at Sebastian being alive and my heartache for what Sinthy had put herself through evaporated as I saw what was playing on the television. Live footage of the aftermath of the attack. I hadn't even given myself time to check and see how many of our own people had been injured or killed. Instead of worrying about the innocent dead, there was only one thing the reporters were focused on. Sinthy.

I clicked through multiple channels. Every broadcast showed the same thing. Clips of Sinthy as she fired balls of fire from her hands, erected defensive bubbles around shifters, and the god-like performance she'd put on to rebuild the surrounding barriers. Witches. That was the only word anyone wanted to talk about. It ran across the ticker on the bottom of the screen; history scholars were brought in, and more than one angry voice talked about how dangerous it was that a shifter clan had a witch in their pack.

Gritting my teeth, I clicked on one channel to hear the entire exchange.

"With us in the studio, we have a professor emeritus from Southern Coast College, Doctor Eli Horowitz. Doctor, what does this mean? Witches were thought to have died out after the trials of the sixteen-hundreds," the anchor said.

The professor was a small, chubby man with thinning hair. He smiled at her and shook his head. "The Salem Witch Trials were, as we all know, brought about by hysteria and fear of real witches. In my book, *Where Are They: The Truth About Witches,* I go into more detail about this distinct era in history. It was my theory that the Spanish Inquisition, which took place from the mid-fourteen-hundreds until the early eighteen-hundreds, was the true driving force that pushed witches into hiding. The

Witch Trials and other anti-metaphysical hatred stemmed in part from the terror and fear of heresy that the Inquisition instilled in many people."

The anchor leaned forward. "So, you're saying that they've always been here? Hiding in the shadows?"

The professor chuckled. "Well, that's a bit grim. Sounds like some conspiracy. Like they've been pulling strings and working behind the scenes. No, not exactly. I think that with them going underground, it became very difficult for them to find like-minded people who shared their distinct power and skill set. As we know, not anyone can become a witch. History tells us that ninety percent of witches are born with the power, and the other ten percent had Wiccan ancestry and could tap into the latent power with study and practice. Any witches alive today are few and far between and probably do their best to hide."

The anchor pointed at him with a pen. "And why would they hide? What is their goal?"

The professor shook his head again, seemingly annoyed with the line of questioning. "What is their goal? To survive, of course. What else? They probably live in abject fear that something like the Inquisition is going to roll around again and truly end them. No one wants to be burned at the stake, drowned, or crushed with rocks. Surely you understand that?"

The anchor appeared to either not understand or not want to understand.

"Well, Doctor…" He pointed at a computer screen. "What we've seen today shows that, perhaps, we did have something to worry about. This witch, who has somehow aligned herself with the Lorenzo pack, has incredible power. It was like nothing I've seen. All this time, we thought that maybe, the Lorenzo wolves had some kind of advanced technology that was protecting them. Now, it seems that it was, in fact, a witch."

Doctor Horowitz leaned on the table and interlaced his fingers, and it was obvious he was glaring at the other man.

"Chuck, I have a very bad feeling that you may be veering away from what should truly be the story. Witches aren't gone. That's miraculous and amazing. Also, these *people*—if one can call them that—attacked innocent shifters who'd done nothing wrong. These terrorists need to be rounded up, arrested, and made to face the full strength of the law."

The anchor was getting worked up. He slammed a hand on the table. "These *shifters* are dangerous. You've seen what Viola Monroe has said about Maddison Sutton. She is a descendant of the werewolf king Edemas. *She* is the one who needs to be arrested and brought in before she can do more damage. The people who attacked that compound are patriots doing what needed to be done." He was red-faced and sweating. There was so much anger in his eyes that the professor leaned away from him. Fear and confusion showed in his eyes.

Horowitz glanced off camera. "Doug? Jamie? What the hell? Is this guy for real?"

There was murmuring from behind the anchor, who spun to address the people talking to him. "No, goddamn it. It needs to be said. Everyone is too damned afraid to talk about it."

I stared in abject shock as two security guards stepped onto the sound stage and grabbed the anchor by his arms, dragging him, screaming, off the set. The professor looked shocked and saddened as the video cut away to a commercial.

Anger boiled inside me like an inferno. It appeared we'd been right when we thought some of Viola's followers were in higher places. A famous reporter was probably the lowest of her devotees. People everywhere who already hated us would start to believe every pack had a witch.

As I tried to calm down, I stomped to the busted-out windows and looked out on the battlefield. My breath caught in my throat at the disaster that reigned over my lands. I'd hoped to limit the bloodshed, and we'd even trained to do our best to hurt but not kill during our simulated training. That had gone out the window when our lives were on the line. At least a dozen dead bodies littered the field and streets of the pack neighborhood. Our own people were collecting the casualties from our side. In the distance, I could hear the wails and screams of grief as family members found their loved ones who had been cut down by psychotic bigots.

The ambulances were sitting outside the gates, tending to the humans who'd retreated. We hadn't allowed any of them in to help us. They couldn't be trusted, plus we had no clue how to let them in with Sinthy down for the count. It had been necessary, but the blood was still on our hands. There was no going back. And I was sure by tonight, some sympathetic TV channel would be showing the faces of the dead humans. There would be stories of all the good things they'd done in their lives. The charities they volunteered for, the houses they built for the poor, and the churches they attended. Yet that didn't change what they'd come here to do.

I was sure there had been Nazis who'd done nice things and gone to church and taken care of people. That didn't change or erase all the terrible things they'd done to an entire race they didn't like. Soulless evil could lurk in the prettiest and most esteemed of costumes.

The time for Viola to be the only voice the world heard was over. We needed to send a message of our own. Chills ran down my spine at the thought. Out in the field, I saw Donatello, smeared with blood and dirt, lift a body into his arms. Even from this distance, I could see the grief in his eyes. If anyone could help me get the word out, it was him. Especially now that he'd seen first-hand what Viola was capable of.

As I headed out to help with the cleanup and to try and board up the windows Sinthy's spell had cracked, I started formulating a plan. Several of my pack rounded up the bodies of the attackers who had fallen and laid them with as much respect as we could muster by the front gate. Whenever Sinthy was back to full strength, we'd have her open a portal in the barrier so we could give the bodies to the authorities.

Thankfully, it seemed my own pack had suffered far fewer casualties than I'd initially thought. Most of the bodies I'd seen strewn about the property had been injured but not dead. Doc had been working overtime extracting bullets from legs, bracing broken bones, and stitching up cuts. While we worked, I thought more about what I was going to do. Even the sorrow of finding my fallen packmates didn't deter me from what I was planning.

Davis, the guard at the shack, had been shot three times in the chest during the initial attack and lay dead by the gate. One of Tiago's pack mates, a young woman named Selena, had also been killed by what looked like a silver knife wound to the stomach. Two more members of my pack had been cut down in the street close to my house. A young man named Joshua and another man close to my age, Tristan had been shot in the back. I'd known him well; he'd dated my cousin Eliza for almost a year, and we'd thought they might become mates. Instead, they'd decided just to stay friends. Seeing their pale dead faces, remembering who they'd been, hurt me deeply. It was like a metal band was wrapped around my heart and squeezed tighter with each second.

As we worked, I kept picturing Sebastian dead in my arms, his last breath hissing out past his lips. Without Sinthy and Maxwell, he would have joined these three in the pack's cemetery. I couldn't abide that. It was time to do what needed to be done, but I had to have the pack's approval. I was alpha, but this was not a dictatorship. I wouldn't do anything the others didn't want.

With the cleanup basically done, I grabbed Gabriel by the arm. "Spread the word. Meeting at the Moon Mate building in two hours. Go."

Gabriel, who had always been so jubilant and had fashioned himself the class clown pretty much since birth, wiped a smear of dirt off his face and shook his head sadly.

"A meeting about what, Nico? Is now really the time?"

I squeezed his arm in reassurance. "It is. I'm done fighting Viola from the shadows. It's time to let the world know what we're fighting against. Go on, tell everyone. I want everyone who isn't injured there."

Resigned, Gabriel nodded before moving off to tell everyone. I found my other siblings and had them give the word as well. By the time I strode toward the Moon Mate building, nearly the entire pack had arrived. Maddy's fingers were twined with mine as we walked. She agreed with my plan—supported it, and I welcomed that because what I had to say was frightening. It might very well end up causing another attack.

Grabbing a chair to stand on, I stepped up on it and turned to address the gathered shifters—both my pack and those from the rescued packs.

I gestured to the area where the hardest fighting had taken place. "The royals have come into our home. They've hurt us and done what we never thought was possible… They've made us feel unsafe in the one place that was truly ours. We've done all that we can in the usual ways, but nothing has stopped them.

"Viola Monroe has used her voice to build a worldwide army that wants us and all of our kind dead. I want to do the same. It's time to send a message to her and the world about exactly what has been happening. I want to tell the world the truth.

"I'm your alpha, but I will not do anything that my pack doesn't sanction. I brought you all here to ask if you agree. Is it time to tell the world what we know? Can we let our voices be the counterweight to what Viola is saying? What do you say?"

It was short and sweet, but it got the point across. To my surprise, the pack didn't take long to think about it. After a few seconds, people called out to me.

"Do it, Nico."

"Tell 'em. Tell 'em everything."

"Yes."

"Yeah."

"I agree."

"Let's do this."

The same sentiment was repeated by everyone. Those who didn't speak, simply gave me silent nods. Everyone was in agreement.

"I'll get to work. Thank you, everyone. I can't tell you how much it meant to me to fight alongside you all. This is our family, this is our home, and this is the place we'll fight for."

A small cheer went up as I stepped down off the chair. Donatello was at my side before I could even take hold of Maddy's hand.

"A message, you say. This sounds intriguing." Donatello smiled. Even smeared with dirt and blood, the man somehow managed to look glamorous.

Wrapping an arm around Maddy's shoulders, I nodded. "Yeah. With Maddy's name out there, there's no use hiding her anymore. I want to tell the world everything. The entire story, not the altered one, the royals have been shoving down our throats for centuries. I think it could help garner more sympathy. I hate to say it, but we have to pit the anti-shifter side against the pro-shifters."

Donatello nodded. "Fight propaganda with propaganda? I like it."

"Well, it's not propaganda if it's true, right?" I asked.

Donatello chuckled and patted my arm. "My dear friend, every side of every conflict thinks they're telling the truth. The only thing we have going for us is that we actually *are* the ones telling the truth. Let me know how I can help."

All through the afternoon and into the early evening, we spent hours going over what we were going to say. We organized it onto notecards I would read on video. I even got Javi to give me details on some of the missions his pack had done under orders of the royals over the years. Finally ready, Felipe set up the camera and lights.

Nerves ate at me as he readied everything. Donatello stood at the back of the room and nodded, giving me a thumbs-up.

"Are you ready?" Felipe asked.

At my nod, he hit the record button.

"My name is Nicolas Lorenzo. I am the alpha of the Lorenzo pack."

I laid it all out for the world. The true story of Edemas, the way he'd been betrayed and finally killed, his two hidden children, and the royals' history. I told them how the royals and Viola's entire family had butchered and killed shifters throughout history to try and find this magical vial of blood. Javi's stories, the facilities where experiments were done, the torture she put Maxwell through, the babies and children she'd had murdered, and the way Maddy had been attacked and left for dead that night in her bar. I painted the true picture of Viola Monroe and pressed home the fact that if anyone was a monster, it wasn't Maddy. It was Viola.

The only thing we held back was Maddy's pregnancy. We'd thought at first it could elicit more sympathy from the world but decided against it at the last minute. The idea of Edemas's heir being pregnant might cause fear about what the baby might be. It was better to keep that information hidden until later.

By the time I was done, the video was over half an hour long, but I'd said everything I wanted to say. I'd even begged the world for help, for protection for shifters and anyone else Viola wanted to exterminate. I didn't lay it on thick, but I did try to make sure anyone watching would know that I was serious and that we were facing serious danger.

"Very eloquent," Donatello said as Felipe stopped recording. "How do you plan to disperse this little home video?"

I shrugged. "We could post it online, but I thought you could help spread it faster."

Donatello rubbed his hands together greedily. "Ah, yes. I think I know a few people who can assist us."

Luis uploaded the video to the regular sharing site, and Donatello gave him some email addresses of fairly high-ranking presidents of news organizations. He sent the video to them along with a short letter from Donatello. It took less than an hour for all hell to break loose.

Before the eleven o'clock news came on, nearly every channel broke into their regular programming with banners reading: Breaking News. Soon my face was on screens, and my voice was echoing across dozens of channels. Within an hour, Donatello and Luis informed us it was being broadcast on the BBC, Euronews, NHK in Japan, Al Jazeera, and News24 in South Africa. The video had gone viral and was being shared hundreds of thousands of times every hour.

"I believe we have done what we set out to do," Donatello said. "I, for one, am going to go to sleep for about thirteen hours. Good night to you all."

The others slowly headed off to bed, and I joined Maddy in ours. We lay there, tired beyond belief but unable to fall asleep. So much had happened in one day. It felt like it had been weeks ago that Sinthy and I kidnapped Maxwell, and all this had gone to shit. How had it only been twelve hours ago?

Sensing my agitation, Maddy rolled over and curled around me. The hug sent a spasm through me, and I wrapped my arms around her, holding her close to me. Her scent filled my nose, enveloping me. As she ran her hands through my hair, a dam within me nearly broke apart. Finally allowing myself to relax, my body shuddered against hers, and all the adrenaline of the day drained out of me.

"You did everything you could, Nico," Maddy whispered.

My eyes stung with tears. "I should have listened to you. Maybe it would have been better if we hadn't gone after Maxwell."

"And if you hadn't, he wouldn't have been here to help Sinthy save Sebastian. Everything happens for a reason. I know you feel guilty about the ones who died or were hurt, but you've done everything right. It's all been for me and your family and your pack. Let it go." She rubbed my back gently. "Let it all go, Nico."

And I did. I sank into her and let it all go. My eyes slipped closed. I didn't even realize I'd fallen asleep until I woke up several hours later. Eyes snapping open, I glanced around the room. Maddy was still breathing deeply beside me. The room was dark, the moon still high outside. What had woken me?

Then the sound came again. A muffled voice from downstairs. It sounded like Sebastian. Frowning, I eased out of bed and tiptoed to the door. Once I was on the landing, I thought I heard the refrigerator door open and close. A glance at my watch told me it was almost three in the morning. Who was getting a snack at this hour?

At the base of the stairs, I saw Sebastian smearing peanut butter on a slice of bread—a jar of jelly sitting beside him. Sensing my movement, he glanced up. Our eyes met, and he gave me an embarrassed shrug.

"I was starving. Haven't eaten since breakfast."

It was the first time I'd seen him since he'd been brought up to the house. He'd slept the entire day, which I couldn't blame him for. He'd basically been dead for about three minutes.

I walked quickly around the counter and latched on to my friend, embracing him hard enough to make him stumble. Happiness, regret, relief, sadness, anger, and hope—every possible emotion I could feel—flowed out of me.

"I'm okay, bro. I really am," Sebastian whispered.

Yanking at him and hugging him tighter, I nodded. "Yeah. I can tell."

I was finally fully at ease. Like I hadn't been able to relax the whole day until right then, even earlier with Maddy, I'd still held on to my worry about my best friend. Having him here, smelling his scent, and knowing he was fine brought relief I didn't know I could possibly feel.

Releasing him, I nodded to his sandwich. "You gonna make me one?"

Sebastian chuckled. "Sure. But I'm not putting potato chips on it like you like. That shit's gross on a PB and J."

The next morning, Dad came in and told me what I'd been expecting. We were sitting around the table eating when he walked in the door and pointed back the way he'd come.

"News vans, Nico. Every-damned-where. The big names, as well as some I've never heard of. They're camped out at the gate."

"Have they said what they want? Or are they just reporting from our location?" I asked.

"Interviews. That's all they're yelling about. You, Maddy, Sinthy, anyone who will come out."

I sighed. I didn't want to do any interviews. Everything I had to say had been said in the video. But I'd known everyone would want a follow-up. I couldn't stop it. They'd push and push until they got what they wanted. It might even help. The more I was out there, the harder it would be for Viola to be the only voice of the crisis.

"Okay, I'll do one interview. One of the bigger national stations. CNN or something. See if you can make that happen, Dad."

He blew a breath out, puffing his cheeks. "I'll give it a shot. Do we know when Sinthy will be back in good health? I want to open a passage through the barrier so we can take the bodies out to a coroner or something."

"I actually heard her moving around in her bathroom this morning," Gabriella said. "I know it took a lot out of her, so I'll check in and see how she feels today. It might not take a lot to do that."

"Good. Let me know. I'll head out and make contact with the media for you."

Dad left us to our breakfast, and I looked across the table at Gabriella. "Have you seen Maddy? When I woke up, she was already gone."

"She went running," Gabriella said as she smeared butter on her muffin. "She seemed upset about something but didn't want to talk about it."

Through our strong connection, I felt her out in the pack lands somewhere. I wanted to be near her. Standing, I tossed my napkin on the table and headed for the door.

"I'm gonna go find her. Let Dad know what Sinthy says."

I closed the door behind me and shifted, sprinting off toward the forest. Maddy's scent and aura pulled me in the right direction, the warm air of the morning fluttering through my fur as I ran. I found her on an outcropping of rock, still in her wolf form.

Shifting back, I walked up beside her. She turned her head and nuzzled against my leg as I eased down to sit beside her. While I sat there, Maddy rubbed her face across my hands and lap and cuddled beside me. I stroked her fur and gave her time. Something had upset her. It could have been a bad dream or something else.

At last, she shifted back to her human form and rested her head on my shoulder. It was then that I could sense what it was that had her so upset. Guilt.

I put my finger under her chin and lifted her eyes to me. "Hey, what's up? Didn't we have this conversation last night when I was the one feeling guilty?"

Maddy huffed and rolled her eyes. "This fated-mate thing is a pain in the ass sometimes. Maybe I want to keep some stuff secret."

"Too bad. So, spill it."

Maddy looked down at her hands. "I can't get over how all this, everything, is my fault. It probably would have been better for everyone if I'd been hit by a car when I was a kid. Without me, none of this would have happened."

Those words sent a spike of fear and sorrow through my chest, and I pulled her onto my lap.

"Absolutely not. Where would I be without you? I'd be miserable forever without you by my side." I placed my hand gently on her stomach. "And this little one wouldn't be getting ready to make an appearance. Everything happens for a reason. None of this is your fault. It was never your fault."

Maddy smiled at me, nestling her head into the crook between my neck and my shoulder. "Thanks. I needed that, Nico."

I stroked her back. The problem was, she didn't believe me. I could feel it. She was still hanging on to that guilt, and I had no clue how to get her to stop. If she kept those thoughts in her mind, she might end up doing something stupid.

Chapter 26 - Maddy

We sat like that for a while, basking in the silence. I had so many emotions flooding through me that it took a while to get them organized enough so I could actually voice them.

Finally, I said, "I know I shouldn't feel this way, but all I can think about is how useless I was yesterday when it mattered most." Nico opened his mouth to say something, but I continued, cutting him off. "I was locked up in that house, behind closed doors, while everyone else was out there fighting and protecting our home. It made me feel so weak."

Nico pulled me tighter. "You aren't weak. Not by a long shot. You've already been through more than most people could even imagine. You're pregnant, but that doesn't mean you're weak. All it means is you have to protect yourself more."

I sighed and shook my head. "I hate talking about it like that. It's like it's some sort of cop-out. *Oh, I'm pregnant. I better stay out of the way*. Ugh."

"That isn't a cop-out," Nico said, gently turning my face to meet his. "Maddy, you're braver than anyone I know. You are protecting our baby by not fighting. You may very well be saving its life by staying away from battles and fighting and all the rest. Just because you're not fighting right alongside all of us doesn't mean you're weak. Anything but. You're stronger than you can ever imagine, and I need you to stay strong for me. For us." He finished by putting his hand on my belly again.

Hearing him say it that way actually did make it a little better. My own hand drifted to my stomach. I still couldn't get over how fast everything was happening. It hadn't been that long ago that I'd found out I was pregnant, but my body was already changing. My belly was hardening, my breasts were getting bigger, and it wouldn't be long before I couldn't hide it anymore.

"Are we good?" Nico asked.

I nodded. "We are. I'm sorry. I keep getting in my own head about things I have no control over." I waved a hand through the air. "Enough about me. How are things going this morning?"

Nico sighed. "The video did the job. Dad told me there is a ton of people out front. No more anti-shifters, but journalists, news stations, bloggers—anyone and everyone who reports news. They're asking for an interview. Dad is going to set one up with one of the big national news channels. I guess my fifteen minutes of fame is getting started."

"Oh wow. Seriously?" I never dreamed Nico would be doing news interviews. Better him than me. That sounded terrifying and nerve-wracking.

"Yup. After what happened yesterday, I think it's necessary. We've got to be an alternative voice to Viola. Someone needs to be the yin to her fucked-up yang. If yesterday proved anything, it's that we can't keep hiding behind the wards anymore. There's an entire war going on out there. Shifters can't live locked up and hiding."

He was right. As awful as things had been for us, we were in a great spot compared to others across the world. We lived in a secure location, and we had one of the biggest packs in the country with plenty of able-bodied shifters to fight off intruders. We also had what appeared to be the most powerful witch of the last millennium. Compared to the smaller, less powerful packs, we were living in heaven. Hundreds of thousands of shifters all across the world were living in hiding, wondering if each day was going to be their last, and so far, all they'd heard or seen was Viola's damned face and the hatred she loved to spew.

"I see what you mean," I said. "Someone has to be the voice of reason. Who better than an alpha, right?"

Nico shrugged and looked uncomfortable. "I'm not trying to be some shifter messiah or anything. I only want the world to know the truth. I don't want any more lives lost, but Viola has to lose this power she has over us. She's orchestrating a genocide against shifters. If no one else is going to speak out and be the... I don't know... figurehead or something, I guess it has to be me."

Those words shot through me, leaving terror in their wake. If Nico really did become the other voice that pushed back against Viola, then the target on his head would only grow. The fight would only get bigger. The next attack would be more aggressive. It would escalate. The only real question I had was where I would be standing when the final fight came. The thought that had been worming its way ever deeper into my mind for the last couple of months surged to the forefront. There was no ignoring it this time. So much had already happened, and who knew what other awful surprises Viola might have up her sleeve? We needed a trump card.

"I think I should drink the vial." The words were out before I even realized I was opening my mouth.

Nico tensed. "What?"

It was out now. I needed to plead my case before he started on me.

"Listen," I said. "I know we were worried what the blood would do to the baby, but this child is also a descendant of Edemas. That tells me that any effect will be minimal. I don't think there will be a negative outcome. Not really. Plus, Isme didn't tell me not to drink it. Remember? She only said that if I did, it had to be done for pure and honest reasons. I don't want to rule or subjugate. All I want is to protect my family and friends. I *have* to protect them."

I don't know if it was the imploring tone in my voice, the desperation he saw in my eyes, or the terror of what happened yesterday, but instead of immediately retorting why it was a dumb idea, he sat in silence. I'd been so ready for the argument to begin that I'd already gotten several rebuttals ready. He'd caught me off guard.

Nico held up a hand. "Let's talk this through. I'm not saying it's a good idea or a plan that I want to implement, but I'm not completely against it like I would have been a couple of weeks ago."

"Are you serious—"

"Don't get ahead of me. This is not something to take lightly. I want to approach this vial like it's… a nuclear bomb or something. Dangerous, powerful, and only to be used at the very last second."

I nodded. "That's exactly what I was thinking. Like yesterday, if things had started going poorly. I could take it to see if it gave us an advantage. Something that would save lives."

Nico nodded wearily. "Exactly. Here are my stipulations. Using the vial is on the table… if it looks like all is lost and there are no other options. When it looks as though we are all going to end up dead anyway, then, and only then, would I be okay with you drinking it. Can we agree on that?"

"Yes. Absolutely."

Nico looked pale, but he pulled me in again.

"I hope it doesn't come to that, but I guess we'll see how things go."

Despite the danger we were in, I felt hopeful again. For the first time in days, I had something to look toward. Having a weapon in our back pocket made everything else seem a little less dangerous, a little less terrifying. I didn't truly want to use the vial but knowing Nico agreed it was a good last option was nice. Sort of like jumping out of an airplane but knowing you had a parachute.

The virtual interview was set up for early afternoon. It had taken a lot out of Sinthy to open a portal so the dead could be handed over to the authorities, and none of us wanted her doing any more magic until she was fully rested. She'd already eaten more than a high-school football team would have consumed and was currently sleeping again.

Luis set up a digital video camera and a small TV monitor so Nico could see the reporter he'd be talking to. It would be awkward, but everyone had gotten used to this type of thing since the pandemic a few years before.

Nico, unsure of what image to present, had opted to wear a suit. The last thing he wanted was for Viola's 'filthy degenerate shifter' message to be used because he was dressed like a slob.

"Are we ready?" Nico asked.

Luis was on the phone with the news station and gave Nico a thumbs-up. "The guy's name is Bruce. He should be on any second."

I was nervous, and I wasn't the one who'd be on screen. My palms were clammy, and my mouth was dry. A moment later, a man appeared on the TV screen.

"Mr. Lorenzo? I'm Bruce Witherspoon. Wonderful to meet you. We'll go live in two minutes."

Nico gave him a hesitant grin. "Yeah, good to meet you too."

Not long after, the actual interview started.

"Good afternoon, everyone," Bruce said. "Today, we come to you remotely from Clearidge, Florida, the site of yesterday's intense attack on the Lorenzo shifter pack compound. With us is the alpha of the Lorenzo pack, Nicolas 'Nico' Lorenzo. You may know him from the viral video posted online yesterday. This video has already received nearly one-hundred-thirty-eight million views as of nine o'clock this morning and is increasing rapidly. In the video, he goes into great detail on the history of The Monroe Group's illegal activities as well as an alternate history of the legendary werewolf king Edemas. He has agreed to an interview today to give us even more insight into what he believes is going on. Welcome, Mr. Lorenzo."

I chewed at my nails off-camera as Nico nodded and smiled. "Hello, Bruce. Thanks for having me."

"First things first, let's get to the heart of the matter. Can you give our viewers, who may not have seen your video, a bit of background on your history with Viola? Where did this vendetta begin?"

Nico cleared his throat. "It started hundreds of years ago when Viola's ancestors, distant relatives to Edemas's queen, turned on the royal couple. I won't get into a history lesson about that—the viewers can see my video for more information on that.

"The current crisis began months ago. My mate, Maddy Sutton, was identified by The Monroe Group, who is known in shifter circles by their ancient title, The Royals, as the last remaining descendant of Edemas. She was attacked and almost murdered in her place of business. My pack and I stopped that attack by sheer chance.

"Since that night, Viola and her group have done everything in their power to get at the secret they think Maddy holds. Maddy, her best friend, and both her adoptive parents, along with her birth mother, have all suffered from kidnapping and were tortured during their time in royal hands. Maddy's friend is suffering from PTSD as a result."

Bruce held up a hand. "Let's dive deeper into this story Viola has woven about Maddy Sutton. If her videos are to be believed, your mate is the next coming of some sort of demonic werewolf shifter. Someone to be feared, to be stopped at every opportunity. Where does this come from? Why does she believe that?"

Nico shrugged and gave the camera a humorless grin. "I have no clue. Maddy is like anyone else. She was a latent shifter and didn't develop her connection to her wolf until recently. *That* is only because her adoptive and birth parents knew she would be hunted and gave her suppression meds. Maddy's life has been one long history of running, hiding, and fear. All because of one woman's psychosis." Nico lifted a hand and gestured for me to step forward and join him.

My eyes nearly bugged out of my head. He wanted me to go on camera? Was that what he was asking? He gestured again. Without any conscious thought, my feet took me closer to him, walking over to join him in front of the camera. Once I was there, Nico draped his arm around my shoulders.

"Does this woman look like a monster? Like some sort of beast that's going to somehow turn all the shifters into an army to subjugate humans?" Disbelief and derision thickened his voice.

Bruce raised his eyebrows and gave a small shrug. "No, Mr. Lorenzo she does not. Hello, Miss Sutton."

"Hello," I said, surprised at the calm in my voice.

"Allow me to play devil's advocate here," Bruce said. "Images can be deceiving. Is there anything about Maddy that could be a threat? Could there be some grain of truth to what Miss Monroe is saying? I'm not saying Maddy is a super being, but perhaps she fears Maddy could become a figurehead of sorts. A freedom fighter who could rally the shifter community to greater heights. Something along those lines?"

If I took the vial, there was a chance I could actually become a werewolf. That wasn't something we needed to discuss here. The odds were low, and there was no need to help Viola's cause. Werewolves hadn't been seen since the time of Edemas, and they'd become a thing of myth and legend even among shifters. What we needed to focus on was the terror and tragedy Viola was bringing to the world.

"Viola Monroe is chasing a fairytale," Nico said. "Maddy only wants to live her life. She has no aspirations to become the next Ghandi or Mandela. What we have here is a powerful and wealthy woman who has brought death and destruction to the world. Children have been murdered. Died, Bruce. Babies. Innocent lives lost because Viola is pursuing this baseless vendetta. That's why I agreed to this interview. I'm here to let her, and the world, know that we refuse to hide anymore."

He gazed intently into the camera. "Everyone watching needs to understand this. I am telling every shifter across the globe that they need to protect themselves. After the attack on us yesterday, it has become evident that people want to follow Viola. To do what she tells them because they are afraid of use—because they refuse to understand us. Every shifter alpha listening right now needs to be ready to defend their homes.

"Any human who feels compelled to follow Viola's instructions needs to listen. This battle is not yours. You are being manipulated into a war that could cost you your lives or freedom. Do not listen to her. Shifters are not coming for your families. We don't want to take over the world, and we aren't a threat to you. All we want is to live our lives like you do. We want to raise our children, wake each morning in peace, and do nothing more.

"For those of you who can't or won't listen to reason, all I can tell you is that we will no longer hide in fear. If you choose to attack us, then I, and every shifter on Earth, have the right to defend themselves. Take this as a warning. If you step foot on any pack land, if you attack any shifter, or if you threaten harm to any shifter, then be prepared for us to push back. And we will push back hard because when it comes to family, nothing is more sacred to a shifter, and we will not hesitate to end any threat. I plead with you to end this bloodshed. Once Viola Monroe is dealt with, I know this war will be over."

"Very well said, Mr. Lorenzo. I, and most of the world, are on your side. One thing that we can't skip over was the attack yesterday and the footage broadcasted from the helicopter. The disturbing images were heart-rending, but in the midst of that battle, something else became apparent: the witch that fought beside you and the other shifters."

Nico sighed. "I knew we'd get to that eventually."

"Indeed. As you and most others know, witches were thought to be extinct for hundreds of years. Many had even decided that they may have never existed. Seeing the power this woman wielded has made many become even more fearful of the so-called *Shifter Threat.* Can you go into some detail on how this woman came to be in your employ?"

"First off," Nico said, "the woman is not my employee, slave, or minion. She is a member in full standing with the Lorenzo pack. Though she is not a shifter, she is a part of my family and under my protection."

"Yes, but how did you find this woman?" Bruce asked.

"She found us. This, as with most things, goes back to Viola. Viola's company murdered her parents, rendering our pack witch an orphan who was, in turn, raised by another witch. They came to us to help in our fight against the royals. Your viewers cannot imagine the horrors this girl has witnessed. Not only that, but we recently took in another individual who has the powers of a witch. He was forced to become one by The Monroe Group. The magical energies of a dead witch were forced into him during cruel experiments overseen by Viola Monroe. I don't want to drag this young man into it, but he is Miss Monroe's own son."

"Umm, I'm sorry? Mr. Lorenzo, are you saying that Viola Monroe abused and experimented on her own child?"

"I am. I'm not going to say his name because it isn't my place to expose him to the world, but everyone needs to know the monster we are dealing with. No one is safe. If it helped her goals, she'd kill anyone, including all these poor deluded people following her. She's even kidnapped his half-siblings and has been holding them as insurance to make sure he does her bidding. The government needs to look into this. They're minors and are in desperate need of help."

The reporter looked a bit shell-shocked at this revelation. Nico had been keen to get the info out to both help the cause against Viola and to force law enforcement around the world to try and find Maxwell's siblings. I wasn't sure if it would work, but there was no use in not trying. If Viola was going to kill them, it was likely she already had. Nothing we said would make things worse for them.

"Mr. Lorenzo, I want to thank you again for joining us today. I'd like to send my deepest condolences to your pack for those you lost yesterday. I truly believe that this interview will open some eyes around the world. Is there anything else you'd like to add before we end?"

"No, Bruce. I think I've said everything I wanted to. All we want is peace. If that isn't possible, then we *are* prepared for war."

"Fair enough. I'm Bruce Witherspoon with TDN News. Thank you."

There was a slight pause, and then I watched as Bruce loosened his tie on the screen.

"That was a helluva interview, Nico. I really do hope it works out for you all. Is there anything else we can do for you?"

"I don't think so. Is that it? When will the interview air?"

Bruce laughed. "Um, I guess my producer didn't tell you. We were actually live."

"Oh." Nico looked like he'd been kicked in the stomach. "Okay, then."

"If I were you, I'd check social media in an hour or so to see what the reaction was. See you all later." Without another word, the video feed went black.

Nico rubbed a hand over his face. "I need to call the other alphas. The ones nearby we couldn't bring in. See how things are going for them. I want to see if they're of the same mind as I am. I'm done hiding. Do you want to sit in on the call?"

I shook my head. "No, I'll be fine. You go do your *alpha* stuff."

Nico went to his office, and Luis started breaking down all the video equipment he'd set up. I wandered out the back door, desperate for some fresh air. To my surprise, Maxwell was sitting in the grass beyond the porch. I noticed his hands and saw that, in all the confusion, Sinthy had never reattached the magic bracelets that held his power back. He was free to use his magic and could have vanished in the night but chose to remain here. Why?

"Maxwell?" I said as I walked toward him.

The young man jerked in surprise. "I'm sorry, Miss Sutton. Am I not allowed to be here? I can go back to my room. It's not a problem."

I dismissed his apology with a wave of my hand. "It's fine," I said as I sat on the grass beside him. "I was wondering why you didn't decide to teleport away when you had the chance." I nodded toward his bare wrists.

He looked down and let out the weariest sigh I'd ever heard. He shrugged. "Where would I go?"

"Well... maybe back to your mother? I know she's terrible, but she's still your mom. Maybe she'd let you see your siblings?"

He chuckled ruefully. "No chance of that." He glanced at me, unable to meet my gaze. "I did try to leave, though."

I blinked in surprise. "You *tried*?"

He nodded. "Late last night. I started conjuring the teleportation spell, but something in my magic... spoke to me. Telling me to stay. There's something different now," he said, staring at his palms.

"Like what?" I asked, truly curious.

Without looking up, he said, "Before yesterday, my magic never really felt like mine. It was always like it didn't belong with me. Have you ever put your underwear on backward in the dark?"

I laughed. "Um... probably. At some point."

"Right," he said, finally looking at me. "It'll work, it covers you and keeps the pants from rubbing you raw, but it'll always feel uncomfortable, and it doesn't make it easy to walk around. That's how it always was with me.

"Yesterday, when Sinthy touched my hands and pulled my magic through her body and fed it into your friend? Something happened. When we saved that guy's life, and it all poured back into me, it didn't seem foreign anymore. It was like... I don't even know... like Sinthy using it, made the power *accept* me or something." He looked into my eyes. "I think I'm supposed to be here. I am worried about my siblings, though. We must get them away from my mother."

The boy—I kept thinking of him that way even though he was clearly in his early twenties—looked like a child. Fragile and broken. I patted his shoulder, and he flinched before calming under my touch.

"It's okay, Maxwell. You're safe here. I promise we'll do anything we must in order to get them back safely."

The only answer he gave was a hesitant grin. The tears that glittered in his eyes told me how much he was holding back. All I wanted was for him and his family to be okay. I'd be damned if I'd let that bitch destroy another family.

Chapter 27 - Nico

Leaving Maddy, I went to my office and called the surrounding alphas. It took some time before everyone joined the conference call, but once we were together, it went smoothly. They'd all seen the interview and were happy with how it went.

"Do we think this is going to give the royals something to think about?" It was Raul, an alpha from New Smyrna.

"If I'm being a hundred percent honest," I said. "I don't think so. What I do think it will do is get more people on our side. We get the conversation started, and there's going to be a discussion happening outside of shifter compounds. If a person is thinking of going after and attacking a shifter, but their wife, mother, or husband says, 'Hang on. I don't think that's the way to go about this'. Then we've done a good job of decreasing Viola's reach and power. That's what I think this will do in the short term."

"I liked what you said about not rolling over and dying," an alpha named Jacob said. "We aren't doing ourselves any favors by hiding in holes. My pack has been stuck in an abandoned factory for weeks now. So far, no one has figured out we're there, but it's only a matter of time. Once the anti-shifters get wind of it, they'll come like locusts. I'm tired of hiding. Fuck, man, I'd love to take a damn walk around Target or something. Go to a restaurant and relax with my mate. The time for hiding is over."

I nodded to myself. "Good. I like hearing that. To tell you the truth, I was worried you all might be upset that I went there with the interview."

"Hell no," Tiago said. He was on the call from his quarters near the Moon Mate building. "I think I speak for all of us when I say that the time is over. None of us want a bloodbath, but after what happened yesterday, I'm done playing nice. We've done everything we could to make peace, but if these psychos are going to keep doing Viola's bidding, the gloves need to come off."

"All right," I said. "If we're all in agreement, then we need to be ready to face the consequences. Are we certain we can push back if it comes to that? I don't mean physically—I mean mentally. It's one thing to say you're going to fight back, but it's another when you're looking down the barrel of a gun or watching a horde of angry people flood your property."

Brevard spoke up. If I wasn't mistaken, he was with a bear clan out of Sarasota.

"Nico, listen, man, I know it's a tough ask, but I don't think you need to worry about it. When I was at your pack lands for that get-together a few months ago, I could already see where this was going. You're right when you say it's different talking about it versus actually doing it, but none of us are afraid. We've got packs to protect. Women, children, and older folks. You aren't a true alpha if you aren't willing to do whatever it takes to protect that. I'm in. Anyone else?"

Murmurs of assent came all around, and it lightened me that they all sounded confident and ready. That was good. I hoped my message would push down the attacks and maybe scare off Viola's followers, but that was probably only wishful thinking on my part.

"Guys," I said, "I need to get my own house in order. Be ready. Now's a good time to add men to your guard rotation. Make sure that wherever you're holed up, it's secure and easily defendable. Get your people ready and prepared. If you've got guns, get those loaded and easily accessible."

Once the call had ended, I sat back in my chair, exhaling heavily and breathing deeply. That was one item checked off my list, and it had gone better than I'd thought. Back when I'd hosted the alpha meeting, things had been a little contentious. A few men had even stormed off and left. Clearly, the events of the past few months had changed some minds.

Before I could get up to leave, my phone rang again. I glanced at the screen. Unknown number. My heart started hammering, slamming forcefully against my rib cage. It had to be Viola. She was calling to tell me about some new horrific idea she had to kill or torture people I loved.

Hesitantly lifting the phone to my ear, I said, "Hello?"

"Is this Nicolas Lorenzo?" It was a deep male voice about as far from Viola as it could get.

"It is. Who's this?"

He cleared his throat. "My name is Doug Brindle. You don't know me, but I'm the alpha of a panther pack in North Dakota. I got your number through… well… a big chain of friends-of-friends. It's almost ridiculous how many people it took."

Frowning, I leaned forward and rested my elbows on the table. "Okay, uh, what can I do for you, Doug?"

"Mr. Lorenzo— "

"Call me Nico."

"Oh, sure. Sorry. Nico, I had to call you. I watched your interview, and I can't get it out of my mind. This is gonna sound dumb, but I want to thank you for what you said."

I let out a little laugh. "I don't really know what to say to that. All I said was the truth. At least, the truth as I see it."

"That's the thing," Doug said, sounding more ardent. "It is the truth. We have to do this. Fighting back is the only way to show these people we aren't going to roll over and die. Since all this started, every alpha I know has done exactly what everyone else has done. Hidden, kept quiet, put their heads down.

"A bunch of folks in my pack watched that interview with me. I'm not ashamed to admit that as you talked, I could sense the emotion in the room. You touched a nerve in my people that even I couldn't. You fired them up. By the time it ended, I could see how much more confident and hopeful they were. Some alphas might take that as slight. Not me. It opened my eyes. Showed me exactly what we needed to do. Thanks to that interview, our pack has already started reaching out to neighboring shifter clans. We're going to pool our resources. Put up a more united front, you know?"

North Dakota? This guy was over two thousand miles away from me, and he'd taken what I said to heart. It boggled my mind that I could say a few words on TV and touch people that far away.

"Well, Doug, all I can say is that I hope what I said helped. Do you feel safer after talking to your neighboring packs? That's what this is all about, really. I don't want to see another tragedy on the news."

"Yeah, we do. I mean, your interview was only an hour ago, but every alpha I've talked to since then has said the same thing. They're talking about you, man. 'This guy in Florida knows what's up.' That's the consensus. I only wanted to call and thank you. You've given people a lot to hope for. Thank you."

I was struck speechless but managed to find my words before the pause got too awkward.

"Doug... I don't know that I can say the right words, but you have no idea how happy that makes me. This all started with protecting my own pack, but the thought that I could help others means a lot. I appreciate you reaching out. My phone is always on if you ever need anything."

"I will. Again, thanks. Stay safe down there."

"You stay safe up *there*," I said, then ended the call.

A dumbfounded grin tugged at my lips, but I didn't have much time to think about the call. Luis ducked into my office with a phone pressed to his ear.

He covered the mic. "I've got a guy on the line. Alpha from Idaho—wants to talk to you. Got my name and number from a guy I worked with a few years back."

I opened my mouth to say something, but my own phone rang, interrupting me. The number showed that it was an incoming call from Maine. It took some time, but after nearly three hours, I'd talked to over two dozen alphas from all over the world—Alaska, Colorado,

Australia, West Virginia, California, Scotland, Belarus, and pretty much everywhere in between. I'd even received a call from the alpha of a lion-shifter pack from a remote area in Africa that required a translator.

I finally had to stop answering the calls and put my phone on do-not-disturb. Exhausted as I was, I felt thrilled. Not in a million years would I have believed I could touch so many people. I did, however, worry about the blowback. I prayed that the humans who were following Viola heard my words and heeded them.

My hopes and prayers were shown to be pointless over the course of the next few days. The morning after the onslaught of calls, a report came in that a bear pack had been attacked overnight. My jaw almost hit the floor when I saw that it was a pack in North Dakota. The news showed the devastation, but unlike before, it wasn't the shifters who'd been caught off guard. It had been the human attackers. The bears had been more than ready. Instead of being asleep, nearly half their fighting force had been on guard duty. They'd thwarted the attack without suffering a single casualty. The humans had gotten out without a death, but many had been severely injured.

I texted Doug to see if that had been his pack— sure enough, it had. His pack had shown the humans mercy rather than killing them where they stood. He again thanked me and told me they would have been slaughtered if my words hadn't stirred them to action.

Maddy and I were glued to the TV over the next several days. An attack on a shifter compound in Nevada had met the same fate as the attack on Doug's pack. No shifter deaths and massive injuries to the attackers. Again, the humans had been spared death. A coordinated attack on a tiger pack in India was thwarted in a similar fashion. I'd never spoken to anyone from there, but their alpha released a statement thanking *me* for helping them realize they needed to prepare for war.

It was astounding, and it looked like we were making headway. The media, which had been toeing the line between both factions, suddenly swung completely pro-shifter. Out of nowhere, they were firmly in our camp. Several regular reporters were missing from broadcasts, and I wondered if they were upset about the change in priorities. Maybe they were closeted anti-shifter activists. The fact that these attacks were still happening, but the shifters were showing the attackers mercy and not killing them, helped sway public sentiment in our direction.

Things had been shaky ever since Viola had used the drug to force us to shift. Those orchestrated attacks, all on video, had done severe damage to the shifter cause. Now, though? It was like all that had been erased. Everyone was starting to see that we were the ones under attack.

Even the government was doing more than lip service. They'd arrested everyone associated with the attacks and were pushing for the most severe punishments. The president and multiple governors had addressed the public, touting the Shifter Crisis as the most pressing issue of the day and promising further assistance where necessary.

We were watching another news bulletin when Felipe came barreling into my house. He was panting, his eyes wild.

I got to my feet, tugging Maddy up with me.

"What's wrong?" I asked, though I already had a suspicion.

Felipe gestured back toward the gates. "Massive group of humans. Almost all of them are armed. Headed this way. One of the guards was manning the drone and caught sight of them. Two miles out. Probably less than a mile by now."

"Shit," I said. "Are Sinthy's wards still up?"

Felipe nodded. "They are, but she's too weak to enhance them. They're nothing like they were before. More like a fence than anything. I'm... hell... I'm not sure they'll hold."

"Come on. Get everyone to meet at the gate. Move." I looked at Maddy. "Stay here."

She looked like she wanted to argue, but she slumped onto the couch, her breath leaving her in a huff as she crossed her arms.

"This is going to be okay. I promise," I said as I left.

For some peculiar reason, I wasn't worried. In fact, as I walked to the gate, I was completely calm. Sinthy's barrier wasn't as strong as the last. If a big enough force tried to push through, they would probably be successful, but they'd suffer for it. It would be painful, and even if they got through, we'd make them pay.

By the time I made it to the gate, it was already a moot point. The rest of my pack had heard the approaching vehicles and headed to the gates. The attacking force had been determined. They'd managed to push nearly a half dozen of their group through the forcefield, but those had been ineffective fighters as the electric shock of the spell—while not as strong as before—was still painful.

My pack had given them a few bumps and bruises to remember us by, then pushed them back through the barrier. It was like watching someone push a person through thick gel.

I stepped close to the barrier, raising my voice. "Go home. There's nothing for you here."

A man in a rather nice suit came stomping forward, nearly pressing against the barrier.

"You filthy motherfuckers! We're here to rid the world of you. Viola Monroe knows what's going on. She will lead us in eradicating your filth. Do you understand?"

Behind him, the flashing blue-and-red lights of cops heading our way lit the sky. I bared my teeth.

"If you're so dead set on it, then come on through. It's a little painful, but I'm ready if you are," I said, staring him dead in the eyes.

The sirens became louder as we stared at each other. Finally, whether he was afraid to put his money where his mouth was or the idea of getting arrested for being a violent bigot got to him, he and the others sprinted back to their cars, jumping in and peeling out as the cops approached.

"Everyone good?" I asked as I turned to my pack.

"All good, Nico," Luis said. "We got this. I'll talk to the cops. You can head on back."

"Okay. Let me know if you need me for anything else. Make sure our people on patrol around the perimeter have enough help. I don't like that they were able to push through the barrier so easily."

"It wasn't that easy," Luis said. "Did you hear them screaming as they went through? Didn't look like fun."

"Yeah, still. Add people if needed."

I was back at the house less than ten minutes later. If I'd hoped to relax, I'd been terribly misguided. It seemed the drama of the day wasn't quite done yet.

My phone rang as I walked in the door. This number wasn't masked, and it wasn't another alpha calling to give me his support. It was Viola. My eyes jerked away from the screen and locked on Maddy's face. She jumped up, sensing my fear and anxiety.

"Is it her?" she asked.

I nodded and answered the phone on speaker so Maddy could hear.

"Hello, Viola," I said with as much calm confidence as I could muster.

"You, Mr. Lorenzo, have become a very large thorn in my side." Her voice was controlled, but I could sense the undercurrent of rage beneath it.

"In what way, Viola? Are you mad that your little sycophants can't murder babies anymore?"

Viola chortled a brittle laugh. "Oh, I don't consider your types human. Killing a shifter baby is no different from stomping on a maggot that churns in the rotting flesh of a rat carcass."

"Lovely to speak to you as always. Each time is a delight."

I wasn't surprised that she'd reached out. She was the face of the anti-shifter movement, and by no planning of my own, I'd become the face of the resistance. It had only been a matter of time before she called. That didn't make things any easier.

"Your little *rebellion* has gone far enough," Viola said. "It's time we settled this once and for all. From the moment you saved that bitch of yours— "

"Her name is Maddy. If anyone is the bitch, it's you, so watch your goddamned tongue when you speak of her."

Viola's breath caught. I'd touched a nerve. She wasn't used to being interrupted, and she definitely wasn't used to being called a bitch. I grinned as I listened to the silence.

Finally, she said, "I want this over as much as you do. We can finish this, and I can finally have what I've always wanted."

"Which is?" I asked.

"An end to shifters. I want the vial so that no shifter can ever take the mantle of werewolf again. Once that is gone, eventually, you all will do what mongrels do, and you'll weed yourself out."

I furrowed my brow, looking at Maddy. She shrugged, a deep crease between her eyebrows.

"I still find it hard to believe that you've done all this simply because you hate shifters."

"Shifters infiltrated my family. They stole the throne from us. Diluted the blood when Edemas pushed his filthy cock into that traitorous queen. His progeny are a blight on the Earth and stole what should have been ours. They made a mockery of the royal name. My family has never recovered from having that animal blood mixed into our family line. That vial might hold the key to restoring the true royal family to what it once was. I want to bring about a renaissance."

"And how do you want to do that? I'm not giving you the vial, and I'm not giving you Maddy. So, explain how you want to end this."

"First things first. You have my son. I want him back."

I jerked back like I'd been slapped in the face. The change of topic was jarring, and I had a hard time believing this woman truly cared for her son or had a single maternal bone in her body.

"Why would I do that, Viola?"

"I will release his siblings. I have no use for them anymore. Worthless as they are, they proved inefficient in my experiments. They are no longer useful to me. I release them, and in return, you give me my son back."

Should I tell her that Maxwell was no longer our prisoner? He'd decided to stay of his own accord. There was zero chance I'd ever force him to go back to his mother. Not in a million years. Instead, I sidestepped.

"That might be possible, but I need to know where this final meeting will happen. What are the terms?"

Viola laughed again, dark malevolence in her voice. "I thought to make it like the olden days. Two armies on a field, facing one another. A battle that will seal the fate of the world. How does that sound?"

"It sounds like melodramatic bullshit, but I'm game. When and where?"

"Your pack lands. I'll even give you the benefit of home-field advantage, as they say. One week from today. I'm sick of these games, and I want to get back to living my life the way I did before that mate of yours showed her pretty little face. Understood? My army against yours. We'll see who has the last laugh."

My stomach flipped and twisted into knots. An end to this whole thing… The very thing I'd been praying for from the start was in sight. At least, it was if she was telling the truth. It could be a trap, but could I keep living like this, standing around, running from fights because I was afraid we couldn't win? No, this had to end. Even if she had some strange shit up her sleeve, we needed to do this. Sinthy was almost back to full strength, and my pack and the surrounding packs were ready. I'd make every call I could and bring in as many shifters as wanted to fight. This would be the end. Every instinct I had told me we would come out on top, but there were no guarantees. Win or lose, it was coming to a head now.

"Fine," I said, "We'll be ready for you."

She clucked her tongue in disappointment. "I do hate that it came to this. I never wanted this blood on my hands. See you soon, Nico."

She was lying through her teeth. This was exactly what she'd always wanted. Even with her living in hiding and being hunted, I had the feeling she was thriving on this. Almost like she'd been desperate for war all these years and was ecstatic that her plan would finally come to fruition.

Maddy bit her lip. "One week."

I nodded. "One week."

That afternoon, Viola released another of her videos. It was broadcast on every channel as usual. She called for every able-bodied member of her movement to get to Clearidge, Florida for a final confrontation that would determine the fate of humankind.

Taking a page from Viola's own book, I had Luis help me release my own video where I called for the same thing. Any shifter who could make it to my pack lands would find safe haven here and would be welcome to fight alongside us.

Needless to say, the authorities were less than pleased, threatening to arrest anyone who took part in the fighting. Even as I watched them announce it, I had a sense that law enforcements and governments around the world were possibly a bit relieved that it was coming to an end. It had been disastrous for months, and if it could be settled in one day, they were more than likely to turn a blind eye when it all came down.

My phone was inundated with texts and calls almost immediately. Most packs couldn't send their entire fighting force to me, but nearly everyone was sending at least a dozen men and women our way to fight. The local packs had promised nearly their full force.

A vague memory of a bible verse kept coming to mind. The one about the end of days. About a great battle between good and evil. It was to take place on a field, and that field was named Armageddon. I looked out my window

at my pack lands and wondered if that was what was about
to happen.

Chapter 28 - Maddy

Shifters started to arrive in carloads, rented box trucks, and on motorcycles the day after Nico's video. There was a surrealness to it as I watched hordes arrive in our pack lands. Nico had made the call, and it had been answered. Dozens of shifters from around Florida, Georgia, Alabama, and the Carolinas arrived first. They were the closest and managed to get here quickly.

When the first string of vehicles had crested the hill in the distance early that morning, a murmur of fear had shot through the pack. Our first inclination was that anti-shifter attackers were descending on us. Nico had rallied our forces, and we were getting ready to defend the gates when the scent hit. Shifters. A new group was coming to ally themselves with us. That had been the beginning, and since then, it had only grown.

The guest houses were all packed, and every home in the pack lands had at least three people bunked up with our members. Hell, even my parents had taken a couple of shifters from an Ohio bear pack into their tiny cabin. The only home that didn't have some of our new guests in it was ours. That decision had been made under protest. Nico had wanted to bring as many in as possible, but the rest of the pack had declined. Luis and Nico's dad said that, as the alpha, he needed a place of respite to gather his thoughts and stay sharp for the battle ahead.

We were so crowded that, eventually, we had to have people stay at off-pack locations. Javi and his pack volunteered to leave the safety of our land to head back to his own land, claiming he'd feel safer there with reinforcements. He took three packs with him when he left—a lizard pack from Nevada, a wolf pack from New York, and a bear pack from Texas. Nico would get in contact with them when it was time to rally together for whatever was coming.

As much as I agreed with Nico and wanted us to pull our own weight, I was grateful I didn't have to worry about entertaining guests. My nerves were at an all-time high, and the stress was getting to me. Apart from that, I was starting to show. My tummy was expanding by the day. Currently, it looked more like I was three plates deep into a Thanksgiving feast, but the pudge would soon be obvious for what it was.

By the sixth day, things had settled down a bit. The influx of shifters had become more of a trickle. Most packs that had enough people to send to the cause had already sent them. Any more that were arriving had to come from far away, and it took them forever. The farthest away had been a group of seven leopard shifters from Belize and a group of polar bears who'd driven from Alaska pretty much nonstop for over four days to join us.

Nico was in his office, talking to Donatello on the phone. Sinthy had sent him back to his island a couple of days before so he could use his communications setup to coordinate with the others in his group. He was still attempting to locate Viola, hoping to end things before an all-out war started.

I left him to his business and went for a walk. The warm breeze helped me calm down, but the rest of the pack lands were chaotic. The noise of so many people alone made it hard to think. Luis, Felipe, and Sebastian were working with Nico's brothers to help the new arrivals get up to speed with our security and perimeter, as well as some of the strategies we'd developed when training with Sinthy's battle illusions.

The buildings were so full that a group of about a dozen people had set up tents near the tree line to the west of the gates, and I could hear their conversations echoing up toward me. That took a backseat to what I saw at the opposite side of the pack lands.

Sinthy and Maxwell. Even in the distance, I spotted Sinthy's long hair fluttering behind her as she led Maxwell into the forest. I smiled sadly as they vanished into the trees.

She'd been taking the boy out every day. It seemed like Sinthy was spending more time in the woods than she was in the house, and most of that time was spent with Maxwell, helping him hone his talents and get a handle on his powers. All around me, people were preparing for war, and I felt like a sitting duck. I ran a hand along my belly before turning around to head back inside.

A familiar voice called out to me before I reached the front door.

"Maddy."

I grinned and turned to see Gabriella jogging up the path.

"Hi. Is everything okay?" I asked.

Gabriella nodded and smiled, but then her eyes narrowed on me. Even though she hadn't raised me, and we'd only reconnected over the last few months, there was something inherently maternal about her. She was giving me a look that told me she sensed my deepest worries.

"What's on your mind?"

For a split second, I wanted to deny that anything *was* wrong, but I gestured feebly to the activity surrounding us.

"I feel like I'm not doing enough. Everyone is getting ready to fight, and I'm just hanging out. It's like I'm waiting for the end of the world." I shrugged half-heartedly. "I wish I was doing more to help, I guess."

Gabriella glanced behind her, then walked over to put her arm around my shoulders.

Pointing out at the activity, she said, "Do you notice anything?"

I scanned the pack lands, stopping on each little grouping of people as they worked or talked. I couldn't tell what she was getting at, so I shook my head. "I don't think so."

"Over ninety percent of the fighting force is men. The packs from around the country sent almost exclusively men. Our own fighting force has some women, but that's out of necessity. If I had to guess, with all these extra fighters, most of the women won't be in the final conflict. The men will do the fighting."

My gaze darted back out across the area I'd looked at a moment before. Gabriella was right. For the most part, it was mostly men doing everything. There were women, but the majority of them were doing things like delivering food and fresh towels or tending to the small gardens and other *feminine* jobs. A sudden rush of heat rose in my chest. It pissed me off.

Gabriella must have caught a whiff of the change in my pheromones because she chuckled to herself. "Calm down. It's not on purpose. It's the nature of shifters. It's not a misogynistic plot. This is how it typically plays out in the animal kingdom. The men protect the pack, and the women protect the families and children, and obviously their mates."

"But we can fight," I said.

"True," Gabriella agreed. "As a last-ditch effort. If wild dogs attacked a pack of wolves and overwhelmed the males, then, obviously, the females would jump in to defend and fight. But that's the last thing they do. What they are supposed to do is stay back and protect those who can't protect themselves," she said and tentatively touched my abdomen.

I remembered the discussion Nico and I had about using the vial—about it being a last option and only to be used if there was no other choice.

"Let Nico protect you," Gabriella went on. "That's his duty—what he's made for. Your job is to protect the child growing inside you."

Before I could mull over her words or decide whether I'd tell her about my decision to drink the contents of the vial if we were out of options, another set of footsteps approached from behind us. When I turned, I saw my mother. She looked embarrassed and a little hesitant.

"Am I interrupting?" she asked.

I shook my head.

Gabriella smiled. "Not at all."

There was an awkward moment when none of us spoke, but Mom finally broke the silence.

"I came up to apologize."

That caught me off guard, and I shook my head in bewilderment. "What? Why? For what?"

Mom twisted her hands together nervously. "Not only to you, Maddy, but to Gabriella. I saw you over here, and I figured there was no time like the present."

I blinked. "Mom, what are you talking about?"

"Your father and I—we've… I guess we've been having a hard time understanding your new life. It's like we're sort of watching you from a distance. From outside. I know it's silly, and we both know that Gabriella isn't trying to take you away from us, but it's difficult. There's been… jealousy. We cannot connect with you in the same way as she can. We can't help you understand shifter things the way she can. We should have been more understanding about what you were going through. Your father and I have been more distant than we should have been, and that wasn't fair to you. Not when there's so much going on.

"I wanted to apologize for any hurt we may have caused to either of you. We don't want to drive a wedge between the two of you. Gabriella is your biological mother, and she gave us so much to keep you safe. It's not right that we try to step between you. That's what I came to say. I'm sorry."

I didn't say a word. Instead, I walked over and wrapped my arms around her. This was the woman who'd held me as a child. She'd kissed my skinned knees and bandaged my cuts and bruises. I'd cried on her shoulder when things didn't go well at school or when a boy broke my heart. She was everything a mother could be and more. The only thing that wasn't there was the blood, and that mattered less than anything. Gabriella had missed out on all those things—she was the one who'd carried me in her womb and had cried herself to sleep for weeks after giving me up. Both these women were my mother. In my mind, I was blessed to have so many people around me that cared for me, and I didn't want any of them to think they held a lower standing in my eyes.

I kissed Mom on the cheek. "You don't have to apologize for anything, Mom. It's good that you love me so much. And I'm glad you said all this. My baby is going to have so much love. They're lucky to have so many grandparents."

Mom's eyes glistened with tears as I turned and beckoned Gabriella over. I took her hand in my left and Mom's hand in my right. Gabriella and Mom shared a brief look before linking their free hands. The tiny circle we formed comforted me more than I thought possible. I hadn't realized how much I'd needed this until that very moment.

Afterward, I spent some time watching a crew of guys, led by Tiago's and Norman's packs, work on clearing a huge patch of land. They cut trees and hauled away brush. They were increasing the size of the training field. Nico and the others had decided to designate it as the battlefield.

Tomorrow, this would all come to a head. Part of it didn't seem real. A tiny portion of my mind had convinced itself that this would go on and on forever like some awful purgatory. Knowing that we were almost to the end was odd. There was no way to know exactly what the end would look like. Who would live? Who would die? Those questions had kept me awake for the last week.

Once the crew finally finished clearing the land, they drifted off to their bunks for one more good meal and then a night of sleep—if they could calm their minds enough to sleep, that was. All I could hope was that they would get the rest they needed.

I stepped into the house after the sun set. The house was silent. Nico was sitting at the dining room table, and it looked like he'd been waiting for me.

"Where is everyone else?" I asked. Luis, Nico's family, and the others had been in and out of the house all day.

"I sent them away," he said.

Looking around and knowing that we were alone, I could feel a crack start to form in my mind. It was all too much—the weight of knowing what was coming; the horror that was about to be visited upon us. I'd done a good job of keeping it locked up behind the dam in my mind, but now that I was alone with Nico, it started to crumble.

He must have seen it in my face because he was up and over to me, wrapping me in his arms in a second. Feeling his strong body against mine, I let it all go. I cried, and everything I was worried about tumbled from my mouth. Our baby, one of us dying, our friends or family dying, what would happen to the world if we lost, and a dozen other things that had been bouncing through my head for days. Nico let me get it all out and comforted me through my entire mini-breakdown.

When it was over, and my tears had mostly dried, he lifted my chin so that he could look at me.

"It will all work out the way it's supposed to."

"How do you know that?" I said.

"For sure? I don't. All I know is that as bad as the world is, it still tends to gravitate toward *good*. Evil does win, but usually in the short term. In the long run, good usually triumphs. Eventually. All I know is that we are on the good side. Whatever power and influence Viola might have, it can't be stronger than being on the right side of history."

He was so confident. Whether he was talking out of his ass or not, his confidence made it seem better. At least a little. He leaned down and kissed me. It was a soft, almost chaste kiss—something a couple of seven-year-olds might share on a playground. The innocence of it sent a raging fire through me.

"I want you, Nico. I *need* you."

A sly smile played on his lips as he took my hand and led me upstairs. My heart pounded as he closed the bedroom door behind us. Somehow, it was like our first time together again. I was nervous and scared and excited all at the same time.

He undressed me in a slow, methodical manner, keeping his eyes on mine most of the time. Once I was naked, I did the same for him. The heat of his body radiated from him as I slid his clothes off. Nico pulled me close, our naked bodies pressed flush against each other. When he kissed me this time, it was hungry, demanding. I tried not to dwell on the thought that this might be the last time I got to be with him. I shoved those thoughts away and allowed myself to simply live in the moment.

As our tongues danced, I slipped my hand between us and took his cock in my hand. He was already hard, and he sucked in a breath as I began to stroke him. I could feel his pulse as my fingers glided up and down his shaft.

Nico caressed my breasts. They were fuller than they'd been a few weeks ago *and* more sensitive. I moaned into his mouth as his thumb slid across my nipple. We stood like that, kissing and exploring each other's bodies.

Right when I thought I couldn't hold off any longer, Nico wrenched his lips from mine and gently lowered me to the bed. My back pressed against the soft blankets, and I stretched languorously as he nestled himself between my legs. He trailed kisses up and down my inner thigh, each pass getting closer to my pussy. I was drenched, desperate to have him inside me, but I wanted this to go on forever. I didn't want it to end.

My back arched slightly as he slid his tongue between my legs, sweeping up across my asshole, then thrusting deep into my pussy, and finally flicking across my clit. Fireworks went off inside my head as he continued the torturous path. His hands found their way up my stomach until they palmed my breast, massaging them as he devoured me. Raising my hips to meet his mouth, I put my hands on his, loving the way his fingers glided across my skin.

When I couldn't take it anymore, I pulled away and tugged at his hands, gesturing him to come up.

"I want you inside me, Nico," I whispered.

He smirked as he crawled up the bed, pressing his lips to my stomach, my sternum, and finally, my breasts. His tongue circled my left nipple before he pulled it into his mouth at the same moment as he slid the full length of his cock inside me. I opened my mouth and breathed out a sigh of pleasure as he filled me. It was like I was complete. When he started to move against me, grinding himself inside my pussy, I lost all awareness. The only thing that mattered was Nico, me, and how we made each other feel.

I wrapped my arms around him, moaning with every thrust and tilt of his hips. His lips left my breasts and drifted up, kissing my chest and neck before his mouth found mine again. I twined my fingers through his hair as he kissed me and fucked me. If I had died right then, those few moments would have been what I experienced for the rest of eternity.

His breathing grew faster, his hips gyrating as his thrust became more intense. It made my head spin, and my own climax began to build. An exquisite pressure started building in my pelvis, and electric tingles crackled through my mind. I was getting close, pleasurable spasms shooting through me.

I pulled my lips away. "Faster, Nico. Faster. Make me come." My voice was barely more than gasping breaths.

Taking my words to heart, he crashed his hips into me. Explosions of ecstasy started to shake me to my core. Even when I'd been in heat, it had been nothing like this. It kept building bigger and bigger inside me. There was fear as well as excitement as I was desperate for the release.

"I love you, Maddy," Nico groaned softly into my ear.

I dug my nails into his back, feeling myself about to slip past the point of no return. "I love you, Nico. I love you so much."

Nico stiffened, and his hips moved spastically against me as he came. He called out an inarticulate moan of pleasure. Hearing him come was all it took for me to crash down into rapture. Everything muscle and nerve I possessed clenched and unclenched as wave upon wave of ecstasy rocked me. I cried out his name, then screamed as it kept going. For a moment, I thought I might black out from the unending pleasure.

Finally, sticky with sweat and gasping, we collapsed together. I didn't even realize it when we fell asleep in each other's arms. I drifted in and out of sleep all night. Even then, it was one of the most restful and rejuvenating nights of my life.

When I woke the next day, I could sense the shift in the air. Even inside our bedroom, locked away from the outside world, I could smell the reek of testosterone and adrenaline. The rest of the pack was awake, and they all knew what was coming. Anxiety and fear were laced through the other scents.

Nico kissed me before he got out of bed and dressed to go check on all the final preparations. After he left, I pulled on my robe and collapsed back into bed. Part of me wanted to do what Nico was doing—go out and check on everyone. I was the alpha's mate, so it was probably expected, but the bigger part of me wanted to stay here, insulated from the impending horror.

Ten minutes later, there was a knock at my bedroom door. Frowning, I said, "Come in."

Sinthy slipped in, glancing guiltily at me. "Sorry. I hope you weren't still asleep."

I sat up in bed. "Really? I'm surprised I was able to sleep at all last night. What's up?"

From behind her back, she pulled a familiar object. The dark wooden box that contained the vial. She stepped forward and held it out to me, staring deeply into my eyes. With a bit of hesitancy, I reached forward and took it. I didn't think I could have given anything more reverence.

"You'll know when the time is right," Sinthy said. "You'll know what you need to do."

The box seemed heavier than it should have. Like it held the weight of the world within its six sides. That was probably appropriate since, for us, it basically did hold our whole world. Our final, last, and best weapon.

I tucked the box under the bed, wishing I could carry it with me the entire day, but that wasn't practical.

"When you're ready, come downstairs. I have something I want to show you," Sinthy said as she left.

Even though it was something I never thought I'd have to think about, I chose an outfit I thought would work well for both fighting and running. The butterflies in my stomach were going crazy, and I wondered how I'd ever get through the day if I was already this stressed out. Once I pulled my sneakers on, I went downstairs. At the base of the stairs, I noticed what Sinthy had for me. She stood next to a very worried Maxwell.

"Maddy, I'll be out with the others during the battle," Sinthy said.

"Right." I nodded. "I wouldn't want you anywhere else."

Sinthy gestured to Maxwell. "While I'm out there, Max here is going to act as your bodyguard."

I raised my eyebrows and smiled at him, delighted when he blushed in response. "Really?"

"I've been working with him on his powers, teaching him to control them. I'm confident he can do what's necessary."

Sinthy turned to look at him, her gaze intent. "You protect this house and especially protect Maddy. Do you understand that?"

Max took a few deep breaths. Still looking nervous as hell, he nodded. "I will. I understand." He looked up at me, and I witnessed the determination in his eyes. "I'll do whatever is necessary to protect you, Maddy. I promise."

Sinthy looked at me, one eyebrow raised in question.

I nodded, smiling warmly at Max. "Sounds good to me."

I was grateful there'd be a witch to protect me, but my mind drifted back upstairs to the box I had hidden under my bed. I hoped this young man was all that I'd need to stay safe. But at the back of my mind, I worried that I would need even more than what he had at his fingertips to survive. To save my loved ones.

Chapter 29 - Nico

Sinthy was just leaving the house when my mother and I reached it. I met her at the door right as she opened it.

"Oh, Nico," she said in surprise. "I didn't think you'd be here for a few more minutes."

Glancing inside, I saw Maddy was in the living room with Maxwell. Gabriella was coming down the stairs.

"Yeah," I said. "I wanted to get my mother here before... well, before."

"Come on in," Sinthy said, sweeping her hand back into the house and smiling at my mom.

Maddy smiled and waved her over. Mom went, giving her a hug. Whatever negativity had once been between them had vanished completely, and that pleased me. There was too much at stake to worry about such petty things.

"I put an additional ward around the house," Sinthy said. "Gabriella, Maddy, and your mom will be here. It's as safe as I can make it. Max is going to stay with them and protect them." Sinthy gave me a knowing look. "Assuming it comes to that. Hopefully, it won't."

"Thank you."

It seemed trite to say it that way. Sinthy had done so much for us, there should be more to say than *thank you,* but I wasn't sure if I'd ever have the words to express what she meant to me and my pack. She'd nearly killed herself to save us and Sebastian during the last attack. She'd put on a brave face and had since recovered, but I'd never seen someone look so close to death and still survive.

"Guys, I need a minute with Maddy." I took her hand and walked over to the quiet corner of the kitchen.

"Is everything okay?" Maddy asked.

"Yeah, I think so. I wanted to talk to you for a minute. Before… well, you know. Things are about to get crazy."

What I refused to say, but what I was worried about, was that this might be the last time we got to speak to each other. There was a possibility, as awful as it was to admit, that one of us might not survive the day.

"Are you going to be okay here? Everything locked up and ready?"

Maddy nodded. "Yeah. Abi should be here in a minute. We're all going to hole up here."

"Good. Javi got here with the others about thirty minutes ago. He said there are lots of people he didn't recognize in Clearidge. I think a bunch of people came to heed Viola's call. I'm worried."

"What's our final number?" Maddy asked, glancing out the window at the group of shifters slowly assembling in the field.

"Nothing official, but Diego and Mateo said they were fairly sure at least three thousand shifters came to join the cause."

Even saying those words made my head spin. Three thousand shifters. From all over the country. Canada and south of the border too. If you'd told me a year ago that this was going to happen, I never would have believed it, but here we were. My makeshift army was assembling like some sort of medieval battle.

Maddy placed her hands on my cheeks and forced me to make eye contact. "Promise me you'll be careful. That you'll stay safe and be smart."

I looked into her hopeful eyes and tried to forget what had happened in Paris and the bullets that had hurtled toward me. The fact that, without Sinthy, I'd be dead. I swore I'd be more careful, and I intended to keep that pledge.

Putting my hands on hers, I nodded. "I promise. As long as you do the same."

With nothing else to say, Maddy leaned forward and brushed a soft kiss over my lips. I took her by the arm and walked her out the front door. I'd have to leave her at the steps, but I wanted to see her as long as possible. I really didn't want to leave her, but there was nothing else to be done. We only had these last few moments before our world got turned upside down.

If I'd been hoping for a few more seconds of calm, I was sorely mistaken. As soon as we stepped outside, Sebastian came jogging up the path toward the house. That would have been fine, but from the other side of the path, Abi was heading to the house as well. Maddy and I shared a look as the two finally spotted each other.

Abi and Sebastian froze ten feet apart, staring at each other. It could go either way. Would they continue needling and poking each other? Would they bury whatever hatchet there was to bury? Would they ignore each other and try to act like nothing had ever happened?

Right when I thought they were never going to do anything, Abi stalked straight toward Sebastian. Her eyes were dark and intense. I was a split-second away from leaping forward. I truly thought she might attack Sebastian, but Maddy clenched my hand tight, holding me in place.

Abi reached forward and grabbed Sebastian by the shirt collar, shaking him gently.

"If you try to die on me again, I swear to Go,d I'll never forgive you. Be careful."

Sebastian looked confused at first, but that faded and was replaced by a warm and happy smile. He chuckled. "I'll be careful."

Then he leaned forward and kissed her. Abi wrapped her arms around his neck and kissed him right back. I let out a relieved sigh. I was happy the two of them had finally gotten their shit together. Though, it was annoying that it took Sebastian almost dying for them to get to this point.

Sinthy stepped out the door, and I knew before she even spoke what she was going to say. Her eyes were stern, but nerves danced in them.

"She's coming. I can sense her," Sinthy said.

Viola. It was happening. She was on the way, and God only knew what horrors she'd bring with her.

"Okay, Abi, Maddy? I need you to get inside," I said, then kissed Maddy one final time. I placed both my hands on her stomach, cradling our unborn child. "You stay put. I'll see you soon," I said, even though I couldn't promise that was true.

The vial was in the house. I could almost feel its pulsating power. I prayed things wouldn't go so poorly that we'd have to use it. Though, I had to admit, it was nice to know we had one last trick up our sleeve if we needed it.

Once Maddy and Abi were locked inside, Sinthy and I walked toward the massive group of shifters gathered at the battlefield. Anxiety permeated the air around the crowd. However ready they were to fight, they were scared. At least they understood what was at stake. My eyes widened as the thousands of shifters turned to watch my approach. Never in all my life did I think I'd be leading an army. It was awe-inspiring yet terrifying.

I nudged Sinthy as we got close. "I want to speak to them. Can you like… amplify my voice or something?"

Sinthy grinned and rolled her eyes. "You could at least ask for something a little more difficult."

I frowned. "Does that mean yes?"

"Yes. Nico. I've got you taken care of."

A pick-up truck was parked in the clearing, and I climbed up into the bed to look down at everyone. Sinthy raised a hand and waved it toward me.

When I opened my mouth to speak, it sounded like I was talking into a microphone with speakers strewn around the field to bring my voice to everyone in attendance, no matter how far away.

"Viola is on her way," I said as the crowd quieted. "I want to thank you for joining us here. I don't think you'll ever know what it means to my pack and me that all of you have chosen to come here for this final fight." I gazed across the multitude of faces and tried not to wonder how many wouldn't live to see another day.

"I feel, deep in my heart, that we will win this day. Tomorrow, when the news reports what happened here, they are going to tell a story. A story about how a few thousand shifters stood up to face a threat. It is not only a threat to our kind but to the whole world. For decades to come, history will remember what we do here today. You will be remembered as the brave few who stood up and fought back against a force that wants nothing more than to see us vanish from the face of the earth."

The crowd began to murmur, and I saw my father's face light up with a smile. I pointed toward the gate where our enemy would meet us soon.

"The royals think they'll win. They think they'll crush us and destroy our race. They think they will erase us from history and then continue doing all the horrible things they've been doing." I curled my hand into a fist and raised it high overhead. "When they step foot on these pack lands? They'll see they bit off more than they could chew. Those who survive will know that they were on the wrong side of history. When they go to sleep each night, they will be haunted by nightmares of the battle that unfolds here today. They will wake in a cold sweat and regret the day they ever tried to say to us that *we don't deserve to live.'* My voice was gaining volume, enhanced both by Sinthy's spell and my passion. It reverberated across the entire pack lands, so loud I wondered if Maddy could hear me.

"I want you to look at everyone to your right and left and know that they are here to defend not only themselves but you and yours. Today, on this patch of ground, there is one pack. One species. We are the last line of defense against the darkness—against the shadow that would fall upon us and eradicate us. This is where it stops. It ends here. As God is my witness, they will know this day as the day shifters stood up and said *no more.*" I looked at the crowd once more. "Do you believe?"

The next moment, I was nearly knocked backward from the scream of agreement that erupted from the army of shifters. The truck on which I stood vibrated under my feet. My chest filled with the rumble of shouts, roars, and bellows of agreement.

I climbed down, and Sinthy and I headed to the gate. There were a half dozen police cars sitting at the gate. Sinthy lowered the barriers enough for me to walk out to meet the Clearidge sheriff. He looked beyond me at the huge fighting force, and his face paled.

"Uh... Mr. Lorenzo? I'm Sheriff Grand. I need you and your people to disperse. There's word of a fairly large force heading this way. We'll be handling that. I don't want any fighting to happen in my city. Do you understand that?"

With a look over my shoulder at my army, I said, "Sheriff, even if I wanted them to, there's no way they'd leave. I also don't think you have the manpower to stop what's coming."

He grumbled and pointed a finger at my chest. "Now, hang on a minute. You don't dictate terms to me. I've put a call into the area National Guard for backup. We'll be fine."

"What was the response?" I said.

Grand frowned. "Huh? Response to what?"

"The National Guard. Did they say they were coming?"

His face started going red. "Well... they... well, they said they'd get back to me, but I know for a fact this is precisely what they are used for. They'll be here."

"Sheriff," Sinthy said. "The government wants this to end. They know this fight is the only way that will happen. They aren't sending anyone. One way or another, they want this done."

The sheriff laughed, but I could tell it was forced. He looked more panicked by the second.

"You expect me to believe that the US Government wants a fucking bloody battle to take place on United States soil?"

"Pragmatism, Sheriff," Sinthy said with a shrug. "It's what governments are good at."

As a distant rumble became audible, all three of us looked down the road. It was the sound of dozens of cars, trucks, and vans headed straight toward us. The sheriff looked like he wanted to puke.

"This isn't your fight, Sheriff," I said. "Go on. This is for us to take care of."

He glanced at us, then back down the road and back again before taking his hat off and slapping it on his thigh.

"Goddamn it." He pointed at me as he left. "Don't say I didn't try."

He and the other deputies got into their cars and sped down the road. I watched as they passed the lead car. It was, of course, a shiny black limo. Of course, Viola would ride in style—even to war.

Above us, new helicopters and possibly military choppers hovered into view. Sinthy raised her hands, and a new ward descended over us. The aircraft vanished from view, but the sunlight still streamed in as though nothing had changed.

"Did you make them disappear?" I asked, looking up in wonder.

"No. We can't see them, and they can't see us. As you said, this is our fight. No one else needs to see this."

I nodded in approval and looked at the cars pulling in. I should have been surprised at the sheer number of anti-shifter activists that had hooked themselves to Viola's train, but I wasn't. Part of me pitied them. Many were probably deluded by fear that had been instilled in them since they were children. As much as I wanted to spare those who had been led down the wrong path, it wouldn't be possible. My family, my pack, and my friends' lives were at stake. These people had been given plenty of time and information to make a better decision. They'd come here with blood on their mind. Unfortunately, they would reap what they sowed.

The limo came to a stop in front of the other cars. The driver stepped out and opened the back door. Viola slid gracefully out of the backseat. She wouldn't participate in the fight. The woman was too selfish to ever put herself in harm's way. She'd dressed the part, at least—not in the silly military fatigues she'd worn in some of her propaganda videos. No, instead, she wore a bright blood-red business suit. At least she wore flat shoes, though I wouldn't have been surprised had she walked toward me in stiletto heels.

From behind me, my entire fighting force growled at the sight of her. The anti-shifter army had begun to pile out of their vehicles, and it was a broad spectrum of people. There were hillbillies with stained jeans and red trucker hats, but there were also people who looked like they would be at home in a law office or accounting firm. There were women who appeared to have probably dropped their kids off at daycare before coming to kill shifters, and everything in between.

Viola's force glared at us with disgust and revulsion but also surprise. There were several looks of anxiety and fear in her group. They obviously hadn't thought this many shifters would be present at the battle. Viola pulled her dark sunglasses away, and behind her stoic calm, I picked up on the hesitant worry in her eyes as she, too, took in the army at my back. She'd probably been anticipating several wolf packs, but seeing so many different species together as one force obviously threw her off her stride.

Sensing the fear in the crowd, a huge number of my army shifted into their animal forms. Lions, bears, panthers, alligators, wolves, and a half dozen others snarled, snapped, roared, and hissed at them. Even I was intimidated by the sound. It was not surprising when several of the humans, facing a force far bigger and more terrifying than they'd expected, turned and ran. A few dozen at most, but it was good to see. The rest of Viola's force looked even more nervous as some of their allies sprinted up the road rather than face near-certain death.

"I warned you," I called out to Viola. "I told you this wouldn't end the way you wanted it to end."

Viola's lips peeled back in a sneer of disgust. "It doesn't matter. You can have all the filthy animals you want at your back, but God, nature, and humanity know that I will come out victorious. Where is my son?"

I glanced behind me, and fifty yards away on the porch of my house, the young man stood, arms at his sides, as he looked over the battlefield, ready to protect the women inside.

Viola saw him, then turned and snapped her fingers at her driver. The big, beefy man opened the back door, and two younger children climbed out. Their eyes were wide as saucers as they took in the scene around them.

Viola grinned at me. "Have my son come down here. Right now."

"Unfortunately, that won't be possible. He has his own duties to attend to," I said.

Viola's smile grew as brittle as glass. "Excuse me? What duties would a prisoner have?"

I crossed my own arms. "I never said he was a prisoner. He's chosen to stay with us. It was his choice."

If Viola had been a cartoon, steam would have spurted out of her ears. The look of shock, rage, and disbelief was so evident that it was almost comical.

Without looking back at the driver, Viola said, "Duncan? Plan A."

The driver slid his hand into his suit, pulled out a pistol, and pressed it into the ear of the youngest child—a pretty girl who looked much like Maxwell.

I raised a hand. "Wait!"

The man grinned at me and cocked the gun. Sinthy was beside me, but I wasn't sure even her reflexes and powers would be enough to stop a bullet at such a close range.

As though she was reading my mind, Viola turned her wicked grin on Sinthy. "Don't think about it, you little hex-casting bitch. We may not understand all your godless powers, but we were able to create a few weapons that even you can't work your magic on. Try if you want, but those bullets *will* find their mark no matter what you do."

Sinthy hissed a breath of frustration. "Damn."

Feet slammed into the grass behind me. I grimaced and closed my eyes, knowing who it was. I'd have done the same had it been one of my brothers.

Maxwell skidded to a halt beside me, his breath leaving him in heavy gusts. "Stop. Please, Mother. Don't hurt her. I'm begging you."

"Beg all you want, you filthy fucking traitor," Viola spat. "If you want these little shits back, you need to fight by my side today. Make your choice. If you decide to align yourself with these vermin, then little Madeline and Devon here will be the first to die. You'll watch as my man there splatters their brains all over my limo, and then you'll die next. Make your choice, boy. Family? Or filth?"

Glancing at Maxwell and knowing he had no other real choice, I said, "It's up to you. I won't hold it against you. Family is everything. Pack is everything. Do what you must."

Maxwell's eyes were wet with tears as he looked from his siblings to Viola and back to Sinthy and me. She nodded sadly at him, but then Maxwell looked at the house.

"But I made a promise. Maddy and the others. I *promised*." The last word sounded so tortured that it broke my heart. He wanted to do the right thing, and that made me loathe Viola all the more.

I clapped a hand on his shoulder. "It's fine. It'll be all right, Max."

Shoulders sagging in defeat, he turned to Viola. "I'll do it."

Viola snapped her fingers again, and the driver thrust the children forward. Madeline almost tripped as she stumbled into Maxwell's arms. The boy, Devon, ran to his older brother, and all three of them huddled into a tight embrace. Max whispered something to them and pointed back to the house. The kids fled and sprinted to my house. Gabriella, Mom, and Maddy stood ready to greet them. When the kids reached them, Gabriella picked one up, and my mother scooped the other child into her arms. Maddy stared at us, and even at that distance, I could see her eyes flashing with fury.

"Oh, there's our little wolf princess," Viola said cheerily. She raised her voice to shout toward Maddy. "I'll be making sure you're the last one breathing, dear. I want you to watch all these mongrels die. Then, right before I slit your pretty little throat and take all that valuable blood of yours, you'll know you've lost."

That threat was all I needed for my rage to overwhelm me. I growled low and deep in my throat as I shifted. Behind me, my army sensed that it was time. As I ran toward Viola's group, the sound of thousands of feet, paws, and growls followed me as my own force descended.

Viola's driver hustled her out of the way as her own army swarmed toward us. She vanished into a sea of angry, screaming faces. When the two armies slammed into each other, it sounded like the end of the world.

Chapter 30 - Maddy

I stumbled backward as Gabriella and Nico's mom took the children inside. The battle exploded across the field as I slammed the door shut. I rushed to the bay window to look down on the fight. It was the most horrible thing I'd ever seen. Even through the walls, the staccato sound of gunfire, the screams of rage and pain, and the howls of the shifter army were so loud it was like the battle was happening inside the house.

As bad as it was, I couldn't look away. My heart ached as I watched bodies fall to the ground, writhing in pain. It was gruesome and terrible. Movies and books didn't do an actual battle justice. This was a nightmare.

When Nico and Sinthy had left, I'd gone upstairs and grabbed the vial. I wanted it near me at all times if something went wrong. Sliding my hands into my pocket, I curled my fingers around the glass container as I watched my loved ones fight.

Nico was my main concern, but I kept trying to steal glances at Sinthy, Sebastian, Luis, and Felipe—all the people I'd grown so close to. I was desperate not to lose any of them. I'd never be able to deal with the guilt.

The battle was pure chaos, and it was hard to pick out who I was looking for. A large group of humans breaking away from the fight broke my focus. They ran, limped, and hobbled back to the cars and gates. They were in over their heads, and some of them looked like they realized it. Running was better than dying. That gave me a sliver of hope. Maybe the shifter army could end this quickly, with as little bloodshed as possible.

A stray bullet slammed into the wooden posts of the front porch, jolting me.

"Get down. Everyone stay low!"

Everyone, including the children, fell into a crouch. The children huddled around and hugged Gabriella. Abi,

Nico's mother, and my mom were holding each other beside them.

Needing to see what was happening, I I peeked over the windowsill to keep an eye on the fighting. I'd been trying to find Viola and Maxwell, but they were nowhere to be seen. If I had to guess, Viola was using Max to protect her in some way with a forcefield, invisibility, or something similar. There was no way she was anywhere near the battle. She wouldn't want to risk breaking a nail. They'd probably retreated down the main road a bit and were watching the fight from a distance like I was.

My wolf thrashed inside my mind. The sounds and smells of battle riled her up. She was anxious, pacing and whining, desperate to join the fight. I tried to calm her to no avail. She couldn't be consoled. Frowning, I realized she was trying to tell me something. There was something she sensed. Something was wrong. Very wrong, but I couldn't quite tap into what she was feeling.

Not caring about the battle anymore but desperate to get a better look at things, I inched over and opened the door.

"Maddy, no!" Mom screamed.

Ignoring her, I crawled out onto the porch, closing the door behind me. The sound of battle was even stronger now. I gazed out at the fight. The shifters seemed to have the upper hand. They were pushing the humans back to the gate. We'd managed to prevent their force from splitting up to encircle our group. It didn't look like it could have gone any better.

Then the wind shifted. The breeze coming from the forest surrounded us instead of the gate. A bolt of fear shot through me. My head snapped around to look toward the forest. Sinthy had dropped all the wards. This had been the final battle, and we'd assumed Viola would bring her entire force to bear here at the gate. We'd been wrong.

Understanding, fear, terror, and hopelessness tore through my mind in quick succession. Before I could scream or do anything to warn Nico and the others, dozens of men and women erupted from the trees around the battlefield. They carried weapons, but… not the typical machine guns or rifles. The weapons looked strange.

Another sound ripped my attention away from the reinforcements. The fighting was nearing the house, and I could hear Maxwell screaming. He was being pulled backward by Viola, who had a pistol to his head. Her bodyguard was there too, armed and blocking her. A patch of red spread across the bodyguard's stomach. One of the shifters had clawed him.

"No!" Maxwell screamed with such furious agony that I was sure my heart would shatter.

"Yes, goddamn it," Viola shouted and jammed the pistol harder into his head. "This is all you're good for. Now do it before I blow your traitor brains out."

My eyes widened, and everything seemed to slow down. Sinthy, at the edge of the fight, caught sight of Maxwell and Viola. She turned in time to see the reinforcements before she looked back at Maxwell.

Sinthy raised a hand, her terrified voice exploding out of her. "No."

Maxwell's lips formed the words *"I'm sorry."* Then he lifted his hands toward the intruders with the strange weapons. He murmured some kind of spell, and then the world exploded. An arc of lightning shot from his fingers. It crackled across the grass, then split into dozens of different smaller arcs until they slammed into the barrels of the strange weapons the anti-shifters had brought. The guns glowed bright, then they fired.

It didn't sound like regular gunfire. Instead of explosive popping sounds, there was a boom like thunder as the weapons fired. Sinthy, already seeking to understand what was about to happen, had pressed her hands into the ground to try and create a forcefield around the fighters. She succeeded—I saw the wavering shimmer in the air as the shield was raised, but most of the magic-infused bullets tore straight through her ward. It stopped maybe one in three. Even from as far away as I was, I could see shifters topple and fall. The bullets passed, magically, around or over the human fighters, leaving them unharmed. I'd never seen anything like it. In seconds, we'd lost our advantage. The humans were rallying and pressing our force backward, and we were in disarray. The shouts and screams of confidence from the shifters had turned into yelps and barks of fear and confusion.

Sweat trickled down my face as I watched the disaster unfold. Panic tore at my heart as I tried to find Nico in the frantic chaos. Luis, blood oozing from a wound in his leg, was back in his human form, limping away as he fired a pistol toward a group of humans following him. Felipe was being hauled backward, a knife sticking out of his leg. Sebastian, in wolf form, had him by the collar and was desperately trying to pull his friend to safety. He had deep gouges in his side as well. Sinthy sprinted across the field toward a man who was on his knees, bleeding from his sides. My breath caught in my throat. *Nico*.

The edge of the fighting was now less than twenty yards from our yard. We were being pushed back. Nico stumbled to his feet and spat a mouthful of blood on the ground as Sinthy put her hands on him, trying to heal him. My eyes burned with tears as I took stock of his injuries. He was cut in dozens of different places, his face and arms bruised. It looked like he may have been shot in the side.

"It's over, Nico!" Viola shouted, her gun still jammed into her son's face. Maxwell was openly weeping as she dragged him along. "I've won. You animals can't fight against our weapons." She pointed the gun toward Nico and Sinthy. "When you fall, they all follow. Cut off the head, and the serpent dies."

Sinthy, teeth bared and seething, threw up her hands, the air crackling around her. Immersed in magic, she never noticed the group of humans descending from behind. They swarmed the young woman, tearing her to the ground. Nico broke away, sprinting toward Viola. He dodged the volley of bullets she fired at him, almost as though he anticipated exactly where each would go. My mate was beautiful, like nothing I'd ever seen before. I watched, mesmerized, as he narrowed the distance between himself and Viola.

I almost didn't see the man with the rifle.

The humans grabbing and tearing at Sinthy were suddenly blasted away in all directions as the witch flashed some kind of spell that left her free. She stumbled to her knees, trying to get to her feet, then her eyes went wide with fear, the little color remaining in her complexion fading.

The only reason my gaze pulled away was because I caught sight of the red laser flashing in my peripheral vision. My eyes flicked over. A man in fatigues had his long-barreled rifle and laser sight aimed at Nico. I snapped my attention back to my mate just as a glaring red dot appeared on his chest. I opened my mouth to scream… but the gunshot silenced any noise I might have made.

Nico jerked backward, blood spraying from his chest, arms flailing as he twisted, spun, and then fell face-down in the grass.

He lay there, unmoving, and my vision blurred, then turned red. A crimson sheen descended on the world in front of me. Rational thought vanished. I could barely process the fury and grief that coiled around my heart. My jaw creaked because I was clenching my teeth so hard. Unbidden, my wolf leaped forward, filling my mind with her own hatred and bloodlust. Now was not the time to think of what-ifs. It was time. There would be no second chance.

Viola turned to me. Her lip curled in victory. She had her mouth open to gloat but froze when she saw what I held—what I was raising to my lips. Her smile faded, replaced by fear, anger, and terror flashing over her face in quick succession. The sudden realization that she'd miscalculated was written all over her face in that last instant before the glass vial touched my lips. She never believed I would have the guts to do it. She never thought, in a million years, I'd have the nerve to actually use the weapon. Proving her deadly wrong, I put the vial to my lips, tilted my head back, and let the thick liquid pour down my throat.

Chapter 31 - Nico

Grass. I could smell grass. That was my first thought when my eyes opened. My face was pressed into the lawn. My fingers curled into the blades of green. I pulled in a ragged breath, but that sent me into a coughing fit. A bolt of pain shot through me, so excruciating I couldn't even cry out in agony. Rolling gingerly to my side, I looked down and saw where I'd been shot. The bullet had hit me in the chest. I should be dead, except whoever had shot me had hit me at a bad angle. The bullet had slammed into the muscle beside my sternum, traveled through the flesh of my chest, and exited beside my nipple. It hadn't gone through my ribcage, but it still hurt like a motherfucker. I'd been shot in the chest and had somehow lived.

The pain was like a never-ending ripple of heat searing across my chest and torso. I could barely think above the agony. The battle around me sounded dull and indistinct, and I tentatively touched my ears to check if I was somehow suddenly wearing earmuffs. As bad as the injury was, I wasn't dead. Not yet. I still had a chance to fight. That was if I could move. I tried to brace myself and get up, but it was like a blazing rope of fire being pulled taut around my ribs. Gasping, I collapsed onto my back. An instant later, Sinthy's cool fingers brushed over my cheeks. My blurry vision righted as I focused on the dirty, blood-smeared face hovering above mine.

"Don't move," she muttered as she ran her hands across my body.

Her magic felt like static electricity as she healed me as best she could. The bullet in my side popped out of my skin and tumbled to the ground, and the wound in my chest went from agonizing pain to brutal discomfort.

"Maddy?" I croaked.

"She—"

A pulse of power cut off whatever she'd been about to say. I was certain this was what it felt like when you were near a nuclear blast. The powerful surge took my breath away. The sounds of battle died away as all the combatants noticed it.

"Well… shit," Sinthy muttered.

A deafening roar filled the pack lands. It reverberated into every inch of the battlefield, and I thought I noticed the earth beneath me shake. It was an alpha's roar, but like none I'd ever heard before. I was an alpha, and even I trembled at the power of it.

Having regained some of my strength, I rose up on my hands and knees and saw her. I wobbled to my feet and gazed at Maddy as she stalked forward. All around me, shifters and humans alike gawked at her.

She wasn't a werewolf. No, she was the biggest damned wolf I'd ever seen. Her shoulders stood taller than a horse. Her head was nearly as large as a grizzly bear's. Pools of blood seemed to have replaced her eyes, they were so red. Bright, razor-sharp teeth glinted in the sun as she panted. They looked like knives sticking out of her jaws.

Viola took a hesitant step backward. "My God," she whispered. Then she pointed at Maddy and screamed, "Kill the beast! Kill her!"

The humans didn't react. None of them attacked. Fear had paralyzed the crowd. Weapons slid from several of their grasps, clattering to the ground.

"Run."

The guttural voice traced an icy finger down my spine. I turned to see Maddy stalking toward us, and as she opened her maw, saliva dripped from the massive fangs, and the voice again erupted from her throat, though the wolf lips and tongue didn't move.

"Run." That single syllable sounded ferocious and terrifying.

The sound was deep and almost seemed to come from within my own head rather than through my ears. It frightened me. My mouth hung open as I watched Maddy walk ever closer to the group of fighters. The fiery eyes did nothing to alleviate my fears.

"Any human who wants to live should run. Now."

A rustle of shouts and screams erupted from the group of human fighters as they took in this gigantic, talking, blood-eyed monster wolf walking toward them. At least half of Viola's army tucked tail and sprinted back to the gates and woods, scattering like the wind.

"Cowards," Viola screeched at their backs as they ran. Not a single one looked back.

The remaining humans must have been either incredibly brave or terribly stupid. It was the latter.

They screamed in rage and rushed toward Maddy. The shifters were all like me, rooted to the ground beneath their feet from the shock of seeing her in her true form. I wanted to run to her aid, to attack the ones running at her, but I seemed to be stuck.

It turned out she didn't need my help.

The first group ran at her, and she lashed out with a massive front paw—damn near as big as the lid of a trashcan—and slammed it into three men, sending them rolling across the ground in a bone-crunching tumble. More rushed at her, but Maddy swatted them away like annoying insects.

Then the gunfire erupted again. I flinched, finally pulled from my stupor as bullets slammed into Maddy's hide. The shots didn't seem to penetrate her, but that didn't quench the fire that erupted in my heart. The sight of my mate and my unborn child being shot at sent me into a rage I'd never experienced. I leaped forward, shifting in mid-air, and barreled into the midst of the shooters. I snapped and bit at them, my teeth ripping at flesh, tearing fingers, ears, and appendages free from bodies.

Once the three men who'd shot at her had been taken care of, Maddy's huge wolf head nuzzled against me. I spun in place and pressed my nose into her side, smelling her, listening. I could still hear our baby's heartbeat. Strong and steady. I looked into the scarlet orbs that were her eyes, and... somehow... I could see my mate inside them. More powerful than any shifter I'd ever met. Stronger and more dominant than anything in history—maybe not even Edemas himself had been this strong.

More shots erupted, and I watched as five slugs slammed into Maddy's side, but the bullets simply fell to the ground, warped and broken. Maddy was unhurt. After a final nuzzle against my mate, she and I both leaped into battle. The other shifters, seeing the tides had turned, joined us. The battle became more of a brawl than anything else—a desperate scrabble by the humans to try and do anything against us. They were unsuccessful. Whatever that vial had done to Maddy, she looked damn near indestructible. She waded into gunfire, shielding me and the others with her body. Her gigantic fangs tore at arms, legs, and necks.

Even through the bloodbath, I heard Viola screaming at the humans to keep fighting.

"Burn her!" she howled. "Burn her like we burned her filthy ancestor."

She wheeled around, looking for help, but her bodyguard had fled. I spotted Maxwell running to my house, to his siblings. Viola was alone, but that still didn't seem to deter her. As I walked toward her, she looked more angry than scared—defiant to the end. The humans were backing away, finally realizing that fighting was pointless with Maddy on our side. They crumpled to their knees, fatigue, heartbreak, and defeat clear in each of their expressions. The dumbasses had really thought they were saving the world. I pitied them for being so easily misled.

Viola snarled at them, her nose wrinkled in disgust. Her perfectly manicured nails twisted into claws as she screamed at them. "Get up. Damn you, get up. The fate of the world rests on us. Fight, for God's sake!"

She looked maniacal. Her hair was disheveled, hanging in tangled strands across her eyes, she'd lost a shoe in the scuffle, and she seemed on the edge of a breakdown. I shifted back to my human form and strode toward her.

"It's over, Viola," I said.

She leveled a glare at me. Anything resembling sanity had vanished from her eyes. Whatever thread had been holding her mind together must have snapped when she realized she was going to lose.

"Fuck them. I'll end this myself." Viola sneered as she raised her gun.

The barrel lifted straight toward me, angled to aim right between my eyes. The bitch was going to shoot me. Probably in some hope that it would give her the victory she wanted. Maddy, however, was having none of that. A howl that nearly split my eardrums burst from her throat as she raced into the field of fire and rushed Viola. Viola's hand trembled as she turned the gun from me and pointed right at Maddy's head. Her finger twitched on the trigger as she fired, but that bullet, too, fell away, leaving Maddy uninjured.

Dropping the weapon, Viola screamed into Maddy's face. Not a scream of terror or horror—one of rage and hate. Maddy snapped her jaws and latched onto Viola's arm, then jerked her head around. I heard Viola's arm shatter, and a yelp of agony burst out of her as she hit the grass with a loud thud.

Almost at once, Viola stumbled to her feet, cradling her shattered arm. She was covered in dirt and grass but was still trying to hold herself up like the royalty she thought she was.

"This settles nothing," she shouted. "I'll be back with a bigger army. I'll never stop. Not until every one of you filthy animals has been wiped off the planet. Do you hear me? You'll never be safe. Your children will die. Your mothers and fathers will die. I. Will. Not. Stop."

Max had stepped out onto the porch, gripping his siblings' hands as he watched the end of the battle. Viola saw him and held her good hand out toward him.

"Max. Come to Momma. Get us out of here," she said. The bitch even had the gall to snap her fingers at him.

Max ignored her, turning his face like he hadn't heard anything.

Viola knew we couldn't let her get away. She was too insane and driven ever to stop. The nightmare would never end unless she was locked up—or dead.

"I am your mother! You will do as I say, you little fucking bastard."

Max turned, ushering his brother and sister back inside, leaving Viola alone to face her fate. For the slightest of instants, I thought we could take pity on her, show her mercy and turn her over to the police. That option was removed for me in the blink of an eye.

With an audible *pop*, Sinthy appeared behind Viola. When the other woman turned to see who was behind her, she jolted at seeing Sinthy. The young witch glared down at Viola with a rage that broke my heart.

"This is for my parents," Sinthy hissed.

She slammed a palm into Viola's chest. A light as bright as lightning flashed, and I had to squint against the glare. Viola flew backward nearly ten feet and rolled to a stop at my feet. I looked down and gazed into the open, lifeless eyes of Viola Monroe.

Chapter 32 - Maddy

It was over. It was finally over. I would have jumped for joy, but I was still stuck in my beastly body. I wanted to run and jump into Nico's arms, but shifting out of this… whatever I was, was harder than usual shifting. Something about the body felt *right*. My wolf felt so at home in this body, she didn't want to give it up. As calmly as I could manage, I spoke to her.

The power excited her, as did the knowledge of what her father had been like. I understood that and told her that. I pushed my thoughts toward her, showing her how much I loved Nico and my family and friends and that I needed to go back to my human form to be with them. We were not *just* wolf, we were human and wolf bound in one body. We had to compromise.

A deep sense of understanding from her reached me, and her grip on the wolf loosened, allowing me to shift back. Even that was strange. It wasn't as simple as usual. Instead of flowing freely and easily between two bodies, it was more like I had to drag myself out of a collapsed tent without knowing where the exit was.

Once I was back in my own body, I staggered toward Nico, lightheaded. I collapsed against him just as he closed his arms around me.

As tired as I was, I still remembered seeing him get shot. I ran my hands across his body, looking for wounds and blood.

"Maddy, it's fine. I'm all right," he said. "The bullet missed my vital organs. Sinthy nudged my healing along. It's okay. Take it easy and rest."

I sighed with relief and looked down at Viola's body. Part of me wanted to be childish and petty and spit on her, but I was a better person than she'd been. Instead, Nico and I turned and limped to our house. The rest of our army had started to spread out, assisting the injured and gathering the dead.

Sinthy strode beside us. As we got to the door, she gestured for us to stop.

"I'm leaving. I'll be back in a day or two."

Nico looked baffled, and I could do nothing but stare at her.

"Where are you going?" Nico asked.

Sinthy glanced back at Viola's body. "I need to take care of some stuff. Not all her laboratories have been found. That research can't get out. I need to destroy every trace of what she and her scientists worked on."

Although I saw her point, there was still so much to do here. So many injured and hurt people. When I mentioned that, she gave me a knowing grin.

"Maxwell will help. I've taught him how to use healing spells. He'll do fine." She put her hand on my shoulder. "A day or two tops. I'll see you soon."

Before we could protest, she was gone, leaving behind a swirl of air. Nico got me inside. As badly as I wanted to help with the cleanup, I was too exhausted to do more than lie on the couch. Gabriella, Mom, and Nico's mother doted on me like I was an invalid.

The next several days were much busier than anticipated. The sheriff, while afraid to take part in the battle, hadn't completely run off with his tail between his legs. He and his men had dropped back and managed to detain nearly all the fleeing attackers. An impressive feat when he'd only had a hundred and the anti-shifter activists numbered over two thousand.

The media were desperate to interview Nico and me. Sinthy's blocking spell hadn't allowed the helicopters overhead to see what happened, and it seemed like every hour, Nico and I were on video with one news channel or another. After a virtual interview on *The Today Show,* I stopped keeping track. Next came the government.

Representatives from the FBI, state police, and the NSA had all come to question us about the battle and the number of casualties. Nico and I were truly afraid that we might be brought up on charges. Dozens of people had died here. That didn't count the nearly five hundred humans and shifters who'd been injured or hurt in some way.

At the end of the week, we'd received the most interesting phone call of our lives. The president of the United States called us to personally extend his apologies and informed us he would be signing a pardon for any and all shifters, humans, or witches who had helped defend the Lorenzo Pack lands. After thanking him profusely, the call ended, and Nico looked at me.

"Am I dreaming? Did that really happen?"

I nodded, my cheeks starting to hurt from smiling so much. "It did. At least we aren't going to jail."

The humans that the sheriff and his men had arrested couldn't say the same thing. They'd all been detained at MacDill Airforce base, and their charges were... heavy. Most of them would probably never see daylight again. The government wanted to send a very clear and *very* strong message to anyone else who wanted to follow in Viola's footsteps. That tamped down and pretty much eradicated the online anti-shifter community. Even though the military had basically turned their backs on us to fend for ourselves on the day of the battle, they were holding up their end now that it was over.

Once the last of the interviews were over, Nico and I slept for days—literally days. We were so wiped that we only got out of bed to eat, drink, and use the bathroom. Even with all that sleep, I was still a bit tired. Changing into that massive monster of a wolf had taken everything out of me. Even my own wolf was hesitant to ever shift into that form again.

That brought forth the question of whether I actually *could* do it again. Would I eventually be able to do that on command? It was a frightening thought.

Nico and I emerged from our bedroom after a few days of rest and rejoined the pack. Sinthy had returned, her work complete—or so she said. The media reported that random factories and office buildings had mysteriously been destroyed practically overnight, and Sinthy had given us some half smiles when the reports came in.

The only way I could describe those initial days was... they were strange. Since the night I'd been attacked in my bar, everything had revolved around the royals, around Viola and her company. We'd been running from, hiding from, researching, planning, and orchestrating against them for so long that it was weird not to have some crisis. To keep us busy, we worked on figuring out how to do the one thing we didn't want to do.

The shifters had suffered a lot of deaths. Many from our pack as well as the ones who'd come to us, had perished, and Nico was planning a sort of memorial service. Nico's father liked the idea and offered to make the arrangements.

Donatello had returned, bringing financial aid for the repairs and rebuilding. He seemed upset that he'd missed out on the final battle. Almost like he felt guilty.

"I feel a bit like the one in a group project who did nothing but still got a good grade," he'd told Nico.

"Don, you've done more for us than you can imagine. One more fighter wouldn't have made any difference. Don't beat yourself up," Nico said, patting him on the arm.

Donatello bowed his head. "Be that as it may, I need to atone for my absence at such an inopportune time. Some paperwork will be arriving in the mail." Donatello gestured at me with a smile. "I've set up a college fund for the little wolf cub growing inside Maddy. I know you all are fairly well off, but..." He shrugged. "College is expensive, and I have money. It's the least I can do for friends."

After Donatello left to help Nico's brothers repair the fences that had been torn down by the retreating humans, I walked out and stood on the lawn. It was the exact spot where I'd watched Nico get shot and fall to the ground. I'd been so sure he was dead. So sure that the man I loved was gone that I hadn't even thought. I'd downed the vial with no heed of the consequences.

The image played in my mind on a loop. The laser dot, the sound of the gun, the spray of blood, and his lifeless body tumbling to the ground. It was all over, but the memory still brought a lump to my throat. I was weeping, and I was so caught up in my emotions, I never heard Nico walking up behind me.

He wrapped his arms around me from behind and shushed me. "It's okay. It's all okay now. I'm fine. Everything is fine now. It's over."

I turned in his arms and breathed in his scent. "I was so scared when I saw you get shot. I didn't even think of the consequences when I drank the vial. All I wanted was revenge. I thought she'd killed you."

Nico, bless him, let me vent my frustrations, worries, and anger. Finally, I got around to my biggest fear.

I looked into his eyes and said, "What if I'm always going to be that massive monster? Is that what I'll be every time I shift now?"

Nico shrugged. "I guess we could test the theory."

I winced. "I'm not sure. When I was like that… it was like I wasn't totally myself. My wolf wasn't fully in control either. It was almost like there was a third presence there. One that might have been as strong as both of us."

Nico brushed a strand of hair from my face and said, "No matter what, I'll always be there to ground you. If you have trouble changing back, I'll help you. Okay?"

"Okay." But I wasn't sure how much I believed it.

That night, after Nico had confirmed with his dad that all arrangements for the memorial services had been made, we went into the woods to test whether or not I was always going to be a monster. He led me to the same creek he'd brought me to months before when I was trying to form a connection with my wolf.

"I'll go first," Nico said. "Then you can change."

My hands were shaking violently. "All right."

Nico shifted and padded around in a circle, then came to sit on his haunches in front of me. I looked into his wolf eyes as he stared back at me. There was no judgment or expectation in his eyes. He was here to help me and nothing else. Here to support me as I tried to shift.

Taking a deep breath to calm myself, I reached out to my wolf and opened up to her. There was a single tremor of fear as she came forward and took control. The familiar, warm tingle flooded across my limbs as my body morphed. When I opened my eyes, I was relieved to find I was in my regular wolf form. I wasn't six feet tall, and my vision wasn't tinged with red. It was how it was supposed to be.

Nico and I took off at a trot that turned into a breakneck sprint. As the forest scents filled my nostrils, I realized something. I might not have been a monstrous Edemas-sized wolf, but I was different. My senses were more heightened, and it was like I was more in tune with my wolf than I ever had been before. I even overtook Nico in our race, leaving him in my dust—I'd never been able to do that before. The contents of the vial had changed me in more ways than one. Even though I wasn't the size of a polar bear anymore, I still felt like I was *more* than I had been. Maybe that had been Edemas's intention all along.

Once we'd exhausted ourselves on the run, we shifted back and lay in the grass of a small clearing. Nico was panting for breath.

"When the hell did you get so fast?"

I giggled. "Guess you'll need to step your game up, won't you?"

"Apparently," he said and settled his head on the grass.

After a few minutes of silence, I rolled over and rested my head on his chest. "I can't believe it's finally over. Can you?"

Nico shook his head. "Not really. I'm grateful it is, though. It's like we can finally breathe. Before, it was sort of like a belt was tied around our chests, squeezing tighter all the time. Like any second could be our last. This is… nice."

I trailed the tips of my fingers over his chest. "We can finally really start our lives together." Moving up, I kissed him. "I'm not sure if I've ever said this, but thank you for saving my life. I'd have been dead a long time ago if not for you."

Nico brushed my cheek with his knuckles. "You think I saved you?" He shook his head. "Maybe, but it goes both ways. You saved me too. I never realized how much I was missing until I had you. I was living a hollow life until the day I met you."

There was a pleasant tension in my chest when he said that. I was wanted and needed. He loved me. It was everything I'd ever hoped for and more. As the moon began to rise, I kissed him again.

Chapter 33 - Nico

A week after Maddy and I had our run in the woods, we held the memorial ceremony. Dad, Maddy, and I decided it wouldn't only be for the lives lost in the battle but for all the lives lost during the royals' rampage. I put the call out to all shifter packs and clans around the world who wanted to attend. I'd thought the influx of people who came for the battle had been big, but in the days leading up, every hotel and rental house within a two-hour drive was filled.

I hadn't completely understood how pervasive the royals' reach had been until shifters from as far away as Tokyo and South Africa came. The royals had ruined lives for centuries, and what had begun in Europe had spread like a plague across the globe.

We held the ceremony at my pack lands. The power of the land coursed through, reaffirming that it was the best place for it. It may have been one of the only places that held the true power of shifters and would do the ceremony justice.

The night of the ceremony, alphas and their entourages arrived in droves, along with the media. I'd wanted to keep them out, but it would be more trouble than it was worth. Besides, the world needed to see this. To know we were still here.

I said a few words, but I honestly couldn't remember what I said. Looking out on a sea of over ten thousand faces had sent shivers of anxiety through me. Whatever I'd said, it must have been good, as there was thunderous applause after I was done. Over the next hour, alpha after alpha went to the microphone and read prepared statements or simply read the names of those who'd been killed, tortured, or driven mad by Viola and her family. It was intense and heartbreaking, especially when a bear alpha from Colombia read a list of names of children killed in a small village. Back in the nineties, a blood test had shown one of the kids was a descendant of Edemas, but records weren't clear on which child. Rather than doing more research, Viola's father had sent mercenaries in to murder them all. It made me even more relieved that the entire family had been wiped out or arrested over the last several months.

At the end of the ceremony, Sinthy had used her magic to cast a dazzling display of fireworks into the sky. They rumbled and crackled across the sky, and everyone in attendance shifted to their animal form and cried out to the moon: growls, roars, and howls. Then we all rushed into the forest, running wild and exultant in our newfound freedom.

Adrenaline was pulsing through my body when we got back. Donatello had arranged an enormous feast. He'd flown in nearly a hundred different chefs and their teams and had to have spent at least half a million dollars on food. Our guests made their way to the huge tents that had been erected to accommodate the meal, but I had different ideas.

I found Maddy at the edge of the forest right as she was shifting. I took her by the hand and damn near carried her back to our house.

She giggled when I scooped her up and carried her through the front door and up the stairs. All I wanted was to have a few minutes alone with her. Now that the danger was gone, I wanted her. I wanted her more than I could ever comprehend.

In the bedroom, I kissed her. There'd never been a time when I'd desired her more. It was as though nothing could satisfy me but Maddy.

We panted as we tore at each other's clothes. She seemed equally as desperate for me to take her as I was to have her. Maddy kissed and sucked at my neck as I yanked my pants down. Once I was finally naked, I laid her on the bed and kissed her again, this time deeper than I had before. I wanted her to know exactly how much she meant to me.

"I love you," I whispered after pulling away.

Maddy ran her fingers through my hair. "I love you too."

We were safe. She and our baby were safe. I could truly believe that this was our happily ever after. We could lose ourselves in each other's bodies for a time. Nothing to worry about but our own love, our own passion. With that on my mind, I kissed her again.

Maddy's fingers ran along my side, down my hip, and across my ass. My breathing grew heavier with her touch. My cock was already throbbing as it lay nestled along her thigh. My own hand drifted down, finding her breast soft, supple, and growing fuller as her pregnancy progressed.

She broke the kiss to suck in a breath as my fingers slid across her nipple, each finger slipping slowly over the dark, puckered flesh. Maddy gripped my ass and pulled me closer.

"I want you inside me, Nico," Maddy whispered with her lips against my collarbone.

I rose onto my knees and gently nudged her legs apart, kissing each of her knees as I did. She looked so beautiful, lying there, looking up at me. I fisted my cock and placed it right at her opening. Maddy's eyes closed as I slid the head of my dick across her clit, down the wetness of her pussy, and back up again. I moved it up and down slowly, never quite sliding inside her.

When I thought she was about to burst, I pressed into her, sliding my full length into her warmth. It was an embrace that would never grow old. I lowered myself on top of her, feeling her breasts press into my chest, then moved my hips. Lifting my ass, I pulled almost free of her, then thrust back inside, letting her envelop me. We moved like that, over and over. Our lips brushing, her hands sliding along my body, my tongue flicking across her nipples. In time, it was like we'd become hypnotized by the movement and the pleasure of each other.

Maddy laid her head back on the pillow and slipped a hand down between us. I could feel her fingers rubbing at her clit. It was so erotic that I grew even harder. My desire urged me on, and I looked into Maddy's eyes as I started thrusting into her faster. The panting of my breath mixed with Maddy's groans of delight.

I was getting close. The rising pressure along my balls and cock increased by the second. I was going to explode at any moment, but I focused on holding off. Maddy's pleasure was my only thought. Then, she gasped, and her hips lifted to meet mine.

"I'm gonna come," she whispered.

I smiled and moved even faster, slamming into her with abandon, rushing toward my own orgasm.

"Look in my eyes, Maddy. I want to see you come."

Our eyes locked. I gazed deep into hers as her mouth fell open, and her body began to convulse and shiver. Her face went red as the power of her orgasm crashed over her.

The connection, the way our gazes held each other, and the way she moved, looked, and felt as she came sent me over the edge. My own climax rocked me to my core. Exquisite pleasure erupted through me, and I continued thrusting in and out of her until the last threads had faded away.

We collapsed in each other's embrace as sounds of the gathering outside filtered into the bedroom. Laughter, shouts of joy, and happiness. I'd been worried I'd never hear it again. After a half hour of enjoying each other, we reluctantly dressed and went down to join the others in their celebration.

Maxwell had disappeared with his siblings after helping to heal the severely injured fighters. There'd been no sign or word from him since. Sinthy hadn't seemed worried about it since her trace spell was still on him.

"I can find him at any time," she'd said as we cleaned up the mess from the memorial service.

"Why not find him now?" I asked.

"He probably needs some time. It's the first time in his whole life he's not had his demon of a mother in control."

That didn't alleviate my worry for him. He had so much to learn about his powers. I didn't want him getting into trouble. Plus, he was so young to have to worry about taking care of his brother and sister. Could he handle it on his own?

My concerns were put to rest a day later when Maxwell came walking up to my front porch, looking for all the world like a dog who was waiting for his master to strike him. His head was lowered, and he wouldn't meet my eyes. Maddy, Sinthy, and I came out to meet him. His little brother and sister were right behind him.

"Umm," Maddy said with a glance at the children. "Why don't you guys come with me?"

Maddy reached out to the children. At Maxwell's nod, the two kids hesitantly took Maddy by the hand and walked farther out in the yard with her to give us privacy to talk.

"I'm sorry I left," he said.

"Where did you go, Max?" I asked.

"I took my siblings somewhere safe. I also... well, I went to one of my mother's houses. A penthouse in Chicago. I remembered she had some money stashed there. Um, a *lot* of money. I, maybe, took it."

I chuckled. "Good for you. You deserve some kind of inheritance."

Max looked up in surprise. He was shocked that we weren't even batting an eye that he'd vanished for over a week.

"The only question I have," I said, "is why you returned. You don't owe us anything. Freeing you was an added bonus to defeating Viola."

Max licked his lips, and I watched as his eyes slid from mine over to Sinthy. She noticed and rolled her eyes.

"Lord," she groaned.

Maxwell's face went beet red, and he looked down at the ground, embarrassed. "No, it's not like that. I only want someone to keep teaching me how to use my magic."

"You want a mentor?" I offered.

Max nodded. "Yeah, basically. I want to control it. I want to do the magic justice. It belonged to someone very dear to Sinthy. I don't want that to go to waste."

His words hit hard. Sinthy was trying to hide how much they meant to her, but I could see the look in her eyes. She was remembering her mother. Although she'd gotten her revenge on Viola, there was still more healing to come. Perhaps working with Max could help.

Sinthy's face was a mask of contemplation. I couldn't read what she was going to decide, but I was curious. I found myself truly hoping that she would help Max. Regardless of his bloodline, the guy was decent. He'd been forced to do awful things, had been abused and experimented on, and somehow still found it in himself to be a good person. If anyone needed help and mercy, it was him.

Sinthy finally raised her hands in defeat. "Okay. I think I can *maybe* give you some help.

She turned to look at me. "As long as Nico is okay with you and your siblings staying in the pack lands."

I looked across the lawn at Maddy, who was chasing the two kids in some sort of game of tag. The boy had to be about ten or eleven, and the girl was a year or two younger. They were smiling and laughing. I also saw the big grin on Maddy's face as she played with them.

Glancing back at Sinthy and Maxwell, I said, "I think we can make that work."

Now that all the drama and danger were over, Maddy and I could finally get to the hospital to have the baby checked. Doc had done what he could in the pack lands, but without an ultrasound and other things, we wouldn't know how the baby was developing and if it was healthy.

Once the appointment was made, Maddy leaned over and nudged my shoulder.

"What are you hoping for?"

"Huh?"

Maddy laughed and punched me lightly. "The baby, dummy. Boy or girl? What are you hoping for."

That was one of the major things you were supposed to think about when you were having a baby, but it hadn't even crossed my mind. What I wanted didn't matter. Fate would determine that.

"Doesn't matter to me. All I want is a healthy baby. I don't care about gender. I'll love it the same no matter what."

Maddy looked genuinely taken aback. "Really? I thought for sure you'd say you wanted a boy. Someone to carry on the Lorenzo name. Then you could train him to take over and be the next alpha."

I shook my head. "No, I wouldn't force anyone to be alpha. That's an honor you should take willingly. It's what my dad did with my brothers and me. It worked out that I was the one who wanted it, and I was the oldest. If my child doesn't want that responsibility, then one of my brothers will surely have a son who will take over. I mean, I hope any son I have would *want* the job, but it's not meant for everyone, and I'd never try to stifle any dreams they had that led them to something different."

"Wow," Maddy said. "I guess I never asked how that worked. That actually makes me really happy."

She leaned in and gave me a kiss. "Well, I'll go ahead and wish for a boy for both of us. How about that? But I think, boy or girl, they deserve a dad like you."

Her words sent a bolt of emotion into my chest, and my eyes stung as I tried not to cry. I wiped at them. Thankfully, Maddy didn't mention my tears.

Three days after Maxwell's return, Maddy and I were nervously sitting in an exam room as a technician ran the ultrasound wand across Maddy's belly. I watched, completely oblivious to what she was doing. She clicked different spots on the screen, took pictures, and made some sort of measurements, but all I could do was stare at the squirming gray form. The heartbeat seemed to reverberate across the room and all the way into my chest.

Shifter babies developed faster than humans, and the baby already had the outline of arms and legs. It moved and twisted in Maddy's belly. The more I watched it, the more love I felt. It was strange to fall in love with something that wasn't even born yet. The lump in my throat told me the feelings were real, though.

"Okay, folks," the technician said. "Baby looks great. Measuring exactly where they should for a wolf-shifter. I got a really good picture of the genital area, so I can say for certain it's—"

"Wait," I blurted.

The technician and Maddy both looked at me in surprise. My cheeks flamed.

"Is everything okay, Mr. Lorenzo?" the technician asked.

"Yeah, are you okay, Nico?" Maddy said, rubbing my arm.

I nodded and smiled. "Yeah. I just thought… wouldn't it be kind of exciting to be surprised when our baby is born? I'd like to know then. What do you say?"

Maddy grinned back at me. "I love surprises."

Chapter 34 - Maddy

Abi was planning our baby shower, and when she heard that we were going to wait until delivery to find out the sex of the baby, she'd been playfully irritated. She'd been hoping for a girl so she could have pink *everything*. A full pink extravaganza. Instead, she had to readjust her plans and go gender-neutral. To say she wasn't a fan of the middle-of-the-road colors of yellow, green, and gray was an understatement, but she still planned a hell of a party over the next couple of months.

It was during the baby shower, while I was filling my plate full of finger foods and appetizers, she sidled up next to me.

"Are you guys still serious?" Abi asked.

"About what?"

She rolled her eyes. "Seriously? The gender, you doofus. You and Nico are still going to wait?"

I laughed. "Yes. We're still waiting. It'll be a big surprise."

"God, you guys are impossible. Where's the fun in that?"

"I don't know," I said. "I think it's fun." I glanced toward Sebastian, who was piling his plate high with food. "Whenever you and that one have a baby, you can find out ahead of time."

Sebastian's hands jerked in shock, and the food he'd been about to stuff into his mouth tumbled back onto the plate. Behind him, Felipe, Luis, and Diego chuckled and pointed at him. On the other side of the room, Nico let out a huge belly laugh.

Sebastian's face went red. "Hang on, now. I'm not ready to be a daddy."

Abi narrowed her eyes at him. "Oh yeah? Well, who says I'm ready to be your baby mama, huh? Besides, before you even think of putting a baby in me, you need to put a ring on this finger first."

"Shifters don't do weddings or exchange rings." His smile grew playful, and he cocked an eyebrow. "We do bite, though."

"Shut up," Abi said and threw a pig in a blanket at him. Sebastian deftly caught it in his mouth and grinned.

It was so nice that the two of them had finally figured things out. As much as they poked and joked with each other, they were the perfect match. I was glad my friend had possibly found her person, even if it had taken a *long* time to get there. Sebastian stole another glance at Abi as she turned to join the rest of the party. He chewed on the inside of his cheek, looking like he was working up the courage to say something, but Nico's voice pulled away my attention.

He'd stepped up on an ottoman and held his hands up for quiet. Once the crowd calmed, he started speaking.

"I wanted to thank everyone for coming today. You'll never know how much it means to Maddy and me to have our friends here at this special time."

I moved over to be at his side as he nodded to everyone around the room. Donatello stood in the corner with what looked like a supermodel draped on his arm. Tiago and Norman raised their glasses from the back. Even the Alabama lizard shifters had made the trip out to give us their well wishes. The room was full of dozens of people, and I couldn't believe how lucky I was to have such a huge extended family now.

"We've been through a lot this last year," Nico went on. "I know it's been difficult, but I know that there's no other group of people I would have rather gone through hell with than you all." Nico cleared his throat as he tried not to get choked up. "I don't think I'll ever be able to thank you enough. Many of you didn't even have to help us. You weren't family before all this, but you are now. If anyone in this room ever needs anything, anything at all, they can count on Maddy and me to be there for them. That's all I've got," he said.

The crowd hooted and clapped for him as he stepped down. Before the festivities could start again, Sebastian jogged over to the ottoman and jumped onto it. "Hang on, one more speech from the godparents. Get over here, Abi."

Abi, looking mortified, put her food down and reluctantly joined Sebastian in front of the many attendees.

"I wanted to let Nico and Maddy know that we can't wait to meet the little guy or girl they've got baking in the oven. Abi and I can't even tell you how surprised we were that you chose us as the godparents— "

"Speak for yourself. I knew my girl was gonna choose me to love on that little baby," Abi interrupted. The crowd laughed.

"Yeah, yeah, okay," Sebastian said. "We want you guys to know that we hope your baby has a full and happy life, and we'll do everything we can to help with that. I swear on my soul that your baby will be as much a part of my family as you guys are. Now, for other news."

Instinctively, I could tell what was coming next. The look in Sebastian's eyes, the way he quickly dug into his pocket… it was all so obvious now. I clasped a hand to my mouth to conceal my squeal. My eyes were already tearing up when I looked at Nico. All he did was give me a knowing smile. I swung my gaze back to Abi and Sebastian. Abi looked confused as Sebastian went to stand before her.

"I have to tell you guys," Sebastian said. "I can't in good conscience take on the role of godfather if I didn't make an honest woman out of the godmother."

Abi's eyes popped as Sebastian sank to one knee and pulled a ring out of his pocket. He'd been right when he said shifters didn't do that kind of thing, but Abi wasn't a shifter. She was human, and like almost all human women, she'd dreamed of the day a man would slip a ring on her finger. She was crying as Sebastian took her hand.

"Abi? Will you be my wife?"

Abi's mouth dropped open, but she was laughing through the tears, nodding like a maniac. "Yes. Yes, you big dumb idiot, of course, I will."

The room exploded with cheers and applause. There was barely a dry eye in the house as the two of them embraced after Sebastian slipped the ring on her hand. I was overjoyed for them.

After eating a bit, I went outside for some fresh air. It was getting rowdy inside as everyone was trying to congratulate Sebastian and Abi. Gabriella sat in the grass right beyond the front porch. She was alone and staring off at the setting sun.

I walked over and sat down next to her. I was *much* more pregnant now and took my time getting on the ground. How would I get up? Gabriella smiled at me and helped me get settled.

"Oof, this belly is getting big," I huffed.

"It tends to do that," Gabriella said.

"Is everything all right?" I asked.

She smiled and nodded. "I'm so happy for you, Maddy." She looked at the sunset once more before turning back to me. "I don't think you'll ever realize how grateful I am to have been allowed back into your life. A year ago, I'd completely given up ever having a chance to even talk to you, much less all of this." She took my hand in hers and rubbed it, almost like she didn't think it was real. "I have so many regrets, but giving you up was the biggest one of my life.

"I know it was for the best, and it was the only way I could protect you, but that doesn't mean it hurt any less. Year after year, knowing I was missing birthdays, Christmases, and first steps. There are so many things I can never get back. I don't know if you have any bitterness toward me about it all, and I know I wasn't there to be the mother you needed, but I hope I'm allowed to be a grandmother to your baby so I can give it all the love I never got to give you."

I squeezed her hand. "Gabriella, I could never hate you or be upset. Now that I'm pregnant, and I can feel this little person growing inside me, I can understand where you came from. If someone told me my child was in danger and giving them up was my only hope to save them, I'd do exactly what you did. It would rip my heart out to do it, and that gives me a better understanding of what you went through for all those years."

Gabriella's lips trembled as tears formed and trickled down her cheeks.

"Thank you for making such a huge sacrifice. Fate works in mysterious ways, and there's no telling what would have happened if you'd kept me. I know I wouldn't have Mom and Dad. I wouldn't have Abi. There's no way I'd have ever met Nico. Hell, you and I would most likely have been dead years ago. I will never hold a grudge against you for doing what was right.

"You are going to be a wonderful grandma. There's no hate, no blame. Please don't think that. All I have is forgiveness. Forgiveness and love. I love you, Gabriella, and we have years to catch up on everything we missed."

Gabriella couldn't speak. Her tears were coming so strong and fast. She sobbed and leaned toward me, clutching me in a hug so tight I thought I might pop. She cried into my shoulder as I stroked her hair. My mother's hair. As I let her release all her feelings, I stared out at the purple and gold sunset, and I couldn't remember ever feeling so at peace in my life.

Chapter 35 - Maddy

Shifter pregnancies only lasted seven months rather than nine months. I was almost to the end of the seventh month. The air was getting cold outside. Well, cold for Florida. There was a refreshing coolness to the breeze, and I was getting excited to meet our new arrival. I had one week left until my due date, so the baby could come at any time.

I went to the nursery to double-check my bag for the hospital. It was sitting on the changing table. Everything was exactly as it should be. I sighed in happiness as I looked around the nursery. We'd decided that *Winnie the Pooh* was a good gender-neutral décor idea.

Felipe, surprising to me, at least, was a fantastic artist and painted a jaw-dropping mural of a *Pooh* scene. It was so gorgeous that I'd have to do something to preserve it whenever our child grew tired of looking at it, which was bound to happen.

I was halfway through checking my bag when I heard the raised voices outside. Abi and Sebastian. I rolled my eyes and hurried downstairs to see what it was this time. Nico leaned back against the kitchen island. Sebastian and Abi were standing in front of him, arguing.

"I know what I saw, Sebastian," Abi said with a smirk.

Sebastian grabbed the sides of his head and gaped at her. "Babe, you fired her, for God's sake. Isn't that a little much?"

I slipped up beside Nico and whispered, "What the hell's going on this time?"

Nico leaned toward me but kept his eyes on the couple. "Just got back from their meeting with the wedding planner."

"You were checking her ass out, weren't you? I saw it," Abi said, crossing her arms.

Sebastian smiled bashfully and shook his head. "Okay... so... you maybe did see me looking at her butt, except— "

"Ha!" Abi jabbed her finger into his chest. "You admit it."

"Let me finish, " Sebastian growled. "So, the chick stood up and... well, I guess you didn't see it, but she had a big smear of paint on her skirt. It caught my eye. That's it, and that's the truth. I seriously don't think firing her on the spot was the best idea."

They kept bickering back and forth. They always liked to pick at each other, but as we got closer to the wedding, they seemed to be enjoying it more than usual. The big day was two months away. I wondered how bad it would get before then.

My smile quickly morphed into a wince. I'd been having minor contractions for days, but this one was tighter and a bit more painful than usual. Then something even more disconcerting happened. A popping sensation deep inside me. I glanced down and saw a thin drip of water sliding down my inner thigh under my dress. The next contraction came a moment later, clenching painfully in my abdomen. The pain was hot and sharp.

My right hand lashed out and clutched Nico's bicep. "It's happening," I hissed through gritted teeth.

Sebastian and Abi went silent and spun to look at me. If I hadn't been in so much pain, I would have laughed at the bug-eyed looks of surprise they gave me. Nico spun and put his arms under my armpits, holding me up.

"The baby?" he asked, already breathless.

I nodded. "Yup. It's coming."

Nico and Sebastian helped get me into the car while Abi sprinted up the stairs to grab our bags. She tossed them into the trunk even as Nico was pulling out of the driveway. Sebastian had called ahead, and Luis and Felipe met us in their trucks to escort us to the hospital.

Everything was happening so fast. It was almost like watching things through a flashing camera lens.

My anxiety was through the roof as we neared the hospital. The contractions were coming faster each minute. They were also getting a lot more painful. After getting hustled through the emergency room and up to Labor and Delivery, the nurse gave me the bad news. I was too far along to get an epidural. The baby was coming and coming fast.

Nico took my hand. "It's gonna be okay, Maddy. You're going to be okay."

The next three hours were some of the most brutal of my life. I'd never been in so much pain or so exhausted. Nico was by my side the entire time, helping me focus, keeping me calm, and always encouraging me. If not for him, I might have gone crazy from the pain.

Finally, after two hours of pushing, I collapsed back on the bed, an exhausted breath huffing out of me as my body rejoiced in being done. A moment later, the doctor placed my baby in my arms. It was so fast, I barely understood what was happening. One moment I was in agony, and now a tiny warm boy was pressed against my naked chest. The moment I felt the skin-to-skin contact, I took in the scent of the baby, and an unbreakable and powerful bond formed. I wept as I looked down at the little wonder in my arms.

Nico stepped up and leaned in to see it. His eyes were wide with awe, almost like a little boy on Christmas morning. Taking a small thin blanket the nurse had given me, I wrapped the tiny bundle and held our son up toward Nico.

Over the last few weeks, we'd decided on names. Since we hadn't been sure what we were having, we decided to settle on a name for each gender. Then, whatever the baby was, we'd already know the name. We picked Seraphina if it was a girl and Nial if it was a boy. Nial had been Nico's grandfather's name.

Holding the baby out for Nico to take, I smiled at my mate. "Meet your son, Nial. Take him, Nico. Hold him."

He reached out and carefully took the bundle. He backed away and pressed the baby to his own chest, bouncing our son gently while he walked back and forth. I lay there on the pillows, feeling more bone-tired than ever before but also elated as I watched my entire world standing in front of me. Nico looked up from the baby and smiled at me, and I grinned.

Everything was exactly how it should be. We didn't have to run anymore. All we had to do now was live our lives. And as I gazed at Nico and Nial, I couldn't help but be excited to see what those lives would look like.

Made in United States
Orlando, FL
12 February 2024

43599676R00189